Marriage

o...

This was not the first time she'd been kissed . . .

A village boy or two had tried to while she was growing up, but she'd never been much moved by the activity. Perhaps that had been due to the kisser, she thought now, because the kisses she'd received in the past had seemed sloppy and uninteresting and had always left her wanting to wipe her hand across her mouth. This kiss was nothing like that.

Cam's mouth was firm as it brushed across hers, and then he nipped at her lower lip, a quick, tantalizing tug that had her mouth opening with surprise. The moment she did that, his tongue slid into her mouth like an invading army, causing chaos and starting up fires at various points throughout her body.

Cam then began to trail kisses across her cheek toward her ear.

"Cam, this is—" This was what? she wondered, trying to recall what she'd been about to say before he'd begun to explore her ear, nibbling and kissing it in a way that had the most unexpected effect. Damn, she couldn't recall, but what he was doing was rather amazing. It was sending shivers of excitement up and down her body in waves of pleasure she'd never experienced before.

Lynsay Sands

To Marry a Scottish Laird

AVON

An Imprint of HarperCollinsPublishers

AVON BOOKS
An Imprint of HarperCollins*Publishers*
195 Broadway
New York, New York 10007

Copyright © 2014 by Lynsay Sands
Excerpt from *Sweet Revenge* copyright © 2000 by Lynsay Sands
ISBN 978-0-06-227357-4
www.avonromance.com

First Avon Books mass market printing: July 2014

Avon Trademark Reg. U.S. Pat. Off. and in Other Countries, Marca Registrada, Hecho en U.S.A.
HarperCollins® is a registered trademark of HarperCollins Publishers.

Printed in the U.S.A.

10 9 8 7 6 5 4 3 2 1

Chapter 1

CAM HEARD THE TROUBLE ON THE TRAIL AHEAD before he saw it. The screams made him instinctively slow his horse as he rounded the bend, but when he saw a young boy being held by the scruff of his shirt and beaten by a big bull of a man, Cam reached for his sword and spurred his horse to move faster. A heartbeat later he'd reached the pair.

The thud of his boots hitting the ground made the assailant glance around, just in time to see Cam's sword hilt before it slammed into the big oaf's head. The fellow went down like a stone, unfortunately falling on the boy and landing with enough weight to bring a grunt of pain from the almost senseless lad.

Wincing in sympathy, Campbell used his booted foot to roll the villain off the boy. The moment the man's weight was removed, the lad opened his swollen and blackening eyes and squinted up uncertainly.

"Ye're safe," Cam said and bent to offer him a hand up.

Instead of taking it, though, the lad glanced past him, swollen eyes widening slightly with horror. Cam instinctively started to straighten, but a blow to his lower back made him stagger. He managed to avoid trampling the lad and regained his footing after a couple of steps, then whirled to confront his assailant.

Assailants, Cam corrected himself grimly as he took note of the three men he now faced. They all had dirty faces and wore ragged clothes. None were as big as the man he'd knocked out, but they were not small either, and each had a different weapon. The bald man on the left held a club, the one with long dark hair on the right held a rusty old sword, and the ginger-haired one in the middle held a knife that was presently dripping with blood.

His blood, Cam realized even as he felt warm liquid begin to trickle down his lower back and leg. He hadn't been punched in the back, he'd been stabbed. Mouth tightening, he raised his sword, pulled a small blade from his waist with his left hand and started forward, knowing he wouldn't have long before the loss of blood weakened him. He had to take care of the men before that happened or he and the boy would no doubt be found dead here on the side of the road by the next traveler to come by.

Cam sent his knife flying at the man with the bloody blade first, waited just long enough to see it find a home in his chest, then swung his sword at the man on the right.

Despite his ragged clothes and filthy condition, the man handled his rusty old sword better than Cam would have expected. Or perhaps he was already weakening, and that—combined with the worry that he would be clubbed from behind by the third man at any moment—affected his abilities. Whatever the case, it took Cam half a dozen swings of his sword to finally fall his combatant.

Amazed that he hadn't already received half a dozen blows to his head and back, Cam whirled to confront the other man, only to find him on the ground. The boy stood over him, the ginger-haired man's bloody blade in hand.

"He was going to hit you," the lad said defensively, dropping the blade when he glanced up to see Cam staring at him.

Mouth opening to thank the lad, Cam took a step forward, but his mouth closed when he found himself suddenly on his knees. He peered down with confusion as his sword then slid from his fingers, and turned bewildered eyes to the boy. But in the next moment he found himself planted flat on the ground and losing consciousness.

Joan stared at the Scot with amazement. One minute he'd been seemingly strong and well and battling her assailants, and the next he was face-down in the road. Stooping to pick up the knife again, she quickly wiped it on the dead man's back to remove the blood, and then slipped it into the belt at her waist and stepped over him to move to her savior's side.

Her gaze immediately found the dark patch on the back of his plaid. She didn't need to touch it to know it was blood. He'd been stabbed, Joan realized, surprised at how serious the wound was. She'd seen the ginger-haired man approach him from behind with the knife raised and had assumed he'd stabbed him, but when her savior had battled so capably, she'd thought perhaps it had only been a paltry wound. The amount of blood on his back and soaking through his plaid from the buttocks down, though, suggested it had been a rather nasty one after all. In fact, she was now amazed that he'd managed to fight at all.

Sighing, Joan sat back on her heels and glanced around. She was pretty sure that three of the men were dead. But the man who had been beating her when her savior had arrived was merely unconscious. She briefly considered rectifying that situation, but Joan was a healer. Killing an unconscious man, even one who had been beating her but moments ago, went against everything she believed in.

Her gaze slid back to her savior and Joan raised his plaid to see the wound. She got an eyeful of his arse first, but this was not the first time she'd tended an injured man and her training kicked in, allowing her to ignore his naked behind and instead turn her attention to his lower back.

"Damn," she muttered, noting the jagged wound. It looked deep and nasty. The knife hadn't plunged right in and out, but Ginger had twisted it, leaving a hole rather than a slice in the skin. Cursing, Joan pushed herself to her feet and rushed to grab her bag from where she'd dropped it while the toothless giant had been assaulting her. She was rummaging inside when he moaned and shifted next to her.

Joan stiffened, her eyes shooting to the man. Toothless was waking, which was the last thing she needed. Mouth tightening, she glanced wildly around until her gaze settled on a good-sized rock nearby. Grabbing it up, she turned to Toothless as he started to push to his feet and slammed it into his head with a good deal of force. He collapsed to the ground with a grunt of pain and lay still.

Joan eyed him briefly, prepared to thump him again if he stirred. Killing a helpless man might go against her nature, but she had absolutely no problem knocking him out, and hopefully with enough force that it would leave him with a grand headache later. Certainly, Joan was going to suffer from his attack for some time. She was already suffering. Toothless had been furious when she'd refused to give up her bag and had taken out that fury on her, pummeling her face and chest with his big, ham sized fists. As a result, Joan's face felt as if it was on fire and hurt everywhere. She had no doubt it was swelling and bruising by the moment. She was also pretty sure she had more than a couple of cracked ribs. If she were standing rather than kneeling, she'd kick Toothless a couple times to ensure he suffered as much as she did when he woke up. However, she had to tend to her savior, so Joan dropped the rock and continued searching her bag until she found the items she needed and then moved back to the Scot's side.

Despite the need to rush, she was careful to clean the wound thoroughly before sewing him up. The moment Joan had finished bandaging him, she checked on Toothless again. The man appeared to still be deep in unconsciousness. She considered giving him another good blow to the head to ensure he stayed that way for a bit, but then turned her attention to the Scot instead. Getting him on his horse and getting them both out of there, and far away from Toothless seemed a good idea. She started out trying to lift him, but the man was huge. After a moment to inventory what she had at hand, Joan then moved to her savior's horse. The mount was a beauty. Only nobility would own a beast as fine. She murmured and cooed to the horse as she approached, caressed his nose when he let her near, and then caught his reins and urged him back to stand beside his owner.

Joan next moved to each of the dead attackers and quickly removed their clothes. They weren't in the best of shape, threadbare in some places, torn in others. It made it easy for her to rip them into strips and quickly tie them into a cloth rope. She only hoped the cloth would hold the Scot's weight.

Toothless was stirring again by that point, so Joan took a moment to hit him over the head again. Satisfied that he was again unconscious, she then tied the makeshift rope around the Scot's chest, under his arms. She threw the free end over his mount's saddle before rushing around to grab it up. Bracing her legs, she then began to pull.

The man was heavy. Joan had to literally bend her knees and curl into a ball and hang all her weight from the cloth rope to accomplish her task, but eventually she managed to get the Scot over his horse, arms dangling down one side, legs on the other.

Sighing with relief, Joan dropped the rope, then ran around to the other side of the horse, reached under its belly to catch the dangling cloth and quickly tied it to the Scot's ankles. It was the only way she could think to make sure he didn't fall off and she didn't have to go through this again. The man might shift and hang under the beast's belly, but he would remain on the horse. And hopefully, with her mounted behind him, she could prevent him from shifting. Rushing to her bag, Joan scooped it up, closed it and then collected the weapons the men had used.

Getting on the beast's back was a trial in itself, but she eventually managed the task. Joan immediately took up the mount's reins, but then paused. She was hot and sweaty, her face and head ached and she was even a little lightheaded now. Rather than risk fainting and falling off the beast, Joan paused to allow her heartbeat to slow down and her head to clear. She watched Toothless the entire time, though, afraid he'd rise up like some nightmare monster and stop them just on the verge of escaping. He didn't, however, and still lay motionless in the road when she kicked her heels and urged the horse to move. Joan tried that three times before acknowledging that there was something wrong with the beast . . . or she wasn't doing it right. She'd never ridden a horse before and had no idea what she was doing. Sighing, she slid off the horse again, moved around in front, and took the reins to lead it away along the path.

She had no idea where they would go, but it seemed a good idea to put some distance between this spot and them. She would walk for an hour or so and then try to find somewhere to stop, somewhere safe, where they could rest while they both healed, and where Toothless wouldn't find them when he woke. After that . . . well, she'd stay with the Scot until he was well enough to take care of himself again, Joan decided. She owed him that much for saving her life.

CAM FELT LIKE HELL. THAT WAS HIS FIRST AWARENESS. His back hurt, his mouth was as dry as dust, and—he suddenly realized—he was lying on his stomach with his bare arse in the air. What the hell? He started to shift, intending to roll over, but a hand pressed down on his back, stopping him.

"Don't move."

Cam glanced warily over his shoulder and let his breath out when he recognized the boy he'd saved on the road. Actually, he didn't recognize him so much as guess it was the lad by his bruised face. The poor boy had really taken a waling. His face was almost deformed, it was so swollen under the wool cap he wore. Cam would guess that the lad was probably in as much, if not more, pain than he was presently suffering. Wincing in sympathy, Cam turned and lay flat, only to wince again, this time in pain from whatever the boy was doing to his back.

"What the devil are ye doin' lad?"

"Cleaning your wound again before I put a clean bandage on." The answer was a bit slurred, no doubt from the swelling around the boy's mouth. "It stings like the devil, I know, but has to be done."

Cam grunted in response, and then stuck his fist in his mouth to keep from screaming as something was poured over his wound that made it feel like the area had been set on fire.

"Breathe," the boy suggested. "You're holding your breath and 'tis easier do you breathe through the pain."

Cam let out the breath he hadn't realized he'd been holding, and sucked in another deep draught that he immediately released. Oddly enough it did help. It didn't exactly relieve the pain, but somehow made it more bearable. He breathed deeply in and out until the burning agony lessened to a nagging ache.

"You'll need to sit up for me to bind you."

Cam removed his fist from his mouth and eased carefully to his hands and knees, and then sat back on his haunches and raised his arms, ignoring the fact that he was completely naked. The boy rubbed something soothing on his wound, then began winding cloth around his lower waist, reaching around his stomach to pass the strip of cloth from one hand to the other and draw it back to wrap around him again. He made three passes before tucking the end of the cloth in to the binding at Cam's side.

"Done."

Cam glanced back to see the lad packing his medicinals and tools back into a cloth satchel.

"You should dress," the boy suggested, nodding past him. " 'Tis chilly today."

Cam glanced forward and noted that he'd actually been lying on his plaid. Grabbing it up, he quickly shook it out and then laid it on the ground and began to fold pleats into it. His gaze flickered upward as he worked. The sun was high in the sky, making it about the nooning hour. It had been late afternoon the last he recalled. He'd obviously been unconscious for at least almost a day. He glanced around his surroundings next, taking note that he didn't recognize the area.

"How long since the attack?" Cam asked as he finished pleating the cloth. Straightening, he spotted his belt and grabbed it to slip beneath the pleated cloth. He then laid on it. Before this, Cam had never noticed how much movement there was to donning his plaid, but with every shift in position causing a shaft of pain to shoot through his back, he was aware now. Lying on the wound was the worst though.

Cam was pulling one side of the plaid around his body when he realized the boy hadn't answered him. Glancing over he noted that the lad was staring at his groin with a wide-eyed fascination that almost verged on horror. A smile pulling at his mouth, Cam shook his head. "Do no' worry, ye're just a stripling. Yers'll get bigger in time."

The boy blinked. "What'll get big—" The words died in his throat as his gaze shot down to Cam's groin with understanding. The boy then flushed and turned away, focusing firmly on the task of repacking his bag.

Chuckling, Cam finished donning his plaid and then eased cautiously to his feet. "Ye did no' say . . . how long has it been since the attack?"

"You've been in a swoon for three days," the boy answered, closing his bag and tightening the tie at the top.

"Three days?" Cam asked with disbelief, and then scowled. "And I did no' swoon."

"All right, you've been sleeping for three days then," the boy said with a shrug. After a moment, he added grudgingly, "You were in and out of fever most of that time. It broke this morning."

Cam grimaced, and glanced around. They were in a clearing by a river. He didn't see a road anywhere. "Where are we?"

"I thought it best to get you somewhere safe to recover," the boy said quietly and straightened with his bag. "Now that you have, I suppose you'll mount your horse and be on your way so . . ." The lad nodded at him. "Thank you for saving me life. I'm sorry you were wounded. Safe travels."

Cam's eyebrows flew up as he watched the boy move over to sit on a small boulder by the river. The lad really expected he'd just get on his horse and leave him here now that he was on his feet. Although, on his feet was a rather generous way to put it. He might be standing, but his legs were shaking beneath him, and he felt extremely weak. He was in no shape to travel yet, and even if he were, he'd hardly abandon the boy after he'd spent three days nursing him back to health.

Spotting his sword and knife on the ground, Cam moved over and bent to pick it up, just barely refraining from crying out as his stitches pulled in his back. Damn. Mayhap he was glad he'd slept these last three days. If this is how it felt on the fourth day of healing, he was not sorry to have missed the first three.

Straightening with a grimace, he eased his sword and knife into his belt and then settled on a boulder next to the boy. He stared at the water moving slowly past and cleared his throat. "Thank ye fer tending me."

" 'Twas the least I could do," the lad said with a shrug. "You were wounded saving me from those thieves . . . and I thank you for that."

Cam eyed him silently, one eyebrow raised. The boy was an English peasant and obviously poor, his clothes threadbare and dirty, his hat in no better shape. All he seemed to have was the bag of medicinals. "What were they trying to steal?"

"Me bag," the boy answered, brushing his fingers over the bag he'd set on the ground between his feet.

"For that they were beatin' ye?" He asked with disbelief, wondering why the men would waste time pounding their fists on such a short thin lad when they simply could have taken the bag and left.

"Nay. They were beating me because first I wouldn't let go of the bag until they forced me to, and then I kept chasing after them trying to get it back," the boy admitted.

"Ye'd risk yer life fer a bag o' weeds?" Cam asked with disbelief.

"They aren't weeds. Weeds wouldn't have saved yer life. They're herbs," the boy said stiffly, and then sighed, picked up a branch lying next to his boulder and began to absently strip the smaller twigs off. "'Sides, 'twas not the herbs I cared about, but a scroll that I am charged with delivering."

"A scroll?" Cam asked curiously.

The boy nodded and began to dig in the dirt in front of his bag with the stick as he said, "Me mother asked me to deliver it on her deathbed."

"Ah," Cam said with understanding. "A death-bed request is a hard one to refuse."

"Or fail at," the boy added grimly. "I have to deliver the scroll. Mother said she'd not rest peaceful in her grave if I didn't."

"I see," Cam murmured, his respect for the boy rising. He hadn't taken the beating to save some small trinket, but to fulfill a deathbed request. He had honor, and obviously loved his mother. The boy's voice had deepened several octaves when he'd spoken of the woman. That thought made Cam realize that the lad still had a higher voice, which meant he was even younger than he'd first thought.

His gaze dropped to the bag and he shook his head. The thieves wouldn't have been interested in the scroll or the weeds in the boy's bag. Had he just given it up, they probably would have up-ended it, spreading the contents on the ground and then—finding nothing of value—would have left him alone and continued on their way. But his refusal to give up the bag, and then his determi-nation to have it back, had no doubt convinced them there was a king's ransom stashed in the small satchel.

"What's your name boy?"

"Joan—Joan-as," the boy answered.

"Jonas?" Cam asked, wondering if the boy had a stutter or some other speech impediment. Perhaps it was just his swollen face affecting his speech, he decided.

"Aye. Jonas," the boy muttered, ducking his head.

"Well, Jonas, I am Campbell Sinclair. Cam to me friends."

"A pleasure to make your acquaintance Camp-bell Sinclair," Jonas muttered, ducking his head again.

"As I said, me friends call me Cam, and since ye saved me life, I think I'll count ye amongst them," he said with a smile.

"Cam," Jonas murmured, and then cleared his throat and said, "You can call me Jo. 'Tis what my friends call me."

"Jo 'tis then," Cam said easily.

They were both silent for a moment and then Jo asked, "Isn't Campbell a clan name?"

"Aye. 'Twas me mother's clan. So she gave me her last name fer a first," he explained.

"Oh," Jonas nodded and then began digging again with his stick.

"Let me see the scroll," Cam said abruptly. When Jonas's head shot up, eyes narrowed, he shook his head and said, "I will no' take it. I do no' even need to touch it. I just want to see it."

Jonas hesitated, but then set down the stick and opened his bag. After rifling through it briefly, he pulled out a small, but thick, scroll. Cam could see the wax that sealed it, but it was just a blob, probably from candle wax dripped on it. There was no mark in the wax, however, as would be on a nobleman's message. But then a peasant wouldn't have a family ring with a crest to press into the wax. On the other hand, parchment wasn't usually something a peasant had either.

"Tuck the scroll in yer shirt," Cam said finally. "'Twill keep it safe, and the next time someone tries to steal yer bag, ye will no' risk yer life to keep it."

Jonas's eyebrows rose, but then he nodded and shoved the scroll down the top of his shirt. It pressed against the loose material, but you wouldn't notice it unless you were looking for it. Satisfied, Cam nodded.

"You're rubbing your stomach. Is it sore or are you hungry?" Jonas asked suddenly.

"Hungry," Cam admitted with a grimace. His stomach felt completely empty. He was sure if he swallowed a coin, they'd hear it rattling around inside his hollow belly.

Jonas nodded and stood. "I'll trap a rabbit and gather some berries."

"I can help," Cam said, pushing to his feet.

Jonas didn't humiliate him by pointing out that he was wavering on his feet like a sapling in a stiff breeze. He merely shook his head. "I'll be faster on me own. Besides, you'll tire easily for the next while. You should rest while you wait."

Before Cam could even respond, the lad had slipped away and disappeared into the woods. He'd also left his bag behind. Cam would have liked to think it was because Jonas trusted him, but knew the truth was the boy now carried the only thing of import that it had previously held. Still, the weeds had come in handy and might again, so Cam stooped to pick up the bag, mouth firming against the pain the action caused. Straightening carefully, he carried it over to set beside his own bag, and then eased his way down onto the ground and lay on his side. A little rest sounded a good idea.

JOAN WASN'T SURPRISED WHEN SHE RETURNED to camp and found Cam sleeping. She'd seen enough injured men to know he'd do a lot of that for the next day or two. Maybe longer. That was all right with her. She hadn't slept much the last couple of days as she'd watched over him. She hadn't dared sleep while he was feverish, and had instead spent her time soaking his plaid in the river's cold water and then laying it over him in an effort to cool him off. It was the only way she'd known to fight the fever. Joan couldn't even guess how many times she'd rushed back and forth from the river to the unconscious man. He'd been so hot, the cloth had seemed to grow warm and dry in minutes. The only other thing she'd been able to do was dribble willow bark tea down his throat along with other tinctures she'd thought might help . . . and wait. Now that the fever had passed though, Joan didn't have to watch over him constantly. It meant she could actually get some rest too.

Settling beside the fire, Joan turned her attention to cleaning the rabbit. It wasn't the first time she'd performed the chore, so the process didn't take long. Once that was done, she started a fire and then found a good-sized branch and skewered the animal on it. As she set it over the fire, Joan couldn't help thinking that a pot would come in handy. Cam would have done better with soup than roasted meat, and she'd come across some wild onions and carrots while catching the rabbit. However, she had no pot, so they would have to make do with roasted rabbit and the vegetables she'd found, wrapped in the large leaves and roasted in the hot coals.

Sighing, Joan removed her hat and ran a hand wearily through her long hair as it fell around her shoulders. She was exhausted, and filthy. She hadn't bathed since setting out on this journey two weeks ago and she itched everywhere. Two weeks and still she hadn't made her way out of England and into Scotland, she thought with a shake of the head. True, her travels had been interrupted a time or two when she'd stopped to help an ailing or injured traveler, but still, she'd expected to be further north than this by now.

Sighing, she slid her hat back on her head and glanced to Cam. He seemed an all right fellow for a Scot. He'd troubled himself enough to stop and save her from a nasty situation. Many wouldn't have. He'd even thanked her for tending to him afterward, something she wasn't used to hearing from nobility. Generally, nobles took what they wanted without a by your leave, or reacted to a kindness as if they were entitled to it. But he'd thanked her.

Mind you, he thought she was a boy, Joan reminded herself. She didn't know if that made a difference or not. Perhaps he still would have thanked her had he known she was a woman. She'd never know, because he'd never know she was a girl. Joan had told the truth when she'd said she was delivering a message as a deathbed request from her mother. The other part of her mother's request had been an insistence that she dress herself as a boy for the journey. It had been a smart idea. After everything that had happened, Joan didn't think she'd have got far on her journey had she traveled as herself. Even as a boy she'd encountered some pretty despicable characters with less than honorable intentions. She'd had some narrow escapes. This last one had been the worst, though.

Joan glanced to Cam again. It was something she'd done often over the last couple of days. It was impossible not to; he was a good-looking man with all that fair hair falling around his handsome face. He was also very well built. The man had muscles to spare. And his behind? Joan gave her head a shake, trying to remove the memory of the man's derriere. She'd managed to avoid looking at it the first several times she'd tended his back, but temptation or perhaps exhaustion had weakened her and, of late, she'd found herself stopping to look at his behind as she'd tended his wound . . . and it was a fine behind. So fine she started to wonder if he had a lady wife. He probably did . . . and if not, then he most definitely had a betrothed. Things like that were arranged when a nobleman was a child.

Joan didn't know why she even bothered to wonder about it. A lord would never be interested in a village lass, at least not for anything more than a dalliance. And Joan had no intention of being anyone's dalliance. Truthfully, she didn't think she wanted to be anyone's wife either. From the time she was born her mother had taken her along to birthings and healings. Joan's first memory was of a birth that had gone wrong. It was nothing but a fuzzy blur of blood and screaming, but that was enough. Since then she'd seen many other examples of what happened when a child was born.

She'd seen women ripped up so badly below that their blood ran black. She'd seen women die with the child still lodged in their bodies. She'd also seen everything in between those two extremes when it came to birthing and it was enough to scare any desire to have children right out of her.

Nay, children were not for her. Joan was content with healing and midwifery and tending the sick. She had no desire to bind herself to another and bear children. No matter how attractive the man's derriere was.

Chapter 2

"*M*MMM. 'TIS GOOD."

Joan glanced sideways to Cam and nodded silently. They were sharing a small log as they ate the rabbit and vegetables by the small fire she'd built. The meal had turned out surprisingly well considering she'd had so little to work with. Or perhaps this meal tasted so good to her because she hadn't had meat since setting out on this journey. Joan hadn't wanted to draw attention to herself, or take the time to bother with a fire while traveling on her own, so had made do with berries and any wild vegetables she'd encountered. She'd also packed two loaves of bread in her bag when she'd set out, but had finished the last of that while watching over Cam.

Of course, he thought it was good too. But then this was the first bit of food he'd had in three days. That was sure to color his opinion.

"So Jo," Cam said suddenly around a bite of rabbit. "How old are you?"

"Twenty," Joan answered without thinking, and glanced up with surprise when the Scot burst out laughing.

" 'Tis sorry I am boy, but ye barely reach me chest, yer face is hairless, yer voice has yet to change, and ye've no' developed a bit o' muscle yet." He shook his head. "If ye've seen more than twelve or thirteen years, I'll eat me horse."

Joan ducked her head, and picked at her meat, but her mind was in a bit of a muddle. She'd briefly forgotten that she was supposed to be a boy. That was a dangerous slip. Not that she believed Cam would harm her if he knew she was a female. She'd saved his life, after all, and that after he'd saved her. It didn't suggest he was the sort to attack a woman traveling alone. Besides, there was little he could want from her. She had no money, and from what she'd seen of her face in the river's surface when she was washing the rabbit, she was a mess. Joan had hardly recognized herself. Her face was almost universally swollen. Her eyes had black circles around them that were just beginning to turn green at the edges as the bruising started to fade. Her upper lip was swollen and cut and there was another bruise on her jaw as well. She wasn't anywhere near attractive enough to move a man to want to attack her. Still, she'd donned this garb for the journey for a reason. 'Twas better to be safe than sorry. Besides, she didn't want Cam to have to eat his horse.

That thought made her smile, which in turn made her wince as her split lip complained at the stretching.

"Who are ye to deliver the letter to in Scotland?" Cam asked suddenly.

Joan hesitated about answering. The Scots were well known for their clan feuds. If the MacKays were an enemy of the Sinclairs, would he try to stop her from completing her task? She frowned at the possibility.

"Ye will no' tell me?" he asked with surprise when she remained silent.

Joan shrugged. "What can it matter to you?"

Instead of responding to that, he suggested, "Tell me about yer mother then."

Her eyebrows rose with surprise. "Why?"

"Why no'?" Cam said with a shrug. "Neither o' us is in any shape to travel, and we've naught better to do than talk. 'Sides, I'm curious to ken what kind o' woman would move a lad to take on a quest like this. 'Tis a large task indeed for a young boy to try to make this journey on foot and with no coin. She must have kenned she was settin' ye a difficult and dangerous task and yet she asked it o' ye anyway."

Joan lowered her head again. The fact that she was a woman made the task an even more dangerous one than Cam thought, and her mother had been aware of it. She'd repeatedly fretted over and warned her about the many and varied dangers. She'd insisted she take every precaution, and she'd berated herself for not handling the matter herself while she'd still been healthy enough to do it. Finally, she'd apologized to Joan, telling her that she loved her, and that she hoped Joan would always remember that and forgive her.

Jo thought about that now, wondering, as she had at the time, what was in the scroll she carried. She also wondered who the MacKays were and what her mother could possibly think she needed forgiveness for.

"Was yer mother a Scot?" Cam asked suddenly.

Joan blinked her thoughts away and shook her head. "English."

"Are ye sure?" he asked. "Mayhap her mother was a Scot and—"

"Nay," Joan interrupted. "She spoke often of my grandparents. They were both English. He was a blacksmith who died when she was a child, and her mother was a healer and midwife like she was. She trained my mother in healing until she died of a lung complaint. Just as my mother trained me until illness claimed her."

"Ah," Cam murmured and when Joan glanced at him in question, said, "I was wonderin' where ye'd got yer healing knowledge."

Joan nodded. "I was her apprentice. She taught me everything she knew."

"Ye were close then," Cam murmured.

"Aye," Joan whispered and peered into the fire as memory overwhelmed her. Maggie Chartres had been a good woman, smart, skilled and loving. She'd been the best mother Joan could have asked for . . . and she missed her horribly. Losing her had felt like the end of her world. Her grandparents had been gone by the time Joan was born, and her mother was all the family she'd had. Now she was alone with no family, no home, and no purpose other than to complete this one last task for her mother.

"Could yer father ha'e been a MacKay?" Cam asked.

Joan smiled faintly, but shook her head. "I don't think so. At least she never said he was. He died ere I was born," she explained and added, "As far as I know he was a simple English stable boy."

Cam nodded. They were both silent for a moment and then he asked, "What are your plans after ye deliver yer mother's message?"

Joan smiled wryly, wondering if Cam didn't have a touch of sight about him. His thoughts seemed to be running along the same lines as hers. Sighing, she shrugged helplessly, and admitted: "I've no plans."

"Will you return to your village?" Cam asked.

"Nay," she said huskily. "The home I was raised in actually belongs to the Augustinian Friary. Mother was allowed to live in it in return for her skills as a healer. She served the monastery, the abbey and the village. Now that she's dead . . ." She shook her head wearily and he finished for her.

"They took back yer home."

She nodded. "I'd hoped to continue Mother's work in the village, and at the abbey and monastery." Joan hadn't just hoped, she'd pleaded with Friar Wendell to allow her to take over the position.

"But they said nay?" Cam suggested quietly.

"According to them I'm too young and need further training," Joan said bitterly. "I told them she'd taught me everything she knew, but he just shook his head and said that God had other plans for me and he had already arranged a replacement for Mother. That he would need the hut for the new healer. Besides, did I not have a task to carry out for my mother?"

"He kenned about your mother's message?" Cam asked with surprise.

"Aye. He visited daily when my mother grew sick. She found comfort in his company." Joan smiled faintly at the memory. She'd often returned to the hut to find them deep in a solemn conversation that ended the moment she entered. It had seemed almost furtive to her. Once, she'd returned earlier than expected from a task and found the man writing on parchment. He'd quickly rolled it up and slid it up his sleeve before leaving, but Joan suspected it was the very parchment that now rested against her belly inside her shirt. One hand unconsciously rising to touch the scroll through the cloth of her shirt, she admitted: "I think he wrote her message for her. Mother was too weak to write at the end."

"Your mother knew how to write?" Cam didn't hide his surprise at this news and Joan supposed she shouldn't be insulted by his surprise. It was rare for someone outside of nobility to know how to read or write.

"Aye, she was taught by one of the nuns in an abbey she worked at before I was born."

"Did she teach you?" he asked curiously.

Joan merely nodded.

"'Tis a valuable skill, boy," Cam said solemnly. "Between that and yer healing abilities ye shouldn't ha'e any problem finding a position once yer task is done."

Joan didn't comment. What he said might be true were she a male as he thought her to be. But she wasn't and that would make things more difficult. Her mother had only done as well as she had because she'd earned the favor of the abbess who ran the abbey in the village where she'd grown up. Joan had thought she had the affection and favor of both the abbess at Wellow Abbey and the Friar at the Augustinian friary, but both had gently but firmly refused her when she'd approached them.

"Mayhap this message yer mother left is a request fer a position fer ye," Cam said thoughtfully. "She may no' ha'e been Scottish, but that does no' mean she does no' have Scottish acquaintances. Mayhap she saved this Scot's life and is hoping their gratitude will move them to offer ye a position."

Joan frowned at the suggestion, but shook her head. "I don't think so. She never spoke of anything like that, or even the name. In fact, I've never heard it before."

"What name?"

"Mac—" Joan cut herself off abruptly and scowled at him. He'd nearly tricked her into naming the recipient of the message.

"Why do ye no' wish to tell me their name?" Cam asked.

Joan's eyebrows rose, not at the question, but at

his expression as he asked. He looked almost suspicious. She understood why when he asked, "Are they enemies o' my clan?"

"I don't know who the Sinclairs count as enemies," she said truthfully, and then admitted, "But if 'twas an enemy, would you try to stop me from delivering it?"

"Nay, o' course no'," he assured her, and then grinned and admitted, "But I wouldn't help get ye there either."

Despite herself, Joan found herself smiling at his words, and then wincing as her split lip complained.

"Come now, tell me who the message is for," Cam coaxed. "The Sinclairs do no' ha'e many enemies. 'Tis more likely a friend and then I can repay yer kindness in saving me life and escort ye there . . . or at least part o' the way if they're too far out o' me way."

Joan peered at him silently. She was too proud to ask for help, but not so proud she wouldn't accept help were it offered. It would certainly make her journey less dangerous were she not alone. She debated briefly and then blew out her breath and just said it. "Laird and Lady MacKay."

Cam's lips split in a wide grin, and he reached out to thump her in the arm. "Ye're in luck, lad. The MacKays are friends to the Sinclairs. Good friends." He shook his head and then added, "Even better, they're our neighbors, so I can see ye all the way there on me way home."

Joan righted herself slowly. His friendly thump

in the arm had nearly knocked her off the log. Managing a small smile that didn't pull too much at her healing lip, she nodded. "Thank you."

They ate in silence for a minute, and then Cam asked, "So no family 'sides yer mother?"

Joan shook her head and swallowed the meat she'd just taken a bite of. "Me father died ere I was born, me grandparents too, and I had no brothers or sisters." She glanced to him curiously. "You?"

"Both parents still alive, two brothers, one sister, and more aunts, uncles and cousins than you can shake a stick at," he said around the onion he'd just bitten into. He grimaced then and added, "I've family coming out me ears. More than anyone wants or needs."

Joan raised her eyebrows at that. She would have loved to be able to claim such a large family. But then she was alone. "You don't get on with your kin?"

"Oh aye," he assured her. " 'Tis just that me clan seems to think being blood means they can interfere in me life at every turn. 'Tis enough to make a man crazy at times."

Joan nodded with an understanding she didn't really have. She'd never had that problem.

"Actually, that interference is the only reason we met each other," Cam said suddenly, a wry smile curving his lips.

"How is that?" Joan asked.

"Me family thinks I should marry again," he added grimly.

"And you don't want to?" Joan guessed.

"Aye. I mean aye, ye're right and nay I do no' want to," he added and then shifted forward off the log so that he could sit on the ground and lean back against it. Eyes focused on the flames before them, he sighed and then said, "After me first wife . . ." He shook his head. "I do no' want to go through that again."

"Your first marriage was so bad?" Joan asked, trying to understand.

"Nay," he answered at once. "She was pretty and smart, a good woman, and marriage was no' so bad."

Joan raised her eyebrows. "Then why would you not want to marry again?"

Dissatisfaction crossed his face, and he stared so long into the fire that she began to think he wouldn't answer, but then he suddenly did. "We were married a year. 'Twas a good year. We got on well and it was a good match. But she got with child, and went into labor a year and a day after we married."

"She died in childbirth," Joan guessed, understanding immediately filling her.

"Aye," Cam murmured, his expression full of regret.

Joan nodded silently.

"She was so small, and the babe was big," he said grimly, and then added, "The midwife said the child was sideways."

"Did the midwife try to turn—"

"Aye," he interrupted. "She tried and tried, but said it would no' turn."

Joan didn't comment. What could she say? She had encountered the same thing herself a time or two. Usually she could shift the baby, but sometimes it was as if the baby was caught on something and—

"It took her three days to die," Cam said grimly. "For three days the whole castle listened to her scream as she fought to push our babe into the world. On the third day her screams were so weak . . . I kenned she was dyin'. My family tried to keep me out, but I forced me way into the room and . . ." He paled, his eyes closing. "There was so much blood."

Joan waited a minute and then asked, "The child?"

"We buried them together," he said heavily. They both stared into the fire now and then he straightened and said firmly. "I'll no' put another woman through that."

Joan didn't comment. She understood. Witnessing something like that . . . well, it had made her decide not to have children. She could understand his not wanting to watch another woman go through it as his first wife had.

"Me family are determined I should wed and give them the heirs they want though," he added with a grimace. "Me mother especially is determined and once the snow melted, started filling Sinclair with any unmarried or widowed female she can find that she thinks might tempt me. By spring's end I was tripping over women everywhere I turned. The woman was making me life a misery," he said with disgust and shook his head. "I finally had to head out and find a battle to fight jest to get a rest and that's where I've been all summer. Offering me services to those in need o' a good sword hand. Well, offering me sword and that o' a couple cousins who went with me."

"Where are your cousins now?" Joan asked.

"We started out together, but stopped in Nottingham for a meal. The tavern wench was a pretty little thing, and very friendly," he said with a grin. "I told me cousins to continue on without me and I'd follow later."

"I see," Joan said and almost winced when she heard the disapproval in her own voice. She was supposed to be a boy, after all, and a young boy would probably listen with eager glee rather than disapproval. But Cam only chuckled at her censure.

"Oh, come, lad. Ye'd have stopped too had she been wiggling her bosoms in yer face and dropping in yer lap to bounce about."

Joan managed a smile and merely said, "Aye, well, 'tis fortunate for me that she was so friendly and slowed your journey else I may not have survived my encounter with Toothless and his friends."

"Toothless?" Cam asked with confusion.

"The big man who was beating me when ye came upon us," she explained.

"Ah." Cam nodded, and then shrugged. "I did no' see his face. I hit him from behind."

"Oh, aye," she murmured, and stood to walk

to the river and kneel at its edge to dip her hands in and remove the grease from the rabbit meat off her hands. When Cam joined her a heartbeat later, she asked, "Are your brothers younger than you?"

Cam glanced to her with surprise. "Aye. How did ye ken?"

She shrugged. "If they were older your parents would not fret so about heirs. As the eldest though, you inherit the land and title . . . so an heir becomes more important."

"Aye. Or I could leave it to one o' me brothers and their heirs," he pointed out, then straightened and shook his hands, removing the worst of the water as he complained, "I should no' be tired but I am."

"You're healing," she said quietly. "You'll tire easily over the next while."

"Aye, well, then I'd best sleep. We'll leave at dawn on the morrow."

Joan mumbled agreement and watched him walk back to the fire. He unwound his plaid as he went, wrapping it about himself like a blanket before lying down on his side, facing the fire. The sight made her wish she had a plaid of her own. It was the end of summer, warm during the day but cooler at night. It would have been nice to curl up in the heavy woolen cloth to sleep.

She straightened, giving her own hands a shake, but then grimaced. Now that her hands were clean, the filth on her skin from the wrists up was more noticeable . . . and tomorrow they would be traveling again and gathering even more dust and

dirt off the trail. Her gaze slid to the water almost
longingly. A quick dip would be lovely. The night
air was cool enough that the river water had felt
almost warm in comparison when she'd washed
her hands. If she moved a little distance up the
shore and was quick . . .

Joan glanced over her shoulder toward Cam,
and then began to move silently along the riverside.

Cam shifted restlessly and opened his eyes to
peer into the fire. He was tired, but now that he
was lying down, he couldn't seem to fall asleep.
His body was exhausted, but his mind appeared
to be rolling over his conversation with Jonas. He
liked the boy. He was smart, capable and brave
enough to take on this mammoth task on his own
and that had earned his respect. Cam did not give
respect unless it was earned, and the boy had
earned it.

Jonas had also proven himself in possession of
honor. The lad could have just left him lying in the
road. It certainly would have been a lot less trouble. He also could have stolen his horse and the
heavy sack of coins Cam had earned during his
summer of mercenary work. But while the saddle
and sack had been removed from his mount, they
had both been set neatly nearby, under a stack
of underbrush to hide them from any would-be
thieves.

It had taken Cam a good bit of hunting to find
the items. He'd actually begun to fear the boy
had sold the one and taken the other when he'd

stumbled over them. Every last coin was still in the sack too. Cam had checked. A sack of coins like that must have been a great temptation. It was more than the boy would probably see in his entire life, but the lad was no thief. He was also a skilled healer. Cam could tell that by the fact that he still lived. He'd gingerly felt around on his back earlier and noted the size of his wound. That plus the amount of dried blood he'd found in his boots when he'd tried to don them told him as much. His plaid had been clean, but the boy hadn't thought to check inside his boots. Cam had set them to soak in the river with a couple of large rocks to hold them in place, hoping that would remove the dry blood.

That recollection had Cam sitting up. Gritting his teeth against the pain that shot up his back, he glanced toward the river, eyebrows rising when he saw that Jonas was no longer at the river's edge. The sudden worry that the boy might have fallen in had Cam getting abruptly to his feet. He had his plaid wrapped about his waist and was at the riverside in a trice. There was no sign of him there, but the river could have taken him downstream. The current wasn't strong, but there was a current.

Cursing, Cam began to follow the river, scanning the surface for the boy's floating body. He'd gone perhaps twenty feet when movement in the shadows ahead made him slow and squint his eyes to see better. Jonas stood ahead, at the water's edge. He was disrobing, obviously intending to bathe.

Cam paused and relaxed, glad he hadn't called out. The boy obviously wanted privacy for the task or he wouldn't have come so far downstream. Cam was about to turn and give him that privacy when the boy took his hat off, allowing long hair to come tumbling out. His eyebrows rose at that. Most peasants kept their hair short to keep it out of the way while working. It was also a sign of their status. Jonas having hair that tumbled down his back almost to the top of his braies was just a bit startling. But that wasn't the only surprise. The boy tugged his tunic off over his head, revealing bandages wrapped around his upper chest in a wide swath.

The sight made Cam clench his fists as Jonas began to unwind the wrapping. He hadn't realized how badly the boy had been hurt in the attack. Here he'd apparently taken a mammoth wound, and yet the lad was the one who had looked after him while he—

Cam's thoughts died abruptly as the last of the bandages fell away and two rather generous breasts popped into view. Shocked to the core, Cam merely stood there gaping like an idiot as he tried to accept what his eyes were telling him. Jonas, the fine young chap he liked and respected, was a girl. A fine figure of a girl too, he saw, as she dropped her braies and started into the water. She had a figure that—

Bloody hell!

Turning abruptly, Cam strode silently back the way he'd come, not stopping or even slowing until he reached the spot he'd been lying on earlier. Pulling the plaid up around his shoulders, he then lay down, pulled the plaid to cover his head and shoulders and then firmly closed his eyes. The moment he did, an image of Jonas stripping off his braies rose up against the back of his eyelids. *Her*, Cam corrected himself. *She'd* taken off her braies.

Dear God, Jonas was a Josephine . . . or perhaps a Joanna, or something along those lines. He had no idea what her real name was. Or how much to believe of the tale he'd been told. Was there really a message to be delivered? He suspected that was true. He'd seen the scroll himself. And lad or not, she was still delivering the message, though whether it had been a deathbed request or not wasn't certain.

On the other hand, Cam reminded himself, she hadn't stolen his gold or left him to die at the roadside, so he suspected he could trust her word and that the majority of the tale was the truth. Actually, it made a lot of sense for her to travel as a boy. Had she been dressed as a woman, he wouldn't have come upon her being robbed, but raped. Which was no doubt the reason for the disguise, he realized. It wasn't safe for a lass to travel alone.

A lass, he thought. Damn. Cam lay still for a moment, but then recovered enough from his shock to decide it made no difference. She had saved his life and tended him while he was ill and helpless. She deserved his aid in getting to her journey's end, more so now that he knew Jonas was a girl.

As for her secret, he wouldn't confront her about it, Cam decided. He still liked the lass. She was a brave bit of goods and smart and able. He would see her to MacKay and allow her to pretend to be a boy on the way there. But now he was curious to see what she looked like without all that bruising and swelling. Would he think her worth a tumble once healed?

Cam rolled his eyes at himself. She had earned his respect as a boy and should be given at least as much respect now that he knew she was a woman. That being the case, it mattered little what she looked like. He would see her safely to MacKay and then continue on to Sinclair without divulging that he knew her secret. Unless of course she came to trust him enough to tell him herself, he decided.

The situation resolved in his mind, Cam shifted to a more comfortable position and closed his eyes to attempt to sleep . . . and again couldn't find that elusive state. Now that he knew Jonas was a girl, he felt he should be standing guard while she bathed. Ensuring no one troubled her, that she didn't encounter difficulty and drown, and then to see her safely back to their camp.

Not revealing that he knew her secret was going to be difficult, Cam realized suddenly. He wouldn't have let her go traipsing off into the woods alone to hunt their supper had he known. Hell, now he was feeling guilty over it. As the man, he should have hunted down their dinner himself.

Oh aye, this was going to make the journey more difficult.

A rustling sound made him open his eyes and turn his head to look over his shoulder toward the river in time to see a small shape move into view. Jonas, or whatever her name was, was returning, he realized with relief. Relaxing into the cocoon his plaid offered, Cam closed his eyes to feign sleep and listened as the girl approached the fire. There was some rustling and movement and then silence.

Several moments of silence passed and then Cam opened his eyes to glance about. The female who had introduced herself as Jonas had picked a spot not far from his own and lay on her side, hands clasped and pillowing her cheek. Her eyes were open though and meeting his gaze, she nodded, murmured, "Good sleep," and then closed her eyes.

Cam stared at her face briefly, but she was so misshapen from her beating he couldn't tell what she would look like once healed. He also couldn't tell what color her hair might be. She wore her woolen cap pulled low in the front, covering even her brows. He continued to stare at her for a long time, simply watching the flames cast light and shadow over her swollen face, and eventually drifted off to sleep.

Chapter 3

"Tell me about your brothers."

Cam raised his eyebrows at that question. They had been chatting about various and sundry since setting out that morning, their likes, dislikes and so on, but this was the first time the conversation had taken a more personal turn. Cam glanced briefly over his shoulder to where Jonas was mounted behind him on his horse. Jo, he corrected in his mind. It just didn't seem right to think of her as Jonas now. Not after seeing her naked. That thought made him grimace. The image of her naked in the moonlight had kept him awake until nearly dawn. It had seemed like bare minutes later when a combination of birdsong and Jo's moving around had woken him. Now he was exhausted, and grumpy, and his back hurt with every step the horse took so that he had kept the mount to a slow trot. They were moving so slowly they may as well be on foot, but at least they were moving.

"Why?" he asked finally.

"Because I'm curious," she said and he felt her shrug where her front pressed against his back. "Besides, 'twill pass the time."

He supposed that was true, and mayhap it would distract him from his own somewhat ridiculous thoughts. He found his gaze continually dropping to where her hands were. She really had lovely hands, long slender fingers, pale, unmarked skin. If he'd taken note of those, he might not have been caught so off guard by the realization that she was female. They were definitely a woman's hands, and a woman who had not damaged them with hard labor. Being a healer, she didn't have the dry, work roughened skin and callused fingers of the average peasant. In fact, her hands could have passed for a lady's.

"What are their names?" Jo prompted and Cam forced his gaze away from her hands again.

"Aiden and Douglas," he answered, glancing over the path ahead.

"And they're both younger than you?"

"Aye. Douglas is three years me junior, he's the eldest of the two."

"And Aiden?" she asked.

"Seven years younger than Douglas. Still a lad, really, though he thinks he's a man at fifteen," Cam muttered dryly. "And like all youth he thinks he knows everything and is invincible."

"Of course he does," she said with amusement and then asked, "Were your brothers not sent to train in the homes of other nobles? I thought that was common amongst nobility."

"Aye, all of us were. Father insisted. But Mother couldn't bear us to be away long and so I was away for two years, Douglas was gone two and a half years and Aiden for three," Cam murmured.

"It got easier for her with each child," Jo noted.

"Aye," Cam murmured and then grinned and added, "That or I was her favorite, Douglas her second favorite, and Aiden a pain in the arse she was happy to be rid of."

"You are awful," Jo said on a laugh, lightly slapping his belly with one of the hands clasping him there.

Her laugh definitely wasn't that of a boy. It was high and tinkling. He liked it, Cam thought, glancing down again at the hands splayed on his stomach. They rested low, just inches above—

"I gather Douglas is your favorite brother then?" Jo asked, interrupting his thoughts.

Cam shrugged. "We are closer in age, but . . ."

"But?" she queried when he paused.

"We have little in common," he admitted quietly and then explained, "Douglas is terribly serious and grim all the time, while I am not."

"Hmm," she murmured, shifting against his back. "'Tis usually the other way around. The eldest is usually more serious and the middle child less so."

"Aye, and that is how it was when we were growing up," Cam admitted.

"What happened?" Jo asked. "When did that change?"

Cam squinted thoughtfully as he considered

the question. He'd never really troubled himself to work that out. Now he did and wasn't sure he liked the answer to her question, but she was waiting for one, so, sighing heavily, he admitted, "After me wife's death."

"Ah," she murmured.

"Ah?" he asked, stiffening. "Ah what?"

He felt her shrug against his back again. "Tragedy often changes people."

Cam grunted, but felt dissatisfied, both with her words and the realization he'd just had. While growing up he had always taken his responsibilities and charges seriously. It had been hammered into him that he should, and so he'd been dutiful about everything, performing every task required of him . . . until his wife, Lacey, had died.

Like him, Lacey had taken her duties seriously and had done all she was expected to without fail. Their marriage had been arranged while they'd both still been in swaddling. When their parents decided that it was time for that marriage to take place, they'd both accepted and gone into it without fuss or ado despite their being complete strangers. Lacey had dutifully welcomed him to her bed, if not eagerly, then with calm acceptance. She'd even got with child quickly, as was expected and carried the child without complaint right up until the day it had killed her. And that was when Cam had begun to throw off the shackles of duty.

"What are your parents like?"

Cam shook off his thoughts at that question

and considered how to respond. "Me mother loves and frets o'er us all. She's a good woman."

"And your father?"

"He dotes on me mother. We all do," Cam answered and then urged his horse off the road, onto a barely visible trail through the woods.

"Are we stopping?" Jo asked and he could feel her shifting behind him, her chest sliding against his back as she looked around.

"Aye. 'Twill be dark soon, and I ken a good spot to stop just off the road. I ha'e camped there on other trips."

"Oh," she said and relaxed against him, her hands slipping a little lower at his waist.

Cam knew it was an unconscious move on her part. She probably wasn't aware her hands had dropped a bit, and certainly it wasn't as if they were anywhere they shouldn't be. He wasn't even sure why he was so aware of their position. He liked the girl, had liked her when he'd thought she was a boy too, but he wasn't attracted to her. At least he didn't think he was. True she smelled nice, he liked her laugh and he enjoyed talking to her, but he didn't even know what she looked like under all those bruises, so he couldn't be lusting after her. Could he?

"'Tis beautiful," Jo breathed as they broke out of the woods and into a clearing.

"Aye," Cam agreed but with appreciation rather than the wonder she was experiencing. He'd been here before after all. But it was a truly beautiful spot. The trees had been cleared away as if someone had planned to build here. In the absence of trees, a field of knee high grass and wildflowers had grown and it was all beside a lovely waterfall that the river flowed over before meandering away toward the south.

Once they reached the center of the clearing, Cam brought his mount to a halt and then twisted just a bit, ignoring the pain it caused and held his hand and lower arm out to Jo. He didn't have to say a word, she took his hand with one, and grabbed his forearm with the other and then held on as she swung herself off the horse and to the ground.

"Thank you," she said with a nod and then turned to walk toward the water's edge as he dismounted.

Once on his feet, Cam leaned his head against his mount and took a moment to let the pain the action had caused to ease. He then led his mount to a tree on the edge of the clearing and secured the reins to a branch before removing his bag, and Jo's. Setting them aside, he then started to unsaddle the beast, and brushed him down before turning to find the clearing empty. Cam frowned, but then realized that she had probably gone to find a secluded spot to take care of personal business and relaxed.

It had been a long ride. They may not have got far because of the speed at which they'd been forced to travel, but they'd ridden from dawn until now, almost dusk. He needed to drain the dragon as well. Scooping up his bag and Jo's he headed back the way they'd ridden in. He didn't want to risk running into Jo and spoiling her secret after all. Besides, seeing her that way once had been enough. He didn't need another vision of her naked to keep him awake.

JOAN LEANED FORWARD, TOOK A DEEP BREATH and lowered her face into the water again. She would have liked to take a dip to wash off the day's dust, but there was no time for that. Besides, it was still light out. She didn't want to be seen and recognized for the woman she was. The water was nice though, and felt soothing on her swollen face, so when she couldn't hold her breath any longer, she lifted her head, took another breath and dunked her head in the water again. Joan did that three more times before straightening and sitting back on her heels to let the water roll down her face and neck.

It had been a good day, the best of this trip for her so far. It seemed her encounter with Toothless and his gang, while painful, had worked out for the best for her. This was the first day she hadn't been anxious and nervous from sunrise to sunset. Traveling alone, she'd had to be constantly on her guard. That hadn't been the case with Cam. She'd been able to relax a bit today and just enjoy the scenery and conversation. The combination had made the journey much more pleasant, and despite the fact that they had ridden slowly and probably hadn't got much further than she would have on foot, at least her feet and legs didn't ache. And Cam had promised to see her safely to MacKay so the rest of her travels were going to be this easy. All in all, what had started out the worst of days when Toothless and his gang had attacked her, had ended up being quite lucky.

A rustling in the bushes behind her had Joan standing up with surprise and turning around. Her abrupt action must have startled the pheasant she'd apparently heard, because in the next moment one suddenly rose up out of a nearby bush and flew into the branches of the nearest tree. The sight made a slow smile stretch her lips, and this time, the pain was minimal. Her face was still misshapen with swelling and bruising, but it was a little better than it had been. At least it had seemed so in the wavering reflection she'd seen in the river water.

Not that it really mattered at this point, she supposed. It wasn't as if she wanted to appear attractive to Cam or anything. After all, he thought she was a boy. Besides, she'd decided long ago that relationships and men were not for her. Getting mixed up with them was dangerous. She had no desire to die in the birthing bed as she'd seen so many women do. Every one of them had gone screaming, or exhausted from screaming if they lived long enough to push the baby out. Nay. She liked Cam, it was true, and yes he was certainly very attractive, but that was as far as it went.

"And you are such a liar," she muttered under her breath. Joan was more than attracted to the man. She'd sat behind him on horseback all day, her arms around him, her face pressed to his back, smelling the woodsy scent of him, and enjoying the caress of his soft hair against her cheek as the wind blew it back toward her.

She definitely had an attraction to the man. It had started as she'd nursed him back to health those three days. While he apparently didn't recall it, Cam hadn't been incoherent the entire time, at least he hadn't been unconscious anyway. He'd been feverish but talking even then and she'd found him amusing and intelligent. An opinion that had only grown once his fever broke and he woke up. Their conversations last night and today had merely increased her liking and attraction to him.

Joan supposed that meant she was lucky that he thought she was a boy. At least this way, he wouldn't be interested in a dalliance to pass the time. Not that he probably would anyway, considering how unattractive she was just now. Still, with both those little matters between them he wouldn't be interested and she wouldn't be tempted to do something stupid.

Pushing these thoughts out of her head, she moved over to stand beneath the tree the pheasant had flown to. It had roosted on a branch about fifteen feet up. She peered at it briefly, imagining how good it would taste cooked over an open fire. The thought made her stomach rumble, reminding her that they hadn't eaten since the rabbit the night before. Joan rubbed her stomach and then glanced around her for a good-sized rock. Finding one that would suit, she retrieved a slingshot from the small bag she'd sewn inside the waistline of her braies.

Joan had always been good with the slingshot. A natural talent her mother had claimed. She hit the bird in the head with the first shot and watched with satisfaction as it toppled off its roost and fell. Her satisfaction died abruptly, though, when the damned thing merely landed on the branch below the one it had been on and lay there.

She waited, hoping that given a bit of time, the bird's weight might make it slip off the branch, but when that didn't happen, Joan heaved a sigh and moved to the tree to begin to climb. Never having climbed a tree before, she was surprised at how easy it was. It didn't seem to take long at all to climb up so that the branch the bird had flopped over was at her chest level. Joan reached for it then, but of course it was out of her reach. Quite a ways out of her reach.

Joan debated the matter and then climbed up until she stood on the branch the bird was on. She then eased to sit on it and pressed her hands down on the branch and straightened her arms. The action lifted her behind enough that she could then swing to the side a bit until her hip bumped against her right wrist, then she lowered herself and performed the action again over and over until she had moved herself far enough along the branch that she could reach the bird.

Smiling at the thought of the meal she was going to make for Cam that night, Joan picked up the bird and moved it to lie between herself and the trunk on the branch she was on. She then began to shift herself back the way she'd come. She was perhaps halfway back when the bird she'd thought she'd killed proved otherwise and suddenly fluttered and squawked beside her. Startled, Joan jerked, one hand slipping off the branch, and then she was falling. Crying out, she grabbed for something to stop her fall, and then cried out again as her head slammed into a branch. Pain radiated through her head, and then through her whole body as she crashed to the ground. Joan moaned as darkness claimed her.

CAM WAS PACING THE CLEARING AND FRETTING over what was taking Jo so long when he heard her scream. He whirled in the direction he thought the sound had come from and by the time the second scream sounded, he was running. The problem was he had no idea where she was, and after the second scream there was nothing to lead him to her. Cam shouted her name several times, but got no response, and then simply had to search the underbrush and area along the river. He did so quickly and methodically, aware that the sun was on its downward journey and he had to find her before dark.

Cam had been searching for what seemed like forever, growing more anxious by the moment when he glimpsed what looked like a bundle of cloth under a tree ahead. Eyes squinting, he moved slowly toward it, but then broke into a run when he recognized that it was Jo, lying on her back.

"Jo?" he said, dropping to his knees beside her. When she moaned and turned her head, relief coursed through him like he'd never before experienced. Her eyes were still closed, but she was alive at least, and she was stirring.

Bending, Cam scooped her up in his arms and straightened. The action brought her eyes open and she moaned again and winced as if the light bothered her.

"Oh, my head," she muttered, turning to press her face against his chest.

"What happened?" Cam asked, carrying her quickly back along the river toward the clearing.

"I fell out of the tree," she admitted on a sigh, raising one hand weakly to the base of her skull. Wincing at her own touch, she pulled her hand away and Cam cursed when he saw the blood on her fingers.

"What the devil were ye doing in the tree in the first place?" he asked sharply.

"Trying to get a pheasant," she admitted, sounding weary. Jo blinked her eyes open to give him a wry smile as she explained, "I knocked it out with my slingshot. I thought it was dead, but when I started to come back down the tree with it, it woke up and startled me. I fell . . ." She shrugged and turned her face into his chest again. "Sorry, I guess we won't be having pheasant for supper as I'd hoped."

"I'll find us supper. Ye should ha'e left it to me to begin with."

"You are still healing," she began and then

suddenly stiffened and turned her face to his, eyes popping open. "Damn. Put me down. You shouldn't be carrying me. You'll open your stitches. Put me down, Cam."

"Me stitches are fine," he growled, tightening his arms around her and ignoring the pain in his back. "They will no' be fer long, though do ye no' stop squirming."

Jo went still at once, but glared at him for his obstinacy. The sight made Cam smile. She looked so cute with her face all swollen and scrunched up like that. It made him think this must be what little evil elves must look like.

"What are you smiling about?" she grumbled, turning her face away to see where they were.

"Ye do no' want to know, la-ad," he stumbled over the word, barely catching himself from calling her lass. He'd have to be more careful about that, he supposed and shook his head as they reached the clearing.

"Let me see your back," Jo said when he carried her to the river's edge and set her down to lean against a boulder there.

" 'Tis fine," Cam assured her and turned to go find both their bags. He'd forgotten all about the damned things in his panic when he'd heard her scream. He should have hidden them the moment he'd taken them off the horse, he supposed and then shrugged the worry away. He'd found her, and the bags were still here which was fortunate since they needed her medicinals.

"Tell me what I should do," Cam ordered as he returned.

"You should show me your back," she said grimly. "I want to see the stitches and be sure you haven't pulled any of them."

"They are fine," he repeated, dropping his bag at her feet and turning his attention to opening hers.

"Then show me," she snapped, and then grabbed for her bag with annoyance. "Give me that."

"Ye're bleeding," he said grimly and rifled quickly through the bag. Sadly, he didn't know a damned thing about healing, so in the end, merely removed a small swatch of linen and then handed her the sack and moved to the waterfall to stick the cloth under the icy running water. When he turned back, Jo was rifling through the bag herself, retrieving item after item. Cam ignored what she was doing and knelt beside her and reached for her head. "Let me see."

"I am fine," she said sharply, jerking back from him and putting one hand to her hat as if to stop him from taking it off. That was when Cam recalled that there was a long mane of glorious hair hidden under the cap she wore. If he tried removing it, her secret would no longer be a secret.

Cursing, he sat back on his heels and scowled. Let her think she kept her secret or tend her injury?

"I am the healer. Why do you not go hunt us up some supper while I tend this?"

The words were couched as a question, but the tone was definitely an order. He had been dismissed, Cam realized, and found it amusing, considering that just moments ago she'd been demanding to see his back to ensure it was all right. It seemed that given a choice between ensuring he hadn't split his stitches and keeping her secret, keeping her secret won out.

"Go on, away with you," Jo said, waving him away as if he were a pesky fly.

Cam hesitated, but then nodded and stood. He would let her keep her secret for now. But he would keep an eye on her, and if she showed any signs of serious damage, he would be tending her himself, secret or no secret.

"But I want to see those stitches when you return," she added fretfully as he strode out of the clearing as ordered.

Cam merely grunted and continued until the woods closed around him, blocking him from view. He made a lot of noise as he moved through the brush to ensure she heard him leaving. But after he'd judged he'd gone far enough that she would think he was gone, Cam paused and made his way silently back. Head wounds were a nasty business, unpredictable at best, and he was determined to be sure she was all right before he would be willing to leave her alone for the amount of time it would take for him to scare up some dinner.

Reaching a tree at the edge of the clearing, Cam stationed himself behind it and leaned to the side to peer at Jo. His noisy exit had apparently reassured her, for she already had her cap off. Cam hadn't been able to tell the color last night, since the sun had set and everything had been in shadow. Now he saw that it was a wave of fine spun gold.

"Beautiful," he murmured, admiring the fair color until he noted the splotch of dark red just above and behind her ear. He scowled at the sight even as she covered it with the cloth he'd dampened at the waterfall.

Cam watched for several moments as she cleaned and then explored the area blindly with her fingers. When the worry on her expression eased and she merely applied salve before carefully catching up her hair in the cap and returning it to her head, he relaxed and slid away. Cam still would have liked to see for himself that the wound wasn't a bad one, but he trusted her skills. Besides, she'd only cleaned the blood away once and hadn't had to do it again before applying the salve. That suggested the bleeding had stopped, which was a good thing.

Glancing around the woods as he moved silently through them Cam briefly debated what to do about their meal. He could catch a rabbit, or hunt down that pheasant who had scared her out of the tree, or even catch fish . . . or he could head to the small village he knew was nearby and fetch them back a meal from the tavern there. While the tavern was small and didn't offer lodging, it did serve some of the finest food he'd found on his travels. In fact, just the thought of his last meal there made his mouth begin to water . . . and that made his decision. The village tavern it was, he decided, and turned his feet in that direction.

It wouldn't take long to walk there and back. It would have been faster on his horse, of course, but he hadn't thought of it while he was in the clearing. Shrugging, he picked up his pace, and distracted himself with wondering what the tavern owner's wife had cooked up that day.

Chapter 4

Jo SOAKED THE LINEN IN THE WATER AGAIN and raised it to press against her cheek until the cloth grew warm from her skin. She then glanced fretfully around as she dipped the cloth in the river water again.

Cam seemed to be taking a long time. The sun was almost completely below the horizon, leaving the sky afire with an orange glow that darkened to deep purple around the edges. Night would soon descend and he wasn't yet back.

Perhaps he was having trouble finding game, she told herself, withdrawing the cloth from the water and pressing it to her cheek again. She didn't have anything better to do while she waited.

Cam's mount shifted where he stood and she glanced toward him, stilling when she noted that the beast's ears were pricked. The animal had heard something, she realized, and began to scan the woods around the clearing, her ears straining to catch any telltale sound that someone approached. Still, she was caught by surprise when Cam suddenly stepped out of the trees and crossed the clearing toward her.

"I was beginning to worry," she admitted.

"No need. It just took me longer than I expected," Cam said easily, dropping the bag she hadn't noticed he carried beside her and then kneeling to quickly wash his hands in the water.

"What's this?" she asked curiously, eyeing the bag with interest as some rather heavenly smells wafted from it.

"Open it and see," he suggested, shifting to sit in front of her so that they faced each other, legs crossed.

Jo didn't even hesitate. The smells coming from the bag were amazing.

"That's what took me so long," Cam announced as she peered at the food inside. "The tavern owner's wife was still cooking the chicken when I got there, but promised it would only be a trice before it was done. Her idea of a trice is apparently a lot longer than mine," he added dryly.

"Chicken," Jo almost moaned the word, but then glanced to him with surprise. "The tavern owner's wife?"

"Aye. I have stopped here many times and there is a village a short walk away with a tavern that always has delicious food. Rather than hunt up our meal, and clean and cook it, I thought I'd simply buy it from the tavern keeper's wife and fetch it back. Fortunately, while she was offering stew to the customers, she had a roast chicken for herself and her husband that I was able to convince her to sell me. A lucky thing since I had no idea how I would have fetched stew back here. It would have soaked through the trenchers before I could make it back."

"Aye," Jo murmured, her face practically buried in the bag as she examined the contents; roast chicken, dark bread, cheese and two ripe apples. It all looked and smelled divine.

"Well, what are ye waiting fer?" Cam asked suddenly. "I've been smelling that all the way back from the inn. Get the food out. Ye must be hungry. I ken I'm starved. We've no' eaten since last night."

Jo hesitated, and then set down the bag of food to reach for her medicinal bag. Aware that Cam was watching her with bewilderment, she quickly pulled out some clean dry linen and set it on the ground. Only then did she start to unpack the food from the inn. The strips of linen might not usually be used this way, but she hadn't wanted to set the food on the ground and be spitting out dirt all night. Besides, the linen could be washed afterward.

"How's yer head?" Cam asked, breaking off a drumstick from the chicken and passing it to her.

"A little sore but fine," she answered. She then took the offered meat and murmured, "Thank you."

She waited until Cam had broken off a leg for himself as well and was raising it to his mouth before taking her own first bite of the meat. The moment she did though, her eyes closed on a little moan of pleasure. She'd thought the rabbit was good, but this was positively heaven. Jo swallowed with a sigh and opened her eyes, the drumstick already rising to her mouth again. She wanted to go slow and savor, but didn't think she could. This was possibly the best thing she'd ever tasted in her life. The truth was, while her mother had been a fine healer, she hadn't been much of a cook, and Jo had learned everything she knew from her mother. Even had they been able to afford a whole chicken to roast, which they wouldn't have, she never could have produced a bird as moist and well seasoned as this. And the bread and cheese were just as good, she found as she sampled those. It must be a popular inn indeed if it served such fine food, she decided.

Hungry as they were, and good as the food was, it didn't take them long to clear away the chicken. Joan was done first and settled back to watch Cam finish off the rest of the bird. There was no sense saving any, it would only go bad. That wasn't true of the cheese and bread though, so after a bite or two each, they'd decided to concentrate on the chicken alone and take the cheese, bread and apples with them to eat on the horse at nooning the next day.

"Well," Cam said, swallowing the last bite of chicken. "That was well worth the walk and wait."

"Aye," Jo agreed with a small smile. "Thank you."

"Me pleasure," Cam said and then raised an

eyebrow when she got to her feet. "Where are ye off to?"

"To wash chicken grease off me hands and . . . er . . . tend to other matters," she muttered, aware that a boy would have said they were draining the snake or some other such thing.

"How's yer head. Will ye be all right on yer own?" Cam asked with concern.

"I'm fine," she assured him. "My head barely aches anymore."

"Hmm," Cam muttered, and then shrugged and said, "Shout if ye need help."

Jo merely grunted and headed off into the woods around the clearing. She hardly needed help relieving herself. Her head wound really wasn't that bad. The bump was a good size, but not alarmingly large, and the ache really was easing. She suspected she'd been knocked out as much from having the wind knocked out of her when she hit the ground as from the blow to the head. In fact, she hadn't lost consciousness until landing in the dirt with such a jolt.

A rustling in the bushes to her left made Jo slow and glance that way, but it was so dark away from the fire that she couldn't see a bloody thing. It had been lighter last night. There was no moon tonight, she noted glancing up. No stars either and she wondered if the night sky wasn't full of clouds blocking them. Whatever the case, it made her eager to return to camp and their fire, so Jo was quick about her business.

Cam already had his plaid wrapped around him like a blanket when she returned.

He lay down as soon as she stepped into the light cast by the fire and offered her a "Good sleep."

"Good sleep," Jo murmured in return and stretched out on the opposite side of the fire. She was just closing her eyes when she realized she'd forgotten to take a look at his stitches on his return. Sighing, she quickly got back to her feet and moved around to his side of the fire. The moment she blocked the flames and cast shadows on him, Cam opened his eyes. He raised his eyebrows when she stopped before him.

"I need to check your stitches," she said firmly, afraid he would again claim he was fine and try to refuse her.

Cam considered her briefly, then shrugged and rolled onto his stomach.

Jo hesitated, but then knelt beside him and gently pulled the plaid down in the back. Her eyes widened slightly when she saw that his shirt was gone. A glance around showed it draped over a stick stuck in the dirt by the fire to dry. It was soaking wet. He'd either washed it, or—

"I waded into the water to wash me hands, slipped and got dunked," Cam said with amusement at his own mishap. "Fortunately, a similar thing happened the last time I stopped here, so this time I took off me plaid ere stepping in else I'd be laying here naked."

The words put an immediate image in her mind of his naked body stretched out before her like a feast. An image that quickly vanished when he glanced over his shoulder at her and added, "Take heed, the river's bottom is flat stone fer a ways after the waterfall, and 'tis covered with moss and slippery. Use caution if ye go in else ye'll end up on yer rump."

Jo nodded quickly, letting her breath out with relief when he turned away again. Giving her head a shake, she turned her attention to his back again. She'd tugged the cloth down just far enough to reveal his shoulders before stopping to look around for his shirt. The skin revealed gleamed golden in the firelight. She tugged the plaid further down, baring his back and noted how the flames cast dancing shadows on it, emphasizing the rippling muscle as he folded his arms under his head and relaxed.

Cam was a beautiful man, she admitted to herself with a little sigh as her gaze ate up all that she'd revealed. She'd seen it before of course, but had been more concerned then with saving his life than the fine figure he cut. Now though, she couldn't seem to stop staring at all that naked flesh.

" 'Tis fine, is it no'?" Cam said suddenly. "I told ye it was."

Jo gave a start at the words, her glance automatically dropping to the wound on his lower back. She immediately frowned. "Your wrapping is gone."

"They got wet too," Cam said, shrugging his shoulders and making the muscles in his back move in an almost mesmerizing way. "They're under my shirt by the fire."

Jo forced her gaze away to glance toward the shirt. She couldn't see the bandages under the large shirt, but had no doubt they were there. Still she continued to look for a count of ten, just to allow herself to regain her composure. She had no idea why the sight of his bare back was affecting her this way. It was beautiful and she had the mad urge to run her hands over all that golden skin. Instead, she clasped her hands together, bit down hard on her lower lip and then turned back, determinedly focusing on his wound.

As he'd said, it was fine. Truly. The man must have a healthy constitution, for it was healing quickly, and she could see no sign of tearing from his carrying her. Still, she leaned to the side to grab her bag and opened it to retrieve her salve. 'Twas better to be safe than sorry, she told herself as she began to smear it gently on the wound. This had nothing to do with her desire to touch him, and everything to do with his healing. Really.

Rolling her eyes at herself, Jo finished with the task, quickly tugged the plaid back up over his shoulders and stood.

"Good?" Cam asked, rolling onto his side.

"Aye. 'Tis healing well," she mumbled, turning away to move back around the fire to where she'd first lain down. "Good sleep."

"Good sleep," Cam responded, curling up in his plaid once more.

Sighing, Jo stretched out on her side and closed her eyes, but her mind was filled with moments from that day. Riding with her arms around Cam's waist, her chest pressed to his back. His carrying her back to camp, his arms and chest surrounding her with heat and making her feel small and safe. His grin of anticipation when he'd watched her open the sack he'd brought back with him from the tavern. Cam lying half naked before her as she rubbed salve on his back . . .

Jo drifted off to sleep with a smile on her face.

Muttering a curse under his breath, Cam shifted restlessly and peered at the woman on the other side of the dying fire. She was sleeping like the dead. He, however, was wide awake. Again. He'd had the devil of a time getting to sleep the night before and should be exhausted now . . . and he was, but that didn't make a difference. He still couldn't sleep. It was Jo's fault. So far today she'd plastered her little body to his back like a leech on his horse, her hands just inches above the part of his body that had woken when he'd accidentally seen her undressing and learned he was a she. Then she'd gone and knocked herself out, scaring him silly and forcing him to carry her in his arms, her warm little body cradled against his. And then she'd moaned and sighed her way through their entire meal like a woman responding to a lover's attentions. She had definitely forgotten she was supposed to be a boy there. No lad would react that way to a bit of chicken.

The *pièce de résistance*, though, was her rubbing salve on his back. It was not the first time she'd done it, and she hadn't done it with any sort of sexual intent, but that hadn't made any difference. His body had reacted as if it were foreplay and now he was wide awake and aching and she, bloody minded woman that she was, was completely unaffected.

A cold drop of liquid hit his nose and Cam blinked and brushed it off with one finger, his gaze moving automatically skyward just as another drop hit his forehead. Great! Now it was going to rain. He should have known. Clouds had been gathering in the sky as he'd made his way to and from the village, and darkness when it had come had arrived fast and hard as it was wont to do when clouds aided in its arrival.

Two more drops hit his face and Cam's gaze slid to Jo. While his plaid was oiled on the outside and water would just run off it so that all he had to do was pull it over his head to remain dry, his traveling companion did not have such protection. She would be soaked in minutes once the clouds opened up. Another drop, on his eyelid this time, started him moving and Cam got quickly to his feet and rearranged his plaid as he moved around the fire to Jo's side. He didn't shake her awake or say her name, Cam just settled on the ground on his side behind her, and threw his plaid over to cover them both, then let his hand rest on her hip.

It took him about a heartbeat to realize that this might have been the biggest mistake he'd ever made in his life. Jo did not wake up, shrieking with dismay at his move. She didn't wake up at all as far as he could tell, but she did murmur sleepily and press back closer against him. He had no doubt she was unconsciously seeking his body heat, but she was also wiggling her bottom into his groin in a most distracting manner.

Cam set his teeth and tried to ignore it, but the fact that they were cocooned in the plaid, leaving him surrounded by her scent, didn't help any. Much to his relief, Jo suddenly murmured sleepily and rolled away from him and onto her stomach. At least he was relieved until he realized that his hand was now resting on her bottom rather than her hip. Cam closed his eyes and counted to ten as he fought the urge to squeeze the rounded cheek under his fingers, then carefully raised his hand. As he set it on his own hip, he acknowledged that it was going to be a very long night.

JO SHIFTED SLEEPILY AND SMILED AT HOW WARM and comfortable she was. The patch of ground she'd chosen was a little lumpy, but softer than she recalled it being last night when she'd lain down. And for a change instead of waking up cold and a little stiff from sleeping on the cold, damp ground, she was warm and . . . moving slowly up and down, she realized, her eyes popping abruptly open.

Darkness surrounded her, confusing her briefly, and Jo lifted her head, feeling something pressing against her head and shoulders as she did. It was like some kind of material was over her, she thought with confusion and was completely befuddled by that. She was also starting to panic a little when the cloth that she'd felt was suddenly

pulled off her head and she found herself staring
down at . . . Someone's chest? A chest that was
moving up and down with every breath. She recognized that chest too, Jo thought and lifted her
head to find herself staring into Cam's open eyes.

Jo opened her mouth, intending to ask how the
devil she'd got on his chest. And how they'd got
on the same side of the fire, but as she noted the
grimace of pain on his face, what came out was
a concerned, "Your back," as she realized he was
lying on it.

Cam reacted immediately, splaying one hand
on her back, catching her head in his other and
abruptly rolling so that she was lying flat on the
ground, and he was on top of her. He quickly
shifted his hands then to allow his elbows to take
his weight, and she expected, to get up off of her,
but instead his head came down and his mouth
covered hers.

Jo was so stunned at the action that she simply
remained still for a moment. This was not the first
time she'd been kissed. A village boy or two had
tried while she was growing up, but she'd never
been much moved by the activity. Perhaps that had
been due to the kisser, she thought now, because
the kisses she'd received in the past had seemed
sloppy and uninteresting and had always left her
wanting to wipe her hand across her mouth. This
kiss was nothing like that. Cam's mouth was firm
as it brushed across hers, and then he nipped at
her lower lip, a quick, tantalizing tug that had her
mouth opening with surprise. The moment she

did that, his tongue slid into her mouth like an invading army, causing chaos and starting up fires at various points throughout her body.

Jo had never experienced anything like this, and was so overwhelmed that it took a moment for her to realize that Cam was kissing her. Her . . . Jo . . . who he thought was a boy. Her eyes immediately popped open and she began to press against his chest, trying to lift her mouth from his. When escaping his kisses upward didn't work, she finally turned her head determinedly to the side. That worked. At least it broke the kiss. However, bereft of her mouth, Cam began to trail kisses across her cheek toward her ear.

"Cam, this is—" This was what? She wondered, trying to recall what she'd been about to say before he'd begun to explore her ear, nibbling and kissing it in a way that had the most unexpected effect. Damn, she couldn't recall, but what he was doing was rather amazing. It was sending shivers of excitement up and down her body in waves of pleasure like she'd never experienced.

If the church knew about this they would no doubt be up in arms, she thought. Nothing that felt this good could be condoned by the church. They tended to disapprove of anything pleasurable and— That thought reminded her of what she'd wanted to say earlier, this kind of thing was definitely not condoned by the church, not just because they weren't married, but because she was a boy. At least, he thought she was a boy. She wasn't of course, but to his mind he was kissing a boy, which was a bit distressing since she was enjoying it, but knew he was a man. She'd seen him naked after all. How disappointed would he be when he discovered she wasn't a boy as he thought?

She'd barely had the thought when Jo became aware that Cam had been easing her tunic up her back and encountered the binding that kept her breasts flat and helped her with her disguise. She expected him to ask what that was about and whether she'd broken her ribs in the beating she'd taken, but instead she felt cold steel against the skin of her back and the binding suddenly gave way. A heartbeat later his hands had shifted around to clasp and cover her aching breasts so that he could squeeze and caress them.

Not so disappointed, she thought dizzily as he suddenly rolled her onto her back and lifted her tunic as he shifted down her body so that he could claim one nipple in his warm mouth.

Why wasn't he disappointed? She wondered with confusion. Or at least startled? And why did that feel so damned good?

Jo moaned as he tugged at her nipple with his lips, drawing all the excitement presently bouncing through her body to that area. That excitement only increased when she felt his knee slide upward between her legs and press against the core of her through her braies. So she almost moaned with disappointment when Cam suddenly raised his head and asked, "Joanne or Josephine?"

"What?" She stared at him blankly.

"Yer name," he explained solemnly. "It has

been driving me mad the last two days since I discovered ye weren't a boy. Every female name I could think of that might fit has gone through me thoughts, Joan, Joella, Joanna, Jocelyn, Jo-"

"Joan," she interrupted, and asked, "You knew I was a girl? How—?"

"I saw ye preparing to bathe that first night," he explained, shifting up her body to settle his weight on his side, leaving his hands free. "Ye let yer hair down, removed yer tunic, and then unwrapped the binding and all that beautiful bounty spilled out and I kenned ye could no' be a boy." Lowering his head then, he claimed her lips even as one hand settled over some of that "beautiful bounty" to palm and caress her.

Joan moaned into his mouth at the combination, her back instinctively arching to thrust her breast more firmly into his caress. She released another moan, but this time one of protest when he once again broke their kiss and stopped caressing her. Jo reluctantly opened her eyes, expecting another question, but then blinked them quickly closed and raised herself slightly, her upper arms rising instinctively above her head as he tugged her tunic up from where it had gathered above her breasts and pulled it off. She started to lower her arms then, instinct making her reach to cover her breasts, but Cam caught her wrists before her hands could finish the action, and pressed them down on the ground on either side of her head as he kissed her again. He shifted over her as he did, not pressing his weight into her, but urging his knee up against her again and allowing the springy hairs of his chest to brush across her sensitive nipples.

Jo gasped and writhed beneath him, legs shifting restlessly before closing around his knee and urging him on, even as she arched to allow her nipples contact with his flesh. She also sucked at his tongue when it shot into her mouth, wanting to keep it there. She had no idea if that was the right thing to do and didn't care, it felt good. But she nearly bit his tongue when one hand left her breast and ran down to slide beneath the waist of her braies until he could cup the center of her.

While his knee had been nudging her there, ratcheting up her excitement, his hand against her bare skin was shockingly intimate and Jo went still, uncertainty claiming her as the shock allowed clarity briefly in to warn her they were messing with fire. This was how babies were made and she had no desire to die on the birthing bed, some part of her mind reminded her. But then his fingers shifted, one pushing in to run along her embarrassingly damp flesh and Jo gasped, her hips jerking at the caress and her mind losing track of the warning it had tried to sound.

With him touching her there, Jo didn't even notice that his other hand had stopped caressing her breast to work at her braies until he broke their kiss and left off caressing her. As he shifted to his knees between her legs, she realized that her braies had been pushed off her hips and were halfway to her knees. Even as she noted that, he caught her legs by the ankles, raised them before him and quickly removed the leather pants.

When he tossed them aside, Jo stared after them wide eyed and almost reached to drag them back with some vague intention of pulling them back on, but then Cam set her legs down on either side of him again. She turned her attention back to him just in time to see his face duck out of sight between her thighs.

"Wha—ohhhh!" she cried out as his mouth took over what his fingers had been doing moments ago. His lips, his tongue, even his teeth came into play as he explored a part of her that no man had ever got near before, and Jo was quickly undone. The ability to think seemed to leave her altogether as sensation took over and her whole body rocked under the assault. Some part of her was vaguely aware that her head was thrashing, rolling back and forth in the dirt as she emitted high, loud, senseless sounds and clutched at his head.

When Cam tapped her hand gently, Jo realized she was pulling at his hair and immediately eased her grip, not wanting to hurt him, but that was the extent of what she was capable of. The man was driving her crazy with what he was doing. But then she felt something pressing into her that was too firm to be his tongue and she glanced down with confusion to see that his head was still buried there and she could still feel his lips and tongue working, but now—Oh, his finger, she thought vaguely, her hips dancing under the tune he was playing as he pushed one finger into her at a maddeningly slow speed.

Her hips rose and thrust and tried to force him along, but he was determined to control this and simply eased his finger back out before letting it slide part way in again. His tongue and lips worked madly as he did, plucking at her until she began to moan and wail so loud that she became aware of it. Jo bit her lip then, trying to silence herself, but that was impossible. She wanted to scream with the need claiming her, wanted to cry out, beg and demand by turn that he bring an end to this madness, and that he never stop. And then it was as if something snapped inside her, some string she had never known existed, and in snapping it released a wave of pleasure so strong she briefly shimmied and convulsed under it. It was while she was still convulsing that Cam left off what he was doing, rose up between her legs, clasped her thighs and drove himself into her.

Jo's pleasured cries turned to a shriek of pain as he encountered and slammed through her maiden's veil. Her mother had told her it was different for each woman, that some hardly felt more than a pinch, while others felt as if he were tearing through a thick layer of skin. For Jo, it was the latter option. She definitely felt more than a pinch. In truth, she would have compared it to someone stabbing her with a blade. Not that she'd ever had that happen, but if she had, this was what she imagined it would have felt like.

Much to her relief, Cam stopped moving when she cried out. They were both still for a moment and then Jo forced her eyes open to look at him uncertainly. He stared back briefly, and then shifted one hand from her thigh to slip it between them just above where they were joined. When he began to caress her again, she nearly released an exasperated sound, quite sure he wouldn't be able to stir up any interest after that shot of pain. But she'd barely had the thought when she felt the first stirrings of her rekindling desire.

Cam still didn't move, remaining fully imbedded in her as he patiently worked to rouse her once more, and in the end it was she who began to move. The pain not quite, but almost forgotten, she began to shift against his shaft, knees rising and heels digging into the ground as she began thrusting into his caresses, unintentionally riding him as she sought that release he'd already given her once.

He let her have her way for several moments, but then Cam gave up caressing her and clasped her hips to control her movement as he began to thrust in and out of her, in and out. At first Jo was disappointed and even a little frustrated, but then he shifted and changed the angle somewhat so that his body rubbed against her core and she closed her legs around his hips to egg him on. This time when she found that release she sought and cried out, Cam cried out with her, his hands tightening on her hips and holding her tight against his body as he poured his seed into her.

Chapter 5

*J*OAN STRAIGHTENED FROM CHECKING ON THE pheasant she had roasting over the fire and glanced to Cam's sleeping face for about the hundredth time. He was still sleeping soundly and the sight made irritation flicker through her before she turned to pace to the water's edge and back. She then did it again. Jo had been pacing all day, ever since he'd made love to her.

All right, it hadn't been all day, she acknowledged silently. Cam had collapsed next to her after they'd both cried out with release. Lying on his side beside her, he'd then thrown one leg over hers and one arm across her chest and promptly fallen asleep. Jo had actually slept too for a little bit. She hadn't been able to help herself. Her body had been trembling and weak in the aftermath of what they'd done and she'd just dozed off there with him. She didn't think she'd slept long though. The sun had still been creeping upward in the sky when she'd woken up sometime later.

Jo had remained where she was briefly, listening to Cam's steady heartbeat next to her ear, but then had eased out from under his arm and leg and got up. The first thing she'd done was dress, and rather quickly too. The worry that Cam might wake up and see her naked making her move with more speed than grace. Then she'd sat beside him, berating herself for acting like such a ninny. The man had seen her naked, most intimately in fact, and yet she was going to go all shy about his seeing her again?

She'd followed that up with berating herself for letting him do what he had, or for doing it with him, since it wasn't like she hadn't been a party to it. Joan had reminded herself that she didn't want to get with child, and that she had no desire to be some dalliance for a noble, and that a dalliance was all she could be to Cam. Certainly nobles didn't marry commoners. That depressing lecture had taken quite some time and left her feeling deflated. Not that Jo had started imagining marriage and happy-ever-afters before that. Still, the cold hard truth was often difficult to swallow and after the incredible passion she'd experienced, being brought down to earth so abruptly was much like falling out of the tree had been. She'd landed with a nasty bump.

Feeling cheap and even a little angry then, Jo had taken herself off to find wild berries to break her fast with. Despite the depression hanging over her, or perhaps because of it, she'd suddenly felt hungry. She'd taken her time, finding enough for both she and Cam in case he was hungry when he woke up. It was on her way back to their camp that Jo had spotted the pheasant. Once again, her slingshot had come in handy, but this time she hadn't had to chase the bird up a tree. It had still been on the ground when she'd shot it. But she'd broken its neck for good measure the moment she reached it, to avoid what had happened the night before.

Cam had still been sleeping when she'd returned to camp, so Jo had plucked and cleaned the bird. When she'd finished, Cam was still sleeping with no sign of stirring, so she'd started another fire, and cut down two large Y-shaped branches to stick in the ground on either side of it and a third straight branch to skewer the pheasant on to lay across the first two branches. She'd been eating the berries she'd collected ever since while pacing and occasionally turning the pheasant. The sun was now past its zenith and on its downward journey; the berries were long gone, the pheasant was done, the fire was dying, and Cam still slept.

Sighing, Jo paced to the water's edge again, her eyes wandering to the waterfall. It was beautiful and the idea of stripping and standing under it to wash had been tempting her every time she'd looked at it. The only thing stopping her had been the fear that Cam would wake and see her. But he was showing no sign of that happening anytime soon, which was a bit worrisome really. If it weren't for the occasional snore that slipped from him, she would have feared he was dead.

Jo had no idea why he was sleeping so long, but

then she had no idea about a lot of things. Like how had she ended up under his plaid with him, sleeping on his chest? And why had he not told her that he knew she was a girl and not the boy she was pretending to be? She might have been a little more prepared for his advances had she known that. Although, to be honest, she might not have been; the last time she'd seen her reflection she hadn't exactly been attractive so wouldn't have imagined he'd lust after her.

Perhaps soaking her face in the cool water last night had rushed her healing along and she looked like herself again, she thought suddenly, and knelt at the water's edge to peer at her reflection in the rippling surface. Joan watched a frown pull her brows together as she got a look at herself. While the swelling had gone down a bit and the bruising appeared more green and yellow than black now, she still looked like hell and had to wonder what had moved him to want to bed her.

Sighing, Jo straightened and got to her feet. Another glance at Cam showed him still sleeping. She was beginning to think he would sleep right through the rest of the day and into night. The only thing she could think was that it was because he was still healing. Perhaps they had overdone it yesterday, traveling so long. Perhaps they should have waited an extra day for him to heal, or at least kept their traveling down to half a day or something. She would have to talk to him about that when he woke up, Jo decided and glanced to the waterfall again.

She had never seen a spot as beautiful as this

one, and wasn't likely to again unless she stopped
here on her return journey. Even then it was
doubtful she'd find this spot on her own. Unfortunately, Jo hadn't taken note of where they'd left the
trail. So if she didn't bathe in the waterfall now,
she would probably never get the chance again.

Glancing over her shoulder, she noted that Cam
was still sound asleep, and then she began to dis-
robe. She would be quick about it, Jo promised
herself.

CAM OPENED HIS EYES TO A BEAUTIFUL SUNNY
day, stretched and yawned and then winced as
the stitches in his back pulled a little. They'd done
that a time or two last night while he was tupping
Jo, too, he recalled and the thought made him
glance to the side for her. She was no longer sleeping beside him . . . and wasn't in the clearing, he
noted, after sitting up to glance quickly around.

Frowning, Cam got to his feet and pushed his
hands through his long hair to get it out of his
eyes as he looked around for any clues as to where
Jo had got to. The smell of freshly roasted meat
drew his attention to the pheasant over the cool-
ing ashes of their fire. That made him relax a little.
Only then did Cam admit to himself that for one
second, he'd feared perhaps she'd been upset by
what he'd done and left while he slept, setting out
on foot alone.

Cam grimaced at the guilt that suddenly beset
him. He hadn't forced her, he knew, but he *had*
been rather aggressive that morning. He'd also

caught her half asleep and no doubt completely unprepared for his advances since she was pretending to be a boy. On top of that, she had been completely inexperienced. That had quickly become obvious, even before he'd broken through her maidenhead. In fact, it had nearly made him stop at one point, but she'd felt and tasted so delicious, and she'd been so responsive that he hadn't been able to reign himself in.

Damn, he thought, Jo had a lot of passion in her. She'd moaned, writhed, gasped and cried out like a wild thing as he'd pleasured her, and it had all just made him want to pleasure her further, wring more cries and pleas from her sweet lips. The memory was enough to make Cam hard all over again, and he glanced down at himself, grimacing when he saw the dried blood on his shaft, further proof of her innocence.

Not that he'd needed to see the blood to believe it, he thought, and decided a quick dip was in order and then he would go in search of Jo. They needed to talk. He didn't know what he would say, but was pretty sure that at the least he owed her an apology. Not only had he taken her innocence, but he'd neglected to withdraw or do anything else to protect her against getting with child. That last part was alarming. He liked Jo, a lot. In fact, he liked her more after knowing her these few short days than he'd liked any woman he'd known, even his wife, whom he'd lived, slept and dealt with for a year. He didn't know why. Perhaps because he'd relaxed and talked with her as a friend when he'd thought her a boy. He'd never spoken so freely with a woman before, but felt, even now, that he could talk about just about anything with Jo.

Whatever the reason, the fact was that Cam liked her and had no desire to see her grow big with his child and then die screaming as she tried to push it out of her body. He should have left her alone, or failing that, used a pig's bladder. That was what he had been doing since his wife's death. He'd carried around a pig's bladder and when the need arose, tied it around his shaft with twine to prevent spilling his seed in a woman.

Unfortunately, the bladder had somehow torn while he was with the tavern wench. Cam wasn't sure how that had come about. He'd discovered it on waking up in the morning. He'd had a sore head at the time, and hadn't been pleased at the discovery. He'd hoped for more than one night in the tavern wench's arms, but he wouldn't risk it without the bladder, so he'd mounted up and left, expecting to catch up with his cousins the next day. Instead, he'd run into Jo and her attackers. He wasn't sorry. Frankly, he would pass up a dozen attractive barmaids for one Jo any day. So, in the end, the bladder tearing was a bit of good fortune, he thought with a grin . . . Except for the fact that he hadn't had it to use with her, some part of his mind reminded him, making his grin quickly fade.

Sighing, Cam pushed his thoughts aside and headed for the water to clean up. He was nearly to the water's edge when he realized that someone was already in it. Pausing, Cam stared. Jo stood under the waterfall, half turned away from him. Her eyes were closed, head tipped back, hair appearing almost alive as the water caught it and moved it about, streaming it over her shoulders and body.

She was beautiful, he acknowledged as his eyes ran over the curves on full display. Her nipples were erect, hardened by the cold water, he noted, and her hands were gliding over her body to aid the water in cleaning her. Water nymphs could not be more beautiful than Jo was to him in that moment and Cam stood, simply staring for a moment, watching enviously as she cupped her breasts and lifted them slightly, as if offering them to the water rushing over her. When she then released them and slid one hand down over her stomach toward the apex of her thighs to clean there, Cam couldn't stand it anymore and hurried into the water to cross to the falls.

The water was cold but did nothing to cool his ardor. Besides, his body seemed to adjust quickly and Cam was quite comfortable by the time he reached the waterfall and climbed up the boulders to join her on the flat ledge she stood on. Eyes closed and with the sound of the pounding water covering his approach, Jo was taken completely by surprise when he reached out and touched her shoulder. Her eyes popped open on a startled cry that ended in a gurgle as she took in water. Then she turned too swiftly, stumbled and nearly fell off the ledge into the pond it ran into.

Fortunately, Cam caught her arm and pulled her against his chest before she could. He then shifted them both closer to the small cliff's wall and out of the downpour. Jo opened her eyes the moment she was able and relaxed a little when she realized it was him, but not fully. He could see the questions forming in her eyes, and knew they should talk, but they were both naked, she was in his arms, his erection was cuddled against her stomach and her hard nipples were poking into his chest and all he wanted to do was—

Cam kissed her. It was not the questing kiss he'd started with that morning, it was a hard, hungry claiming. He wanted to devour her and his kiss said as much as he urged her lips apart and drove his tongue in to plunder the passion he now knew resided in her. Jo didn't fight him off, in fact she seemed too stunned to react at all at first, and that wasn't good enough for him. Cam wanted her hot and wanting him as much as he wanted her. He wanted to hear her gasps and moans in his ears, wanted her clinging to him, her nails scoring his shoulders, her body arching and thrusting.

Urging her back against the cliff face, he pinned her wrists to the rock on either side of her head and slid one knee between her legs, rubbing it against her core as he broke off kissing her to drop his mouth to one breast.

Jo said something as soon as her mouth was free, but he couldn't tell what it was with the sound of the rushing water so loud around them. Ignoring what could have been either a protest or a plea, he caught her nipple between his teeth and then closed his lips around it, drawing eagerly until she stopped trying to free her hands and arched into the caress. Cam released one of her wrists then so that he could reach down between her legs and caress her, and much to his relief, she immediately clutched at his shoulder with the free hand rather than push him away.

Continuing his caresses there, Cam released her nipple and straightened to claim her mouth again. This time she kissed him back with all the passion she'd shown him that morning, her own tongue meeting his and wrestling with it briefly before giving that up to instead suck on it when he urged one finger inside her wet warmth while continuing to run his thumb around the nub of her excitement. Her body was not still, her thighs were alternately tightening around his wrist and hand as if trying to keep him from removing it, and easing apart to keep from restricting his touch, as her hips moved, eagerly riding his fingers.

Concentrating on what he was doing, Cam was caught completely by surprise when she suddenly moved her own hand between them to wrap it around his erection. Breaking their kiss on a gasp, he threw his head back, his teeth snapping together as her fingers began to move on him. Her touch was tentative, she obviously wasn't sure of what she was doing, and he closed his free hand around hers, urging her to use a firmer grasp, and then immediately regretted it as his cock jumped

in her hands. Cam nearly found his release right
then, and soon would if she continued at what
she was doing. To ensure that didn't happen, he
dragged her hand away and then caught her by
the backs of the legs, spreading her thighs even as
he used his hold to raise her against the cliff face.

Jo instinctively caught at his shoulders and
leaned her upper body forward to avoid it being
scraped across the rock. It put her head by his ear,
which was the only reason he heard her moan
as he eased her down onto his erection. Cam
caught the last of the moan with his mouth, kissing her as he began to thrust in and out of her at
an angle that allowed him to rub against her core
as he withdrew and surged back in. Jo's kisses
were hot and wet in response, her legs wrapped
around him, crossed at the ankle and drove into
his behind egging him on, and her fingers knotted in his hair and tugged almost painfully with
demand as she sought the release she now knew
waited for her.

It excited the hell out of Cam and made him
drive harder and faster into her. Even so, he didn't
think either of them were prepared for release
when it came. It hit hard and fast, exploding over
him like lightning so that he clawed his fingers
into her hips and broke their kiss on a shout of
triumph that drowned out Jo's own scream.

When it ended, Cam was left sagging against
Jo, pinning her to the cliff face with his body as he
rested his forehead against the cold stone beside
her head. He felt weak as a kitten, as if every last

drop of strength in his body had been sucked out of him. He was even trembling. Afraid his legs might give out beneath them did he stay here much longer, Cam eased away from Jo. She immediately unhooked her legs and let them drop to the ground to take her own weight, but her head didn't move from his shoulder and her arms remained clasped around his upper back. After a brief hesitation where he debated whether he could manage the feat or not, Cam scooped her up in his arms and turned to jump off the large boulders that made up the ledge they stood on. The water in front of the falls was about shoulder deep. They were both briefly submerged as he instinctively bent his knees to reduce the impact of the landing, but it was very briefly. Fortunately, Jo had apparently been prepared for that. At least she didn't come out sputtering and spitting up water when he straightened and the water dropped to shoulder level.

The water was taking some of her weight now and Jo was barely more than floating in his arms, so Cam paused briefly to allow his muscles to regain some of their strength. Not that she was heavy, but weak as he was, he was concerned about carrying her out of the water otherwise.

When he paused, Jo lifted her head to him in question and Cam couldn't resist lowering his head to kiss her again. He'd meant it to merely be an affectionate brushing of lips, but the moment his mouth touched hers, something began to fizzle inside him and he found himself deepening the kiss. Jo responded in kind and that just made the reawakening passion explode back to full blown life between them.

The returning passion brought his strength back with it, and even as he kissed her, Cam began moving through the water toward shore. By the time the water fell away, leaving him to bear her full weight, he had no problem carrying her and in a trice he was laying her on his plaid and coming down on top of her.

Jo welcomed him with open arms, legs spreading when he nudged them with one knee and Cam settled between her open legs, his quickly growing erection nestling against the heat of her. He started to lower his head, intending to kiss her again, but spotting a drop of water trembling on the tip of her nipple, he changed direction and licked the deep rose tip instead, catching the droplet on his tongue. Jo shivered and released a little sigh at the teasing caress. When she then cupped his head in her hands, urging him on, he stopped to attend the breast more fully, laving and suckling at it before letting it slip from his mouth so that he could turn his attention to the other breast as well.

His hips were rocking between hers as he did, his shaft rubbing against her without entering, and Jo was moaning and gasping by turn in response. The sounds were sweet music to Cam's ears. He loved to hear her laugh, but he loved these sounds more. They seemed to feed his soul, so he was disappointed when she suddenly pressed on his shoulders, pushing him away.

Frowning, he gave up what he was doing and pulled back, then sat up on his heels between her legs when she kept pushing.

"What—?" he began with worry, but paused when she shifted to her own knees before him and began to explore his chest with fingers and lips. A small smile pulled at the corners of his mouth, and he almost told her gently that this had little effect on a man and she should concentrate her attentions lower if she wanted to please him, but he enjoyed her hands roaming over the muscles of his chest, squeezing and massaging here and there. And when she closed her lips over one of his nipples and began to tease it with lips and tongue, he was rather shocked to feel a string of excitement pull tight within him.

Damn, I like that too, Cam realized, eyes sliding closed. He then stiffened, eyes popping open when she released the nipple and began to kiss her way down his chest and across his stomach. He caught his hand in her hair and stopped her just as she reached his manhood, and Jo peered up at him, eyes wide and wounded and said, "But I want to please you like you did me."

He stared into her wide, pleading eyes, glanced to her full sweet lips just inches away from his shaft, and then let go of her hair and tried to steel himself against what was to come as her lips moved toward his erection. It had been semierect in the water, fully erect as he'd kissed and caressed her on his plaid, but now was so big the skin was stretched almost painfully tight. That situation only increased as she began to press tentative kisses to his hot flesh. The woman didn't have a clue what she was doing, and that didn't matter worth a damn. Just watching her mouth moving over him was so damned erotic he was having trouble holding back his release. He had to shift his gaze to prevent that, but it didn't help much when his eyes moved down her back to the two curves of her behind.

When Joan took him into her mouth experimentally, he could take no more. Cam caught one hand in her hair again, and grabbed her upper arm with the other to draw her upright and kissed her almost punishingly. When she slid her arms around his shoulders and kissed him passionately back, he released her arm to reach between her legs and caress her again, eager to bring her to the boiling point, as he was.

It didn't take long to get her there, within moments she was breaking the kiss and shifting to straddle him. Cam helped direct her onto his erection and then clasped her hips to aid her in raising and lowering herself at a rhythm pleasing to them both. The position put her breasts in front of his face and he couldn't resist catching one in his mouth and covering the other with one hand to caress her as she rode him.

Joan's cry of pleasure as she found release caught Cam a little by surprise, but the way her muscles spasmed around his cock had him following on her heels, his own shout coming before hers had ended.

Chapter 6

JOAN BREATHED A LITTLE SIGH OF RELIEF WHEN she found the road they'd been traveling on. She hadn't been at all sure she'd be able to find it on her own when she'd set out, but in the end it hadn't been that hard. Cam obviously wasn't the first to find the waterfall and there had been a narrow trail through the underbrush to follow.

Setting off in the direction they'd been headed before leaving the road, she began moving more quickly, eager to get as far away as possible before Cam woke up. Jo wasn't sure that was even necessary, he might be glad to be relieved of her company when he woke. On the other hand, he might have been planning on bedding her all the way to the MacKays and might be angry to lose the opportunity. She just didn't know. She didn't even know why he had done it in the first place, or the second or third. Her face was still a horrible mess, her clothing was less than attractive, and she hadn't got the chance to ask him. She'd meant to speak to him first thing on his waking, but then he'd startled her under the waterfall and then he'd begun kissing her and . . .

Biting her lip, Jo forced those memories determinedly from her mind, afraid that if she thought too much about it, she'd turn around and head right back to camp and wake Cam up for a fourth go around. The man was temptation in a plaid . . . and out of it. Honestly, he made her feel things she'd never before experienced. Things she'd never even imagined existed. The moment he kissed her, she forgot that he was a noble and she a commoner. She forgot that she was just a dalliance for him, that this was a sin. She even forgot her long-lived fears of the birthing bed as something began to quiver deep down inside her, and then erupted into a hunger that wouldn't be denied. She lost all good sense around the man.

That's why when he'd pulled her down to lie with him after the last time they'd done it, she'd waited for him to fall asleep and then had slipped out from the cocoon of his arms, dressed, collected her bag and set out on her own. Since she couldn't seem to resist the temptation he offered, it seemed better to avoid that temptation altogether.

Sighing, Joan glanced to the sky, trying to judge how much time she had left before the sun set and she had to stop traveling. Not much, seemed the answer, she decided with disgust as she noted that the sun was already approaching the horizon. An hour, maybe less was her guess and that couldn't be good. Chances were, Cam would sleep until dark. At least, that was her hope, and then he surely wouldn't set out tonight, another hope of hers. Still, even if she got lucky and both hopes were fulfilled, he would no doubt be up and on the road first thing come sunrise. Even if they started out at the same time, he was on horseback, she on foot. He would overtake her rather quickly.

Joan had barely had the thought when she heard the thunder of a fast moving horse. Not horses, horse, she realized. For one moment she was so panicked at the realization and the fear that it might be Cam that she froze on the road like a deer before oncoming hunters. But then her brain kicked in and sent her scurrying to the side of the road and the bushes that waited there. She dove into them without looking back, then hunkered down, trying to make herself as small as possible so that the bush would hide her. She knew she'd failed when the approaching horse suddenly slowed and then stopped just on the other side of the bushes.

"Joan?"

"No," she instinctively blurted and then could have kicked herself. No? For the sake of the good Lord, what was the matter with her? She should have kept her mouth shut and hoped he'd ride on. Surely he hadn't seen her? And if he had, he'd only caught a glimpse and couldn't have been sure it was her. At least not until she'd said no, not even bothering to try to disguise her voice.

"Are ye comin' out? Or shall I come join ye in the bushes?" Cam asked calmly.

Joan closed her eyes briefly and then sighed and stood up to scowl at him. "How did you know I was here?"

"I saw ye rush over and throw yerself behind the bush," he answered quietly.

"Well surely you only caught a glimpse. I could have been anyone," she pointed out with irritation.

"Aye," he allowed. "Except that yer behind was poking out of the bush, and I'd know that derriere anywhere, under any circumstances."

Aware she was blushing, Joan scowled at the man and then made her way back around the bush and walked stiffly to the road. Coming out just ahead of him, she turned her back and started walking as if he wasn't there. But Cam merely urged his horse up beside her.

"Come on. Up with ye," he ordered, holding his hand down to her.

Joan shook her head, refusing to do more than glance at the hand. "No, thank you. I'm fine walking."

"Why?" he asked, and she knew he didn't just mean why wouldn't she get on his horse. He wanted to know why she'd run off and left him behind too.

Joan bit her lip, and then glanced to him apologetically. "I appreciate your help with Toothless and his men. Thank you."

"Ye're welcome," he said solemnly. "And thank ye fer savin' me life."

She nodded to acknowledge his words and

then said, "But I think 'tis best do I travel on me own from here."

"Ye ken I can no' allow that Joan. 'Tis no' safe fer ye to travel alone."

"'Tis safer than traveling with you," she said, and then grimaced. She hadn't meant to be accusatory. Sighing, she paused and turned to look up at him, not surprised when he immediately stopped his horse. "I—we shouldn't have . . . why did you—? I mean, I'm not very attractive just now, yet you—"

Pausing, she stared at him helplessly. Joan hadn't expected this to be as difficult as it was turning out to be. She was a healer, which meant she'd had to discuss some very personal things with her clients. After years of training, she now could do so without any discomfort or embarrassment, but trying to talk to Cam about their having sex? Well, she was stammering, blushing and floundering like . . . well, like the virgin she'd been until that morning. Dear God, she thought suddenly. Had it only been that morning that she'd lost her innocence? And she'd lost it twice more since then already?

Well, okay, she reasoned, she had only lost her innocence once, but he'd bedded her three times. In one day. And it wasn't even over yet, she thought with dismay and then gasped with surprise when Cam suddenly leaned to the side, caught her under the arms and pulled her up on his horse before him.

"First o' all," he said patiently as he urged

his horse to move again. "Ye're right. We should no' ha'e. I should ha'e realized you were an innocent and left you alone. I also should ha'e pulled out or used something to keep ye safe from getting with child. Howbeit I did no' think. I wanted ye so bad I could no' think," he corrected himself and then said grimly, "As fer this nonsense about yer no' being attractive and why did I . . . Well," he shook his head. "It should be obvious I find ye very attractive. So attractive in fact, that 'tis hard to keep me hands off ye."

When Jo shifted to glance up and over her shoulder at him with surprise, he nodded solemnly, and added, "Even now, I'm fightin' the urge to raise me hand just that little bit needed to cup and fondle yer breasts."

Jo glanced down at the hand he'd placed around her waist just below her breasts. Glancing back to his face, she blurted, "They're bound right now. You couldn't feel anything anyway."

"Thank ye fer tellin' me that. It helps me resist," he said, his lips twitching with amusement.

Jo merely frowned at his words and asked, "But how can you find me attractive? I am far away from my best. My face is all swollen and bruised, my hair stuffed under my hat, and my clothes are not exactly flattering."

"Ye're jesting, are ye no'?" he asked with disbelief. "Woman, ye're wearing tight braies that do nothing but emphasize what a fine behind ye ha'e. As fer yer hair, while I can no' see it now, I've seen it down and ken it's there. And yer face grows better every day."

"Aye, but—"

"I like ye, Jo," he interrupted quietly. "I like talkin' to ye, and travelin' with ye. I like the way yer mind thinks, I like yer laugh, and I like ye as a person." He shrugged helplessly. "It makes me want to hear ye laugh more, and find out what yer thinkin', and it makes me want to strip yer clothes away one by one and sink me cock into yer warm wet body over and over and over again."

Joan stared at him wide-eyed, unconsciously licking her lips as his words bounced around inside her head, forming images that made butterflies flutter low in her belly.

"But I ken I should no'," he added solemnly, raising his hand to run one finger lightly over her lips in the trail left by her tongue. "And I shall try to behave meself fer the rest o' the journey, but I must insist ye ride with me. Ye saved me life lass, and I'll no' make ye risk yers by travelin' alone because ye're afraid o' me."

"I'm not afraid of you," Joan admitted on a sigh as she turned her head away. "I'm afraid of myself. I don't seem to be able to resist you and know I should. It seemed better to avoid the temptation than to fail again at resisting it."

"Well, I ha'e no' helped with that. But from here on out, I'll do me best to keep me hands to meself. Deal?" he asked.

Joan glanced back to him, managed a smile and nodded.

"Good," he said and then urged his horse off the trail.

"Where are we going now?" she asked with surprise.

"Back to our camp. When I realized ye'd left, I mounted up and hurried after ye without thinkin' to grab me bag or the pheasant."

Eyes widening, Joan glanced around, wondering how she could have missed that he'd turned back the way they'd come when he'd taken her up before him. Obviously, she'd been distracted, Joan thought, not really that surprised. The man had a powerful effect on her . . . and she knew she was foolish to give in and not continue on her own, but she just couldn't seem to say no, slip off his mount and walk away.

Joan rationalized it away by telling herself that it wouldn't happen again, that now that they'd talked, they would resist the attraction they had for each other. But she knew that was a lie even as she thought it. If Cam kissed her, she would kiss back, and there was no doubt in her mind where it would go from there. She also knew that he would kiss her eventually. It might not be tonight, it might not even be tomorrow, but eventually, he'd kiss her and they'd both be lost again. She knew all of that, but it was easier to lie to herself so she did.

"The pheasant is still here."

Jo glanced around as they rode into the clearing and noted the pheasant still over the fire, as well as his saddle bag beside the dead fire, but she merely nodded and slid off the horse as he brought it to a halt. Once on the ground, she simply stood there, unsure what to do. Were they staying, or just gathering the pheasant and bag and setting out?

"We'll stay here again tonight and set out at first light," Cam announced as he dismounted and began to unsaddle his mount.

Well that answered that, Jo thought wryly, but found herself staring at Cam as he worked. He hadn't bothered with his shirt when he'd dressed to come after her. In fact, his plaid was merely wrapped around his waist rather than donned properly. It left his chest and back bare and she couldn't seem to stop watching the play of muscles in his back as he worked. The man was a feast for the eyes.

And this was going to be a very long journey indeed, she thought grimly as her gaze dropped to his naked legs below the plaid. There was no way she was going to resist him. She may as well just give in and enjoy him while she had the chance. Joan was pretty sure no other man would stir her as he did. Cam would probably be the only lover she ever had, a fond memory to keep her warm on countless cold nights. She may as well make as many memories as she could, she reasoned.

"If ye do no' stop looking at me like that, lass, ye're likely to bring on something ye do no' want," Cam warned suddenly, turning to eye her with his hands on his hips in a manner that suggested he was annoyed.

"Mayhap I'm wantin' to start something," Joan said quietly.

Cam stilled briefly and then tilted his head, confusion playing on his face. "Did we no' just agree we'd try to behave?"

"Aye," she said and then shrugged helplessly. "But I don't want to. That's why I was leaving, because I knew so long as I was with you I'd want you. And it just seems to me we aren't likely to succeed at behaving, at least not for more than a day or two. Then we'll give in to it, but we'll have wasted those two days, so why bother? Besides, 'tis not as if you can put the eggs back in the shell once you've cracked them."

"Eggs?" he asked blankly, and she clarified.

"My innocence is gone, and I can't get it back. Denying ourselves will not change that. 'Tis a long journey and—"

That was as far as she got before Cam closed the distance between them and drew her into his arms. Joan went willingly with only a pinch of regret and self-recrimination. There would be much more of that at the journey's end she was sure, but for now, her conscience was content to wait.

"WAKE UP, LASS. WE'RE IN SCOTLAND."

Joan blinked her eyes open and peered sleepily around, confused at first as to where she was. But then she realized she was sleeping in Cam's lap on his horse. She'd obviously dozed off and shortly after they'd set out, from what she could

tell. At least she didn't recall being awake for long
after they'd broken camp and set out. Joan wasn't
terribly surprised that she had, they'd been up
most of the night as Cam had taught her several
ways to find the release he gave her.

"I'm sorry," she murmured, straightening in
front of him.

"Fer what?" he asked with surprise.

"For falling asleep on you," Joan explained.
"You must be tired too after last night."

"I slept all day yesterday," Cam reminded her
gently. "I am fine. And ye've naught to apologize
for. Ye need yer rest. In fact, I only woke ye because there is an inn just around the bend that
I was thinking we could stop at fer the nooning
meal."

"Oh," Joan said with surprise and smiled. "That
sounds nice."

"Aye. I thought so," he said with amusement
and urged his mount to move faster now that she
was awake.

The inn they stopped at was a pretty little building that sat all by itself on the side of the road.
There must be a village or town nearby, but Joan
had no idea where it was. She couldn't see any
other buildings about. Cam left his horse with a
stable boy who ran out to greet them, then ushered Joan inside. The door led into a good sized
great room lined with rows of trestle tables and
a stairwell leading upstairs where she was sure
there would be bedchambers to rent. The great
room was empty when they first entered, and

Cam was seating Joan at one of the benches that ran the length of the table when a door at the back of the room opened and a big bellied man with a wide smile stepped out to join them.

"Good day, good day, sirs, and what can I get fer ye on this fine day?" the man said cheerfully as he bustled over to them.

"Ale fer myself," Cam said.

"And fer the lad?" the man asked when he hesitated and glanced to Joan in question.

"The same," she said, trying for a deeper voice than her own. It wasn't until the man used the word boy that she recalled how she was dressed. Funny how she managed to forget about that around Cam.

"And would ye be wantin' something to eat too?" the man asked happily. "Me wife has made a fine chicken stew and a bean pottage."

"That'll do," Cam said when Joan nodded. "Two please."

"Good good," the man said rubbing his hands together. "Sit down, me laird, and I'll let me wife ken to serve up two trenchers, then fetch the drinks."

Nodding, Cam settled at the table. Once the man was out of earshot, he half-whispered, "I keep fergetting ye're dressed as a boy. Truthfully, now that I ken ye're a girl I'm amazed I ever believed otherwise, braies or no braies."

Joan smiled faintly at the compliment and shrugged. "As me ma always said, people see what they expect to. See someone in braies, and most would automatically count me a boy."

"Aye, I suppose so," Cam murmured, but shook his head just the same, suggesting he still didn't understand how everyone didn't at once recognize her as a woman.

Their host returned with their drinks, followed closely by a curvaceous little woman carrying their food. The stew was delicious and hearty and after commenting on how good the meal was, they mostly ate in a companionable silence until Joan asked, "How long do you think 'twill take us to get to MacKay?"

Cam was silent for a moment, and then shrugged mildly. "A week and a half or two weeks."

His answer made her eyebrows rise. She'd expected it to take that long walking. They were on horseback.

"With the two o' us on his back, I do no' want to make me horse go too quickly," Cam explained and then grinned. " 'Sides, why rush? I ha'e nothing to hurry home fer." He paused and then asked, "Is there a rush on delivering the message? Was it to be there by a certain time?"

"Nay," Joan admitted.

"Good." He relaxed and smiled. "Then we shall take our time and enjoy the journey."

Joan nodded and returned her attention to her food, but she knew he meant to enjoy the journey in more ways than one. She also knew she would enjoy it too, so didn't mind. In fact, she was rather pleased to know she had another week and a half of his company, or maybe even two weeks.

"Have ye thought on what ye plan to do once

ye've delivered the message?" Cam asked suddenly and Joan glanced to him blankly.

After a pause, she shook her head slowly. "Nay. Return home to Grimsby I suppose."

"Grimsby, aye, ye said ye were from there," Cam murmured, his gaze on his food.

Joan didn't comment. She'd told him she had been born and raised in Grimsby during one of their earlier conversations.

"But ye've no family there, do ye?" he asked.

"Nay," she admitted. "Me mother was the only family I had."

He nodded, and then took a deep breath and said, "Ye're a talented healer. 'Tis a valuable skill. Mayhap ye should consider settling at Sinclair and working there."

Joan paused and lifted her head slowly to look at him, but he was peering at his food with a concentration that was completely unnecessary. Avoiding her gaze as he made the suggestion? Did that mean he wanted her to stay at Sinclair or not? Was he just making the offer because he felt bad for her? Or because he didn't want this . . . whatever this was, to end?

Joan didn't say anything to that. In truth, his suggestion had quite taken her by surprise. She hadn't expected it. Joan hadn't even considered that this relationship they had, whatever it was, might continue beyond this journey. And she wasn't sure that it was a good thing if it did. She had no desire to be his mistress, so there was no future for whatever they were sharing just now.

"I'll be right back," Cam said suddenly and she glanced up to see him getting up from the table. Joan nodded and watched as he walked over to the tavern owner. Her curiosity rose when he put his head close to the other man's to murmur in a voice she couldn't hear. Joan actually caught herself straining to hear what he was saying, but it was impossible from this distance. Forcing herself to relax, she turned her attention to finishing the last of her meal and was just swallowing the last bite when Cam returned.

"If ye're all done we should head out," he said gently.

Nodding, Joan stood and started toward the door, but stiffened and glanced nervously around when he put his hand on her back to direct her. The tavern owner was nowhere in sight, however. She relaxed slowly and allowed him to usher her out.

"Wait here. I'll fetch the horse," Cam murmured as they stepped outside.

Joan nodded, and watched him cross the courtyard to the stables at the side of the building. He was quick about it, seeming barely to enter when he was coming back out, leading his mount. He hadn't taken more than a couple steps though, when the tavern owner rushed up to him with a small sack in hand. Cam took the sack and turned to hook it to his saddle. He then reached into his saddlebag and retrieved something that he turned and gave the tavern owner. Judging by the man's beaming smile, she'd guess it was probably coins and wondered what Cam had bought as she watched him nod at the man, before mounting and continuing over to collect her.

Joan took the hand he offered, and settled herself on the saddle behind him when he pulled her up. She didn't ask why he'd placed her behind him. She already knew. The tavern owner was watching. She was supposed to be a boy; sleeping cuddled in his lap wasn't the usual spot a peasant boy would ride with a laird. So she simply settled herself in a comfortable position and slipped her arms around his waist.

They rode until late afternoon before Cam found a spot for them to make camp. Another clearing, but this time without even a river nearby let alone a waterfall. It would do though, she supposed as Cam helped her off his mount.

"I'll go hunt up some dinner," she announced as Cam dismounted.

"No need," he said at once, retrieving the three bags hooked to his saddle and setting them on the ground. "I bought some roasted mutton from the tavern keeper ere we left. We're set fer sup tonight."

So that's what he'd bought, Joan thought with a smile. It would be nice not to have to look for their dinner for a night. Besides, mutton beat rabbit any day. Bending, she picked up the smaller bag she'd seen the tavern owner give Cam and quickly opened it to look inside, wondering if the tavern keeper had included bread or anything else with the meal. The first thing she saw was a smaller sack on top of the food. Eyebrows rising, she pulled it out and opened it as well, then tipped the contents onto her hand.

"What—?" she began with confusion and then glanced up with surprise when Cam was suddenly there taking the item from her.

"Ye wercn't supposed to see that," he said with what sounded like embarrassment as he tucked the item back in its little bag.

"Pig intestine?" she asked with amusement.

"Sheep intestine," Cam muttered and then sighed and said, "I ken 'tis a bit late, but I thought if we had no' already got ye with child, then I should don the intestine and prevent—"

He paused when Jo covered his mouth with her hand. For a moment she didn't speak. His thoughtfulness touched her. It showed at least some caring on his part. Although, to be fair to the man, he had been terribly solicitous of her nearly from the start.

"Thank you," she said finally, taking her hand from his mouth. "But there's no need for that. I have been chewing Devil's plague seeds every day since our first time together."

"Devil's plague?" he asked with confusion.

"Some call it bird's nest or wild carrot," Joan said, but he still looked blank. Apparently, no one he knew had used the seed before, or didn't tell him if they did. "It stops a man's seed from planting and bearing fruit."

"Oh," he murmured eyebrows rising. "Yer mother . . . ?"

"One of many things she taught me," Joan said

quietly and then handed him the bag of food and slipped past him. "I'll gather wood for a fire."

"Wait," Cam said suddenly, catching her arm before she could move away. When she paused and turned to him in question, she found him frowning. "It is no' dangerous is it? I've heard o' women taking things for such a purpose and dying, poisoned from the—"

"Nay. 'Tis safe," she said reassuringly. "The women you've heard of probably took hemlock or some such thing, which will dislodge a babe but can kill the mother too. Devil's plague won't."

"Oh . . . good." He let his breath out on a sigh, and then held out the bag of food again and said, "Take a look and see what we have. I'll fetch the wood."

Joan automatically took the bag, but merely watched him walk away, wondering why the conversation had seemed to sober them both so much.

Fear had made Joan chew the seeds the day before. She hadn't thought of them until she'd been preparing to leave him to set out on her own. In fact, she hadn't even considered the fact that what they'd done could leave her with child until that point. Her concerns had been more about what had happened and why. She'd begun to fret and worry that she was just a convenience to him. That any female he'd found himself with would have received his attentions. Despite his claims that he liked her, she didn't understand how he could want her with her face swollen and bruised.

Joan had forgotten that concern once he touched and kissed her, however. She couldn't seem to think of anything but the sensations he caused in her when he did that. It was only afterward, when she was awake and he was sleeping that she'd admitted that she just couldn't resist the man. One touch and she was lost. So it was better to travel alone and avoid the temptation he offered altogether. That was when other considerations had managed to surface in her mind . . . like the fact that she was now no longer untried. That hadn't bothered Joan so much. She never planned to marry anyway so hadn't worried about a future husband's upset at her lack of purity. But the possibility of being with child had occurred to her then as well, and that *had* worried her. Actually, it had scared her silly, and Joan had immediately dug through her bag of medicinals for the wild carrot seeds she knew were in there.

Fortunately, she had a lot of them, hopefully enough to last out the rest of the journey, because she was quite sure she'd need them.

Chapter 7

JOAN NESTLED CLOSER AGAINST CAM WITH A sleepy sigh and smiled when his hand immediately slid down her back, massaging her through the material of her tunic. The smile slipped away and she wrinkled her nose, though, when he pushed the plaid they were cocooned in down to their shoulders, exposing their heads and shoulders to the cool morning air.

" 'Tis chilly," she complained with a little shiver, trying to burrow closer.

"Aye. The nights are growing cooler. Summer is ending," he added, not sounding pleased.

Joan smiled at the complaint in his voice and shrugged as she said philosophically, "Everything comes to an end."

When Cam went still beneath her, she lifted her head to peer at him in question.

Cam stared back, his expression dismayed.

"What's wrong?" she asked.

He hesitated, shook his head, and then suddenly blurted, "Come to Sinclair with me after ye deliver yer message."

Now it was Joan's turn to go still. She stared back at him silently, her mind suddenly abuzz. He had mentioned the possibility of her working as a healer at Sinclair at the first tavern they'd stopped at in Scotland. But that had been two weeks ago now and he hadn't mentioned it since . . . until now. Although, this time he hadn't said anything about her working.

"As a healer or as your mistress?" she asked quietly.

"I do no' care, I just ken I do no' want this to end," he said quietly, caressing her cheek with the fingers of one hand. "I need ye, Joan."

She lowered her eyes unhappily, wondering what she'd hoped he would say in answer to her question. Had she hoped he'd ask her to come to Sinclair as his mistress? As a skilled healer who would be valued? Or as a wife?

In the end, though, it didn't matter what she'd hoped for, Joan supposed. The truth was, the last two weeks had been the best of her life. They'd set out late, stopped early, traveled at a snail's pace and had made love at every opportunity, turning a journey that could have been accomplished in three days at speed, into a two week orgy of pleasure. It hadn't just been their lovemaking that had brought the pleasure; talking, laughing, bathing, walking and even eating had been pleasurable with this man. There had never been a time in Joan's life when she'd laughed as much, or smiled so often. Her cheeks actually ached by day's end from all the laughing and smiling they did on a daily basis. She couldn't imagine a life more wonderful than one spent with this man.

But she couldn't have him. She was a commoner, he a noble. The best she could hope for was to be his mistress, existing on the fringes of his life, waiting for him to come visit her and bring her to life. Joan would be miserable in that existence, and even more miserable when he tired of her and stopped visiting. Then she would suffer endlessly, watching him with other women. Perhaps he would even eventually give in to his parents' pressure and marry again, having children, grandchildren . . . No. She simply couldn't do it. She wouldn't put herself through that.

Letting her breath out on a small sigh, Joan met his gaze and repeated what she'd said earlier. "Everything comes to an end, Cam."

"Not this," he said at once.

Joan hesitated, but then pushed herself up off him. Realizing the plaid had come with her leaving him in naught but his shirt, she untangled herself from it, intending to drop it back on him, but he was already on his feet.

Catching her arms he pulled her close and kissed her gently. He then rested his forehead on hers and whispered, "Not this, Joan. I do no' want this to end."

"But I do," she said quietly and he jerked his head back as if she'd struck him. Joan almost apologized and explained that she didn't mean that she really wanted it to end so much as she didn't want it to continue and then end. Before she could, however, the sound of someone clearing their throat distracted them, and they both turned their heads toward the direction of the sound.

Joan stared blankly at the man standing on the edge of the small clearing they'd stopped in last night. As tall and wide as Cam, but dark-haired where he was fair and perhaps a couple decades older, the man eyed them with an expression that was part uncertain welcome and part discomfort.

"Laird MacKay," Cam said, releasing Joan and turning to face the man. " 'Tis a pleasure to see ye again."

Joan's eyes widened as she recognized the name of the man she'd traveled so far to see. This was the MacKay her mother had wanted her to deliver a message to.

"And fer me," Ross MacKay said, though Joan couldn't help noticing that his eyes danced away from them as he spoke the words.

Cam didn't seem to notice, however, and asked, "What are ye doin' wanderin' yer woods at this hour?"

"The men on the wall reported seeing a fire in the night," Ross said quietly. "So a couple men and meself set out this morning to see what was about."

Joan glanced sharply to Cam. It had been mid-afternoon when he'd decided they should stop the day before. He must have wanted one more afternoon and evening with her, she realized, because they had to be very close to MacKay for the small fire they'd built the night before to be seen. Close enough that they hadn't needed to stop at all. She supposed she should be angry that he hadn't told her they were so close and continued on, but she wasn't.

"Where are your men and horse?" Cam asked.

"We left the horses back a ways and searched on foot fer yer camp. I did no' want to warn any enemies o' our arrival. But when I saw 'twas ye and the lad here, I sent the men back to fetch our horses."

The MacKay definitely looked uncomfortable as he gestured to Joan. It was his calling her lad that reminded her she was disguised as a boy. While Cam had removed his plaid to wrap around them both to sleep and was now wearing naught but a shirt that barely covered his naughty bits, she had pulled her clothes on before going to sleep to help fight the cold night, including her hat which her hair was stuffed up under. She understood the man's discomfort now. He'd come upon them embracing, and sex between males was considered a mortal sin by the church, punishable by death.

Joan tugged her hat off, allowing her fair hair to spill down over her shoulders and back. Only then did Cam say, "Ross, this is Joan. She saved me life when I was stabbed by a bandit and tended me until I recovered. When I learned she was on her way to MacKay to deliver a message to yerself and yer lady wife, I offered to escort her safely here."

"Oh, thank bloody hell fer that," the MacKay

breathed with relief, his stance relaxing. Shaking his head he admitted, "I was fretting o'er what to do. I ken damned right well one o' me men would ha'e reported ye to the priest to save himself a couple hail Marys and then . . ." He shook his head, and strode forward, hand extended. "I'll take the message and then leave ye two be. It looked as if I was interruptin' something when I made me presence known."

"Oh," Joan glanced at his hand, but didn't pull the scroll out of her shirt where it rested. Instead she said apologetically, " 'Tis addressed to Lady MacKay. My mother said you were welcome to read it as well, but that I should ensure Lady MacKay read it first."

"I shall see she gets it then," the MacKay assured her, hand still out.

Joan hesitated, but then shook her head. "My mother was very specific that I deliver it into Lady MacKay's hands myself."

He started to frown at her refusal, but then surprise crossed his face as her words seemed to register. "Yer mother?"

"The message is from her mother. She was on her deathbed when she gave it to Joan," Cam explained, and then added solemnly, " 'Tis a deathbed request and 'tis sure I am Joan wants to follow her mother's instructions to the letter and deliver it to yer wife in person."

The MacKay frowned over that, and then pursed his lips and asked, "Who's yer mother, lass?"

"Maggie Chartres," Joan answered promptly.

"Maggie Chartres?" Ross repeated, and it was obvious he didn't recognize the name.

"She was a healer," Cam offered helpfully, but the man merely shook his head. It wasn't ringing any bells for him.

"In Grimsby," Joan added, hoping that might help, but the man shook his head again and then sighed.

"Well, ye'd best come back to the keep with us then and deliver it to Annabel and I together as requested," he said solemnly, then glanced to Cam and teased, "Ye might want to put yer plaid on first, Campbell. The women'll already be all atwitter over the way we found ye when the men start in gossiping about it. There's no need to give 'em a show to further excite 'em."

Cam scowled at the teasing and knelt to grab and shake out his plaid, then begin pleating it. He was nearly done when several men rode into the clearing with the MacKay's horse. Joan was extremely glad she'd revealed herself as a girl when she saw the expressions on their faces. They'd obviously seen her and Cam embracing too and come to all the wrong conclusions. Their reactions to learning she was female varied from relief to lascivious grins.

Aware that she was blushing, Joan began to wring her cap in her hands and lowered her head to watch Cam work.

"Stop gawking and saddle Laird Sinclair's horse fer him while he dresses," the MacKay barked suddenly.

Joan gave a start at the harsh order, but nodded and turned to hurry across the clearing to where Cam had tied the horse's reins to a tree, but the MacKay caught her arm as she passed, bringing her to a halt as he said kindly, "I was talking to me men, lass."

"Oh," she murmured, noting only then that two of the men had dismounted to rush to do their laird's bidding. One grabbed the saddle and set about putting it on, while the other collected both Cam's bag and her own and carried them over, waiting to hook them to the saddle.

"Maggie Chartres from Grimsby," MacKay murmured suddenly, and Joan glanced to him hopefully. She was rather curious herself to know how her mother knew this powerful laird and his wife, but she could tell at once from his expression that the name still hadn't sparked any memories. Meeting her gaze, the MacKay looked her over and asked, "Do ye favor her in looks?"

"I don't think so," Joan said apologetically.

"Are ye sure?" he asked, examining her features. "Ye put me in mind o' someone." He frowned. "'Tis wiggling at the back o' me mind like a worm, but I can no' put me finger on it yet."

Joan frowned but said, "My mother had dark hair and green eyes rather than my fair hair and gray eyes, and no one ever said we looked alike. I think I must have taken my looks from my father."

"Hrrmph," The MacKay muttered and then glanced to Cam as he approached.

"Shall we?" Cam asked, taking Joan's arm

firmly in hand and pulling her away from the MacKay.

Ross MacKay arched an eyebrow at what could have been construed as a jealous action, but nodded and turned toward his horse. "Let's away."

"Aye," Cam murmured and urged Joan to his horse. Once there, he mounted, and then leaned down to catch and lift her onto the beast before him. He was silent the entire time. That, combined with his stiffness, told her he was angry. She suspected it was about her saying that she did want this to end. Explaining what she'd meant when she'd said that probably would have eased his anger if not banished it altogether, but she didn't do that. It seemed better to her for him to be angry. It would be easier on both of them. There would be no emotional parting now. He would probably drop her at the keep doors and leave for home at once. In fact, she was surprised he hadn't just handed her over to Ross and left already. Especially when she realized just how close they had camped to the MacKay castle. It seemed to her that hardly more than a couple moments passed before they were riding out of the woods into a valley that covered the last little distance to the castle wall.

Terribly aware of the silent gawking the MacKay warriors were doing, Joan was grateful for the short ride. It made her wish she'd had a chance to change before encountering them. Not that she had a dress to change into anymore, but their stares made her wish she did.

And despite the fact that Cam's being angry would make their parting easier, Joan wished he wasn't angry with her and that she could talk to him. While he had become her lover, they had started out friends when he'd thought her a boy, and she was suddenly very nervous about what might be in the message her mother had given her. A message she had insisted Joan deliver in person despite the risky journey that entailed. She ached to talk to him about it, but she couldn't. To do that she had to explain her earlier comment and ease his anger, and if she did that . . .

Joan swallowed and glanced down at his hands on the reins. If she explained, he would surely know just how important he had come to be to her. He would know how tempted she was to stay with him, and he might very well use that against her. A kiss, a caress, and a few sweet words and she knew she would find it hard not to throw caution to the wind and go to Sinclair with him. It was something she was already struggling with. The only thing keeping her from it was her fear of the future, her fear that despite her precautions, his child might settle in her belly. And her fear of the inevitable day when he would tire of her and move on.

A sudden image came to her of standing in the cold and snow, a bairn in her arms, watching Cam kissing and caressing another woman behind a stables. It would break her heart to go through that, Joan knew. No, she assured herself, it was better to treat their relationship like an infected limb and simply cut it off now rather than wait for the rot to spread to the rest of the body. It was going to hurt either way, but this way at least she might save herself some pride and perhaps a little piece of her heart.

"Leave yer horse. The men'll tend him," the MacKay said as they reigned in before the keep stairs and dismounted.

Cam glanced around to nod at those words. He then turned, intending to lift Joan down, but she'd already slid off the beast by herself.

Could she not even bear for him to touch her now? He wondered bitterly as she hurried to follow Ross up the steps to the keep, neatly avoiding his taking her arm to escort her. It seemed now that he'd got her here safe and sound she was done with him. It made Cam wonder if her allowing him to bed her hadn't simply been a means to secure his protection for her journey. Certainly, she'd made it clear that she had no desire to further their acquaintance.

No' this, Joan. I do no' want this to end.

But I do.

His words and her response had echoed through Cam's head repeatedly on the short ride to the keep. In his memory, he sounded like a lovesick lad pleading for her attentions. And she like a heartless harpy, slapping him down. He'd thought at the very least they were friends, but after all their talk, laughter, and passion, she'd refused him outright and without a second thought.

Mouth tight, Cam followed them up the steps.

He really wanted to get on his horse and ride home to lick his wounds, but pride wouldn't allow it. He would stay to find out what was in the message, and perhaps partake of the meal he knew Lady MacKay was sure to offer. Then he would head home as if it were the most natural thing in the world and he wasn't heartsore and angry.

"Nay! Jasper nay! Stop! Do not—Oh! Give me that, you horrid dog you!"

Cam glanced around curiously at those distressed calls as he followed Joan and Ross into the keep, his eyes finding Lady MacKay across the great hall, chasing their dog, Jasper, around the chairs by the fire. His eyes widened slightly, but then he noted the cloth in the animal's mouth and realized the problem just as Jasper spotted them and bound in their direction.

Ross bent to catch the dog as it charged forward, but the animal was fast and veered around him, right into Cam's arms.

"There," he murmured, gently tugging what appeared to be a shirt from the animal's mouth, even as he struggled to hold on to the wiggling beast. The dog was wagging his tail so hard, his whole lower body was waving back and forth like a snake's and he was hard to hold onto.

"Thank you, Cam," Annabel said with an exasperated sigh as she hurried over to them. "I swear this dog will be the death of me."

Cam smiled slightly, but remained on one knee to pet the dog with one hand as he handed the shirt up to Lady MacKay with the other. "When did Jasper start stealing clothes? And what the devil are ye feeding the beast? Last time I saw him he seemed old and tired. Now he's as frisky as a pup."

"He *is* a pup," Annabel said, accepting the shirt.

"We lost Jasper the Second at the end of winter," Ross explained. "This is Jasper the Third. He's about seven months old now."

"Aye, and he is as fond of chewing up clothes as Jasper the First was of cheese," Annabel said with irritation.

Cam shifted his gaze back to Jasper III, eyebrows rising. At seven months old the pup was still growing, yet he was already easily as big as Jasper II had been full grown. The beast was going to be huge.

"Thank you for rescuing Payton's shirt. I had just finished mending a tear in it when Jasper decided he should take it," Annabel said wryly, checking the shirt now. "Fortunately, he doesn't appear to have done any damage . . . this time."

"Me pleasure," Cam said, giving the dog one last pet and straightening.

" 'Tis nice to see you, Cam," Annabel said. "How is your mother?"

"Fine as far as I ken," Cam said with a grimace.

"Oh, aye, you have been away all summer," Annabel recalled, and then smiled. "She will be glad to see you home."

"No doubt," he said quietly.

Annabel nodded and then peered curiously at Joan, blinking when she noted her hair flowing down her back. No doubt Lady MacKay had thought her a boy at first glance, Cam realized and could hardly blame her. While Joan's hair was now down, it wasn't immediately obvious pushed back over her shoulders as it was. She also wore the braies and tunic she'd been wearing when he'd first encountered her. Anyone would have thought her a man at first glance.

"Wife, this is Joan," the MacKay said quietly. "Cam encountered her on his way home and when he heard she was coming here to deliver a message, he offered to escort her."

"Oh, that was kind," Annabel said, and offered Joan a smile. "Well, welcome to you both. You must be tired after your journey. Come sit yourselves at the trestle tables and I will go ask one of the maids to fetch us some food and drinks."

"Thank ye," Cam murmured, and took Joan's arm to usher her after Annabel when Lady MacKay turned to lead them across the great hall. Their hostess paused briefly at the trestle table, gesturing for them to sit, and then bustled off toward the door to the kitchens.

Ross shook his head as he watched Jasper hurry after her. "That bloody dog follows her everywhere," he said with disgust, and then smiled wryly and added, "Well, when he is no' following Annella."

"Annella?" Joan asked curiously.

"Our daughter," Ross explained. "One of them at any rate. We have two daughters and a son, Annella, Kenna and Payton. Annella is our oldest daughter, though her brother Payton is three years older."

"Oh, I see," Joan murmured as she settled at the trestle table.

"Annella and Annabel spoil the dog," Ross added with a small smile. "They both feed him treats at every turn, but Annella lets him sleep on the foot of her bed, so if she is around, he follows her. When she is not, he does no' leave me wife's side."

"Ah," Joan murmured with understanding.

"Where are Annella, Kenna and Payton?" Cam asked curiously.

"Payton is in the practice field and I believe his sisters were going out to the courtyard behind the kitchens to see if the apples are ready for picking. They've a mind to ha'e Cook make them apple tarts."

"Ah," Cam said with a faint smile as he settled on the bench beside Joan so that she sat between him and Ross. It was then he noted the bulge of the scroll she had kept tucked in her tunic through most of the journey. The only time she'd removed it since his suggestion that she keep it there was when she wasn't wearing the tunic. They'd always been careful to roll it in the cloth though to keep it safe then . . . well, there had been a time or two when they'd been a little too distracted to bother, he acknowledged, and for a moment he was awash in memories of those times when passion had overwhelmed them both.

At least, Cam had thought at the time that they

were both overwhelmed by passion, but now he wondered if Joan had truly felt anything at all, or if she'd been feigning enjoyment to please him and gain his aid. For Cam, their passion had been all consuming and addictive. He not only wanted it to continue, he felt as if he needed it, as if he wouldn't be truly alive without her nearby. She, apparently, didn't feel the same way, he thought grimly, and then glanced around at the sound of the kitchen door squeaking open. Annabel was returning with two servants on her heels; one carried a pitcher and tankards, and the other bore a tray with pastries on it.

"Here we are," Annabel said brightly as she reached the table and settled on the bench beside her husband.

Cam smiled at the woman. He'd known Lady Annabel most of his life. She was at least four decades old, but had aged well. Still, she had aged in the twenty years since he'd first met her as a boy. Her always curvy figure had grown a little rounder, her dark hair was now dusted lightly with gray, and her pretty face held the traces of laugh lines around her eyes and mouth. Despite that, he thought she was a beautiful woman, but then he knew her to be kind and caring and perhaps that colored his perceptions.

His gaze slid next to Joan and he let his eyes travel over her face. She had healed during the journey. The swelling was long gone and only the faintest hint of bruising now remained. What was left was a woman as beautiful to him as Lady Annabel. When he had seen her, Joan's eyes had been so swollen they had appeared slits. Now they were large and wide open, revealing that they were a beautiful blue gray color. The cut on her nose had healed but left a small scar that would fade with age, but it was small, barely noticeable to him, and the cut to her lip had healed as well, leaving a similar faint line. Her mouth was beautiful just the same, well formed and full enough that did he not know better, Cam would have thought they were still a little swollen.

"So," Ross said once the servants had finished setting food and drink before them and headed back toward the kitchens. "Joan has a message fer ye."

"For me?" Lady Annabel asked with amazement. "Who would send me a message?"

"Her mother," Ross answered. "Maggie Chartres."

Annabel frowned, but then shook her head and said, "I do not know that name."

Ross nodded as if he'd expected as much and then turned to glance at Joan expectantly. "The message?"

"Oh," Joan murmured suddenly and stood up.

"Is something amiss?" Ross asked, eyebrows rising.

"Nay, I just . . ." Joan flushed, her hand rising to cup the scroll through her shirt. She then grimaced, shook her head, stepped over the bench and moved a couple feet away.

"She kept it on her person to keep it safe durin' the journey," Cam explained quietly when Laird and Lady MacKay stared after Joan with curiosity. "When I came upon her on the road, bandits were trying to steal her bag with the message in it, so I suggested she tuck it in her tunic instead."

"Ah," Lady Annabel murmured with understanding while her husband merely nodded and relaxed.

Cam glanced back to Joan then, noting that she had the scroll out, but was just standing there staring at it. After a hesitation, he stood and moved over to join her. "Is something amiss?"

Joan glanced up, a startled look on her face, almost as if she'd forgotten he was there, Cam thought. But after a moment she shook her head. "Nay. I just . . . my mother . . ."

She ducked her head to hide the tears that suddenly swam into her eyes and Cam almost sighed to himself. He was angry and hurt just now, but couldn't stand by and watch her suffer without trying to comfort her. Mouth tightening, he pulled her against his chest to pat her back awkwardly. " 'Tis all right."

"I don't know why I'm getting all weepy," Joan sniffled against his chest.

"Ye've carried that message since yer mother's death," he pointed out. " 'Tis yer last connection to her. O' course ye'll feel sad giving it up."

"Aye," Joan muttered, raising a hand to dash at the tears on her face. He was right of course, this was the last connection she had to her mother, and she was experiencing some grief at having to give it up. But it was more than that. Delivering this message had been her sole purpose since her mother's death. Once she handed it over, that duty would be done. She would no longer have a purpose and Joan had no idea where she would go when she left here. Friar Wendell had made it plain she was not needed in Grimsby. She had no home to go to. No family to take her in. And on top of all that, handing over this message truly meant the end of her link with Cam too. He had promised to see her safely here and he had. He could leave anytime. In fact, she was still surprised that he hadn't already left. But once she handed over the scroll that would surely be the end of everything between them.

All of that combined made her want to just sit down and weep. Instead, Joan took a deep breath, wiped the tears from her face again and straightened her shoulders. Lifting her face, she nodded solemnly at Cam. "Thank you. For everything."

He opened his mouth to say something, but then abruptly snapped it shut, nodded stiffly and gestured for her to lead the way back to the table.

Joan hesitated, wanting to say something, anything to ease his stiff expression and make him at least smile, if not laugh. But she suspected the only thing that would accomplish that was to agree to go to Sinclair with him and she couldn't do that. She just couldn't, so sighing, she nodded and turned to walk back to the table.

"Thank you," Annabel murmured, taking the scroll when Joan stopped behind her and held it out.

Joan merely nodded and moved back to reclaim her seat beside Laird MacKay. The moment she was seated, Cam settled beside her. She noted that he turned to watch Lady Annabel open the scroll then. Laird MacKay was watching his wife curiously as well. Joan just picked up her drink and took a sip. She was curious too as to what was in the message, but didn't expect to find out. Her own mother had refused to tell her. Why would Lady Annabel?

A gasp from Lady Annabel made Joan set her drink back and glance to the woman.

"What is it?" Ross asked, concern drawing his brows together.

"Maggie Chartres was a healer in Bedfordshire. She served the village and Elstow Abbey. She knew my sister, Kate," Annabel murmured, her eyes still moving swiftly over the words written on the scroll.

"Hmm," Ross muttered, not seeming happy at this news. He then turned to Joan almost accusingly. "Ye said ye were from Grimsby. Ye made no mention o' Bedfordshire or Elstow Abbey."

"We lived in Grimsby all my life," Joan said helplessly. "And my mother never made mention of Bedfordshire or Elstow Abbey."

Ross scowled, but glanced back to his wife as she whispered, "Oh no."

"What's about?" he asked at once, and looked braced for anything.

"Kate died twenty years ago," Annabel whispered, still reading.

Much to Joan's surprise, Laird MacKay actually looked relieved at this news and said, "Well at least we'll no' ha'e to worry about her coming here to cause trouble again."

When Joan instinctively glanced wide-eyed to Cam, he tipped his head to hers and murmured, "She robbed them and tried to kill Lady Annabel when she and Ross were first married."

Joan gaped at this news, but then glanced sharply to Lady Annabel when she gasped again.

"What?" Laird MacKay asked sharply and the man was clenching his hands as if fighting the urge to snatch the message from his wife and read it for himself.

"She was with child when she got to the abbey. Grant's child," Annabel said, still reading. "She died on the birthing bed."

Ross MacKay stiffened and then turned slowly to stare at Joan, an odd expression on his face.

She shifted uncomfortably under his stare, unsure of the reason for it.

"The abbess wrote to Mother and Father at the time to let them know, but they responded that the only daughter they had was me. Kate was dead to them and they were not going to be saddled with the burden of her child," Annabel continued grimly, anger flashing across her face.

"Bastards," Ross breathed, still staring at Joan.

"Maggie suggested the abbess write to me to tell me of Kate's death and the baby, but the abbess refused," Lady Annabel said, sounding horrified as she continued narrating. "She said we had paid for Kate to be taken away and would hardly be interested in her daughter. She also said that while the abbey had been given a dower to take in Kate, she did not feel any responsibility toward Kate's offspring and had no intention of raising her."

"Old bitch," Ross muttered, still staring at Joan.

"So she gave her to Maggie to take away," Annabel continued as she read. "And Maggie . . ."

Joan tore her gaze from Laird MacKay's strange stare and glanced curiously to his wife when she paused. Lady MacKay continued reading for a moment and then lowered the scroll and lifted her head to peer straight at her.

It was Laird MacKay who guessed, "And Maggie named the babe Joan and raised her as her own."

Chapter 8

"*W*HAT?" JOAN ACTUALLY LAUGHED AT THE suggestion, a short nervous laugh, but a laugh just the same. The idea was just so ridiculous. She shook her head. "Nay. I am Maggie Chartres's daughter, not this Kate person's," she assured him.

"Ye remember I said ye put me in mind o' someone, do ye no'?" Laird MacKay asked quietly. "Well, I kenned who, the minute me wife mentioned Kate was with child when she got to the abbey. Ye're the spitting image o' yer mother."

Joan shook her head in denial, and then glanced up with a start when Annabel was suddenly behind her.

"My husband is right. You are a mirror image of Kate," the woman said solemnly.

Still shaking her head, Joan stood to avoid having to crane her head so far around and took a step back from the woman. "My mother was Maggie Chartres. She raised me."

"Aye, Maggie raised you and loved you as a

daughter, but you were born from my sister," Annabel said quietly. "You are Kate's daughter with her husband Grant. My niece."

"Nay," Joan insisted, backing away another step as if distance would make her denial true. "She would have told me."

"She did not wish to see you hurt," Annabel said softly. "My parents had rejected you and she feared we would as well. She ended her letter saying that she had never planned to tell you, ever, but when she realized she was dying and that you would be left alone in this world, she decided to send you to us with this message. She asked that if we felt as my parents did and had no interest in claiming you, to please simply send you on your way so that you would never know that you were not wanted."

Joan simply stared at her blankly, her mind struggling to accept what she was being told. Her mother wasn't her mother? She was the child of Lady MacKay's sister, Kate? A woman who had apparently tried to kill the kind woman before her. Joan turned abruptly away to head for the keep doors. "I should go. I've delivered the message and should let you be now."

"Nay," Annabel protested, catching her hand and stopping her. "You cannot go."

Joan turned back and peered at her with bewilderment. "Why? If it's true that your sister was my mother, you can't want me here. Cam said she tried to kill you."

When Annabel turned to scowl at Cam at this

news, he grimaced apologetically. "Sorry. I did no' ken she was her daughter when I said it."

Annabel sighed and then turned back to Joan and squeezed her hands gently. "That was a very long time ago, Joan, and your mother was just . . ." she hesitated briefly and then finished, "confused."

Ross snorted, but stood abruptly when his wife glared at him and moved to join them.

"I would no' say yer mother was confused exactly, but me wife's right, it was a long time ago. And it does no' matter anyway. We do no' hold ye responsible fer yer mother's actions. Ye're our niece. Family . . . and ye're welcome here."

"See." Annabel beamed at her husband, her smile just as wide when she turned to Joan. Squeezing her hands, she announced, "You will stay here. Your cousins will be so pleased to meet you and—" She paused abruptly, eyes widening. "Oh dear. We should see you bathed and changed before they—" Halting again, she turned to her husband, mouth opening.

"I'll ha'e the maids bring up the bath," Ross said before she could say anything.

"Thank you, husband." Annabel leaned up to kiss his cheek. Taking Joan's arm then, she began to usher her toward the stairs, adding, "Have them bring it to the empty room. Joan can have it for her own."

"Ye'd best put her in Kenna's room fer now," Ross countered. "Cam will be in the empty room."

"Oh." Annabel paused to turn back and Joan did as well, as surprised at this news as the older woman proved to be when she said, "I am sorry, Cam. I did not realize you were staying."

"I had no' realized either when I first arrived," Cam said quietly.

"Oh, I see," Lady Annabel said, but her expression made it clear she didn't understand. Neither did Joan. She really had thought he'd leave now and this was the last thing she'd expected. Well, no, not the last thing, she acknowledged. The last thing she could have expected was learning that her mother wasn't her mother and she was a niece to the MacKays.

Her mind still grappling with this knowledge, Joan let her worries about what Cam was or wasn't doing slip away for now and listened as Lady Annabel announced that she was about the same size as her daughter Annella and could borrow one of the girl's gowns until they could make her some of her own. And while she couldn't sleep in the empty room until Cam left, she could move into it then and it would be hers.

Family, expensive gowns, her very own room . . . it was enough to make a girl dizzy, at least a girl who had grown up in a hut that was simply one room with a fire in the corner, a rickety old table, two chairs and space to lay out pallets for herself and her mother at night. A hut that had stopped being her home when her mother, her last surviving family as far as she'd known, had died. Until moments ago Joan had been without family, possessing nothing but the clothes on her back and the herbs in her bag, and now . . .

She shook her head with bewilderment, overwhelmed by the changes taking place so swiftly in her life.

Cam watched Joan until she disappeared into one of the rooms on the upper landing with Lady Annabel, and then turned slowly to find Ross watching him.

"Ye ken why ye're staying?" the older man asked.

"Aye," Cam said simply.

Laird MacKay cocked his head and eyed him with interest. "Ye're no' going to protest that ye did no' ken she was me niece so should no' bear the consequences?"

"Nay," he answered and shrugged. "That matters little. She is yer niece. I took her innocence, and I shall marry her."

Ross relaxed and gestured to the trestle table. "Sit down and drink yer ale. I've no doubt ye need it about now. I'll jest order the bath fer Joan and warn the cook to prepare a feast and then join ye. I could do with an ale or ten after today's revelations meself." Shaking his head, he turned away and headed for the kitchens muttering, "Kate had a daughter. I hope to hell she's nothing like her."

Cam winced at those words, then moved to sit at the trestle table again. He didn't pick up his mug right away though. He was feeling a little peculiar at the moment and just sat waiting for his world to right itself. Cam had known the moment Ross guessed that Maggie Chartres had kept Kate's child, named her Joan, and raised her as her own that he was right. He'd also known in that moment that he'd have to marry the lass. As he'd said, she was the MacKay's niece. He'd taken her innocence. Ergo, honor demanded he marry her. It was that simple.

What wasn't so simple was how he felt about that.

In truth, Cam wasn't at all sure how he felt. He supposed he should be happy. He had wanted to keep Joan with him and their having to marry certainly ensured that would happen. On the other hand, she'd rejected his request that she come to Sinclair with him, and hadn't just refused, but when he'd said he didn't want what they had to end, she had responded with, "But I do." Though Cam was loathe to admit it, more than his pride had been hurt by those words. Yet now they were to marry.

And how would she feel about that? he wondered. Cam suspected Joan didn't yet realize the plans her uncle had for them. She'd seemed so overwhelmed by everything she'd learned that he doubted it would occur to her that they would be expected to marry until someone told her. It left him wondering how she would react.

She might be pleased, he acknowledged. He was a wealthy man, the heir to a very powerful Scottish laird. Her life would be much different from now on. She would go from being a poor peasant to having riches, servants, and eventually, several castles . . .

Aye, she might be more willing to suffer his presence with all that on offer. Unfortunately,

Cam wanted her to want him, not the wealth and comfort he could give her. However, neither of them had a choice now.

"OH MY," LADY ANNABEL BREATHED AS SHE stood back to look at her.

Joan peered at her uncertainly. She'd been bathed, perfumed and dressed, and had sat still while her hair was brushed dry and pinned up on top of her head in a fashion that was bloody uncomfortable. She only hoped it looked better than it felt because it felt like torture and it had all seemed to take forever. She didn't know how Lady Annabel could stand all the fuss let alone having her hair like this.

"You look so like your mother," Lady Annabel said softly.

Joan shifted uncomfortably. Lady Annabel meant her sister, Kate, but while they could insist that woman was her mother, in her mind, Joan would always be the daughter of Maggie Chartres.

"I think you may be a little lovelier though," Annabel said thoughtfully. "Perhaps 'tis because you have a natural kindness she lacked."

Joan blinked in surprise. She had never considered herself lovely, ever. But aside from that—"I've hardly said a word since you brought me up here. How could you know whether I'm kind or not?"

"You have kind eyes, dear," Annabel said gently and then smiled and added, "And Maggie's letter said that you were. She said you were smart and kind and brave and that she was ever so proud of you."

Tears blurred Joan's eyes at these words and she turned away, blinking repeatedly to keep from crying. She had always loved and respected her mother, so it was good to know the woman had thought highly of her in return.

"Besides, she also said that you had followed in her footsteps and become one of the finest healers she knew. Healers tend to be kind by nature, at least good ones in my opinion," Annabel announced, and then said thoughtfully, "You are more like me in that regard. Your mother did not have any skills in that area that I know of."

"But you do?" Joan asked with surprise.

Annabel smiled and nodded. "I used to work in the stables at Elstow Abbey. Sister Clara was in charge of them and taught me all I know about healing. We worked mostly with animals, but treated the other sisters' ailments too and she taught me much in that area as well." Her expression turned thoughtful and she murmured, "Sister Clara was very old though. The abbess must have brought in Maggie to help her when I left . . . or to replace her when she died," she said softly and then sighed and shook her head as if to remove a sad thought.

Joan merely nodded. While she had been silent during her bath and the fussing that had followed, Lady Annabel chattered away about many things. One of those had been the fact that she'd grown up in Elstow Abbey, expecting to become a nun. Fate could be fickle, however, and her circumstances had changed so that she'd ended up married to Laird MacKay and bearing him three children instead.

"Come, we should go below and—" Lady Annabel paused and turned toward the door with surprise when it suddenly banged open. Two young women burst into the room, skirts flying, only to come to a shuddering halt after a couple steps as they took note of Joan. When they simply gaped at her, she shifted uncomfortably and glanced to Annabel to find her smiling faintly.

"Well?" Lady Annabel said with amusement. "Are you not going to greet your cousin?"

"Cousin!" the younger one squealed, rushing forward to throw her arms around Joan. "Father told us we had a cousin, but we could hardly believe it and had to come see ye fer ourselves. We've never had a cousin before, ye see. We've never had any family at all besides Mother and Father and each other. Oh, and Uncle Fingal," she added, pulling back to peer at her as she explained, "We did have Uncles Ainsley, and Eoghann too, but they were both very old and died. Uncle Fingal's old too, o' course, but he still works as a blacksmith in the village and Mother said that keeps him healthy and strong."

"Stop and breathe, Kenna, or ye shall faint from lack of air," the other girl said with amused exasperation as she moved forward.

Kenna rolled her eyes, and then grinned at Joan and said, "She's always sayin' that, but I've ne'er fainted yet, no' once."

"Oh, well that's good," Joan said weakly, her gaze moving between the two. With dark hair and rosy cheeks, both girls were versions of their mother at different stages in her life. At twelve, Kenna was the youngest of Annabel and Ross's children, while Annella was the middle child at sixteen. Something else Joan had learned from Lady Annabel's happy chatter during her bath.

"That dress looks much nicer on ye than it e'er did on me," Annella commented, drawing her attention and Joan shook her head.

"Nay. I'm sure it doesn't," she said solemnly. "But thank you for letting me borrow it. I shall clean and return it soon as I'm able."

"Ye're welcome, but ye do no' ha'e to give it back. It really does look better on ye than me," Annella assured her.

"Thank you," Joan murmured self-consciously.

"Well, I suppose we should go below stairs." Annabel said and then smiling wryly, added, "What with rushing you up here to bathe and change, you never did get the chance to break your fast."

"Oh, then ye have no' tried Cook's pastries," Kenna said excitedly, catching Joan's hand. "Ye must try them."

"Nay, ye should no'," Annella countered dryly, and confided, "They're horrible."

"Aye," Kenna agreed, turning to her sister, "That's why she must try them." Turning back to Joan she added, "There is no' a worse pastry cook in all o' Scotland than our cook. Father says so and he's always right."

"Aye," Annella agreed. "But he makes the finest stews and cakes, better e'en than our old cook."

"But our old cook used to make the loveliest pastries," Kenna said on a sigh and turned back to Joan to tell her, "I love pastries."

"So do I," Joan admitted with a smile.

"Oh no!" Kenna said with dismay. "Then 'tis a shame our old Cook died. He would have made fine pastries fer yer wedding."

"Wedding?" Joan and Annabel asked as one, each sounding as amazed as the other.

"Aye," Kenna said with surprise. "To Cam."

"YE DO NO' THINK THE GIRLS'LL SAY ANYTHING?" Cam asked suddenly. The apples had been ripe for picking. Kenna and Annella had picked two baskets full, but when they'd delivered them to Cook in the kitchens, they'd overheard the servants talking excitedly about the wedding and the feast they were to prepare. The girls had come rushing out of the kitchens all atwitter, wanting to know who this Joan was that Cam was marrying and why he was marrying here rather than at Sinclair. So Ross had explained that she was their cousin. The girls had been so excited to learn they had a cousin, they'd forgotten their other questions and had rushed upstairs to meet Joan.

"About what?" Ross asked. "The wedding?"

"Aye. I'd rather tell her meself," Cam said quietly.

Ross nodded solemnly, and then grimaced and stood up. "We'd best get upstairs then, ere they tell her fer ye."

Standing abruptly, Cam followed him to the stairs and started up with him.

They were nearly to the top before Cam said, "I'd like to speak to her alone."

Ross nodded as they started along the landing. "O' course. If the girls have no' already told her, I'll send them below and—"

"*What?*"

Cam stopped and glanced to Ross when that shriek rang out.

The MacKay grimaced, and then said apologetically, "I'm thinkin' me daughters may ha'e said something."

Cam merely started forward again, moving more swiftly this time.

"*Marry* him?" came the next cry as he was approaching the door. "Nay!"

"Aye, they definitely said something," Ross muttered, catching his arm. He waited until Cam turned to peer at him and then said, "And I think ye'd best wait below while I talk with me niece."

Cam stood still, mouth tight, Joan's horrified shout seeming to echo in his ears.

"Campbell," Ross said firmly.

Cam sucked in a breath, his head raising, shoulders straightening, and then nodded silently, turned on his heel and headed back downstairs. The good news was, she definitely would not be marrying him for his wealth. Apparently even that wasn't enough of a lure to tempt her.

"Now, Joan, I am sure the girls have this a little muddled up," Annabel said, a small frown on her face as she tried to calm her.

"Nay, Kenna is right, Mother," Annella said quietly. "Father said Cam and Joan were to marry. Here. After the nooning. Cook is preparing a feast as we speak."

"You must have misunderstood, Annella," Annabel said firmly. "Cam would hardly marry without his parents present and by the time a messenger reached Sinclair . . ." She shook her head. "There is no way they could get here in time."

"Cam said he did no' wish his parents to attend," Kenna announced.

Joan vaguely noted the way Annabel frowned at this news, but was too distracted with her own thoughts to care. Cam didn't want his parents at their wedding? Not that she was marrying him, she assured herself. But if they had been going to marry, why would he not want his parents to attend? Was he ashamed of her? Because she was brought up a peasant?

"I am sure you are mistaken," Annabel insisted. "Your father would hardly agree to marry off your cousin to Campbell Sinclair without at least talking to me first. And her, of course," she added with a diplomatic smile for Joan.

"But he said—"

"Annella, Kenna, go below please."

All four females glanced toward the door at that order in a deep voice. Joan scowled when she saw Ross MacKay in the now open door. Her gaze then shifted to her cousins as Kenna reluctantly released her hand, which she'd still been holding, and followed her sister dutifully out of the room.

Annabel waited until Ross had closed the door behind her daughters, and then hurried anxiously across the room. "Husband, the girls said that you have arranged for Cam and Joan to marry."

"Aye," the MacKay said solemnly, clasping her upper arms soothingly. " 'Tis sorry I am that I did no' talk to ye about it first, wife. But it would ha'e made little difference. They ha'e to marry. After what the men and I saw this morning when we found them . . ." He shook his head. "Honor demanded he marry her."

Joan grimaced, aware that she was blushing. But she protested, "We weren't doing anything. We were talking."

"Cam was bare arsed and ye were in his arms," Ross said grimly.

"He wasn't—" she began and then changed directions with her argument because his shirt did not always cover his entire behind and he may very well have been bare arsed. "We were only talking."

"Oh?" Ross asked with obvious disbelief. "Cam agreed that honor demanded he marry ye. Ye're saying otherwise?"

Joan's mouth tightened. He had agreed for honor's sake. Not exactly flattering.

"So if Annabel were to examine ye, she'd find ye still a maiden?" he asked calmly.

"Ross," Annabel protested.

"She's our responsibility now, wife. We ha'e to see to her future," he said quietly, and then pointed out, "She could be with child even now."

"Nay, I ha'e been taking Devil's plague to ensure that didn't happen," Joan said quickly, and then knew by Annabel's expression that it had been the wrong thing to say. She'd as good as admitted she'd given Cam her innocence. Sighing, she shook her head. "This has nothing to do with you. I have managed on my own since my mother fell ill and can continue to do so. I will not marry him. In fact, this," she gestured to the gown she wore, "was a mistake. I'll change back to my own clothes and leave you be. You can pretend I never came here and gave you that message."

"Oh, Joan, no, you cannot!" Annabel protested at once, hurrying back to her side.

"Me wife's right," Ross said grimly. "Ye may ha'e managed on yer own ere this, lass, but that's only because we did no' ken about ye. We do now. Ye're our niece and as such yer our responsibility." He paused briefly and then added, "And as yer uncle, I'm tellin' ye, ye're no' going anywhere. Ye'll stay here and marry Cam as has been arranged."

"But he doesn't want me," Joan protested at once.

"Does he no'?" Ross asked, eyebrows rising. "And yet he was quick to say he should marry ye when ye women came above stairs."

"That's just because he knew you would expect him to," she argued wearily. "He had no intention of marrying me ere finding out that I was your niece."

"Mayhap not," Ross said with a shrug. "But ye are me niece, and ye'll marry because 'tis the right thing to do."

The MacKay turned on his heel and strode from the room then, leaving Joan glaring after him.

" 'Twill be all right," her aunt said quietly, rubbing Joan's arm soothingly, her gaze on the door her husband had left through.

"How can it be?" Joan asked miserably, and then blurted, "I can't marry him. I'll not live my life in fear."

Annabel turned back to her with surprise. "You're afraid of Cam?"

"Aye. Nay. I do not mean that I fear he would hit me or such," she added quickly when Annabel frowned.

"Then what do you mean?" her aunt asked, trying to understand.

Joan tried to find the words to explain, and then finally admitted, "When your husband came upon us, Cam had just said he didn't want what we had to end and asked me to go to Sinclair with him after I delivered your message and I said no."

"You did not want to go to Sinclair with him?" Annabel asked with a frown.

"Oh, aye, I did," Joan assured her. "I wanted desperately to go."

Confusion clouded her face. "Well then—"

"I was afraid," Joan admitted unhappily. "I still am. I've never felt like this. The more I'm with him the more I want to be with him. I feel so happy with Cam, no matter what we're doing. Walking, talking, sitting quietly by the fire, and . . . everything else," she finished lamely, and then sighed. "I've never been so happy as I was this last two weeks. Ever," she admitted quietly, and then added, "But when he asked me to go with him . . ." She shook her head. "As happy as I've been these last two weeks, when he asked me to go with him, all I could think was how miserable I would be when he tired of me for mistress and turned his attentions to another."

"You love him," Annabel said gently.

"Mayhap," Joan said wearily.

"You do," Annabel assured her. "But you do not have to be afraid anymore, Joan. You will not be going to Sinclair as his mistress but as his wife. He cannot throw you aside for another."

"Nay," she acknowledged. "But he never wanted to marry again. He told me so himself. And now he's being forced to." Joan shook her head hopelessly. "He'll hate me for our having to wed. And how awful do you think it will be being married to him, when he hates me?"

Annabel sighed and pulled her into her arms for a hug. Rubbing her back, she said, "I know it does not seem like it now, but life has a way of working out."

"You're right, it doesn't seem like it," Joan said unhappily.

"I felt much the same when I was told I was to marry Ross," Annabel said solemnly. "I thought he would be disappointed in me as a wife. I had been raised to become a nun. I had no training as a wife. I did not know the first thing about running a keep or—"

"Dear God," Joan cried, pulling free as horror rolled over her. "I didn't think of that!"

"What?" Annabel asked with bewilderment.

"I have no training either, but not just to run a keep. I was raised in the village. I don't know the first thing about even being a lady. 'Tis no wonder he doesn't want his parents at the wedding. He is embarrassed by me and they will be horrified the minute they—"

"I'm sure that's not true, Joan," Annabel interrupted quickly, and then added. "Besides, unlike me, you are not alone. I will not abandon you as my mother did me. I can teach you all that you need to know. It will be all right."

Joan stared at her silently. She wanted to believe that everything would be all right, but in her experience, things rarely turned out all right in this life.

Chapter 9

"Do ye plan to sit here all night? Or will ye join yer new bride in bed?"

Cam glanced up from his contemplation of his ale at Laird MacKay's question and heaved a sigh. "I suppose I should retire."

"So eager," Ross said dryly and then shook his head. "I do no' understand the pair o' ye. Ye seemed cozy as could be in the woods this morning, and ye've admitted ye bedded the lass on the journey here. Yet now ye're both acting like marrying each other is the worst punishment available."

"'Tis no' me who sees it as a punishment," Cam said dryly, turning his tankard on the tabletop. "In case ye hadn't noticed, she looked like a lamb on the way to the slaughter this afternoon during the ceremony."

"Aye, she did," Ross agreed. "But then you looked as grim as if ye were at a funeral so mayhap she was just reacting to that."

Cam shook his head wearily. "She does no' want me for husband."

"Hmmm." Ross took a drink of his own ale and then shook his head. "That's the same thing she said about you."

"What?" he turned on him with amazement.

"Aye." Ross nodded. "She said ye didn't want her and were only marrying her fer honor's sake."

Cam scowled at this news. "Well then she's daft. Hell, when ye came upon us in the clearing I'd just asked her to come to Sinclair with me after she delivered her message . . . and she said she did no' want to."

Ross considered that, and then asked, "What were ye asking her to go to Sinclair as?"

"What do ye mean?" Cam asked with a frown.

"Well, were ye planning to marry her? Did ye invite her to work at Sinclair? Or were ye suggesting she go as yer mistress?"

"I . . ." Cam paused. He hadn't even considered marriage. He'd said he would never marry again so often that it had become a truth, although really it was the risking a wife on the birthing bed that he didn't want. But to his mind that meant never having a wife since all women wanted children. Except Joan. She feared the birthing bed, and like him, didn't want to risk it and had the knowledge to avoid it. In truth, she would be the perfect wife for him in that regard, and yet he hadn't considered marriage. After all, she was a commoner and he a noble and that just did not happen. At least, not often.

"Annabel thinks the lass loves ye," Ross announced suddenly, effectively bringing an end to Cam's ruminations.

He glanced to him sharply. "She does? Why?"

Ross shrugged. "She did no' say why she thought it, just that she did."

Cam turned his gaze to his tankard again, his mind racing. Did she love him? That would be— He halted his thoughts and glanced back to Ross. "If Lady Annabel is right, why did Joan refuse to come to Sinclair with me?"

"Pride?" Ross suggested and then grimaced and shrugged. "Who can tell with women? I ha'e been married more than twenty years to one female and reared two more and much as I love them all, still do no' understand why they do what they do most o' the time." He took a drink of his ale, then added, "In truth, I do no' think even they ken why they do much o' what they do. They're very emotional creatures, and there often seems little logic to their decisions until they explain them and then it usually boils down to their being tenderhearted. At least it does with me Annabel and the girls."

"Women," Cam sighed with mild disgust.

"Aye, they can be a trial," Ross agreed and then smiled and added, "but they can be heaven as well and I would no' give up me Annabel or our daughters fer all the gold in England and Scotland."

Cam smiled faintly, knowing that was the absolute truth. Ross MacKay loved his wife and his children dearly. And they in turn, loved him back.

He was a lucky man. Cam had given up any hope of having that when his first wife had died, but if Joan loved him—

"I suggest ye no' worry about her saying she did no' want to go to Sinclair," Ross said quietly. "The fact is, ye're married now. She will be going, and what happens between ye from here on out is up to the two o' ye." When Cam merely nodded and continued to stare into his ale, Ross added, "However, I should point out that yer dallying down here rather than going up to bed her is no doubt just reinforcing her belief that ye do no' want her."

Cam's head jerked up at the suggestion. The man was right, of course. Standing, he said determinedly, "I am going up."

"Good. Then me wife will stop comforting her and come down," Ross said dryly, then caught his arm as Cam stepped over the bench. "A moment."

"What?" Cam asked with a frown. Now that he'd decided to go up, the delay was a bit annoying.

"Ye're satisfied she was innocent the first time ye were together?" Ross asked, eyes narrowed.

Cam stiffened. "Aye. I told ye that when we first talked o' me marrying her. She still had her maiden's veil."

Ross nodded. "But there's the matter o' the sheet fer proof."

Shoulders relaxing, Cam nodded. "I shall see there is proof."

"Good," Ross said releasing his arm. "I shall see ye in the morning then."

Cam nodded and turned to leave the table, but

halted abruptly to avoid crashing into Payton, Ross and Annabel's son. The nineteen-year-old stood with several men behind him, a wide grin on his face.

"'Tis time we took ye up to yer bride," the young man announced.

Cam stared at him blankly, then turned to peer at Ross for help.

"Well, I was gonna let ye get away without this indignity," the MacKay said with amusement. Getting to his feet, he added, "But, what the hell? I had to suffer it, so why no' you too?"

"Damn," Cam muttered as the men suddenly converged on him.

"WHAT IS TAKING THEM SO LONG?" ANNELLA asked with irritation.

"He's not coming. Cam doesn't want me," Joan said unhappily, watching her cousin pace the room. She would be up pacing with her if she weren't completely naked. They hadn't even allowed her a shift to sleep in, claiming the bedding ceremony called for her to be stripped and put abed, and then Cam to be as well. Who knew nobles were so barbaric? Joan thought. She had never slept naked in her life . . . well, barring the few times she'd fallen asleep after Cam had bedded her. Before that she wouldn't have even considered it. The hut she and her mother shared had been too chilly at night once the fire went out; she'd have frozen to death had she slept naked. It was indecent.

"O' course he wants ye," Kenna said with amazement, rushing over to sit on the bed and claim her hands. "Why ye're beautiful, and smart and nice. How could he no' want ye?"

Joan smiled faintly at the girl's words and pointed out, "I'm pretty enough but not beautiful, and how would you know I'm smart or nice? You only met me today."

"Aye, but ye're me cousin," Kenna pointed out.

"So I must be nice and smart?" she asked with amusement.

"Aye," Kenna said simply.

Joan smiled, but then sighed and shook her head.

"Kenna, dear," Lady Annabel said suddenly. "I forgot to ask the servants to bring up wine, cheese and bread for Joan and Cam. Could you—?"

"I'll get it, Mama," Kenna interrupted, popping up off the bed.

"She's such a good girl," Annabel said with affection as the door closed behind her youngest child.

"Aye," Joan murmured.

"Both of my girls are," Annabel added, smiling at Annella. The sixteen-year-old smiled back and then moved to the bed and sat where Kenna had been a moment ago.

"Ye don't really believe Cam does no' want ye, do ye?" Annella asked with a frown, rubbing Joan's cold hand between both of her warm ones. "Kenna's right, ye're beautiful, and ye do seem smart and nice."

Joan grimaced. "It matters little if I am nice or smart. Raised in the village as I was, I don't know the first thing about being a lady, let alone running his keep or . . . I'm sure he fears I shall embarrass him in front of his parents . . . and I probably will. "

"Ye were raised in a village?" Annella asked with amazement.

Joan blinked, surprised the girl didn't know that, but then realized that all Annella and Kenna knew was that she was their cousin and was marrying Cam.

"Yes, dear," Annabel said when Joan remained silent. "Your Aunt Kate, my sister, died giving birth to Joan. Fortunately, the midwife, a healer from the village, was a kind and loving woman who raised her as her own."

"In an English village?" Annella asked with dismay.

Joan couldn't tell which horrified the girl more, that she was raised in a village, or an English one.

"Aye, in Grimsby," Annabel said calmly.

"But why was she no' sent here?" Annella asked, turning to frown at her mother. "Ye and father should ha'e raised her."

"Aye," Annabel agreed. "But we did not even know she existed until today."

"How could ye no' ken she—"

"Not now, Annella," Annabel interrupted quietly. "We can talk about this later."

The girl hesitated, obviously curious to have her answers, but then suddenly turned to Joan and hugged her. "I'm sorry."

"What for?" Joan asked with amazement, hands automatically rising to hug her back.

"Ye should no' ha'e been raised in a village with strangers. Ye should ha'e been here with us. We are yer family."

"There's nothing for you to feel bad about," Joan said, hugging her with more feeling now. "My mother was a good woman. She loved me and taught me much, and we did better than most. We were rarely without food, and usually had wood for the fire. I was lucky," she assured her, but for some reason her assurances seemed to upset Annella. She could see it in her expression and tell by the way her grip on her hand tightened.

"We will teach ye how to be a lady," Annella announced suddenly, and then glanced to her mother. "We will, will we no'?"

"Aye, of course," Annabel said, smiling with pride on her daughter.

Nodding, Annella turned back, "I shall teach ye to dance, and play music, and all those things, and Mother can teach ye how to run a castle and such. I can help with that too but she is better at it, and—"

"They are coming!" Kenna squealed, bursting into the room with a tray of food and drink in hand. She rushed to the table by the fire to set it down, adding, "The men were lifting Cam onto their shoulders to carry him up here as I reached the stairs."

"Off with you two then," Annabel said, ushering her girls toward the door.

Joan frowned as she watched the girls leave the room. The moment her aunt closed the door behind them and turned back, though, she asked with dismay, "He wouldn't come on his own? Was he so reluctant the men had to drag him up like a—?"

"'Tis part of the bedding," Annabel interrupted soothingly. "The women lead the bride up and put her abed, then the men carry the groom up, strip him and put him abed next to you."

"You mean a bunch of men are going to come in here and—?" Her words died as the door suddenly burst open and a dozen MacKay soldiers spilled into the room, bearing Cam overhead like a wild boar they'd hunted down. They had obviously celebrated the wedding well and were the worse for drink. They nearly dropped Cam when they started to lower him to the floor, and then she suspected they unintentionally hurt him a time or two as they tore off his clothes . . . and it could only be described as tearing them off. They certainly didn't strip him as calmly and carefully as her aunt and cousins had done with her.

Joan watched the whole thing with something akin to horror. Perhaps she'd had a sheltered upbringing, or perhaps this was a Scottish tradition. She'd never attended a wedding in England, not even between commoners, so couldn't be sure this didn't happen in England as well, but it all seemed terribly barbaric to her.

Fortunately, it was also fast, and Cam was quickly naked and tucked into bed next to her. The men then began to file out, the laughter and ribald jokes that had accompanied them into the room fading as they moved off down the hall.

"Well, thank God that's o'er."

Joan glanced to Ross MacKay at that comment, noting only then that he'd been amongst the men and hadn't left but stood by Annabel, his arm around her waist. The man—her uncle, she reminded herself—gave her a wink that she suspected was supposed to cheer her. It didn't, any more than Annabel's reassuring smile reassured her, but she forced a smile and the couple slipped from the room, pulling the door silently closed behind them. She and Cam were alone.

Joan breathed out slowly and shifted her gaze to the furs and linens covering her, almost afraid to look at Cam and see anger there. After a moment, she couldn't stand the silence any more. She could actually feel Cam looking at her, and couldn't bear that either.

"There is wine and cheese on the table by the fire if you're hungry," she blurted, desperate to break the silence.

"I'm hungry," Cam admitted. "Jest no' fer wine or cheese."

Joan glanced at him uncertainly. He didn't appear angry. "Then what would you rather have?"

"You."

"You want *me*?" she squeaked

"Aye, ye daft woman," Cam said. Clucking his tongue with impatience, he sat up beside her in bed. "I could no' keep me hands off ye the last two weeks, Joan. Why would it be any different now?"

"I—You're not angry that my uncle made you marry me?" Joan asked uncertainly.

"Nay," he assured her solemnly, tugging the linens and furs down to reveal her shoulders and breasts. Reaching out, he cupped one round globe, allowing his thumb to flick gently back and forth over the nipple as he said in a husky voice that sounded a little distracted, " 'Sides, he did no' make me do anything. I was the one who first said anything about marrying ye."

"But only because you learned I was his niece," Joan pointed out and then gasped as he suddenly bent to close his lips over the nipple he'd been toying with. He suckled at it, his tongue continuing the flicking his thumb had been doing a moment ago and Joan's hands rose of their own accord, one clasping his shoulder, the other cupping the back of his head to urge him on as her body responded to the caress.

Releasing the nipple he'd been nursing, Cam raised his head.

"What does it matter?" he growled as he glanced down and flicked the linens and furs completely off of them both. Raising his gaze, he watched her face as his hand slid down her body.

"We're married." Cam growled and gripped her hip briefly, squeezing. He then shifted his hand between her thighs urging them apart, before finally finding her core.

"Ye're me wife," he breathed, lowering his head so that his hot breath brushed her lips as he spoke.

His fingers ran lightly over her warm, wet flesh once, then again before stopping to circle the nub where the pleasure he was raising in her seemed centered.

Joan moaned and shifted restlessly, her body beginning to strain toward the release that she knew he could give her. She was tugging on his hair and shoulder, trying to bring him down for a kiss, but his mouth remained tantalizingly out of reach as he whispered, "And I'm ye're husband."

"Aye," she gasped, her hips shifting and rotating now under his touch.

"Ye'll come to Sinclair," Cam continued, applying a little more pressure and Joan began to twist her head. He was driving her crazy; her release like his mouth was just out of reach and if he would just . . . she stopped digging her nails into his shoulder and reached instead for his staff, relieved to find it hot and hard.

Cam stiffened at her touch, and then abruptly stopped caressing her and shifted over her to settle between her legs.

Joan moaned in relief as he drove into her, even as he groaned his pleasure. Once fully in though, he paused and kissed her, a hot, wet, demanding kiss. Then he broke that off and raised his head as he began to move, pulling partway out of her again.

"God," he growled as he sank back into her. "Ye feel so damned good, and now ye're coming to Sinclair and I can drown in this pleasure every night."

Cam began to move in earnest then, his body

pounding into hers. Joan held on to him, her hands clutching his shoulders as he drove them both toward release, but for the first time since their first time together, she wasn't wholly engaged in what they were doing. Some small part of her brain remained separate and wondered about the days. How pleased will he be to have a wife good only for bedding?

The thought ran around and around inside her head until Cam suddenly gasped, "Stop yer fretting."

Startled, Joan focused on his face just as he claimed her mouth again. He thrust his tongue in rhythm with his hips, but also reached between them to caress her again and Joan's worries retreated under the onslaught. Her passion quickly returned to a full burn and it wasn't long before they both cried out their pleasure.

Afterward, Cam pulled up the linens and furs as he shifted to his side. He then caught Joan around the waist and pulled her back against him when she turned onto her side as well. A heartbeat later a small snore sounded by her ear and Joan realized he'd fallen asleep. Envy slid through her. She was suddenly wide awake herself, all sorts of worries crowding her mind. Most of them about how displeased Cam would be when he realized how ignorant and unprepared she was to be his wife. But she was also now fretting about what he'd said. He seemed happy that she was coming to Sinclair because he could continue to bed her, but was that the only reason? Was there nothing else about her that pleased him? And, if not, then what would her life be like when he grew bored with her? It was no better being his wife and watching him bed another than being a discarded mistress watching him move on. Actually, she thought suddenly, being the wife was worse. As a mistress she could have simply moved away and saved herself the heartache. As his wife, she couldn't. She would be expected to bear it she was sure, and Joan wasn't at all sure that she could do that.

"One problem at a time," she muttered under her breath. Annabel and Annella were going to teach her to be a lady wife. She would start tomorrow, Joan decided determinedly, and learn everything she could before they left for Sinclair. That thought made her wonder how long she had before they left MacKay. No one had said, but she was sure they would stay a couple days at least. After all, she'd just met her family, just learned they existed. Aye, they would surely stay a couple days or perhaps a week ere traveling on to Sinclair, Joan assured herself as she finally drifted off to sleep.

"TODAY?" JOAN SQUAWKED WITH ALARM, WIDE eyes on her aunt.

"I know. I was hoping for more time too," her aunt Annabel said soothingly, patting her hand where it rested on the table. "But Cam is concerned that his family will be worried about him. He says he was originally traveling with his cousins."

"He sent them on ahead," Joan recalled with a frown. She also recalled him telling her that he'd done so because of a tavern wench and felt a twinge of jealousy, which was just ridiculous. They hadn't even met yet.

"Well," her aunt continued, "I gather he told them he would follow in two days. But he said your journey here took much longer than expected?"

Joan bit her lip and nodded. "He was injured when he saved me from those bandits on the road. He slept for three days afterward, and then it took us two weeks of travel to get here."

"Two weeks?" Annabel asked with surprise.

"Aye. We did not travel very quickly," she muttered uncomfortably.

Annabel nodded with understanding. "Of course. He no doubt needed to take it slow while healing from such a wound."

"Hmm," Joan murmured, avoiding her gaze. It hadn't really been his need to heal that had slowed them. All in all the man had healed quickly once awake. In fact, after the first couple days he'd seemed right as rain to her. Certainly, he'd not seemed to have any problem with . . . er . . . vigorous activity.

"Well, Cam is now two weeks later than he was expected. He worries his family will be fretting and fears they may send out a search party. He thought it would be better just to take you home right away and reassure everyone."

"But—"

"Mother!" Kenna's cry interrupted Joan and made her glance around as the young girl rushed up, dark hair flying and cheeks hectic with color. "Cook just told me he is preparing food for Joan and Cam's journey."

"Aye, dear, I asked him to," Annabel said patiently. "'Tis a half day's travel to Sinclair and I thought they may like to stop on the way for a picnic."

Kenna shook her head and turned to Joan, "But ye can no' leave. Ye just got here. We want to get to ken ye."

"It was Cam's decision, not Joan's," Annabel said gently.

"Well he can just change his mind," Annella announced arriving at the table. "We are supposed to show her how to be a lady. We promised."

"I know," Annabel said unhappily. "But what can we do about it? Cam is her husband now and he has decided that—"

"Then I shall ha'e to go with her," Annella interrupted firmly and when her mother looked as if she were about to protest, added firmly, "Father has always said a promise made is a promise to be kept, and we promised we would help her learn to be a lady."

Annabel blinked and then a slow smile slid over her lips. "Aye, he does say that, does he not?"

"He does," Annella said, grinning now.

"Oh, I promise too. I promise too," Kenna said at once. "I can help. Please, Mama, can I go too?"

"Aye, you can," Annabel said, patting her shoulder. "We shall all go. That way we can get to know Joan better and keep our promise too."

Joan watched wide-eyed as they all smiled, then Annella warned, "Father'll be fair froth o'er our all leaving."

"Then he can come too," she said lightly and stood up. "Come along, girls. We must pack quickly else Cam will leave us behind."

Nodding, Annella turned and gave Joan a quick hug, assuring her, "We'll be quick."

"Do no' let him leave without us," Kenna added, hugging her next before rushing after her mother and older sister.

Joan stared after the trio as they bustled away, feeling just a bit dazed by it all. A lady rather than a commoner, married, and an aunt and cousins who were willing to risk the MacKay's wrath to help her . . . and while she didn't know him well, Joan suspected her uncle's anger might be a thing better heard about than suffered or even seen.

Shaking her head, Joan turned to the table and picked up her goblet of cider. So this was what having family was like? The thought immediately made her feel guilty. Maggie Chartres had been her family for twenty years, in fact her only family. And she had been a wonderful woman who would have fought to the death on her behalf she was sure, but life with her had always been calm and peaceful. Even in a healing emergency her mother had remained unflappable. There had never been frantic cries, or whirlwinds of activity, or mini rebellions as the one her aunt and cousins were about to hold on her behalf. This was different. Her life was now different in many ways.

For instance, last night was the first time in her life that she'd slept in a bed rather than on a pallet on the floor, or the cold damp earth . . . and it had been heavenly. It was also the first time she'd slept in an actual bedchamber. Not a corner of the hut where there was room for her pallet, but a room that had actually been created for just the purpose of sleeping and nothing else. It was the first time she'd woken in the middle of the night to find anyone, especially a handsome, virile, naked man like Cam, picking her up out of bed and carrying her to a mound of furs on the floor where a picnic of wine, cheese and bread had waited. And it was definitely the first time she'd had a man injure himself for her honor.

Her gaze slid to the bloodstained bedsheet hanging over the upper hall railing. Cam had cut his hand and dripped the blood on the sheet as "proof of her innocence" last night after they'd finished the food and wine Kenna had fetched for them earlier. He'd then made love to her on the furs before the dying fire. Later he'd carried her to bed and made love to her again there.

It seemed to her they'd spent the better part of the night seeking pleasure, so when there had been a knock at their door in the morning, she'd merely moaned and tried to burrow back into the linens and furs. Cam had scooped her out of bed so that her aunt and uncle and the MacKay priest could collect the bloodstained sheet. Joan had been so exhausted, she'd fallen right back to sleep the moment they left and Cam set her back in bed between the upper linen and furs.

She'd woken up some time later to find him gone and the bed cold where he should have been. Joan had got up, dressed and come below to find only Lady Annabel at the trestle table waiting for her. She'd asked where Cam was and her aunt had explained he was down at the stables, saddling his mount. She'd then told her that he had decided they should leave today. Joan's heart had seemed to drop right out of her chest at this news. She'd thought she had time, both to get to know her new aunt and uncle and their children, and to learn at least a couple necessary lessons on how ladies behaved, before leaving.

She didn't though. They were leaving for Sinclair today . . . and she would meet Cam's family. The thought was a daunting one. The only thing keeping her from all-out panic in that moment was that her aunt and cousins would be with her. She hoped.

Chapter 10

"How far are we from Sinclair now?"

Cam sighed at that question from Kenna. She had asked it at least twenty times since they'd set out from MacKay that morning. She had also chattered nonstop the entire way. The girl was driving him mad.

And how the devil had he ended up saddled with the MacKay women and a retinue of soldiers for this journey anyway? It was supposed to be just him and Joan on his horse. He'd planned a leisurely ride home, exchanging kisses with his new bride, mayhap sliding his hands inside her gown to enjoy her bounty. Perhaps even easing one up under her skirt to make her moan and whimper in his lap as they rode. He'd found that thought oddly arousing, though he'd never before had any desire to try such a thing on a horse. It was more likely to see them bounced off the beast's back than anything if he got Joan too excited and she began to writhe as she usually did when he touched her like that.

It hadn't mattered in the end though, because when Cam had gone to saddle his mount, Ross MacKay had come out to present him with the first of many gifts, a horse for Joan. She would not need to ride with him. Cam had quickly adjusted his fantasy to suggesting they stop in a pretty little valley he knew that was on their way home. He would feed her the food and drink that Lady Annabel had promised she'd have her cook prepare, and then he would ravish his lady wife in the woods. Perhaps he'd even ravish her twice before continuing on with their journey, he'd thought, marveling at the fact that after two weeks of repeated sexual escapades, he still couldn't get enough of the woman. If anything, he wanted her more and more.

That last fantasy had been scotched when he and Ross had returned to the keep to find out that Lady Annabel and her daughters intended to join him and Joan for the journey. They wanted to get to know Joan, they claimed, and were quite firm about it, but when Ross had begun to protest over their leaving, Lady Annabel had pulled him aside and whispered feverishly and at length about something that had eventually made the MacKay reluctantly give in. Cam had no idea what argument she'd used to sway her husband, but he'd caught the word *promise* several times and each time he'd seen the MacKay frown and slump a little more until he'd nodded in agreement.

Ross had then called Cam over and asked politely if his wife and daughters might accompany them home so that they could visit with Joan and get to know her. He would send men to guard them for the journey, and would collect them himself whenever Cam wished.

What could he say? Of course he'd agreed, and then he'd resigned himself to a half day's ride with the women chattering away, completely oblivious to the fact that they'd ruined his hopes for seducing his bride. He'd consoled himself with the reassurance that they would reach Sinclair just shortly after the nooning and then he could leave the MacKay women to visit with his mother while he dragged Joan away to show her a waterfall not far from the keep where he would then seduce her.

While he'd waited for the women to finish their packing, Cam had sat at the trestle tables, nursing a tankard of ale and thinking of all the things he wanted to do to Joan by the waterfall.

However, he'd eventually come to realize they were taking an inordinate amount of time about their packing. He'd understood why when the servants began to carry the chests down from above stairs. It had looked like they were moving in rather than visiting, until Lady Annabel had explained that some of the chests held wedding gifts for him and Joan. Linens and such, she'd said, smiling happily.

"I am sure 'tisn't much farther now," Joan said soothingly, making Cam realize he hadn't answered Kenna's question.

"She's right, 'tis just over this hill," Cam said now, his gaze dropping to the woman settled on his horse before him. Joan couldn't ride, of course. Something that hadn't occurred to him. Or to the MacKay, obviously. So he'd had to take her up on his horse before him after all. He hadn't minded in the least, until the first time she'd shifted before him, her little behind rubbing against his groin through their clothes. He knew she wasn't doing it on purpose, but the woman was killing him. Every time she moved, she rubbed against him, waking the beast under his plaid and making him harden, and it seemed to him that every time the beast under his plaid finally began to deflate, she'd shift once more, stirring him all over again.

"There it is," Lady Annabel said cheerfully, drawing Cam's attention away from his wife's behind and his aching erection, to the fact that they'd crested the hill and were now looking down on Sinclair Castle.

"Is it no' beautiful, Joan?" Kenna asked excitedly. "I ha'e ever thought it the prettiest castle."

Cam grimaced at the description. Only a female would call Sinclair beautiful and pretty. It was a damned masterpiece of fortification with an outer wall that was fifteen feet thick, was twenty-five feet high and had a wide dry moat before it filled with sharpened wooden posts to discourage getting too close. Inside that was the outer courtyard, separated from the castle itself by another moat, this one filled with water. Then came the gatehouse and towers to protect the first inner courtyard, and then the keep. There was a second inner courtyard behind the keep, of course.

Sinclair was large and a well-designed castle, but not a beautiful one to him.

"Aye, 'tis beautiful," Joan agreed in a dismayed whisper.

Cam glanced down curiously, wondering why she seemed to sound upset. Unfortunately, all he could see was the top of her head, so he couldn't be sure he hadn't misheard her.

" 'Tis big though, don't you think?" she added weakly.

Nope, he hadn't misheard. There was definitely dismay in her voice.

"Aye, big and beautiful," Kenna agreed as they rode down the side of the hill.

"Is something amiss?" Cam murmured by her ear.

Joan immediately straightened before him and shook her head. "Nay. Of course not. Sinclair is lovely."

He winced at the description, but let the subject go for now and concentrated on negotiating the trail down the hillside.

Cam wasn't surprised when half a dozen warriors appeared on horseback, on the bridge at the outer wall. He had expected as much. Their party was big enough they would have been easily seen as they crested the hill. Well before that, probably, he thought as he glanced over his shoulder to the wagons and soldiers behind them. The riders would be sent out to see if they were friend or foe.

The riders waited until they started across the sixty foot area where the trees had been cleared away in front of the outer wall before starting forward. Cam continued forward, unconcerned. Not slowing until the two parties reached each other.

"Brother." His younger brother, Douglas, greeted him solemnly as he reined in before him. "Ye finally decided to wander home . . . and ye brought guests," he added, eyes narrowing on Joan where she sat in Cam's lap. Curiosity flickered briefly across his expression and then his attention turned to the other members of the party. His eyebrows rose and respect filled his face when his gaze landed on Lady Annabel. Giving a half bow in the saddle, Douglas murmured, "Lady MacKay."

"Good afternoon, Douglas," she greeted him with a smile.

"Is Laird MacKay here as well?" he asked, his gaze shifting over the soldiers accompanying them.

"Nay. He could not make it right away, but he will come to collect us in a week's time," Annabel answered.

"A week?" Douglas asked with surprise, his narrowed eyes shifting to Cam with what he suspected was displeasure lurking in their depths.

"They are my invited guests," he said simply, and not wholly honestly. He hadn't exactly invited his in-laws to come home with him, though he supposed he should have thought to do so. After all, they had just been introduced to Joan and would no doubt want to get acquainted with her. And she probably would want that too. He should have thought of it and arranged it himself. He also should have thought to ask MacKay to send a messenger ahead to warn his family that he would arrive soon and was bringing company with him so that rooms could be prepared. But with everything that had happened, Cam hadn't even considered it.

"I'll warn Mother to prepare for more guests," Douglas growled.

"More?" Cam asked, but his brother had already turned his horse and charged away with the other Sinclair warriors following. Frowning now, Cam urged his horse forward again, hoping to God that his mother didn't still have a castle full of women waiting to descend on him the moment he entered. Dear God, she couldn't have kept them there all summer, could she?

Knowing his mother as he did? *Aye, she could have*, Cam thought with a sigh.

Sinclair was huge and crammed full of people moving every which way, Joan noted, gawking about as they crossed the drawbridge into the outer courtyard. She wasn't the only one gawking. Every person in the courtyard seemed to pause and turn to stare at them as they rode past, and every set of eyes seemed to be settled on her, in Cam's lap. At least until they'd passed, then their curious gazes seemed to take note of Lady Annabel, her daughters and the MacKay soldiers and wagons that followed.

Uncomfortable under all those staring eyes, Joan was relieved to reach the bridge across the

inner moat and ride under the gatehouse. At least
until they came out in the inner courtyard and
she noted almost as many people in this area, all
of whom mimicked those in the outer courtyard
and stopped to gawk at them as well.

"Chin up," Cam murmured by her ear. "Ye're
Lady Sinclair now. These are yer people."

Joan raised her chin, and tried to look serene,
but it was difficult when all she wanted to do
was crawl inside Cam's plaid and hide. Especially
when she noted the people spilling out of the keep
and gathering on the steps. Her gaze was immediately drawn to a well-dressed couple on the top
steps. The man had salt and pepper hair, at his
side was a tall, long-necked woman of about Annabel's age, her blond hair sprinkled with gray.

"Your parents?" she asked under her breath.

"Aye."

Joan nodded and let her gaze drift over the
other people on the stairs, most of whom were
women. There were a couple of older women
amongst them, but most were Joan's age or
younger, and every single one was pretty. Cam
had said he only had one sister and Joan guessed
that she was amongst the people on the stairs, but
suspected the rest were not his cousins. At least,
not all of them, she thought, and she remembered
Cam saying that his mother had filled the castle
with unattached women, hoping he'd marry one
of them.

His mother was about to be terribly disappointed, Joan thought on a small sigh as Cam

stopped his mount at the foot of the steps and dismounted, then reached up to lift her down. When he then turned to aid, first, Lady Annabel, and then each of her daughters, Joan glanced to her mother-in-law's expressionless face again.

Aye, she'd be disappointed, Joan thought again, more grimly. How could she not be? Any one of the pretty women on the stairs would undoubtedly make a better wife to Cam than she would. No doubt they were all trained in whatever it was that made a woman a good wife to a noble laird. Certainly, they already had the manners and such mastered, while she did not.

"Courage," Annabel whispered once she was on the ground. She also slipped her arm around her waist and hugged her briefly to her side.

Joan managed a smile for her aunt, appreciating the supportive gesture.

" 'Twill be all right. Lady Sinclair is nice," Annella whispered encouragingly, appearing at her other side and taking her hand. "She will like ye."

"Shall we, ladies?" Cam murmured as he finished lifting Kenna off her mount and led her over to join them. He frowned briefly when he realized that there was no room for him beside Joan, then relaxed, shrugged slightly and ushered them up the stairs en masse.

"Annabel," Lady Sinclair said, moving down a couple steps to greet them. Her previously expressionless face broke into a smile of greeting that made her absolutely beautiful and much more approachable. "What a nice surprise."

" 'Tis lovely to see you again, Bearnas." Annabel smiled widely and retrieved her arm from around Joan's waist to take the hands Lady Sinclair held out and then hug her in greeting.

"And I, you," Bearnas Sinclair assured her and then as they stepped back from each other, she glanced to Cam and added, "Especially since ye brought me son home to me safe and sound. I was beginning to fear he'd been beset by bandits on the road."

"I was," Cam said, stepping up to hug his mother as Annabel moved sideways on the step to greet Laird Sinclair with a hug as well. It seemed the Sinclairs and MacKays *were* close friends, Joan thought.

"What?" Lady Sinclair pulled back from her son with alarm. "Are ye all right?"

"Aye, thanks to Joan," Cam assured her and then turned to hold his hand out to her as he added, "She saved me life. Twice. First taking out one o' me attackers fer me, and then watching o'er me while I lay unconscious and defenseless. She mended me, else I would no' be standing here now."

Forcing a nervous smile as she took his hand, Joan stepped up next to him.

"Well, 'tis definitely a pleasure to meet you then, dear," Lady Sinclair said solemnly, looking her over. "Joan, is it?"

"Aye, Mother," Cam said. "This is Laird and Lady MacKay's niece, Lady Joan Sinclair."

"Niece?" Lady Sinclair echoed and turned to Lady Annabel with surprise. "I did no' ken ye had—" She stopped suddenly and then turned slowly back to Joan and Cam, confusion clouding her eyes. "Joan Sinclair?"

"Aye. We were married at MacKay yesterday. She is me wife," Cam announced. A moment of silence passed where everyone seemed frozen, then one of the women on the stairs made an odd choking sound and apparently fainted. At least, the blond dropped and began to roll down the steps. Fortunately, a younger version of Cam, his brother Aiden, Joan guessed, moved to the side so that she rolled into his ankles and came to a halt.

"Thank you, son," Lady Sinclair said on a sigh as the young man bent to scoop up the unfortunate woman. "Please take Lady Murine inside."

Joan instinctively started to move toward them, ready to help the woman, but her aunt caught her arm and shook her head. "I shall tend her."

Nodding, Joan reluctantly relaxed and remained where she was, but she had to fight every instinct she had to do so.

"I would have thought you'd sent the possible brides home by now," Cam said dryly as he watched his brother carry the woman into the keep with Annabel on his heels. "I have been away all summer, after all."

"Aye, and I did," Lady Sinclair admitted on a sigh as the keep doors closed.

"And then she sent fer them again when Roderick and Bryson returned with the news that ye were on yer way home and should arrive in a couple days," Douglas announced, drawing Joan's gaze his way. The man was as grim as Cam had claimed. He was also dark haired like his father, rather than fair like his mother and two brothers. He then added dryly, "That was two weeks ago, by the by."

"Leave off, Douglas. Cam already said he was beset by bandits and needed nursing," Laird Sinclair admonished, speaking at last. Shifting his attention to Joan then, he stepped down and pulled her into an embrace, adding, "Thank ye fer saving me boy, lass. And welcome to the family."

"Thank you," Joan murmured, managing a real smile when he released her and stepped back.

Laird Sinclair glanced to his wife briefly and his lips quirked up at the edges as he took in her expression. Turning back to Joan, he added, "I ken me wife welcomes ye too, she's jest too stunned right now to speak. We were beginnin' to think the lad would ne'er marry again. Ye must be something special to ha'e tempted him back into that sacred state."

Joan flushed and ducked her head with embarrassment. She suspected the man would be less welcoming if he knew the circumstances behind the marriage, but had no intention of telling him what they were.

"Well, come, let's move this inside and get off these stairs before someone else tumbles down 'em," Laird Sinclair said gruffly, taking Joan's arm to usher her inside.

Joan went willingly, but glanced over her shoulder as she did. Kenna and Annella were directly behind her, and Cam was behind them with his mother on one arm and a younger blonde who looked much like his mother on his other arm. His sister, Aileen, Joan guessed. The rest of the women followed silently, unhappy expressions on their faces. She couldn't blame them. Cam was handsome, smart and kind. She would guess that put him head and shoulders above most of the men out there who were not already betrothed or married.

Joan turned her face forward again, but couldn't help wondering where Lady Sinclair had found so many pretty young women. Weddings were arranged while noble children were still in swaddling, or at least while they were still young. To be available to marry, these women had to be either widowed, or still single because they were unlucky enough that their betrothed died ere marrying them. She wouldn't have thought there'd be that many young and pretty woman available and close enough to make it to Sinclair before them.

Although, they *had* taken more than two weeks to get here thanks to their dallying, Joan recalled. She supposed that was long enough for messengers to be sent and women to have traveled from as far away as England.

"So ye're Annabel and Ross's niece?"

Joan glanced to Laird Sinclair and nodded at that question as they crossed the great hall, heading for the trestle tables.

"Yer accent is English, lass. Ye were raised there?" the Sinclair asked.

"Aye," Joan answered.

"Well, ne'er fear," the Sinclair said, patting her hand where it rested on his arm. "We'll no' hold that against ye."

"Oh," Joan said nonplussed, and then added an uncertain, "Thank you?"

Nodding, he ushered her to the table and saw her seated, then settled beside her before glancing around until his gaze landed on his daughter. "Aileen, go tell the servants to bring ale and mead fer everyone, and warn them we ha'e guests fer dinner."

"Aye, Father," Cam's sister murmured and moved off to do her father's bidding.

"So." Laird Sinclair turned back to Joan. "Tell me about your journey. Ye saved me son?"

"Oh, well, in truth he saved me first," Joan said honestly.

"Her traveling party was beset by a gang o' bandits," Cam said, drawing her gaze to where he was seating his mother on the other side of his father.

Traveling party? Joan thought and stared at him blankly.

"By the time I arrived, Joan was facing four o' them alone," he added, moving around to settle in the empty space next to her so that she was sandwiched between him and his father. Her cousins Kenna and Annella had left room for him, and Douglas had settled on Annella's far side.

"Took out her soldiers, did they?" the Sinclair asked, not seeming surprised. Shaking his head, he muttered, "Englishmen."

"Ye intervened, son?" his mother asked as her daughter returned and settled next to her.

Cam nodded. "Aye. I could hardly leave such a brave lass to be beaten and assaulted by four big men. I took out three o' them, but was stabbed in the back in the doing. I thought sure the fourth would finish me, but Joan grabbed up a knife from one o' the other men and stabbed him."

"Smart lass," Laird Sinclair complimented, patting her shoulder.

Joan forced a smile, and then glanced to Cam as he continued.

"I was felled by me wound. Slept three days. She sewed me up, tended and guarded me the whole while. Then she saw me back to health when I woke. Had she no' done that, I'm sure I would ha'e died there, alone, on the side o' the trail." He turned and smiled at Joan, his hand moving to cover hers on the tabletop and squeeze before he continued, "When I learned she was traveling to MacKay, I offered her me escort."

"And fell in love along the way so ye married her when ye reached MacKay."

Joan blinked and glanced toward his sister when she sighed those words. The young woman beamed at her, popped up from her seat and rushed around to hug her from behind. "Welcome, sister. We are fortunate to ha'e ye in our family."

"Thank you," Joan murmured, automatically raising a hand to pat the arm around her neck, but her gaze was on Cam.

"Me sister, Aileen," Cam said with amusement.

" 'Tis so romantic," Kenna said now, drawing Joan's gaze to where her cousin sat with her sister on the other side of Cam. "I can no' believe no one told us this ere now."

"Aye," Annella agreed, and then smiled wryly and added, "Although, we did no' really give anyone the chance. We were so happy to learn we had a cousin and to meet her we hurried off to find her ere Father could ha'e, and then there was all the rush arranging the wedding feast, and then the wedding itself . . ." Annella shrugged. "Everything has been a bit rushed since they arrived."

"Why was it all so rushed?"

Joan stiffened and glanced toward the woman who had spoken, one of the ladies she had guessed were possible brides for Cam. She was the tallest of the prospective brides, with long black hair, a thin but pretty face and a plunging neckline on her dark red gown. A widow, Joan guessed, sure an untried woman wouldn't bare so much flesh.

Having garnered everyone's attention, the woman shrugged delicately. "Laird and Lady Sinclair were no' even given the chance to attend. Surely ye could ha'e waited a day for them to be sent for? Or ye could ha'e held the wedding here. After all, Lady MacKay and her daughters traveled here with ye. Then no one would ha'e missed the wedding."

"Father would ha'e missed it," Kenna put in.

Ignoring the girl's comment, the dark-haired woman raised her eyebrows and asked, "If Lady

Joan's traveling party was killed by the bandits, did the two o' ye travel alone the rest o' the way? Without e'en a maid fer chaperone?"

The insinuation was impossible to miss. The wedding had been necessary to save Joan's reputation, and she was right of course, Joan thought unhappily bowing her head.

"'Tis my fault we married so quickly," Cam said grimly, his hand moving to Joan's back and rubbing soothingly. "I was eager to get home and reassure everyone I was well, but I wanted to bring Joan as me wife. 'Sides, 'tis me second wedding so I saw no reason fer a big fuss."

"Aye, but did ye travel alone with her the rest o' the way?" the black-haired woman repeated insistently, apparently determined to force the admission that this marriage had been forced by circumstance.

"Finola!" Lady Sinclair snapped, and Joan guessed that was the black-haired bitch's name, because she reluctantly turned her gaze to Cam's mother, one eyebrow arching in question. Lady Sinclair glared at Finola for a full minute before saying, "How circumstances forced them to travel does no' matter. They are married now, and as much as I would ha'e liked to be there fer the wedding, I'm jest glad me son found someone he was willing to marry. The good Lord kens I was failing miserably at the task, obviously picking all the *wrong* women to tempt him with."

Finola's eyes narrowed at what could have been construed as an insult, and then she smiled coldly and turned to Joan to ask, "How were ye available to marry? Or were ye? Is there a betrothed out there somewhere who will be disappointed?"

"Nay," Joan said quietly. "I didn't have—"

"We had not yet had the chance to arrange a betrothal for my niece," Annabel announced, approaching the table with Aiden on her heels. Joan glanced to her, noting the anger on her face, and could only assume she'd heard a good part of the conversation as she'd come below.

"Which was me son's good fortune," Laird Sinclair said firmly, and then stood up as he added, "Now, I suspect our new guests would like to retire for a rest after the long journey here, and I ken me wife has some messages to send." He cast a glance to Lady Sinclair that seemed to be full of meaning as he said that and she nodded, expression grim. "In the meantime, I would ha'e a word with me sons, so . . ." He arched his eyebrows expectantly and the women all got up. Aiden immediately settled where his mother had been.

"I'll show ye to yer rooms ere I start me messages," Lady Sinclair announced, smiling from Joan to her aunt and cousins as she ushered the women away from the table. Her gaze then shifted to the other women before moving to her daughter as she suggested, "Aileen, perhaps ye can take the other ladies to the solar to relax?"

"Aye, Mother," Cam's sister said easily and started for the stairs.

Most of the women smiled and nodded and rushed after her. Finola, however, paused to sneer at Joan before following the others at a much more sedate pace.

Lady Sinclair scowled after the woman, and then sighed and forced a smile as she turned to Joan and her aunt and cousins. "All the rooms are taken up just now with . . ." She waved vaguely toward the women disappearing up the stairs. "Howbeit, Cam's room is available fer ye to clean up and rest in and, hopefully, I can have rooms available fer ye quickly."

"'Tis fine," Annabel assured her, slipping an arm through the other woman's as they started to walk across the great hall. "We arrived unexpectedly so shall be happy with what is available."

"Bless ye, Annabel," Lady Sinclair murmured as they started up the stairs. "And bless ye fer having a niece me son was willing to marry. I was beginning to think I would never see the day he'd marry again."

"That was entirely my sister," Annabel assured her. "She is the one who blessed us with Joan."

"Aye, well, bless her then," Lady Sinclair said on a laugh.

"Was it scary when yer party was beset by bandits?" Kenna asked suddenly, hooking her arm through Joan's as they followed the two older women.

"Of course it was," Annella answered for her with a roll of the eyes. Slipping her own arm through Joan's free one, she added, "'Twas brave o' ye to kill the fourth man. I do no' ken that I could ha'e done it."

"Aye, 'twas very brave," Kenna agreed. "And how lucky Cam arrived to save ye."

Joan merely nodded in agreement. She had certainly been lucky he'd appeared. Joan suspected Toothless would have beaten her to death if he hadn't.

"Here we are," Lady Sinclair said a moment later as she showed them into Cam's room. "As I said, if we're lucky at least one or two o' the girls will leave by the day after next now that Cam is no longer available. It may take until the end of the week to be rid o' the rest, but at least they'll soon be gone." She had paused at the door, and now smiled at Joan as she moved past her into the room, adding, "We shall all be forever grateful to ye fer that."

"Not enjoying the company, Bearnas?" Annabel asked with amusement.

Lady Sinclair snorted at the suggestion. "I used to think it would ha'e been nice to ha'e a passel o' daughters, half a dozen or so, but this has opened me eyes quite a bit. 'Tis amazing how horrible females can be in herds. Most o' them ha'e been fine, but a couple o' them . . ." She shook her head with disgust. "Arguing, insulting each other, and e'en trying to sabotage another by cutting up gowns and such."

Annabel arched an eyebrow. "Finola?"

"Until yer arrival I would ha'e said no. Aileen said she'd overheard Finola insulting one o' the girls and that she was no' as nice as she seemed, but I did no' believe her at the time. The woman has acted as sweet as pie ever since arriving, always offering to help me, and wearing pretty, sedate gowns. Then Douglas returned with the news that Campbell was riding up with guests and the women were all aflutter. They all rushed to their rooms to freshen up. Me eyes nearly fell out o' me head when Finola came down in that gown she's wearing. And then the way she acted at the table . . ." Lady Sinclair shook her head. "It makes me wonder what the other girls are really like."

"Hmmm," Lady Annabel murmured sympathetically, and Lady Sinclair sighed and shrugged.

"I should go start writing me messages and sending them to the families. The sooner they send riding parties to collect their girls, the sooner they'll be gone." She turned to the door, adding, "I'll ha'e servants bring ye food and drink and water to wash with."

"So? Tell me."

Cam raised his eyebrows at his father's words, and then glanced around as servants rushed out of the kitchen with the requested drinks for everyone.

"Leave a pitcher o' ale and four tankards here," Laird Sinclair ordered. "The rest go up to Cam's room and the solar."

He waited for the servants to head up the stairs, and then turned and surveyed his three sons before settling his gaze on Cam. "The truth this time, lad. And all o' it so we ken what we're dealing with. Who is the girl?"

Cam sat back slightly and took a drink o' ale, swallowed, then shrugged. "Most o' what I said was the truth. Joan is Laird and Lady Annabel's niece."

"Impossible," Douglas said at once. "Neither Laird MacKay nor his wife had siblings."

"Lady Annabel did," Cam's father said quietly. "Kate, her name was as I recall, and she caused a passel o' trouble fer those two back in the day."

"What kind o' trouble?" Aiden asked.

"The lass was the one originally contracted to marry the MacKay, but she ran off and married another. The parents presented him with Annabel in her place," Artair Sinclair recounted.

"Sounds more like good fortune than trouble to me," Douglas commented. "Laird and Lady MacKay are very happy together."

"Aye, they were from the start," their father murmured. "But then the sister, Kate, showed up at their door in tears, claiming she regretted her choice and such. It was all bullocks," he added dryly. "She just wanted her pie and the cake too. She wanted the Scottish stable boy she'd married and the MacKay coin as well. She cried her way into MacKay castle and her sister's good graces, then she and her man stole the coin and kidnapped Lady Annabel too."

"What happened?" Aiden asked with fascination.

"The MacKay caught up to them. He got Annabel and the coin back, but the husband was killed in the skirmish, and Kate was sent to an English abbey for punishment."

"It does no' sound like much o' a punishment to me," Douglas muttered.

"Nay?" Artair Sinclair asked with amusement. "We've had a passel o' women here at Sinclair this last week or more. How ha'e ye liked it?"

Douglas grimaced. "It's been hell."

"Aye, well imagine living with hundreds o' them, and ye can no' just get on yer horse and leave, no e'en for a minute's respite."

"Oh, aye, that's punishment, all right," Aiden breathed, obviously horrified at the thought. Cam couldn't blame him. It had been hell the first time his mother had filled the keep with women. That was why he'd gone off to find work as a mercenary. Better war than a castle full of women.

"And this Kate is Joan's mother?" Douglas asked, frowning.

Cam nodded. "Aye. She was carrying Joan when she went to the abbey. She died giving birth to her."

"Who raised her?" his father asked at once.

Cam hesitated, but then decided there was nothing for it and admitted, "The abbess gave Joan to the midwife to be rid of her. The woman was a healer as well as a midwife and raised her as her own, teaching her all she knew."

"And now that the lass is grown she went looking fer her rich relatives?" Douglas suggested cynically.

Cam shook his head. "The woman never told her who she really was. Joan had no idea she was related to the MacKays when I met her. She did no' ken that until yesterday."

"Then why was she on her way to MacKay when ye encountered her?" Aiden asked.

Cam sighed, and quickly explained about the deathbed request and the sealed scroll. He also explained the true version of how he'd encountered Joan and come to be traveling with her. Well, a slightly edited true version. It was none of their business that he'd been acting like a randy bull the last two weeks. When he finished, he stared into his tankard, waiting for his father's pronouncement.

Cam half expected the man would rear up with outrage, upset that he'd married the daughter of a thief and would-be murderer and demand he annul the marriage. Which would mean a holy argument because he had no intention of doing that.

"So, she's half Scot," his father said finally, and Cam glanced up quickly with surprise.

"Aye, I suppose she is," he said slowly.

"And she was raised by a healer in the village, not that Kate woman, so will no' be spoiled and greedy like her mother," Aiden pointed out.

"She is no' spoiled," Cam assured him. "In truth, she's smart, and funny and a skilled healer. She's no' afraid o' hard work."

"She's brave too, setting out alone to deliver her mother's message," Douglas decided reluctantly. "Foolish, but brave."

"Aye," Cam agreed. It had been foolish—brave, but foolish. She could have died. Would have died had he not happened upon her and her attackers when he had.

"It was clever of her to dress as a boy fer the journey," Aiden commented, and then grinned and added, "I wish I'd seen her dressed as a boy."

The comment made Douglas turn on Cam with disbelief. "How the devil could ye mistake the lass fer a lad? Even in braies I'd ken she was a woman on first sight. Her bosoms are—"

"She had her breasts bound," Cam growled, not liking his brother mentioning Joan's breasts, let alone knowing he'd taken note of her generous curves.

"Oh," Douglas said, but then shrugged. "Still, there's her face. She has a pretty face. Nothing like a boy's."

"Her face was swollen and bruised from the beating the bandit was giving her when I came upon them," Cam said impatiently. "She still has a little bruising on her temple by her ear."

"Aye, I noticed that," Douglas murmured and then shook his head. "It's been how long since the attack? Roderick and Bryson ha'e been home fer more than two weeks."

"Two weeks four days," Cam said, quickly adding the two week journey, the three days he'd been unconscious, and then today.

"Two weeks four days," Douglas murmured and shook his head. "She must ha'e taken a hell o' a beating to still ha'e bruising after this much time has passed."

"Aye. It was bad," Cam said. "Her face looked much like Bryson's after Comyn got done with him that time he caught him with his wife."

"Oh, that's bad," Aiden said with a grimace. "She must ha'e been in terrible pain."

"Aye," Cam agreed and then marveled, "She never once complained, though."

"Well," his father said suddenly and pushed himself to his feet. Raising his tankard, he held it out in front of him. "To Cam's new wife, Lady Joan Sinclair."

Cam breathed a sigh of relief when his brothers immediately stood. His father and brothers were accepting Joan and the wedding. All would be well then, he thought and stood as well to lift his tankard.

"To Joan," they all said together.

They all drank, then his father slapped him on his back as they reclaimed their seats and said, "Congratulations son. It sounds like ye've found yerself a fine woman. I'm happy fer ye."

Cam nodded and smiled to himself. He'd never expected to marry again, but now that he had, he didn't mind. He had found a fine woman. One he really enjoyed bedding . . . and would enjoy bedding right then in celebration of his family's acceptance, he decided, gulping down the last of his ale and slamming the tankard on the table.

Standing up, he stepped over the bench, saying, "Well, I think I'll join me wife to rest. It was a long ride."

"I doubt there'll be room fer ye what with Lady

Annabel and her girls in yer bed too," his father said with amusement.

Cam had started away from the table, but stopped at that and turned back. "What?"

"Were ye no' listening to yer mother ere she took the ladies upstairs?" Artair Sinclair asked with a frown.

Cam shook his head slowly. No, he hadn't been listening to his mother, he'd been fretting over the coming talk with his father.

"All those bloody women she brought here to tempt ye with are filling up all the spare rooms," his father explained. "So she put Lady Annabel and her daughters in yer room with Joan."

"Nay," Cam breathed with horror as his newly risen plans to indulge in some houghmagandie with his wife died a quick death.

"Aye," his father said solemnly. "I fear they'll be in yer room until we can get some o' these girls on their way home."

Cam stared after him with dismay, and then asked, "But where am I suppose to sleep?"

"Do no' worry, brother. There's plenty o' room in the barracks," Douglas said mildly.

"Aye," Aiden agreed, and explained, " 'Tis where we ha'e been sleeping since Mother gave our rooms to the women she brought here fer ye."

"Bloody hell," Cam muttered.

"Don't fret, lad," Artair Sinclair said. "I'm sure yer mother'll have the women cleared out soon enough. A week at most."

"A week?" Cam echoed with dismay.

"Well, with so many ladies, there was no' enough room fer their families and soldiers to stay here too, so it was agreed the girls would be left here in yer mother's care with just her and their maids to act as chaperone," Laird Sinclair explained. "That being the case, fer them to leave, a messenger has to be sent to each family, and then their families'll send soldiers to come collect the girls and take 'em home."

"Damn," Cam breathed.

"Here, boy, have another drink." His father poured fresh ale into his empty tankard and added with amusement, "Ye look like ye could use one."

Chapter 11

𝒥OAN TURNED SLEEPILY ONTO HER BACK, HER eyes blinking open when she rolled off her pallet and onto the cold, hard wooden floor. For one moment, she wasn't sure where she was. The ceiling overhead wasn't the straw ceiling of the hut she'd grown up in, or even the branches of trees as it had been during her journey.

Sitting up, she peered about the room and then relaxed with a wry little smile. It was Cam's room in Sinclair Castle. She'd slept on a pallet on the floor rather than in the crowded bed with her aunt and cousins.

All three of her relatives had protested when she'd asked a servant for a pallet, horrified that she would even consider it, but she'd assured them she would rather sleep on the floor on a pallet anyway. It was what she was used to after all, she'd pointed out. Besides, the bed, big as it was, was a bit crowded with the four of them in it. She suspected that was the only reason they'd relented in the end for they'd been pressed up against each other with no room to move. She was sure it had been more comfortable with just the three of them in it. Certainly, she'd been more comfortable on her pallet, though she did regret not getting to enjoy the comfort the bed offered.

Pushing off the furs that had kept her warm in the night, Joan quickly got up and glanced to the bed, eyebrows rising when she saw that it was empty. Her aunt and cousins had already risen to meet the day, it seemed. She wondered briefly why they hadn't woken her, but then was grateful for it. It had been late when Cam had returned her to the room last night, she recalled, a smile curving her lips at the memory.

Her first day at Sinclair had gone well. Meeting his family had not been as bad as she'd feared. At least they had not screamed in horror and cast her out. That was good, especially considering what her mother had done, Joan thought, recalling the conversation she'd had with her aunt after Lady Sinclair had left them alone in the room. She'd waited until her cousins had laid down to rest, but then had joined Annabel where she'd sat by the cold hearth and had asked her to tell her about her mother. Her aunt had been kind, but the long and short of it was that her mother had been a jealous cow who had tried to rob her aunt and uncle and had kidnapped Aunt Annabel with the intent of killing her.

Oh, Annabel had assured her that she didn't think her sister truly would have killed her, but

Joan was equally sure she would have. Her true mother sounded a horrible woman, which just made her even more grateful that Maggie Chartres had been the one to raise her. She just wished she could tell her that. There were many things she wished she could talk to her mother about, but that wasn't possible.

Sighing, Joan pushed her fingers through her hair in an effort to give it some order, and then brushed down her skirts to remove the worst of the wrinkles. It didn't help much and she wished she had another gown to wear, but this was the only clothing she had available at the moment. Joan used to have two dresses that she'd switched between. She'd packed them in her bag when she'd set out on her quest dressed as a boy, but had cut the first one up for bandages for Cam when she'd mended him. She'd cut up the second one to replace the binding around her breasts after Cam had sliced it off that day by the waterfall. She now had no dresses but the one she presently wore, and that was Annella's really. Although the girl had said she could keep it.

A good thing, Joan decided as she noted the grass stains on the skirt. It seemed Cam had caused the ruin of another gown, she thought, but wasn't terribly upset. How could she be when she had been a party to its ruin? After their talk, Joan and Annabel had lain down to rest for a bit too, which was when Joan had discovered the bed simply was not big enough for them all to sleep comfortably. She'd actually been relieved when a servant had come to inform them that the evening meal was ready and everyone was gathering in the great hall. It was then that Joan had asked for a pallet to be brought up for her. The servant had assured her there would be one there by the time she retired that night. Her aunt and cousins had argued with her briefly, but only briefly. She guessed from that they hadn't slept comfortably either.

Cam had greeted her with a smile when they'd gone below and ushered her to sit beside him. He'd then served both himself and her from the trays the servants had brought around. The meal had been a lively one, a celebration of sorts for the wedding the Sinclairs had missed. Joan had been quiet, shyness and uncertainty holding her tongue as the others had laughed and chatted. Still she'd enjoyed listening and laughing along with the others and it had seemed that in no time everyone was retiring.

Joan had blushed when Cam kissed her good night in front of everyone. He'd then hugged her as well, which caught her off guard. While she was used to his holding her in his arms as he kissed her, he did not usually just hug her. She understood why he had when he whispered by her ear to meet him below once everyone was asleep. Nodding, she'd slipped from his arms and dutifully followed her aunt and cousins to his room. But she'd worried the whole way, wondering why he wished to see her.

The pallet had been waiting as promised and

Joan had lain down when the others had retired, but had not slept. She'd waited until she thought they were asleep and the noises from the great hall stopped, and then had silently left the room. Cam had been waiting at the bottom of the stairs for her. Catching her hand, he'd led her silently to the doors to the kitchens, through the still warm room and out into the courtyard behind it, where vegetables and fruit trees grew.

They'd made their way by moonlight to the back of the courtyard where the trees were, and then he'd turned to kiss her. It was only when he began to tug at the top of her gown, pulling it down to free her breasts that she realized why he'd brought her here. Relaxing into his embrace, she'd kissed him back more eagerly.

It had been nearly dawn when she'd crept back to the room and slid beneath the furs on her pallet, which was no doubt why she'd slept so late. But she still didn't understand why her aunt and cousins hadn't woken her.

Shrugging that concern aside, Joan made her way below stairs. There were servants in the great hall but she didn't see anyone else, and no one was seated at the trestle tables. It was late enough that everyone had broken their fast and left, she guessed with a little sigh. She briefly debated going in search of Lady Annabel and her cousins, but the rumble of her stomach sent her to the kitchens instead.

Joan had expected to slip in, pinch a fruit and slip out, but that didn't happen. Her arrival in the kitchen brought an abrupt end to the work going on in there as every servant peered around to see who had entered and then stopped what they were doing to stare at her.

"I just thought to fetch some fruit or something to break my fast," Joan said uncertainly, letting the door close behind her.

"No need, m'lady. Jinny'll fetch it for ye," a man she presumed was the cook said. He then turned to glance at a small, pale woman who immediately rushed forward.

"Aye, m'lady. Please go sit yerself at the table. I'll bring food and drink out to ye to break yer fast."

"Oh, but I didn't want to trouble anyone," Joan protested. "I can fetch it myself. After all, I'm the one who slept late and—"

" 'Tis no trouble, m'lady," Jinny said, smiling as she urged her toward the door. "No trouble at all. Pray, go seat yerself and I'll be right out."

Joan gave in with a little sigh and allowed the woman to usher her out of the room. She wasn't used to being waited on, and wasn't at all comfortable with it. But everyone in the kitchens had looked at her as if she had two heads. Apparently, ladies didn't serve themselves that way.

Aware that Jinny was watching, she moved to the trestle tables. She was halfway to them before she heard the kitchen door close. Apparently the woman had wanted to be sure she wouldn't return before going about her task.

Joan settled at the table to wait, her gaze wandering over the great hall. It was a large room and well tended with colorful wall hangings, and clean fresh rushes on the floor. From what she'd seen, Sinclair Castle was huge, prosperous and well tended. Lady Sinclair ran her servants as efficiently as she imagined Laird Sinclair ran his warriors.

The sound of the kitchen door opening distracted her and Joan smiled at Jinny when the girl rushed out with a tray in hand. The maid headed first for the table at the end of the room, the one that sat a little higher than the others, but changed direction when she noticed Joan sitting at one of the lower side tables.

"Here ye are, m'lady," the woman murmured, pausing beside her. "The pastries are fresh. Cook just pulled them out before ye came into the kitchens. And this cider is from the first batch of the season and I brought ye an apple too. I hope 'tis all right."

"It's lovely," Joan murmured. "Thank you."

"Me pleasure, m'lady," the maid curtsied, then turned and rushed away, disappearing back into the kitchens.

Joan began to eat. She'd finished perhaps half her food when a mean laugh made her pause and glance around to see Lady Finola approaching from the stairs.

"I can hardly believe he had the nerve to bring ye home to his family," the woman said with cruel amusement and when Joan stared at her blankly, said, "'Tis no' bad enough yer the daughter of a thief and murderer, but look at ye, sitting at the low tables, yer gown and face filthy, yer hair a mess."

Sneering, Finola braced her hand on the table to lean toward her as she hissed, "Mark me words, once he's sated his lust fer ye, he'll ha'e the marriage annulled and toss ye aside as he should." Straightening, she looked down her nose at her and added coldly, "Ye do no' belong here. Yer no' lady. All ye'll do is shame the name o' Sinclair."

Movement behind and to the side of Finola caught her eye and Joan noted her aunt approaching from the stairs just as the woman said, "And yet Lady Sinclair told me just yesterday that she is grateful Campbell married Joan and not you, Lady Finola. So, apparently, she does not share your opinion."

Joan bit her lip and watched Finola warily. The woman had turned at the first word from Lady Annabel's mouth so she couldn't see her face, but the woman was terribly still, her hands balled into fists. For a minute, Joan thought she would attack Annabel, but in the end she merely hurried back up the stairs without uttering a word.

"Nasty bitch," Annabel muttered, watching her go.

"Mayhap," Joan murmured, and then added on a sigh, "But she's right."

"What?" Her aunt spun around to peer at her with concern. "Nay, Joan, she's not."

"I am the daughter of a thief and murderer."

"Nay, not a murderer," Annabel protested at once.

"She killed her husband, my father," Joan reminded her. That bit of news had been rather shocking when she'd learned it. Her mother had pummeled the man with her fists, he'd lost his balance, fallen and broken his neck.

"Aye, but 'twas an accident. Your mother loved your father. Truly she did, Joan. She did not mean to kill him."

Joan shrugged that away. "It matters little. As Finola said, I'm no lady. I don't know the first thing about being a lady. She said I was at the low table as if it was a disgrace, but I don't even know what a low table is. Or why I shouldn't sit at it. I mean, I know this table is lower than that one, but why should I not sit—"

"Nobles sit at the high table," Annabel murmured quietly. "The one on the end that is taller than the others. Servants and commoners sit at the lower tables."

"I see," Joan said wearily and stood up. "I think perhaps I should—"

"Joan," Lady Annabel said gently, catching her arm as she started to move past her. "Do not let what Finola said upset you. There are just a few things you need to learn, and that is why Annella and Kenna and I came with you. We can and will teach you these things."

"That won't change the fact that I'm the daughter of a thief and murderer," Joan pointed out unhappily.

"No, but then I am Kate's sister. Should I walk in shame over that?" she asked solemnly.

"No, of course not," Joan said at once. "You were her victim.

"As are you in a way," Lady Annabel said quietly. "You did not pick her for mother, Joan. And no one holds you responsible for the things she did. At least, no one who matters."

"You don't know that," Joan said at once. "It might matter to Cam's mother and father. In fact, I suspect it probably would if they knew."

"I am sure they do know," Annabel said quickly.

"How could they know? Cam could not even tell them the truth about how we met. I had no traveling party."

"Cam had to say that for the benefit of the women who are visiting here. It was to protect you, Joan, against their spreading gossip. But I am sure he told his parents the truth afterward. In fact, that is probably why his father wanted to talk to him and his brothers and sent us all away. He no doubt suspected Cam had altered the story somewhat because of their guests and wanted the true story.

"Joan," she continued gently, taking her hands. "You are your mother's daughter, not your mother. Your uncle and I do not hold you responsible for what she did, and no one else has the right to." She squeezed her hands. "Cam's parents are good people. I am sure they will not hold you responsible either. Besides," she added, smiling crookedly, "Lady Sinclair is so grateful Cam has finally wed that I suspect she will champion you no matter what."

Joan sighed and lowered her head unhappily, brushing at a spot on her skirts.

"We will sew you more gowns," Annabel assured her. "In the meantime, you can borrow a couple of Annella's. And we shall speak to Lady Sinclair about arranging for a lady's maid for you. I would have done so myself ere we left MacKay, but with everything going on, there was no time. The rest is a simple matter of teaching you what you need to know."

Joan hesitated. "How quickly can you teach me enough that I won't embarrass Cam?"

"As quickly as we can," Annabel assured her, and when Joan still hesitated, she caught her hands again and said, "Joan, please, do not let Finola eat away at your confidence and spoil the happiness you have a chance at here. It is what she meant to do. Do not let her. You and Cam could have a good life if you just trust in yourself and give this a chance. All right?"

Joan nodded solemnly. It wasn't as if she had much choice. She was married now. Her only option besides trying to run was to try to make it work. She would do that first. She could always run later if she had to.

"Good." Annabel smiled at her widely. "Then why do you not take your food and drink upstairs. I shall go speak to the girls and send them to start your lessons while I speak to Lady Sinclair about a lady's maid for you."

Nodding, Joan gathered the tankard and food the maid had brought to her, then turned and hurried upstairs with them. Once she reached the door to Cam's room, though, she paused, frowning at the items in her hands.

"Let me help."

Joan glanced around quickly, eyes widening as a petite redhead rushed toward her from the stairwell. It was one of the women Lady Sinclair had brought here for Cam to consider.

The young woman smiled at her as she reached her side. "Yer hands are a bit full."

"Aye, I slept late and . . ." Joan shrugged helplessly, terribly self-conscious now about her clothing and hair. She bit her lip briefly, and then blurted, "I should have fixed my hair and gown ere I went below, but I—"

"But ye lost everything in the attack by the bandits I imagine," she guessed with a little frown, but then patted her arm and added brightly, "But 'twill be all right. I'm sure Lady Sinclair will arrange a maid fer ye, and perhaps I and the other girls could help sew ye new gowns," she offered. "If all of us work on it, we should be able to get at least a couple done ere we leave Sinclair."

Joan's eyes widened with surprise at the kind suggestion. "Thank you—"

"Garia," the girl said when she paused uncertainly. "Me name is Garia MacCormick."

"Well, I thank you, Garia," she said quietly. "I appreciate your kindness."

Garia shrugged. "You have been through much losing your soldiers and servants and all your clothes to the bandits. If I can make things a little easier fer ye, I'm happy to." Turning then, she opened the door for her and pushed it wide. "Now, why do you not go and break yer fast. I'll go talk to the girls about sewing some gowns."

"Thank you," Joan murmured again as she slipped past her into the room. "I really do appreciate it, especially since you came here in the hopes of marrying Cam and I rather ruined that for everyone."

"'Tis me pleasure." Garia assured her and then grinned. "I never expected to win Cam anyway with all these lovely ladies to compete with. At least this way, I will have made a friend, and friends are oftentimes more valuable than gold, do ye no' think?"

"Aye, I do," Joan said solemnly.

Garia nodded. "I'll come back later and let ye ken what the other girls said," she promised, then pulled the door closed, leaving Joan alone.

Cam glanced around the great hall as he hurried inside, but other than servants going about their business, the room was empty. He'd expected as much, however, and continued to the stairs and up to the solar, expecting Joan to be there with the other ladies.

Women's voices raised in argument made him slow as he approached, though, and he paused in the hall just out of view to listen when he heard his name and Joan's mentioned.

"Why the devil would we help sew gowns for the little peasant Campbell has brought home? 'Twill no' benefit us."

Cam didn't need to see who was speaking to

know it was Finola MacFarland. The widow had expected to inherit her very old husband's wealth and castle on his death, but he'd willed it all to his brother's son instead. Just to add insult to injury, the MacFarland had requested his will be read before all on his death and in it had listed her many infidelities during their marriage as the reason why his nephew gained all and she received nothing. She'd been a selfish, careless wench before that, but had become a bitter, cold-hearted bitch since. Her attitude now surprised him not at all.

"The poor girl lost everything on the journey north thanks to those bandits," someone argued earnestly, and Cam shifted closer to peer around the door and into the room to see that only the prospective brides were present and the speaker was a petite redhead he didn't know. "Besides, 'tis no' as if we have anything better to do. 'Twould help pass the time until our families send traveling parties for us and 'twould help her at the same time. She seems nice and really needs our help."

"Do no' be a fool, Garia," Finola snapped with disgust. "O' course she's nice. She's a peasant being allowed to sit at the nobles' table. She's so grateful she'd probably lick yer boots. But mark me words, she'll no' last long. She does no' e'en ken enough not to sit at the low table. Campbell'll tire o' her quickly and toss her aside."

"They are married, Finola," Garia said quietly. "He can no' set her aside."

"Aye, he can," Finola said sounding triumphant. "Her father was a common stable master, her mother a murderer and thief. All he has to do is claim he kenned none of that and the wedding can be set aside."

Cam stiffened and scowled at the woman's words, wondering how she'd learned about Joan's mother and father. But then, the tale had been a subject of gossip at the time and told by the hearth for many years afterward. He had known about Annabel's sister, after all, so why shouldn't Finola? Actually, many knew the story and he had no doubt the gossipmongers would stir the story back to life now that Joan had made an appearance and married him. He would have to see to it that she did not hear and was not hurt by it though.

"I'm sure Cam would not set her aside," Garia said earnestly. "They love each other. Ye can see it in the way they look at each other."

Cam blinked at that. Was Garia seeing love between them? Was there love between them? He wasn't sure about his own feelings. He knew he hadn't wanted to lose her at the end of their journey, that he'd wanted what they had to continue. But Joan hadn't, and yet Ross MacKay had said that his wife thought Joan loved him.

"Love!" Finola spat the word as if it tasted bitter in her mouth. "What could he possibly love about her? She's a commoner. No education, no skills and with precious little to talk to him about, I'm sure."

Actually, they'd talked often and long during

their journey here, Cam thought. Joan might not have been educated in the way a noblewoman would have been, but she was intelligent just the same, and while he had thought her a boy when they'd first chatted by the fire at night, their talks had continued after he'd learned she was a woman. It was how they'd passed the time while traveling, and by the fire at night while recovering in each other's arms, and as they'd broken their fast in the mornings. They'd talked quite a bit.

"Nay. What yer seeing in their eyes is lust, and that ne'er lasts long. He'll tire o' her quickly, and then he will set her aside," Finola said with certainty. "All I have to do is bide me time and wait for that day."

"Well, ye can bide yer time all ye want," Garia said quietly. "Howbeit I am going to sew."

"Aye, but then ye would, ye're a fool," Finola said dryly.

Cam turned on his heel and moved silently away, unwilling to listen to any more of the woman's venom. Sadly, there was little he could do to keep her from espousing her nonsense. He could have made his presence known and silenced her for now, but the moment he'd left, she'd no doubt have started back in. The best thing to do was ignore it and hope her people arrived quickly to take her away. Although, frankly, it might be worth it to arrange for half a dozen Sinclair soldiers to escort her home now, he thought, and then glanced over his shoulder at the sound of footsteps pattering quickly up the hall behind

him. Cam hesitated, but then paused when he recognized Garia.

"Oh, m'laird." She smiled at him uncertainly,
her footsteps slowing as she reached him. "If ye're
looking fer Lady Joan, she's in yer room with her
aunt and cousins. I was jest heading that way
meself to tell her the good news."

"Good news?" he queried.

"Aye, I talked to the other ladies, and all but
one want to help and start on some gowns fer her
while we're here," she said, beaming happily.

Cam didn't have to ask who the one unwilling
to help was. "Thank ye, Garia. Fer championing
me wife and convincing the women to help like
this. I do appreciate it."

"Oh, 'tis nothing, m'laird. I'm happy to help
Joan. She seems lovely, and I'm happy the two o' ye
found each other," she assured him with a smile.
"Now I should go tell her the good news and take
her measurements so we can get started."

"Oh, aye, o' course," Cam murmured, a small
frown pulling at his lips.

"Is something amiss, m'laird?" Garia asked uncertainly.

"Nay, nay," he muttered and then forced a
smile. "I was just going to take Joan out and teach
her to—" He paused abruptly. He'd planned to
use the excuse of teaching her to ride to get Joan
away from the keep and get her alone for some
houghmagandie. But he didn't want to mention
teaching Joan to ride to Garia. She would wonder
why a noblewoman had to be taught to ride. Shak-

ing his head, he urged her to continue walking and said instead, "I was just going to suggest a ride to her. But it can wait. Measuring her for the gowns is more important."

"Oh," Garia said with a small frown as they continued down the hall. "Are ye certain? We could always wait to start and—"

"Nay," Cam interrupted quickly. "She's in desperate need o' gowns. I can take her fer a ride anytime."

"All right," Garia murmured as they stopped at the door. "If ye're sure?"

"Aye," he said and raised a hand to knock at the door for her only to have it open before he could.

"Oh!" The maid who had opened the door smiled nervously from him to Garia. "I was jest tidying the room while 'tis empty."

"Empty?" Cam asked, glancing past her to see that the room was indeed empty. "Where is me wife?"

"She went down to the bailey with her aunt and cousins. I believe they were going to practice their archery," the maid said.

Practice archery? Cam suspected Joan had never even seen a bow before, but merely nodded. "Thank ye."

When the maid nodded and slid past them to head downstairs, he turned to Garia and smiled. "Why do ye no' go on back to the solar? I shall find Joan and send her in to you ladies."

Nodding, Garia turned and hurried away. Cam watched until she slipped back into the solar, and then headed downstairs, wondering where the ladies might have gone for this practice. He doubted it would be in the practice area with the men. In fact, he suspected it would be somewhere no one was likely to see them and realize Joan didn't know an arrowhead from the fletching.

Chapter 12

"Now, aim fer the target, breathe out and release," Lady Annabel instructed.

Nodding, Joan squinted at the target, took in a deep breath, released it and let loose the arrow. She then sagged with disappointment as it sputtered and fell to the ground just feet in front of her.

"'Tis all right," her aunt said and patted her shoulder. "You just need to pull further back on the bow. Come try again."

Sighing, Joan notched another arrow, took a deep breath, pulled the arrow back and let it loose even as she released her breath. This time she did much better. The arrow flew high and far. It didn't hit the target, however, instead landing in the dirt ten feet to the right of the target and just inches from her approaching husband's feet.

"Oh dear," she and Annabel breathed together as he stopped short and stared down at the arrow.

Joan lowered the bow and bit her lip as she

watched Cam pick up the arrow and continue toward them. "I'm sorry, husband. I—"

"'Tis me own fault," he interrupted. "I ken better than to approach a target from behind. I just did no' ken ye'd set up a target here in the back courtyard to practice with," he said wryly. "I should ha'e. The maid said ye'd gone out to practice archery after all, but that was over an hour ago—"

"Ye've been looking for us for an hour?" Kenna asked with wide eyes.

"Aye. This was the very last place I thought to look," he admitted. "And when I did no' find ye in the practice field I thought perhaps ye'd changed yer mind about the archery, but I should ha'e approached more carefully anyway."

"We thought it better to teach her away from the others," Lady Annabel said quietly. "And no one comes back here but for the servants."

"Ye're right, o' course," he murmured."

"Not that it matters," Joan said with a sigh. "We have been out here for over an hour and I've yet to hit the target even once."

"But you are getting better with each shot," her aunt said encouragingly. "With enough practice you will do well."

"I'm afraid practice'll have to wait fer now," Cam said with a faint smile. "Garia has talked the ladies into helping to sew ye new gowns and they need ye in the solar to take yer measure."

"Oh, that's wonderful!" Annella cried, jumping up from where she and Kenna had been sitting, sewing as their mother tried to teach Joan to shoot straight. "We can get gowns done much more quickly with their aid."

"It is wonderful news," Lady Annabel agreed, smiling faintly. "And we have practiced enough at archery today. Let's go in and let the ladies have your measure, then we will switch to music or dance I think."

Joan managed not to grimace at the suggestion. While she liked Garia, she wasn't eager to meet the other women, especially Finola. She also wasn't eager to move on to training in music or dance. Joan had never had much time for such pursuits while growing up. She'd always been trailing her mother around, learning her skills, so knew darned right well she would be as bad at those pastimes as she was with the bow and arrow. In truth, all today's lessons had taught her so far was that she was indeed a peasant, a peasant playing at being a lady.

"ARE YE DONE?"

Joan glanced to Cam with surprise and then back to her empty trencher. She'd been considering having a bit more pheasant, but supposed she could do without it. She didn't need to gain weight and not fit in the gowns the ladies were planning for her. The thought made her smile faintly. Garia, as it turned out, was not the only one of the ladies who were nice. Several of them were. Of course, a couple weren't too. Finola wasn't the only one with a less than pleasant personality, but Joan had mostly enjoyed her time with the women that afternoon before her aunt pulled her away to start dancing lessons.

That thought made Joan's smile die as quickly as it had grown. She was no better at dancing than archery. Truly, she had stomped on her cousin's toes so many times she would not be surprised did they not refuse to help with those lessons in future. Joan didn't mind if they did. She had not enjoyed the lessons. She'd felt awkward and clumsy and the whole ordeal had left her hot and sweaty and miserable.

"Joan?" Cam prodded with a small frown.

Forcing a smile, she nodded and opened her mouth to say aye, she was done, but snapped it closed and glanced around as Lady Sinclair called her name.

"If ye're done eating, dear, I would ha'e a word with ye."

Joan's eyes widened and she glanced to Cam uncertainly.

"Go ahead," he said with a sigh. "I can wait."

Nodding, Joan stood and walked along the table to her mother-in-law as the woman got to her feet.

"Lady Annabel and I had a chat this afternoon," Lady Sinclair said, slipping her arm around Joan to usher her to the stairs. "And she reminded me that ye're in need o' a lady's maid. So I asked one o' the maids to wait fer us in Cam's room so ye can see if ye think she'll do."

"Oh," Joan murmured blankly.

"The girl has ne'er held a position as lady's maid as her main position, but she has acted as one in the past when we've had guests without their own in accompaniment. They ha'e said she was surprisingly good. And o' course, me maid, Edith, and Lady Annabel's maid too, shall help train her if ye think she'll do after ye've spoken to her."

"Thank you," Joan murmured. " 'Tis very kind."

"Not at all, dear," Lady Sinclair said. "I am just sorry I do no' ha'e a fully trained lady's maid to offer ye."

" 'Tis fine," Joan said quietly, and it truly was as far as she was concerned. What was more fitting than for her to have a maid in training? After all, she was a lady in training.

Joan was still smiling over that thought when they reached the bedchamber she was presently sharing with her aunt and cousins. As Lady Sinclair had promised, a maid waited there for them, and Joan's eyes widened as she recognized her. It was the young pale woman named Jinny that the cook had ordered to bring her food to break her fast with that morning.

"I shall just wander down to the solar to wait while ye confer with her," Lady Sinclair announced. "Ye can find me there when ye're done and let me know if she'll do or no'."

"Thank you," Joan murmured as her mother-in-law pulled the door closed. Turning back to the maid then, Joan managed a smile, hesitated and then gestured to the chairs by the fire. "Let's sit, shall we?"

The maid nodded, but waited for her to lead the way. Once seated, they peered at each other silently, the maid waiting expectantly, and Joan wondering what the devil she was supposed to do now. Finally, she cleared her throat and asked, "Would you like to work for me?"

"Oh, aye, m'lady," Jinny answered eagerly.

"You would?" Joan asked, vaguely surprised at her enthusiasm. "Why?"

"Why?" Jinny seemed equally surprised at the question. "Every maid in the castle would love to be yer lady's maid, m'lady. 'Tis a prime position. I'd answer only to ye. I'd ne'er ha'e to work in those hot kitchens again, and cook wouldn't dare pinch me bottom were I yer lady's maid and not just one o' the kitchen girls."

"The cook pinches your bottom?" Joan asked, frowning.

"Aye. And worse. He's a nasty, randy old—" She stopped abruptly and covered her mouth, eyes wide with alarm. After a moment she lowered her hand and whispered, "Oh, pray ferget I said that, m'lady. Cook is fine. I just would prefer working fer ye to working in the hot kitchens is all. Truly."

Joan eyed her solemnly, and then heaved a sigh. She had no idea what else she should ask her. The girl wanted to work for her, so her taking her on as lady's maid wouldn't be taking her from a job she preferred. That was really the only thing that mattered to her. Or it had been. Now that she knew she'd be helping the girl escape the Sinclair cook's lascivious attentions . . . well, that was good too. She never could stand bullies and people who abused the power they had.

"Very well," Joan said, getting to her feet. "You're my new lady's maid."

Jinny blinked and stood up. "I am?"

"Aye."

"Oh." Rather than look pleased, Jinny looked troubled at this news.

"Is there something wrong?" Joan asked with a frown.

"Nay, nay, I just . . ." She shrugged helplessly. "I expected more questions I guess."

"What kind of questions?" Joan asked curiously, wondering herself what she should have asked.

"I do no' ken," the girl admitted wryly. "Just more."

Joan nodded. "Well, if I think of any more questions, I'll ask them as we go along. All right?"

Jinny nodded quickly. "Aye, m'lady."

"Good." Joan headed for the door.

"Excuse me, m'lady."

Pausing, she turned back in question.

"Do I return to the kitchens to help with cleanup, or . . ." She glanced around uncertainly, obviously not sure what she would do here.

Joan frowned at the question and then asked, "Where is Lady Annabel's maid?"

"She was here when I arrived, but when I explained Lady Sinclair sent me, she said she would go take some air and give us the room to ourselves."

That didn't surprise her. Annabel's maid was very good at judging when she was needed and at making herself scarce when she wasn't.

"Well then, nay, you're not to return to the kitchens. Just wait here for her to return and take your lead from her on what you're supposed to do," Joan suggested.

Jinny nodded, obviously relieved not to be sent back to the kitchens, but stopped her again as she turned back to the door. "M'lady?"

"Aye?" Joan asked, turning back once more.

The maid hesitated, wringing her hands as she did, then pleaded, "Pray, do no' tell cook what I said. He has a bit o' a temper and he's really no' so bad. 'Tis just his way, and at least he does no' beat us."

Joan swallowed the anger rising in her throat, and nodded solemnly. "I'll not repeat what you said."

"Oh, thank ye, m'lady." Jinny beamed at her with relief.

Managing a smile, Joan slipped from the room and made her way down to the solar to talk to Lady Sinclair.

"There ye are," Lady Sinclair said when Joan entered the room, setting aside the deep red material she'd been examining. "I was just looking to see how far the girls have got with your gowns. They're moving along rather quickly. A good thing too. I expect three or four will be leaving us tomorrow, and another three the day after. A couple will be here longer, but most will be gone within the next three days and we'll have to finish on our own." She stood up and smiled expectantly. "Well? Will Jinny do?"

"Aye," Joan said and smiled. "Thank you, my lady."

"Not at all, dear." Lady Sinclair moved forward and slid her arm around her waist to urge her toward the door. "Ye have to have a lady's maid. 'Sides, I should be thankin' you. I was beginning to fear I would never see grandbabies from me son. Now I ha'e that hope alive within me again."

"Oh," Joan breathed, guilt immediately rising up within her. She was still afraid of the birthing bed, and knew Cam had no desire to risk losing another wife there, so had continued to use the wild carrot despite the wedding. Which meant Lady Sinclair was going to be very disappointed when no children were produced by the union.

CAM SLOWED AS HE NEARED HIS ROOM, EYES widening with dismay as he heard the caterwauling coming from inside. It was mid-morning, the nooning meal would not be for a couple of hours yet, and he'd hoped perhaps his wife could take some time from her lessons for a little break with him. The sounds coming from his room, however, suggested she was in dire need of those lessons.

"Nay, nay, stop dear," Lady Annabel's voice sounded, bringing an end to the off-tune shrieking taking place in the room. "Listen to Kenna again."

Cam smiled faintly as Kenna began to sing. The

girl had the voice of an angel, he thought, as she began to sing a slow sweet song about a maid's love for a brave warrior. It was a well-known song, but Cam only recognized it now. Joan's version had been decidedly unrecognizable.

"There," Lady Annabel said with satisfaction when Kenna's voice died away. "Now you try, dear. But try to sing from here, from your chest rather than through your nose."

The caterwauling started up again, this time in a tone a little lower than the nasally sound that had come out before, but it was still an off-tune caterwauling that made Cam wince. Singing, it seemed, was not Joan's forte, he thought, but then he didn't mind. He wasn't much of a singer himself, he thought, and raised his hand to knock—

"There ye are."

Cam paused without knocking and glanced to the side at that comment to see Aiden moving toward him from the stairs. Turning away from the door, he walked forward to meet him. "What's about?"

"Da wants to talk to ye," Aiden announced.

"Oh." Cam glanced back toward the door to his room, and then sighed. "Where is he?"

"Down at the stables having two horses saddled up fer the two o' ye," Aiden answered absently, his gaze shifting past him to the bedroom door as Joan's attempted singing continued.

Nodding, Cam moved past him toward the stairs, but paused at the top step to glance back.

Aiden was staring at the bedroom door with a sort of horror. "Are ye coming?"

"Oh, aye," Aiden turned and moved toward him, but glanced back over his shoulder as he came and muttered, "What the devil are they doing in there? Skinning a cat?"

Cam just shook his head and started down the stairs. Joan wasn't that bad. She was bad enough though, he acknowledged and decided it was good he didn't care if she could sing or not.

"NAY, DEAR. STOP," LADY ANNABEL SAID, HER smile a little forced now.

Joan stopped singing at once, and was relieved to do so. Sighing, she shook her head. " 'Tis useless. I can't sing."

"That's not true," her aunt said at once. "You have a lovely voice, you just need to learn not to put so much energy into your singing," she added almost apologetically. "You are bellowing rather than singing, dear, and it makes it difficult for you to carry the tune."

Joan shook her head, quite sure she could never sing as beautifully as Kenna.

"Let us try it again. This time though, sing as softly as you can. Whisper even, and then we will—" She paused and glanced to the door as a knock sounded. "Kenna, will you . . . ?" Lady Annabel let the question die, Kenna was already halfway to the door.

"Good morn," Lady Garia said brightly when Kenna opened the door. Spotting Joan, she smiled and said, "One o' the dresses is near being done and we thought to ha'e ye try it on ere we finish it."

"Oh, of course," Joan said and stood quickly to move to the door. She was more than eager to quit her singing lessons for now. In fact, she would not mind stopping all the lessons altogether. It was terribly disheartening proving she could not do any of the tasks her aunt and cousins seemed to think were so important for a lady to know.

"I think ye'll like it," Garia said as she led her quickly down the hall to the solar. "At least I hope ye will," she added wryly.

"I'm sure I will," Joan assured her, and truly believed that. She was wearing another borrowed gown of Annella's at the moment and while it was lovely, she was ever conscious that it was borrowed and she had to be careful not to stain it. A much more difficult task than one would expect when her husband kept dragging her out to the back courtyard at night to roll around in the grass. When she and his mother had returned below last night, most of the others were just rising to retire. Cam had pulled her aside for another good night kiss and hug, telling her to meet him again once everyone was asleep.

Joan had gone eagerly, but there had been a nip in the air last night, and she had been so worried about Annella's gown . . . well, it would make things much easier when a few of the girls left and she and Cam could share a bed again.

"What think ye?"

Joan blinked her thoughts away as she halted in

the door to the solar and saw the gown two of the women were holding up. It was a masterpiece of deep red with a square neckline and drop sleeves. Gold trim had been added under the bust, and at the upper arms.

"We made a matching chaplet too," one of the women announced, holding up a wreath of red velvet with the gold trim crisscrossing it all the way around and then dangling down the back.

"Oh," Joan breathed. It truly was a beautiful gown. She was a fair hand with the needle, but knew she could never have managed this wondrous creation herself.

"Try it on," Garia urged. "So we can see what must be done."

Joan moved forward and was immediately beset by the women, all first eagerly undressing her, and then just as eagerly dropping the new gown over her head and doing up the stays before all stepping back to consider their efforts.

"Oh my," Garia sighed and the comment was followed by several murmurs and sighs by the other women.

Joan peered down at herself, gently running her hands over the soft cloth. It looked beautiful from her perspective, but she couldn't see the whole picture. She frowned slightly as she noted that the hem was extremely long, and gently lifted the skirt a bit so that it wasn't dragging on the ground.

"Do no' worry about that," Garia said at once, brushing her hands away so that she released the skirt. "We knew 'twould be too long still. Finola said she had the same measurements as you in the bosom and waist and offered to act as yer substitute while we made it."

"She did?" Joan asked with surprise.

"Aye, we were surprised too," Garia admitted, but then shrugged. "Still, it was all she was willing to do and it did help. But we made it to her height to get the full effect, planning to hem it and add gold trim to the bottom when we were sure the rest fit properly."

"And it does, 'tis perfect." Joan glanced to the speaker, recognizing her as the lady who had fainted on the steps the day they'd arrived. Murine, she thought Lady Sinclair had called the blond woman.

"Aye," a petite brunette said. Her big brown eyes moved over their efforts critically and then she suggested, "But we should pin it for hemming while she's wearing it to be sure it's absolutely perfect."

There were general murmurs of agreement all around and then Garia raised her eyebrows. "Would ye mind standing still in it long enough to pin the hem?"

Joan opened her mouth to agree, but then hesitated. Her aunt expected her to attend her lessons. It was the reason her aunt and cousins had gone to all the trouble of packing their belongings and traveling here, leaving her husband and son behind. She could hardly just shirk those lessons and—

"Of course, she will."

Joan glanced with surprise toward the door at that announcement and stared wide-eyed at her aunt. "Really?"

"Aye," Lady Annabel said with a smile and then looked her over slowly and shook her head. "You look more beautiful than I could have imagined, Joan. Of course, you must help them finish it." Moving forward, she kissed her cheek lightly, and whispered, "Maggie would be so proud to see you like this."

Joan blinked away the tears those words brought to her eyes and hugged her aunt, which immediately brought protests that she would wrinkle the gown.

Laughing, Lady Annabel stepped back, holding her hands up as if to fend them off. "All right then, you girls go ahead and get started and I shall see if I cannot get one of the servants to bring you up some pastries and cider for all your hard work."

Joan smiled as she watched her aunt leave.

"Oh dear," Garia said suddenly behind her.

"Is something amiss?" Joan asked glancing around to the woman.

"We only ha'e two pins left," Garia said slowly, peering at the items on a small table behind her. "The rest appear to all have been used in the other two gowns we have started." She tapped her hand against her skirt briefly, then turned and headed for the door. "I'm sure I ha'e some tucked away in me chest in me room. I shall go fetch them."

Once Garia left the solar, the feeling in the

room changed somewhat, it filled with an awkward silence that made Joan uncomfortable. After a moment, she couldn't stand it and blurted, "Thank you so much for doing this. I realize it must be— I mean, you all came here to meet Cam with the hopes of . . ." She waved vaguely rather than verbalize that they'd come hoping to marry her husband. "And then he showed up with me and yet you all . . ." She bit her lip briefly and then said sincerely, " 'Twas very kind of you all, and I do appreciate it."

"Ye're welcome," the petite brunette said solemnly, then stepped forward and offered her hand. "I am Saidh Buchanan."

" 'Tis a pleasure to meet you," Joan said sincerely, clasping the offered hand and squeezing gently.

"Murine Carmichael," the pale woman with the tendency to faint introduced herself.

"Edith Drummond." A tall redhead took her hand next.

They introduced themselves one after another then, giving her name after name until Joan thought her head would spin with them all. There were twelve women after all. Her brain managed to hold on to the names of the first four women, but after that all she could recall were the last names Frasier and Graham, and the first names Glenna and Lorna, and she had no idea if they went together and whose face fit the names.

Fortunately, a servant arrived then with the pastries and cider that Lady Annabel had promised to have brought up. The girls all rushed to pour themselves a drink and select a pastry, but Joan held back, afraid to drop crumbs or spill cider on the new gown. She was thirsty though and tempted, but resisted.

"I found them!" Garia announced triumphantly as she entered the room a moment later, and then spying the girls just moving away from the tray on the table, rushed forward, crying, "Ooooh, lovely."

Joan smiled crookedly as the petite woman hurried up to the table.

"Why are there two goblets still?" Garia asked. "Has one of these already been used, or did some-one not get some?"

"I do no' think Joan got a drink," Murine said, glancing to Joan and back.

"I didn't wish to risk spilling anything on the gown," she explained with a grimace.

"Oh." Garia glanced to her and back and then asked, "Are ye all right no' drinking?"

Joan grimaced and admitted. "I'm thirsty, but I'd rather no' risk it."

"What if we placed some cloth over her chest?" Murine suggested. "Then she could drink safely."

"Aye, that might work," Garia agreed, turning to pour a second drink.

"Here, one o' these might do." Saidh bent to begin digging through a basket of cloth rem-nants, and straightened a moment later with one she considered suitable. "We'll just tuck this in yer neckline."

Joan glanced down to watch her tuck the cloth

between the gown and her chest and then glanced around behind her when Garia cried, "Careful Murine."

"Sorry, did ye spill yer cider when I bumped ye?" Murine asked with concern.

"Nay, 'tis fine," Garia said with an apologetic little sigh. "Just be sure to be careful around Joan when she has her drink, else the cloth Saidh gave her will no' make a lick o' difference."

"Aye, o' course," Murine said unhappily. "Can I take her drink to her for ye?"

"Aye. Please. That way I can get us both pastries," Garia murmured.

"Can ye raise yer arms, Joan? We ne'er checked yer seams there to see that they were all right."

Joan glanced around at Saidh's request and automatically raised her arms, peering at the seams herself even as the other woman did.

"I'll set yer drink here on the table next to ye, Joan, so ye can drink when ye're ready," Murine announced from her other side.

"Thank you," Joan said, glancing to her again.

"Keep yer arms up," Saidh ordered, making her realize that she'd let her arms droop a bit as she'd glanced around. The woman moved around her then, explaining, "I just want to see how it sits in the back."

Joan nodded, and waited patiently.

"Lower yer arms," Saidh instructed, and a moment later said, "Raise 'em again."

"How is it?" Garia asked around a mouthful of pastry.

"Good," Saidh decided.

"Great!" Garia said cheerfully, brushing her hands together to remove any crumbs. "Then we can start pinning the hem."

"Should I stand on a chair?" Joan asked. "Would that make it easier?"

Garia paused to consider the question, but then shook her head. "Nay, 'tis better this way. We need to judge the distance to the floor and the chair would be under yer feet, no' under the skirt."

Saidh nodded agreement and held her hand out for some of Garia's precious pins, asking, "How do ye want to do this? Shall I start in the back and ye in the front?"

"Nay, mayhap we should start in the front and ye go one way around and I go the other," Garia suggested. "What do ye think?"

Saidh nodded and knelt in front of Joan. She peered down at them silently as Garia set the first pin, then the two women began to work, moving away from each other. Joan watched for a minute, and then glanced for her drink. Spying it on the table where Murine had said she'd set it, Joan carefully picked up the cider and took a big swallow, and then nearly spat it out. Good Lord, it was bitter. Not at all what she was used to. Usually it was sweet and—

"Try to stand still, Joan," Garia muttered around the pins she'd placed between her lips.

"Sorry," Joan apologized after swallowing the mouthful of liquid. She held on to her goblet rather than turn again to set it down and unintentionally move her dress. She glanced around at the women surrounding her and after a moment, asked, "So, you're all without a betrothed?"

Silent nods were her answer and Joan bit her lip. No one was casting her accusing looks, but she felt guilty just the same. They'd come here hoping to win Cam's interest and marry him, but she'd sort of stolen him before they could even meet him. Joan took a quick drink of the cider to avoid their gazes and immediately grimaced as the bitter liquid flowed over her tongue. She'd forgotten how bad it was. Swallowing the liquid, she reached to set the goblet on the table beside her, despite the risk of moving her gown. She didn't want to drink it again by accident.

"Finola is widowed," Saidh informed her now. "But the rest o' us ha'e ne'er been married."

"And probably ne'er will be," Murine said with a little sigh. "Likely we'll all end up in abbeys."

"Speak fer yerself," Saidh growled with disgust and paused in her pinning to scowl up at the woman. "I shall ne'er take vows."

"Sorry," Murine breathed timidly, her hand rising to her neck as if she feared Saidh would suddenly produce a sword and hack at her with it. She also swayed on her feet and Joan eyed her with alarm. Murine was a sweet girl, but she also had a tendency to faint at the drop of a chaplet. Honestly, she'd fainted on the front steps when Cam had appeared with a bride in tow, and then had fainted twice more while they were measuring Joan the day before, just from getting overexcited. She was looking overexcited now too, Joan noted with concern. "Sit, Murine and have some more cider. Mayhap something sweet'll keep you from fainting."

Murine nodded and picked up the pitcher, but set it down just as quickly. "The cider is gone." She grimaced and sat down, waving away her concern. " 'Tis all right. I'm fine."

"Nay, you're pale," Joan said with a frown and then picked up her own goblet from where she'd set it on the table and held it out. "Here, drink this then. I've had enough. It's a little bitter for me."

"Are ye sure?" Murine asked.

"Of course," Joan assured her, holding it a little higher. "I was no' thirsty anyway."

"Thank ye." Murine accepted the goblet and took a gulp, her nose wrinkling. "You're right. 'Tis bitter."

"Really?" Saidh asked. "I found mine sweet, a bit too sweet fer me liking."

"Mayhap all the sweet settled to the bottom and it needed a good stir," Garia said, her tone distracted as she pressed another pin into the hem.

"Mayhap," Saidh picked up her own goblet and held it out to Murine. "Have mine instead if ye like."

"Thank ye," Murine said, taking the goblet with her free hand and then holding out Joan's goblet. "Do ye wish to have this one then? It may be more to yer likin'."

Saidh accepted the goblet and took a swallow, her eyes widening and mouth puckering with distaste. "Ew, nay, this is more bitter than I like.

It tastes like . . ." She shook her head. "'Tis off or something."

"Do no' be a ninny, Saidh," Edith said with a faint smile. "It came from the same pitcher as the rest o' ours did and mine was fine. It can no' be so bad."

"Nay? Then try it," Saidh challenged, holding out the goblet.

Shrugging, Edith took it and swallowed some, wincing as she lowered the goblet. "My apologies. 'Tis bad."

"Oh, heaven's, let me see," Garia said, sitting back on her heels and reaching for the drink. When Edith handed it over, she too took a drink, her face immediately twisting with displeasure. "Oh, aye, 'tis bad. But my drink did no' taste like this." She glanced toward the pitcher and shook her head, before handing back the goblet to Edith. Turning back to continue her work, she suggested, "Mayhap there was something in the bottom of the goblet ere we poured the cider in."

"Mayhap," Saidh agreed and then tilted her head and asked, "Are ye feeling fine Joan?"

"Hmm?" Joan glanced to her, slow to comprehend what she was asking.

"Are ye feeling okay?" she asked. "Ye're rubbin' yer stomach."

"Am I?" she asked faintly, peering down to see she was indeed rubbing her stomach. Why was she doing that? Joan wondered, and then realized that it was aching. No, not aching exactly, she decided. That was the wrong word. It was . . . she felt like she was going to heave up everything she'd consumed. What had she consumed? Oh, aye, she'd only had a bit of cider—

"Joan, if ye want a straight hemline, ye must stop moving and—" Garia paused as she glanced up at her. Concern crowding her expression, she straightened slowly. "Joan?"

Joan opened her mouth to assure her that she was fine, but before she could get the words out, darkness seemed to fall over her.

Chapter 13

"*W*HAT?" CAM ASKED WITH DISBELIEF, BUT didn't wait for the answer. Instead, he pushed past his brother to hurry up the keep steps, desperate to get inside and see Joan. "Where is she?"

"Yer room," Aiden said, following hard on his heels. "'Tis all right, Cam. Lady Annabel said she'll be fine. They all will."

"They all?" Cam echoed with confusion as he threw open the keep doors and rushed inside. "Who all?"

"Several o' the ladies fell ill at the same time," Aiden explained, moving up to his side as they hurried across the great hall. "'Twas no' just Joan, Ladies Carmichael, MacCormick—"

"I do no' ken who is who, Aiden," Cam interrupted with a frown. He hadn't bothered to get to know the prospective brides his mother had collected. He had a wife. Not that he would have been interested anyway. "How many o' them are ill?"

"Three I think," Aiden answered, then frowned and said, "Nay, four." He seemed to count them out on his fingers as they started upstairs, and then nodded. "Aye, four. And Joan makes five, o' course."

Joan was the only one that mattered as far as Cam was concerned. He was sorry the others were ill, of course. But they were nothing to him. Joan was his main priority. She was his wife and he had already begun planning a long future with her. It was what he'd been doing with his father all day. They'd ridden out to Inverderry, a castle along the coast and the smallest of the three castles belonging to the Sinclairs. A chatelaine had been running it for years now, but when his father had taken him there today, Cam had expected to be told that he and Joan were to move there and take it over. Instead, his father had announced that he was ready to slow down and carry less responsibility, and so was Cam's mother. His parents planned to move to Inverderry castle and leave him the responsibility of the main castle, while Douglas would tend to Dunlorna, the second largest of the three castles. Aiden would eventually get Inverderry, while their sister Aileen would inherit the Lansend House as her dower, though she would continue to live with their parents until she married.

All the way back from Inverderry, Cam's mind had raced with plans for himself and Joan as Laird and Lady of Sinclair Castle. So it had come as something of a shock to arrive to learn Joan had been struck down by illness. She'd seemed healthy and well the last time he'd seen her, and had certainly sounded hale enough while caterwauling away at her lessons.

"What made them ill?" Cam asked with a scowl as they stepped off the stairs and started along the landing.

"I'm no' sure," Aiden admitted apologetically. "They just started dropping. Lady Annabel is tending them."

Nodding, Cam pushed through the door to his chamber and came to a halt. Joan lay asleep on the furs on the bed, her face appearing almost colorless above the deep red gown she wore. Annella sat on the side of the bed with her and glanced to him when he entered.

"Oh, Cam!" Annella stood, and offered an anxious smile. "Thank goodness ye're here."

"How is she?" Cam asked, moving to the bedside.

"Mother says she will be all right, but she has no' woken yet and three o' the other girls ha'e," Annella said worriedly.

"Four of the other girls," Annabel said quietly as she entered the room. "Joan is the only one who is still asleep."

"But she will wake, will she no'?" Cam said with a frown, settling on the side of the bed to peer at her pale face.

"I believe so. But I think she drank more than the others," Annabel said with a frown. "Not enough to seriously harm her, though, I think."

"Drank what?" Cam asked, turning to peer questioningly at the woman.

"Cider," Annabel answered, moving up to the bed to peer over his shoulder at Joan. "They were hemming the gown she is wearing. I had a servant take up some pastries and cider and Joan complained hers tasted bitter. The other girls who fell ill tried it too. Joan may have had more than the others though. Murine thought she saw her drink from it twice, while the other girls only had one drink each."

"Do ye ken what was in the cider?" Cam asked.

"Her goblet was knocked over when the girls all began to faint and the other girls sent for a servant to clean it up. There was nothing left by the time I realized it was the only thing they'd all had and went looking for it," Annabel said on a sigh and shook her head. "But I think she will be fine too."

"But ye do no' ken for sure?" Cam asked.

"Nay," Annabel admitted unhappily, concern creasing her face as her gaze shifted to Joan. "I wish I knew what was in her cider."

"It was only in her goblet?" Cam asked with a frown.

"Apparently," Lady MacKay said with a shrug. "At least hers was the only one that tasted bitter according to the girls. But they all drank from the same pitcher."

"So it was no' in the pitcher, but her goblet specifically?" Cam murmured, turning his gaze back to Joan.

"Aye," Annabel said heavily. "I had come to that conclusion myself."

Cam's mouth tightened and then he asked, "How many girls left today?"

"As your mother hoped, the Sutherlands, Mac-Leods and Frasers received her messages yesterday and came for their daughters today. They stayed for the nooning meal and then all left early this afternoon."

"Lady Sinclair was going to give us each one o' their rooms, but Mother said nay," Annella told him, bringing Cam's head around with alarm.

"I thought it was only fair that your brothers get their rooms back, so I had her put my daughters and I together in one chamber until another is available for the girls to share," Lady MacKay said soothingly. "Our things have already been moved to the room Lady Fraser was using and yours have been returned up here. So at least you can stay here with Joan now."

"Thank ye," Cam said on a relieved sigh and turned to peer at his wife, thinking that his brothers would be glad to get out of the barracks as well. He was certainly happy to know he would be able to stay here with Joan. At least he would be, were he certain she would recover from whatever it was she and the other girls had drank.

"Mother?"

Cam glanced past the woman to the door she'd left open. Kenna stood there, uncertainty and worry on her face as she peered at Joan.

"Aye, dear?" Annabel asked, moving to her daughter.

"One o' the ladies asked me to fetch the red dress. She said they want to hem it," Kenna said quietly. "They thought it would be nice if 'twas ready for Joan to wear when she wakes up."

"Oh." Annabel glanced to Joan, and then nodded and moved to the bedside. "Aye, that would be nice."

Cam stood at once to help with the effort and with the two of them working, quickly slid the gown off Joan and tucked her under the linens and furs.

"Here you go, dear," Lady Annabel said, laying the gown in her daughter's arms. "Thank the ladies for us. I am sure Joan will appreciate having a gown of her own to wear."

Nodding, Kenna turned and rushed away. Lady Annabel turned back toward the bed, but paused when she noted Annella still there. "There is no need for you to sit with her anymore, sweetling. Why do you not go take Kenna outside for some fresh air? You have both been stuck inside, helping to watch over the ladies for hours."

Annella hesitated, her gaze sliding to her cousin, but then she nodded and silently left the room.

"They are both such good girls," Lady Annabel said with a smile as she watched her daughter go. "I am very blessed."

"Aye," Cam agreed as he moved to the chairs by the fire. He carried one back for her, and then returned for the other for himself and they settled down to watch over Joan.

They were both silent at first, but after a moment Lady Annabel shifted in the chair on the other side of the bed and said, "Campbell?"

He stiffened at once. Being called Campbell rather than the shortened Cam usually indicated he was in trouble or about to get a lecture of some sort or other. Raising his gaze warily to the woman, he said, "Aye?"

"Did Ross force you to marry Joan?"

He blinked in surprise at the question, as well as the worry on the lady's face. "Nay," he said finally. "I wanted Joan to come with me to Sinclair even before I knew she was your niece."

"Wanting her to come as your mistress and having to marry her are not exactly the same thing, are they?"

Cam flushed, his gaze shifting back to Joan. After a moment, he sighed and admitted, "'Tis true. At first I was no' even considering wedding her. I ha'e been so determined no' to marry again that . . ." He shrugged. "But once I realized she was your niece, I kenned we had to marry e'en before Ross said anything to me."

"So you did marry her only because she was my niece," Annabel said, sounding sad at the knowledge.

"Nay," he assured her, and then frowned and admitted, "Mayhap. I am no' sure. When I realized she was yer niece, I was glad. I thought, Ah ha! Now she'll ha'e to marry me and come to Sinclair."

"So you were pleased to get your way?" she suggested slowly.

"Aye." Cam grimaced as he heard how that sounded. "It was no' just getting me way that made me happy. I wanted her with me." He paused and then shook his head and said, "But she did no' want that. When I asked her to come with me, she did no' just say no to me. She said she did no' want to." The memory made him scowl at the unconscious woman.

"You were hurt," Lady Annabel said slowly, realization dawning on her expression.

Cam straightened in his seat and shrugged carelessly, unwilling to admit it.

Lady MacKay was silent for a moment and then said, "Joan told me that when you asked her to come with you, she wanted more than anything in the world to say yes."

He stilled, even his heart seeming briefly to stop, and then Cam sat forward again, asking, "But then why did she say she did no' want to?"

Lady Annabel smiled apologetically. "I can not betray her trust and tell you that. I fear you will have to wait until she is ready. I only told you that she wanted to come with you because I feared thinking she did not want to would affect how you act with her." She paused and then said solemnly, "Just as her thinking that you only married her because you were forced to by circumstance is no doubt affecting her actions around you."

Cam sat back, understanding sliding over him. He would have liked to say that thinking Joan didn't really want to be here hadn't affected his behavior around her, but he knew that wasn't the case. In truth, other than their nighttime trysts, he had been avoiding her. Oh, he'd made a couple of desultory efforts to see her during the day, but had quickly given in when other things had intervened. Between her lessons and his responsibilities here he had found it easy to avoid time alone with her. But they had spent every moment together during the journey here, talking and laughing and working together, and if not for that one moment in time when he'd asked her to accompany him to Sinclair and she'd refused, Cam knew he would have been doing any and everything he could to ensure that continued. Or, at least, that he was able to spend as much time with her as possible, if not alone, then in the company of others but with her at his side.

For instance, he would have liked her to have been with him today for the journey to Inverderry with his father, and no doubt would have used the excuse that it was a perfect chance to teach her to ride away from the keep and others as the reason. Instead, he hadn't even suggested it.

Cam had also been letting people and things come between them since she'd said no to him. When they had realized that Annella and Kenna had given away that he and Joan were to marry, he had let Ross send him away, instead of insisting he talk to her himself. The night of their wedding, he'd delayed going above stairs until Ross had finally said something, and then once he had gone up, he'd made sure there was no time to speak, kissing her every time she'd opened her mouth for fear she would say something he didn't want to hear. And in the morning, he'd left her sleeping rather than wake her and possibly have to talk.

Once here he had continued this behavior, allowing her to be separated from him and sleep with her aunts and cousins. Cam knew if not for those couple of moments in the clearing outside MacKay, he would have insisted they set up a temporary sleep chamber in the solar, or that he and Joan could make do with one of the few empty cottages on Sinclair land for a couple nights, or even stay at one of their other castles rather than be separated.

Mind you, he couldn't go without making love to her. Cam had dragged her off each night to do that, but he'd also made sure she didn't get the chance to talk each time he did. And then he was up early in the mornings, breaking his fast before the others and off in the bailey ere she could possibly wake.

If his own behavior had been affected by thinking she didn't want to be with him, how would hers have been altered by thinking he had only married her because he had to?

He glanced to Lady Annabel. "Ye're sure she wanted to come with me?"

"She said she wanted desperately to go with you," Annabel told him solemnly. "That she had never been so happy as she was during those two weeks with you."

Cam let his breath out slowly and then glanced toward the door Annella had left open as he became aware of the increasing noise coming from the great hall. "It sounds as if they're gatherin' for the sup. Ye should go below and eat."

Annabel hesitated, but then stood. "You will let me know when she wakes?"

Cam nodded silently, his gaze moving back to his wife as he began to sort out what he should say to her when she woke up. Those two weeks traveling with her to Scotland had been the happiest of his life too, and he had also wanted desperately for her to come here with him. But then he'd said as much, it was she who had refused. Cam didn't know why she'd said she didn't want to come with him, but perhaps if he asked she would explain. And perhaps they could sort this all out and they could return to the easy, happy relationship they'd had before those moments in the clearing at MacKay.

Campbell considered several different approaches to the talk he wanted to have with Joan as he sat watching over her, but eventually the late nights and early mornings caught up to him and he began to nod off in the chair. When he woke up some time later, it was to find his mouth dry as stone, his chin covered with drool, and his neck sore from sleeping sitting up.

Grimacing, he rubbed a hand around the back of his neck, trying to ease the crick there, then let his hand drop and glanced to Joan. The fire had burned down to glowing embers, and the candle on the bedside had burned down so that it was now a puddle of wax with a weak flame flickering and about to sputter out. It was enough light for him to see that she was still sleeping, but that was about it. He needed to fetch another candle and build up the fire if he didn't want to sit in the dark.

Yawning sleepily, Cam stood and moved quietly out of the room. In the hall, he walked to the railing to peer down into the great room below. He'd intended to get the attention of one of the servants and have them fetch him a fresh candle, but the great hall was silent and still, the fires burning down, leaving the room nearly dark. Despite that, Cam could see the servants sleeping on pallets on the floor below. It was late enough that everyone had retired. How long had he slept?

A yawn interrupted this concern and Cam debated simply returning to his room, crawling into bed and sleeping, but Joan hadn't woken yet and he wanted to be there for her when she did. He wanted to be awake though, not sound asleep beside her, so he continued toward the stairs, pausing there to glance further along the hall when one of the doors opened.

Squinting in the dim light, Cam tried to see who it was, but could tell little more than that it was a woman until she stopped at one of the guttering torches and lit a candle he hadn't noticed she carried with her. When she then turned and continued toward him, the candle held up before her, Cam recognized Lady MacFarland. Not wanting to deal with her, he turned to continue on his way.

"Campbell."

Surprised as much that she'd used his first

name as that she'd called out to him at all, Cam
stopped and turned slowly to wait for her, sure he
was going to regret it.

JOAN'S HEAD WAS POUNDING WHEN SHE WOKE.
Grimacing, she sat up, blinking when she realized she was in the bed. Wondering what she was
doing there and where her aunt and cousins were,
Joan started to get out of bed only to freeze when
she realized she was naked.

Dropping back on the bed, she pulled the linen
around herself and tried to recall how she'd got
this way, but the throbbing in her head wasn't
helping with that endeavor. Letting go of the
matter for the moment, Joan hesitated, but then
tugged the linen out from under the furs and
wrapped it around herself, tucking the end into
the front to secure it as she stood up.

How she had got this way could wait until
she'd eased the ache in her head. That was more
important at the moment. Desperately important,
she thought, one hand going to her forehead, and
fingers rubbing in an effort to ease the pain.

Her medicinal bag was on the table by the fire
where she'd left it and Joan started toward it, but
paused as she realized she would need a drink
to mix her herbs into. Obviously she couldn't go
below like this though. Joan shifted on her feet
briefly, debating what to do, but then headed for
the door. She might not be willing to go below like
this, but perhaps she'd be fortunate enough to spy
a servant in the hall.

That thought in mind, she opened the door a crack and peered out, surprised to see that the hallway was quite dim with just two flickering torches still lit. It must be quite late, she realized, and then noted movement near the stairs. She squinted, trying to see who it was and then glanced past them as she noticed a light moving up the hall. Someone carrying a candle, she realized, able to see the red of the gown they wore, but not their face. Even as she noted that, they lifted the candle, revealing more of the gown and then their face. Joan recognized her gown just before she was able to see the woman and recognize that it was Finola.

Well, that explained where her gown had gone. Now the question was how the devil had the woman got it off her? The last thing she recalled was wearing it as the girls pinned the hem for her. Joan couldn't see the hem of the gown now, the candlelight didn't reach that far, but she suspected it was just as long as it had been before the women had started to pin it.

Damn, Finola had stolen her dress, Joan thought, mouth tightening. She was about to barge out in her linen to demand to know what the woman thought she was doing in her gown, when Finola got close enough for her candle to cast light on the man at the top of the stairs.

"Cam," Joan breathed, the name barely a whisper of sound as the woman walked straight up to him until their bodies pressed together. Even as Finola leaned into him, she raised a hand to catch him by the back of the head and pulled him down as she rose up on her toes to kiss him . . . and Cam wasn't fighting her off.

Silently closing the door, Joan turned to walk back to the bed. She settled on the edge of it, her mind a complete blank. This was her nightmare come true, Cam turning to another and her having to stand by and watch.

Joan couldn't be sure how long she simply sat there, but after a moment she slipped under the furs, still wrapped in the linen, and closed her eyes. She didn't want a drink anymore, or herbs to ease her aching head, she just wanted to pretend this had all been a nightmare and that she would wake up to find it had never happened.

CAM SHOOK OFF THE SURPRISE THAT HAD BRIEFLY held him still and caught Finola by the shoulders to push her back. Cold anger sliding through him, he demanded, "What do ye think ye're doing?"

"Oh, come, m'laird," Finola murmured, smiling seductively. "Surely ye do no' expect me to believe ye really enjoy being married to the peasant? I ken ye were forced to marry her by the MacKay. But ye can ha'e it annulled, and then ye can ha'e me." She leaned back slightly and held the candle closer to herself so that the glow fell over her from head to knees.

Cam opened his mouth to tell her to go to hell, but then paused and allowed his gaze to travel over her in the gown as he recognized it.

"Am I no' more beautiful than her?" Finola asked with a triumphant smile.

"Nay," Cam said coldly. "And is that no' me wife's gown?"

Finola blinked. "What?"

"The gown ye're wearing," he said succinctly. "Me wife was wearing it when she fell ill. We stripped it off to give to Kenna because she said one o' the women claimed they wanted to sew the hem."

"Ye were there?" Finola asked with alarm.

"Aye," he said dryly and then tilted his head. "I'm guessing ye were the woman who asked fer it. I'm also guessing ye ne'er planned to finish the hem at all. Ye just wanted to steal her dress and then use it to try to seduce me?"

Finola pressed her lips tightly together with anger, and then snapped, "Well, 'tis wasted on her anyway. It looks better on me. And you would do better with me too. At least I'll no' embarrass you and yer family with me ignorance like she will."

Cam stared at her with something that was a cross between disbelief and bewilderment as he tried to sort out how she could think her behavior would be attractive to a man. First, she behaves no better than a village slattern, throwing herself at him, and then she tries to win him over with insults to his wife and boasts of her own supposed beauty? Sometimes he simply did not understand the reasoning skills of others, or the lack of said skills.

"Lady MacFarland," Cam said solemnly, "Joan may very well make mistakes in the future, but they'll no' embarrass me. *She* will ne'er embarrass me. You on the other hand, embarrass yerself, yer clan and me with yer behavior and *ye've* no excuse fer *yer* ignorance."

"Bastard," Finola hissed and raised her hand to slap him.

Expecting it, Cam caught her by the wrist and warned. "I would never hit a lady, Finola, but since ye've proven ye're no' one, I'll give ye fair warning; if ye slap me, I'll slap ye back."

He stared at her silently for a moment, and then released her.

Finola glared at him with impotent rage, her hand balling into a fist, but then she lowered her hand without a word.

Cam nodded. "I'll arrange fer some men to escort ye back to MacFarland on the morrow. Ye're no longer welcome here," he said grimly, and then turned on his heel and continued downstairs. He had no more time to waste on the woman, and couldn't wait to send her on her way.

And he would see to it that Joan never wore that gown again, Cam decided grimly as he made his way carefully through the people sleeping in the great hall. Joan had looked absolutely beautiful in it, but he would not see her wear anything that woman had tainted with her touch.

The kitchen fire was burning low when Cam entered. Something that smelled delicious was bubbling in a large pot hanging above it. The scent reminded him that he hadn't eaten the evening meal and Cam decided he should grab some bread and cheese to take back upstairs with him.

But not now. After he'd retrieved the candles he'd come for, he thought, turning toward the door to the storeroom. Cam unlocked the padlock, lifted the bar and pulled the door open. The room was dim, with just enough light making it through the open door for him to see the candles resting on a shelf on the right, halfway to the back wall. Stepping inside, he moved toward them and was just closing his hand around a couple of the candles when the door suddenly slammed behind him.

Startled, Cam whirled around and stared into the darkness where the rectangular opening should have been, then rushed forward and felt around until he found the door latch. He lifted it and tried to push the door open, but it wouldn't budge.

"What the hell?" he muttered, trying again. Nothing. Pounding on the door now, he called, "Hello? Is someone there? Hello?"

Silence met his call and Cam tried again, pounding and shouting louder, but the door didn't suddenly open, bathing him in light and freedom. Pausing, he stepped back and considered trying again, but the truth was no one would hear him. In the summer, the kitchen staff slept in the great hall with the other servants to avoid the heat that remained after cooking all day. All except the cook, who had a room at the back of the very long and large kitchens. But the man was well known for being impossible to wake once he fell asleep. Cam suspected it had a lot to do with the drink he indulged in at night. But it was none of his business what Cook did when he wasn't working and usually it wasn't a problem. Right now, being locked in the storeroom and needing someone to let him out was a problem . . . but not the cook's.

Sighing, Cam eased to a sitting position on the floor and leaned back against the shelves. Once the kitchen staff were up and about he should have no problem attracting attention and gaining his freedom. It looked like he would be stuck here until then though . . . which meant Joan would be alone if she woke up before morning.

The thought made him pause. While the bar could have fallen back in place once the door was closed, it couldn't have closed on its own. Someone had closed him in here and probably dropped the bar back into place too. Deliberately. Why?

Cam wouldn't put it past Finola to have done it. She was no doubt angry that her plan to seduce him and convince him to annul his marriage for her had failed. She probably wasn't pleased with what he'd said to her either. And he knew she was up while the rest of the castle appeared to be sleeping.

He began to tap his fingers on the stone floor, thinking. So long as this was the extent of Finola's revenge he would let it go, arrange her journey home and just get her on her way. But that was only so long as she didn't do anything else. And that was what worried him. What else could she do? And what else had she done?

Cam fretted over that briefly. Joan and four other women had been made ill after drinking from Joan's goblet. She'd been drinking from the same pitcher as everyone else, so there had obviously been something either in her goblet before her drink was poured, or put in her drink after it was poured. Had Finola been behind it? Had she planned to remove Joan, to clear the way for herself? And if she had, what might she do now that Joan was alone, unconscious and basically helpless?

Not that he thought Finola could possibly still hope that he would turn to her should anything happen to Joan, but she was a bitter and nasty bit of work. Would she hurt Joan to hurt him? Cam wouldn't put anything past the bitch.

Jumping to his feet, he felt his way to the door and began to hammer on it and shout again, then took several steps back and threw himself at it.

Chapter 14

"OH, M'LADY! YE'RE UP!"

Joan turned from the window and forced a smile for her maid, Jinny. "Aye. I'm up, and in desperate need of clothes, Jinny. I think the gown I wore yesterday is still in the solar . . ." Her voice trailed away as Jinny raised her hands, drawing her attention to the dress she held. The same one Joan had worn the day before to go for the fitting. "You have it."

"Aye." The maid grinned and hurried forward. "One o' the maids brought it to yer room last night and I took it below to press the wrinkles out o' it. It looks good as new now."

"Aye, it does," Joan murmured, moving forward to touch the gown. It was one of Annella's gowns, and she was grateful for it. She would never wear the red and gold gown again . . . if Finola even bothered to return it. She hadn't so far. She hadn't returned her husband yet either.

Joan had lain awake all night waiting, unsure

what she'd say or do when, or if, Cam came back
to the room they were to share. She'd debated between feigning that she was sleeping and saying
nothing, or slapping his face the minute he
showed it. But in the end, she hadn't had to decide
between the two. He'd not come back.

When the sun had risen and he still hadn't
returned, Joan had got up and moved to the
window to peer down into the bailey. She'd stood
watching the castle begin to stir and wondering
why she wasn't crying. She should be crying, she
even wanted to cry. It might put an end to the
numbness that had claimed her and seemed to be
locking her in an emotional cocoon, but her eyes
remained as dry as bone.

Jinny suddenly moved away, taking the dress
with her.

"I'll just set this over the chair and fetch yer
basin o' water. I left it in the hall," the maid said
happily, moving to the chairs by the fire to lay the
gown over one. Hurrying toward the door then,
she added, "I ha'e much to tell ye while ye tend
yer ablutions. So much has happened."

Joan's mouth tightened. She already knew one
of those happenings. Did the whole castle know
that her husband had already tired of her and
moved on to Finola?

"Lady Finola is dead," Jinny announced as she
returned with the water.

Joan stiffened and then turned slowly. "What?"

"Aye," Jinny said almost breathlessly as she set
the basin on the table by the fire. "She was found

at the bottom o' the stairs this morning. She tumbled down them and broke her neck. And the nasty cow did it in *yer* dress!" Jinny announced with outrage. "Can ye imagine? Lady Annabel said she and yer husband removed the dress from ye because Kenna came asking fer it. One o' the ladies approached her saying the others were going to hem it fer ye ere ye woke. It turns out, Lady Finola was the one who told Lady Kenna that tale. The other ladies said there was no such plan. That they were all too worried about ye and the other lasses to think o' hemming anything. Well, since Lady Finola was wearing it when she died, 'tis obvious she lied so she could steal the gown right off yer back!"

Jinny scowled ferociously at the cheek of the woman, and then said, "Now I'm thinking her falling down the stairs was God striking her down fer stealing it. Aye." She nodded firmly. "God smote her for her sins."

"When did Lady Finola fall?" Joan asked, her mind churning up all sorts of nonsense.

Jinny shrugged. "She was cold as stone and stiff when they found her this morning, so some time in the night."

"And no one witnessed it?" Joan asked reluctantly.

"Nay. At least no one's come forward to say so," Jinny said with unconcern, moving up beside her to hold out soap and a scrap of linen to her.

"Thank you," Joan whispered and moved to the basin of water to begin to wash.

"M'lady?"

"Hmm?" Joan asked absently, dipping the linen in the water.

"Should I no' take the bed linen?" Jinny asked. "It might get wet do ye no' take it off."

"Oh, aye." Joan unwrapped the linen she'd worn since waking and handed it over to the maid, then turned back to frown into the water as she began to lather the soap. The scent of lime and herbs drifted up to her as she worked. It was a scent she loved, but she hardly noticed. Lady Finola had fallen down the stairs? And no one had witnessed it? The last time she'd seen Lady Finola the woman had been kissing her husband . . . by the stairs, that she'd then apparently fallen down . . . without anyone, not even he, witnessing it.

She shook her head slowly. Something was terribly wrong. More than one thing actually, Joan thought as she recalled all Jinny had said. The woman had blurted it out so quickly and then she'd been more interested in the news about Finola, but now . . .

Turning to where Jinny was making the bed, she asked, "You said the women were too worried about myself and the other ladies to think of hemming my gown?"

"Aye," Jinny said absently and then glanced up to peer at her wide eyed. "Oh, o' course, ye do no' ken about the other ladies. Ye were the first to take ill, and had already fainted ere the other women did."

"Fainted?" Joan asked with a frown. She had

no idea what the woman was talking about. She recalled going in to try on the gown, and she remembered them asking her to remain in it so they could pin. Cider and pastries were fetched, she had some cider and then . . . well, actually her memory got a bit fuzzy after that.

"Aye. Ye had a bad batch o' cider and it made five o' ye ill," Jinny explained, concern on her expression. "Do ye no' recall?"

"Nay," Joan admitted on a sigh, but that explained the headache she'd woken up with. Fortunately, it had dissipated on its own in the time since she'd woken up.

Jinny frowned at this news, then glanced to the door when a knock sounded. Straightening from the bed, she moved over to open it and then curtsied and stepped quickly to the side to allow Lady Annabel to enter.

"Oh, you are awake," her aunt looked amazed, and then glanced to the empty bed and scowled with displeasure. "Where is Cam? Why did he not let me know when you woke up? He promised he would. In fact, when I came up here I assumed he was still here watching over you. Where is he?"

"I don't know," Joan admitted quietly, turning back to the basin of water to quickly finish her ablutions so she could dress. Her aunt had seen her naked several times now, but that didn't mean she was comfortable with it.

"You do not know?" Annabel asked with surprise and then frowned. "Was he not here when you woke up?"

Joan shook her head, but didn't say that her husband had been away for the last half of the night.

"That is odd. He was most concerned about you. He and I sat with you for hours and then he sent me away. He did not even eat the evening meal."

Joan didn't comment, but this news simply added to her confusion. He'd been concerned? Sat with her for hours and then gone out and kissed Finola? Well, to be fair, she supposed Finola had kissed him, but . . . now Finola was dead and he had never returned to their room. Where the devil was he? And had he had anything to do with Finola's fall down the stairs?

She rolled her eyes at her own thoughts. First, she spent hours thinking he was off philandering with Finola, and then she worried that he killed the woman. Joan was so confused.

"I told her about the bad batch o' cider, but she does no' recall getting ill herself," Jinny said suddenly, concern obvious in her voice.

"Do you not?" Lady Annabel asked, and while she didn't exactly sound concerned, Joan could hear a frown in her voice.

"Nay," Joan admitted and dropped the linen in the bowl, then turned to pick up her dress. Jinny immediately rushed to her side to help her don it.

"If ye'll sit in the chair, m'lady, I'll fix yer hair," Jinny said, moving to get the brush once she'd finished tying her stays for her.

"I shall do it, Jinny. I would like to talk to Joan anyway," Lady Annabel said quietly and suggested, "Why do you not go break your fast?"

Jinny hesitated, her gaze sliding to Joan.

" 'Tis all right. Go ahead," Joan said with a nod.

Jinny handed the brush to Lady Annabel and slipped from the room.

"Sit," Lady Annabel said lightly, gesturing to the chairs by the fire.

Joan settled in one of the chairs and stared at the long cold ashes in the hearth.

"It was not a bad batch of cider," Annabel announced as she began to run the brush through Joan's hair. "The servants were just told that to prevent gossip."

Joan raised her eyebrows. "What was it then?"

"I'm not sure, but it was something in your goblet alone," her aunt admitted.

"Mine?" Joan asked with surprise. "Then how did the other girls . . ." She let the question die as she recalled offering the goblet to Murine.

"Aye. All five of you drank from your goblet. You had two sips, and then offered it to Murine. The girls said you thought she was on the verge of fainting," her aunt explained, not realizing that she was recalling now. "The other girls tried it because you both said it was bitter. They only had one drink. You had two. You all fainted after drinking it, but you stayed asleep longer while the other girls woke by the evening meal."

"We were poisoned?" Joan asked quietly.

"It would appear so," Annabel said and then frowned. "But I wonder if whatever was in the drink was meant to kill you or just make you ill. None of you took very ill in the end, so I began to think perhaps it was just meant to make you sleep for a while, but . . ."

"But?" Joan asked when she paused.

"But now Lady Finola is dead," Annabel said on a sigh.

"I thought her death was an accident. Jinny said it was," Joan said solemnly, peering at her hands where they lay in her lap.

"Most people seem to think that," Annabel agreed.

"But you don't?"

"I think 'tis odd that Lady Finola would be up and about and wandering around the castle fully dressed after everyone else had retired."

Joan lowered her head. She knew exactly what the woman had been doing up at that hour . . . kissing, and who knew what else, with her husband. She didn't say as much however.

"Also," her aunt continued, "I went to look about in her room after we found her and there was only one candle in a holder in her room. Yet our room has two candles, a holder on either side of the bed, so I asked Lady Sinclair and she said that there should be two of them in Finola's room as well. There is not, and there was no candle holder found near her or on the stairs."

Joan raised her head slowly. She distinctly recalled Finola carrying a candle as she'd approached Cam in the hall. "What about at the top of the stairs?"

"Nay."

Joan bit her lip. "You think someone is attacking the women?"

"Nay." The brush paused in her hair and then her aunt admitted apologetically, "I fear someone is attempting to hurt you."

"What?" Joan squawked and whirled around on the chair to peer at her. "But five of us were made ill from the cider, and Lady Finola is the one who—"

"Five of you were made ill from drinking *your* cider," Annabel pointed out grimly. "And Lady Finola was wearing *your* gown."

Joan stared at her blankly, her mind beginning to whirl with thoughts now. The fact that the girls had all got ill from drinking her cider suggested someone had planned it for her, and Finola *had* been wearing her gown, she'd seen that for herself. And Cam had no doubt seen that as well, but if someone else had pushed her down the stairs . . . well, when she'd first seen Finola she'd been holding the candle low and out before her, leaving her face in darkness. Someone could have mistaken Finola for her because she was wearing the red and gold gown.

But Finola had been with Cam when she'd last seen her, she thought again. And she'd had the candle, but the candle was now missing and so was—

"I need to find my husband," she said suddenly and got to her feet.

"But I have not finished with your hair," her aunt protested.

Joan swung back, but grimaced and asked, "Do ladies always have to have their hair piled up on top of their head like a bird's nest? It gives me a headache."

"Oh, I am sorry. You should have said something. Perhaps we are setting it too tightly. Or it might just be that you are not used to wearing it up." She grimaced and admitted, "But ladies always wear their hair up, Joan, especially once they are married."

Joan hesitated, but then sat back down in the chair with a little sigh of resignation. If married ladies wore their hair up, she supposed she'd have to as well. She was supposed to be a lady now.

"I will try to make it looser today," Annabel assured her. "Then we will see how it goes."

"SON? SON."

Cam came awake with a start when someone shook his shoulder. Opening his eyes, he peered blankly at the man standing over him. "Da?"

"Aye. What the de'il are ye doing sleeping in the storage room?"

Cam began to struggle to his feet. "Joan."

"She's fine. She's awake."

Cam glanced past his father to the half dozen servants peering into the room and recognized his wife's maid, Jinny, as she finished: "Lady Annabel is fixing her hair fer her right now."

"Thank ye, Jinny," he said wearily. He'd pounded at the door and shouted for what had seemed like hours, giving up only when he began to lose his voice. Then he'd sat down to wait, intending to try again to rouse someone's attention once his throat recovered. Instead, he'd drifted off to sleep leaning against the shelves.

"What the de'il were ye doing sleeping in here?" his father asked, repeating his earlier question.

Cam grimaced and stretched to remove the kinks from his back. "I came down to get fresh candles and someone closed the door behind me. I shouted and pounded, but everyone was sleeping."

"When was that?" his father asked sharply.

Cam shrugged. "Late. The fire in the great hall was nearly out."

"Ye did no' happen to stumble o'er Lady Mac-Farland's body at the bottom o' the stairs, did ye?"

"What?" Cam asked with bewilderment.

"Ne'er mind. Lady Finola must ha'e taken her tumble after that," Laird Sinclair muttered almost to himself. "What the de'il was she doing up at that hour?"

"Lady Finola took a tumble?" Cam asked with amazement.

"Aye. Broke her neck in a fall down the stairs," his father said on a sigh and shook his head. " 'Tis a good thing it was her and no' one o' the other lasses. Sad as it is to admit it, the MacFarlands'll no' miss the lass." Grimacing, he added, "In fact, I do no' think anyone will."

"Aye," Cam agreed solemnly. The woman had not troubled to endear herself to anyone as far as he could tell. And while he should be sorry to hear of her demise, he wasn't terribly sorry to have her out of his hair.

"Well, come, ye must be ready to break yer fast after the night ye had," his father said, urging him toward the door.

Cam nodded, but paused and turned to first gather the candles he'd come for last night.

"I'll take 'em up," Jinny offered, stepping forward as he reached the door.

"Go on, give 'em to the lass," his father suggested. "We need to discuss who should take the message to the MacFarlands. A simple messenger won't do for news like this."

Sighing, Cam reluctantly handed the candles to Jinny and followed his father out to the trestle tables. They were about to sit down when he suddenly glanced around and, spotting Jinny heading for the stairs, called her over.

"Ye said Joan is fine, but how fine is she?" he asked when the maid reached him.

Jinny considered the question briefly and then shrugged. "She seems good as new."

"Well enough to take a ride with me?" Cam asked.

Jinny nodded. "I think so."

"Thank ye," Cam murmured, and turned to settle at the table. He hadn't forgotten what Lady MacKay had said to him last night. He needed to talk to his wife, away from the castle and its people. He would use riding lessons as the excuse to get her away, and then say what needed saying to her.

"You are awfully quiet, Joan. What is on your mind?" Annabel asked as she braided her hair.

Joan hesitated, but then blurted, "She had a candle."

"What?" Annabel bent and twisted around to see her face. "Who did?"

"Finola," Joan admitted, biting her lip.

Annabel dropped the braids she'd been making and moved around in front of her so that she could see her face as they talked. "Last night?"

Joan nodded.

"You saw her last night?" Annabel asked slowly, as if wanting to be sure they understood each other.

"Aye. I saw her last night," Joan said wearily and lowered her head. "I woke up alone. The candles were dying, but I had no clothes. I wrapped the bed linen around myself and looked out in the hall. I was hoping to hail a passing servant to ask to fetch the candles, but the hall was in near darkness, 'twas obvious everyone had retired . . . and then I saw someone standing by the stairs."

"Finola?" Annabel guessed.

"Nay. The person was in shadow, I couldn't see who it was at first, and then candlelight appeared from further up the hall, moving toward the stairs."

"It was Finola with the candle?" Annabel prompted when she paused.

Joan sighed and nodded her head.

"Who was the person by the stairs?" Annabel asked.

"Cam," she whispered and then rushed on. "Finola raised the candle, I saw it was her and that she was wearing my dress. And then she—

she kissed Cam," she got out, her voice cracking as she said it.

"Oh, sweetling," Annabel murmured, bending to hug her. Rubbing her back soothingly, she asked, "What did he do?"

Joan shook her head and admitted, "I didn't see. I just closed the door and got back in bed." She cleared her throat as Annabel straightened to peer at her sympathetically and then added, "I waited for him to return to bed, but he never did and I thought they must be . . ."

Annabel reached out and squeezed her hand.

Joan smiled weakly, appreciating the supportive gesture. "Now I'm not sure what to think. Finola's dead and Cam is missing, and the candle—" She snapped her mouth closed and glanced quickly to the door when it opened. Jinny slipped in.

"Is something amiss, Jinny?" Joan asked, noting the excited flush to her cheeks.

"Someone locked yer husband in the storeroom last night," she blurted, almost dancing on her feet.

"What?" Joan and Annabel asked together.

The maid nodded excitedly. "Aye. Laird Sinclair went to get something out of the storeroom just moments ago and noticed it was unlocked, but the bar was down. When he opened it he found yer husband inside, sleeping against the shelves. It turns out he came down in search of candles last night after everyone retired, but someone closed the door behind him and dropped the bar in place. He says he pounded and yelled, but everyone was asleep and no one came to let him out."

Joan glanced to Annabel to find her peering back.

"Oh, he asked me to bring these up." Jinny held up the candles she carried. "I should clean out the holders and put the new ones in."

"Did he have a candleholder with him?" Annabel asked suddenly, her gaze still firmly on Joan.

"Yer husband?" Jinny asked and shook her head. "Nay. He was in the dark when his father opened the storeroom door and there were none about that I saw."

"Thank you," Annabel murmured and moved behind Joan to continue with her hair as Jinny quickly cleaned the melted tallow off the candleholders and placed the fresh candles in them.

"You thought Cam might have pushed Finola down the stairs?" Joan asked as soon as Jinny left the room again.

"Nay," Annabel answered calmly and when Joan turned to peer over her shoulder at her, added, "I knew *you* did though, and thought you should hear the answer to that question."

Joan turned slowly forward again and then asked, "You really didn't think he—"

"Nay," Annabel assured her solemnly. "And I do not think he encouraged or responded to Finola's kiss. But then I have known Campbell for most of his life. I know what kind of man he is. You have only known him for weeks, and while I think you have a good understanding of what kind of man he is, of course you will doubt yourself if given evidence like seeing another woman kissing him."

Joan let her breath out slowly and nodded. In truth, she never would have imagined that Cam might have had anything to do with Finola tumbling down the stairs before she'd seen the woman kiss him. She didn't think she'd really believed he could even afterward, which is why she'd been so shocked when Lady Annabel had asked her question about whether Cam had the candleholder with him when found in the storeroom.

"Joan?"

"Hmm?" She tore herself from her thoughts and glanced over her shoulder in question.

"Cam and I sat together for quite a while waiting for you to wake up, and while he did not say it, I am quite sure he feels deeply for you. And I know you feel deeply for him."

"I do," Joan admitted, and then sighed and lowered her head. "But he has hardly spoken a word to me since we arrived at Sinclair. The only time I see him is—"

"When you slip out at night to meet him?" Annabel suggested with amusement.

Joan glanced swiftly around. "You knew?"

"Aye," she said with amusement. "At least I assumed that was where you were slipping off to at night."

"Aye, well," Joan turned to face forward again. "He doesn't speak to me then either."

"He was hurt when you said you did not want to come to Sinclair with him," Annabel murmured quietly. "He is unsure of your feelings and fears you resent him for the forced marriage."

"What?" She turned with surprise again. "I thought he—"

"I know," her aunt interrupted quietly, setting a chaplet on her head and weaving the braids she'd placed Joan's hair in through it. "You both seem to be assuming a lot about each other that simply is not so. The two of you need to actually talk to each other and sort these things out. If someone is out to hurt you, the two of you need to work together. 'Tis better if these issues between you and Cam are resolved.

"There," she added, stepping back as she finished with Joan's hair. "How does that feel?"

"It's less tight," Joan admitted.

"Let us hope that it resolves the issue of your headaches," Annabel said on a sigh. "Now, come. We should go below, break our fast and find out if anything else has occurred that we should know about. These things often happen in threes," she added dryly as she led the way to the door.

Chapter 15

"I'M SORRY I WAS NO' THERE WHEN YE WOKE this morning."

Joan glanced around when Cam whispered that apology by her ear. He was standing behind where she sat at the trestle table next to her aunt and she wondered briefly how he'd approached without her noticing. He hadn't been at the table when she and Annabel had come below moments ago, but his father had explained that Cam was out at the stables seeing his brother off. It seemed that he and a small group of Sinclair warriors would carry the news of Finola's death, as well as her body, back to MacFarland. It was thought that a member of the family should deliver the sad news rather than just a clan member. Douglas had volunteered to perform the deed.

"Ye have no' already eaten, have ye?" Cam asked.

"Nay, we just sat down," she admitted.

"Good." Smiling, he held out his hand. "Come with me."

Joan hesitated, but then took the offered hand and let him help her up from the bench. He didn't release her then as expected, but continued to hold her hand as he led her to the keep doors. Distracted as she was by that fact, it took her a moment to notice the two saddled horses waiting at the base of the steps. Once she did, however, her eyes widened with alarm.

" 'Tis all right," Cam said at once. "Ye'll ride with me."

"Then why is the mare my aunt and uncle gave us here too?" she asked worriedly.

"He's tethered to the back of my saddle," Cam pointed out gently.

"Aye, but why?"

"I thought we'd go for a ride, break our fast, talk and then perhaps get in a quick riding lesson ere we come back," he explained.

"That's what I was afraid of," she said unhappily and Cam chuckled at her expression.

" 'Twill be all right," he assured her. "We'll go slow."

Forcing a smile, Joan nodded and let him lift her up onto his horse. He then mounted quickly behind her and took up the reins.

"Ease yerself," Cam said once they were out of the bailey and crossing the open area to the trees. "Ye're stiff as a log."

"Sorry," Joan muttered and tried to make herself relax. It was difficult though. It wasn't just her anxiety about riding lessons that had her tense. She was also concerned about the coming talk he'd mentioned. She knew they had to talk, Annabel was right about that, she was just worried about what she might learn once they did.

"Joan, I really did want to be there when ye woke," Cam said suddenly. "I sat with ye from the minute I returned to the keep and learned ye were ill, but—"

"I saw you kissing Finola," Joan blurted.

Cam reined in, bringing both beasts to a halt, and then caught her by the waist and lifted and shifted her so that she sat sideways in front of him and he could see her face. Tipping her chin up with his fist, he peered solemnly into her face and said, "I did no' kiss Finola. She kissed me."

He paused briefly, but when Joan didn't respond, he added, "She took me by surprise with her boldness, and I didn't immediately react, but then I pushed her away and let her ken I was well satisfied with me wife and no' interested in stolen kisses with a wench in a stolen dress."

"I was rather insulting about it," Cam admitted quietly. "She tried to slap me, I caught her wrist and warned her if she did that, she could expect to be slapped back. Then, I told her she was no longer welcome at Sinclair and that I would arrange for men to return her to MacFarland today. After that I left her there on the landing and went below to fetch the candles I'd started out in search of in the first place."

"At least, I thought I left her there," he added

suddenly. "But she followed me below and locked the storeroom door behind me."

"You saw her close the door?" Joan asked with surprise.

"Nay, but it must have been her. Everyone else was sleeping," Cam reasoned and then frowned and added, "She must have tripped over her skirts or something on the way back upstairs. I gather they found her dead at the foot o' the steps this morning, her neck broken from the fall."

"Aye, I heard that," Joan said thoughtfully, taking in everything he'd said.

She believed him. That might have been just because she wanted to, but Joan did believe him and now considered the possibility that Finola had simply lost her footing and fallen down the stairs as he seemed to think. She wouldn't put it past the woman to have been the one behind locking him in the storeroom. It would have been fine retribution for his insulting and rejecting her, but that didn't explain the missing candle and holder.

"Did Finola set her candle down during your exchange?" she asked now.

"What?" Cam asked with confusion.

"She had a candle with her when I saw her approach you last night. Yet they did not find one near her, nor at the top of the stairs when she was discovered this morning," Joan explained. "Did she set it down somewhere?"

"Nay," he said slowly, obviously thinking back to last night's events.

"Perhaps Finola set it down in the kitchens to

free her hands to close the storeroom door," Joan suggested.

"Aye, but she would no' have then left it behind. The stairs were in complete darkness. She would have needed it to make her way back upstairs to her room," Cam pointed out, frowning now.

Joan nodded solemnly, remembering that Cam had nearly disappeared into the shadows when she'd seen him at the top of the stairs. Even if Finola had forgotten the candle in the kitchens, she would have returned for it once she reached the stairs, she was sure.

"Ye're sure there was no candle with her?" Cam asked with a frown.

"Aye. Aunt Annabel is the one who noticed. She said she went to Finola's room and noticed that there was only one candle beside the bed. There are two in ours and she asked your mother about it. Lady Sinclair said there should be two in Finola's room as well, that there are two in each chamber. So aunt Annabel checked by the stairs and asked about it as well but no one had seen a candle anywhere near the stairs or the upper landing," Joan explained. "She thinks Finola had help falling down the stairs and that whoever did it took the candle with them."

Cam was silent for a moment, but then grimaced. "Well, I suppose I should no' be surprised. The woman was unpleasant at the best o' times, and I gather she did no' make friends while she was here. She—"

"—was wearing my dress," Joan interrupted.

He glanced to her sharply. "Aye. She told Kenna the ladies wanted to hem—"

"I know," Joan interrupted again. "But Aunt Annabel put that together with the cider incident and is worried that Finola was pushed down the stairs because she was wearing my gown and was mistaken for me."

Cam's breath left him on a slow hiss as he rocked back away from her in the saddle, and then he straightened with a hissed, "Damn. I did no' think o' that."

They both sat still and silent for a moment, then Cam stirred himself and urged the horse to move again.

"Where are we going?" Joan asked.

"Nowhere. We're here," he announced as they broke through the trees into a clearing.

"Oh." Joan glanced around at the small clearing he'd brought her to. It was a shady spot with large old trees offering covering from the sun, and a small brook running through it. It was quite pretty. Not as awe inspiring as the waterfall, but still lovely, she thought, as Cam dismounted and helped her down.

"Here, lay this out for us to sit on," he instructed, handing her a large animal fur.

Joan accepted the rolled up item and glanced around, then moved to the center of the clearing to unroll and lay it out. By the time she'd finished, Cam was there, carrying a small sack in hand.

"I brought bread, cheese and fruit," he explained, sitting down and opening the bag. "I brought a skin o' cider too and—" He paused abruptly when he noted her expression, and then said wryly, "But mayhap cider was no' the best option."

Joan gave a faint laugh and shook her head. "Nay. I will make do without cider for a bit, I think."

Smiling, he nodded and set the cider aside, then broke the bread in half and offered her a piece. He then gave her cheese as well and they began to eat. Silence fell over them and seemed to grow. Joan tried to think of something to say to break it, but didn't know how to start the conversation she knew they had to have and the silence soon became almost palpable between them. It was a sharp contrast to every meal they'd had on their journey to Scotland. They'd seemed to talk so easily then, laughing and teasing and chattering away. But it had been different then, they'd both been free and simply enjoying the moment. Now they were married, and she at least was afraid of being hurt. Perhaps Cam was feeling the same way, but whatever the case, the silence began to drag on Joan and affected her appetite so that she merely picked at the food he'd brought.

A glance to Cam showed him doing much the same thing, until he finally set his food aside and quickly repacked everything. Setting the bag aside then, he peered at her, cleared his throat, opened his mouth, closed it and then sighed and said, "Perhaps we should start yer riding lessons."

It was a sign of how uncomfortable she was

that Joan actually nodded almost eagerly, prefer-ring another round of lessons she would no doubt fail at in a spectacular way than have the discussion she knew they needed to have.

"Right," he muttered and stood up, then moved to his own horse to untether her mount from it, saying, "The first lesson should really be to teach ye how to care fer a horse. But we'll do that when we get back."

"How to care for it?" Joan asked. She'd stood and followed him over, but now stood a couple feet back, eyeing the horse warily. She wasn't exactly afraid of horses. Joan had no problem riding on them with someone else or tending them, but the idea of trying to control it herself was intimidating.

"Brushing it down, saddling and unsaddling it and so on," Cam explained, turning to her with the reins in hand. "But as I say, we'll tend to that another time. Fer now, we'll start with mounting and dismounting."

Joan relaxed a little at that. She'd mounted Cam's horse all by herself when he was injured. She could do this, she thought with relief and moved to her mare, grasped the saddle and raised her leg to put her foot through the stirrup. Unfortunately, she hadn't been wearing a gown the last time . . . and Cam's horse had stood still for her, whereas her mare whinnied and shifted the minute she put any weight on the saddle.

"'Tis all right," her husband said patiently. "Ye're nervous and the horse is picking up on that. Just take a deep breath, hike yer skirt up a bit and . . ." His voice died as Joan yanked her skirt up and tucked it into the belt around her waist, leaving her legs bare almost to the thighs.

Joan wasn't nervous: she'd done this before, she could do it again. She had just needed to get her skirt out of the way, she thought determinedly, and reached for the saddle again. This time her skirt didn't get in the way and she easily slipped her foot in the stirrup, but again her mare whinnied and shifted, this time trying to move away from her. Foot caught in the stirrup, Joan hopped to keep from tumbling and then launched herself determinedly upward, threw her leg over, and landed on the saddle.

That's when her world seemed to tip. The mare went crazy. Joan wasn't even settled in the saddle properly before the mare let out a panicked whinny that sounded more like a scream, and reared. Joan threw herself forward, clutching at the mare's whithers and neck with her hands and clenching her thighs around the saddle and sides of the horse, holding on for dear life as the mare tried to throw her off.

The animal came down hard on its hooves, still screaming, the jolt rattling painfully through Joan's body, and then the mare reared again. Joan could hear Cam shouting and caught a glimpse of him pulling on the reins he still held, trying to force the beast back down while dodging her slashing hooves. Then the reins snapped. The mare came down with another bone jarring jolt and then began to run, charging out of the clearing and into the woods.

Still clinging to the beast, Joan closed her eyes, but then just as quickly opened them again when she felt something brush against her leg. A tree trunk, she realized, glancing behind her. The horse was moving so fast that it was narrowly missing—

Joan gasped with pain as they rushed past another tree, too close. Closer even than the last time and her leg was skinned against the trunk. She saw the blood begin to bubble on her outer leg, and then shifted her gaze forward. Another tree was coming up, and rather than try to avoid it, her mare steered toward it, as if she wanted to hurt her. Or scrape her off her back, Joan realized . . . and this time she was going to take one hell of a hit. By her estimate, she wouldn't just receive a scraping, the whole front of her leg would be hit by the tree. If it didn't drag her off the horse, it would drag her leg off of her, or crush it.

None of those options sounded like good ones and Joan desperately released her grip on her mare and tried to throw herself off the beast. Too late, she realized even as she did it. But there was nothing she could do but close her eyes as she flew through the air. Her entire side hit the tree rather than just her leg, still it wasn't with the same speed, but it was enough.

Joan cried out on impact, the trunk slamming into her from her hip up to just below her still upraised arm, and then she crashed to her stomach on the ground and lay gasping for air she couldn't seem to drag into her body. She could hear Cam shouting her name, but was too distracted trying to catch her breath to respond, and then he was kneeling beside her, turning her over.

"Joan?"

Her response was an almost airless groan as she slid onto her back.

"All right, love. 'Tis all right," he muttered soothingly as he bent to examine first her side and then her leg. She heard him curse, but air was finally making its way into her and she was too busy sucking in large drafts to ask what was wrong.

Sighing, Cam straightened and clasped her hand, simply waiting as she regained her breath. Once her breathing had eased though, he squeezed her hand, drawing her gaze to him. "I have to pick ye up, love. It might hurt, and I'm sorry fer it, but I have to get ye back to the castle."

Joan nodded, knowing he'd have to. She could hardly lie there in the woods while her bruises healed, and that was mostly what she'd received from her latest catastrophe in these lessons to make her a lady: scrapes and bruises. Joan was pretty sure of that. She'd got the wind knocked out of her too, but that was it, she decided as she did a mental inventory of herself, cautiously moving fingers and toes, hands and feet, arms and legs. Nothing was broken. But damn, everything hurt, she acknowledged, gasping in pain as Cam slid his arms under her and scooped her up.

"I'm sorry, love," Cam said grimly as he carried her to his horse.

He'd chased after her on his own horse, Joan realized and wondered how she'd not heard the thunder of his horse's hooves.

"I'm so sorry," he repeated as they neared his mount.

"Nay, I'm sorry," she said unhappily. " 'Tis useless. I'm a complete failure as a lady."

"Nay, ye're not," Cam said firmly.

"Aye, I am," she insisted miserably. "I can't dance, I can't sing, I can't shoot a bow. I didn't even know I wasn't supposed to sit at the low table and still wouldn't if Finola hadn't let me know in her less than charming way."

"None o' that matters," he assured her.

"Cam," she said, reaching up to touch his cheek and make him look at her. "I'm sorry. I love you but can't be a proper wife to you. I don't know the first thing about running a keep, or being a lady. Finola's right, I'll embarrass you and your family, and you should have the marriage annulled."

He had stopped walking and now stared at her. In fact, he stared for so long she began to think he was having some sort of fit or something, and then he said with wonder, "Ye love me?"

"What?" she asked blankly.

"Ye said ye love me."

Joan shook her head, "Nay, I—"

"Aye, ye did," he insisted. "Ye said I love ye but can't be a proper wife. It's what you said. Ye can no' take it back now. Besides, I love you too."

"I—" She blinked. "You do?"

Cam nodded. "I realized it yesterday while I watched over ye. Lady MacKay insisted ye'd wake up, but I just kept thinking what if she was wrong and ye didn't? I felt such guilt and regret over me first wife's death, Joan, but that would be nothing next to how I'd feel if ye died. A part o' me would die with ye, and I do no' think the rest o' me would even want to carry on without ye."

"But I shall embarrass you with my lack of skills, and I don't want to do that. I don't want to embarrass your family either. Mayhap we were only ever meant to be lovers. Perhaps ye should annul the marriage and move me to the village and just visit me from time to time and—"

"Joan," he interrupted firmly. "There's no damned way I'm annulling the marriage. I do no' care if ye can sing or dance or shoot a bow. Either ye'll learn those things over time, or ye will no'. It does no' matter to me. I do no' even care if ye learn to ride. Ye can ride with me if necessary. Those are no' the things I came to value about ye on our journey north. I value yer honesty, yer courage, and yer spirit. I like that yer smart, and that we could talk about anything under the sun and laugh together. That's what I want from ye. That's why I wanted ye e'en with yer face a mess and in braies. Ye've an inner beauty and spirit that shines through everything, and I love ye fer it."

Joan stared at him wide-eyed. Her whole body ached, and his arms were inadvertently pressing against her injured side leaving her head spinning and making her nauseous, and all she could think was how wonderful this man was.

"Joan, say something," Cam said quietly.

"I—" She paused and swallowed, trying to hold on to consciousness.

"Joan?" he asked with concern.

Unfortunately he also, unintentionally she was sure, tightened his hold on her, sending shafts of excruciating pain through her. A moan slid from her lips and then she fainted.

Cursing, Cam hurried the last couple of steps to his horse and then paused briefly as he realized he couldn't mount with her in his arms. Not liking that he had to do it, he laid her gently over his horse, then quickly mounted behind her and scooped her back up. Once he had her settled in his lap, he put his heels to his horse, determined to get her back to the castle as quickly as possible.

The clearing wasn't far from the castle, and the ride out had passed quickly enough. However, the ride back seemed to him to take forever. Cam knew that was no doubt just a result of his worry and not a true measure of the time it took, but he was vastly relieved when he passed under the gatehouse into the inner courtyard.

He spotted Joan's mare by the steps of the keep, his father and the stable master soothing the beast. Anger at the beast immediately joined Cam's concern for Joan as he peered at the animal, but common sense managed to reign over the other emotions churning through him by the time he reined in beside the mare.

"She came back just moments ago and we were just discussing sending out a search party," his father announced, leaving the stable master to hold on to the mare's reins as he walked around to take Joan from Cam so that he could dismount. "What happened?"

"The mare went crazy when Joan mounted her," Cam announced, dropping to the ground and taking his wife back. He paused long enough to glance to the horse and said, "Something's wrong with the animal. Check her carefully ere ye stable her," he ordered the stablemaster.

Laird Sinclair scowled. "There's something no' quite right going on here, son. First Joan and the other lasses fell ill, then Lady MacFarland took her tumble down the stairs, and now this?" He shook his head. "This is one too many accidents to me mind." Clapping a hand on his shoulder, he said, "I'll look at the mare meself. We'll sort out what happened. You tend yer wife."

Cam just grunted, he was already starting up the stairs with her.

Lady Annabel was seated by the fireplace with his mother when Cam entered with Joan. The two women glanced over and started to smile on seeing him, but those smiles died, replaced with alarm when they noted Joan in his arms.

"What happened?" Lady MacKay cried, lunging out of her seat and rushing toward him as he headed for the stairs. His mother was so close on the other woman's heels he was surprised she wasn't tripping over her skirt.

"I was giving her a riding lesson and there was an accident," Cam said quietly.

"Did she hit her head?" Annabel asked, reaching out to feel her head for bumps as they walked.

"Nay," Cam assured her. "It was her side and leg."

Lady MacKay merely nodded and rushed on ahead of him up the stairs. By the time he reached the top step, she had his bedchamber door open and disappeared inside . . . to pull the linens and furs down, he saw as he carried his wife into the room a moment later.

"We'll need to strip her so that I can see her side," Lady Annabel said as he laid Joan in the bed.

"I'll help," his mother said at once, urging him out of the way. "Why do ye no' go below, son? I'll come tell ye what's what once Lady Annabel—"

"Nay," Cam interrupted firmly. He wasn't going anywhere.

"Well, go sit by the hearth then," his mother said impatiently. "Ye'll just get in the way here."

Cam retreated to the foot of the bed, but that was as far as he was willing to go. It allowed him to see everything without having to dance about trying to look over his mother's shoulder as the two women quickly and efficiently stripped his wife. They removed her gown and the tunic she wore under it and then turned Joan on her uninjured side and raised her arm over her head so that they could look at her side. Cam wasn't surprised they hadn't needed to ask which side was injured, the scrape on her leg was the size of a hand and bleeding freely now. As for her side, he winced and then ground his teeth together as he noted the size of the bruise already forming there. It covered a large area, from just under her arm down to her hip and he could tell already that it was going to be as black as night.

Joan's aunt took one quick look at it and then straightened and started around the bed. "I need water, linens, bandages and my medicinals."

"I'll get everything," Cam's mother announced, waving her back. "Ye stay here. Ye ken better what to do."

Lady MacKay nodded and moved back to the side of the bed, and then bent and began to run her hands along Joan's injured side, feeling for broken ribs, he guessed. "The horse threw her?"

"Aye, I think so," Cam answered, although it had almost looked to him like she'd leapt off to avoid being crushed against a tree.

"She didn't hit the ground," Annabel muttered, examining the forming bruise now.

"Nay. She hit a tree," he admitted.

"And her leg?" Annabel asked, shifting her attention to the large abrasion.

"The horse scraped her against another tree first."

"I will need to clean it well, then," Annabel said on a sigh and straightened with a shake of the head. "She tries so hard, but these lessons are making her miserable."

"She does no' need them. I do no' care if she can

sing or dance," Cam said grimly. "If I'd wanted a lass who could sing and dance I'd ha'e married one. I want her. And I'll tell the daft woman that again when she wakes up. There'll be no annulment."

"Annulment?" his mother gasped and he turned to see her frozen in the bedchamber door, horror on her face and a passel of servants on her heels. "I should say not. Who the devil said anything about an annulment?"

"Joan," he growled. "She fears she'll embarrass me because she does no' ken how to sing and dance and nonsense like that."

"Oh, well that's just nonsense," his mother said with disgruntlement as she continued into the room. "This is all Finola's fault for attacking her the other morning when Joan sat to break her fast at the low table. In fact, Finola said something then about the marriage being annulled."

"You heard that?" Lady Annabel asked with surprise.

"Aye. I had slipped into the kitchens to have a word with Cook. I saw Joan at the table on my way there, and I suppose I should have explained then about the high table and had her move, but I didn't want to embarrass her so said nothing." Sighing, she shook her head. "If I had, it would have saved her the humiliation of Finola's attack."

"Finola attacked her?" Cam asked grimly, wishing the witch was still alive so he could throttle her.

"No' with her fists or anything," his mother said

quickly. "She just was very, very cruel, calling her ignorant and saying she'd embarrass us all." She glanced to Lady MacKay and added, "I was about to intervene when I saw ye coming down the stairs. I kenned ye would handle it though, and thought Joan might be less embarrassed was it you and no' me so I eased the kitchen door closed and waited until I thought it was over."

She glanced to Joan and a soft smile curved her lips. "She loves ye son if she's offering annulment to keep from embarrassing ye. I've been trying to find ye a wife, but ye found yerself that and more, a partner who loves ye will work to make ye happy." Her mouth firmed. "There'll be no annulment."

"Nay, there will no'," Cam agreed solemnly.

"What the devil's taking so long, Bearnas?" Artair Sinclair complained, suddenly in the doorway. "Ye were supposed to send Cam out to— bloody hell!" his father barked, spotting Joan. "What'd ye do? Paint her with pitch?"

"Son, yer father is in the hall and wants a word," Lady Sinclair said calmly, shifting so that Joan couldn't be seen from the doorway.

A startled laugh slipped from Cam's mouth and he stepped up to his mother to kiss her cheek. "Thank ye," he said solemnly and then moved to urge his father out of the room and into the hall.

"She's a muckle mess," Artair Sinclair said grimly.

"Aye," Cam agreed on a sigh.

"Well, this is why," he announced grimly, holding up a small object. "We found this in the mare's saddle."

"What is it?" Cam asked, taking the tiny sword.

"'Tis a hatpin," his father said grimly. "I only ken because I bought one fer yer mother once from a traveling merchant."

"And it was in the mare's saddle?"

"Aye, it was set in the underside o' the saddle so that weight on it would stick the horse in the back."

"So when Joan mounted . . ."

"The horse was stuck by the pin and was desperate to get her off," his father said dryly.

"And it's Mother's?" Cam asked with disbelief.

"Nay. Her's had a different hilt," his father said at once, and then frowned and shifted to the side to make room for the servants who had brought up the water and linens as they now left the bedchamber. Once they'd all hurried past and started downstairs, his father continued, "I showed yer mother though. She was coming out of the kitchens when I came inside. She says Lady MacFarland had one just like it."

"Finola," Cam muttered.

Laird Sinclair nodded. "And we ken it could no' ha'e been her."

"Nay. It could no' ha'e been her," he agreed. "But someone's out to hurt Joan."

Laird Sinclair let his breath out on a disappointed sigh. "I wondered if that were no' the case. Yer mother helped Lady MacKay tend the lasses when the cider made them ill, and she mentioned to me that it was Joan's cider that had something wrong with it. And then when Jinny came out o' the kitchens and saw Lady Finola she said the wench was wearing Joan's gown." He smiled faintly and added, "She was more upset that the woman had gone and died in Joan's gown than she was that the woman was dead." Shaking his head he gestured to the hatpin Cam held and added, "And now this."

Sighing, Artair ran a hand through his hair and shook his head. "I'll arrange for men to guard yer chamber door while Joan is recovering, then to accompany her everywhere once she's up and about until we resolve this. If 'tis all right with you," he added.

"Aye." Cam said, glad to have her guarded.

Nodding, his father turned away. "I'll let ye get back to her then. Keep me informed on how she's faring."

"Aye," Cam murmured and turned to slip back into the bedchamber.

His mother and Lady Annabel were just pulling the linens and furs up to cover Joan as he entered the room. Lady Annabel glanced to him as she straightened and announced, "I cleaned the wound as well as I could, and put some salve on her bruises to help them heal quickly. Now all we can do is wait."

"I'll watch over her. Ye two go on back to what ye were doing," Cam said at once, moving up to the bed to peer down at his wife.

"Are you sure?" Lady Annabel asked. "I do not mind sitting with her.

"Nay. Go on. I'm fine," he assured her.

Annabel hesitated, but then nodded and began to gather her items.

Once they'd left the room, Cam peered down at Joan, then removed his weapons and plaid, lifted the furs covering his wife and slid into bed next to her. If he was going to wait and watch over her again, it was going to be from the comfort of the bed . . . and with her in his arms, he decided, and caught Joan's arm to pull her over to rest against his chest. This time, he would be the first thing his wife saw when she woke up.

Chapter 16

$\mathcal{J}$OAN OPENED HER EYES AND FOUND HERSELF peering at her husband's sleeping face. A smile immediately pulled at her lips. This was a sight she'd woken up to more than once during their journey to MacKay and she'd enjoyed it each time. Cam looked young and untroubled in sleep, not at all the ferocious warrior, or the laughing friend, or the seductive lover, all of which he could be by turn when awake. Campbell Sinclair had many facets, and Joan liked every one of them. There was not a side to her husband that she did not love.

And he had told her he loved her, she recalled and briefly closed her eyes at the memory. Cam loved her. The thought was a thrilling one, and made her want to squeal with glee, but she didn't want to wake him up that way.

"Cam loves me," she whispered with wonder. "And I love him."

Her aunt had said as much the day they'd married, but Joan had merely shrugged off the suggestion. She supposed she hadn't been ready to accept it, or maybe she'd been afraid to accept it because if she loved him and he didn't love her . . . the pain that could have involved would be devastating, she knew.

Sighing, Joan opened her eyes and peered at him again, her smile slowly fading. Now she need only fear that his love would wither away once the first heat of passion died and he began to care more that she couldn't do all those things true ladies were trained to do.

The thought was a depressing one, and she wanted to quickly push it away, but didn't allow herself to. Instead, she started thinking of ways to avoid that. Joan didn't want to have her marriage annulled. She did love him and she wanted to be his wife, she just had to learn to be the wife he needed and was expected to have. And surely if she practiced hard and often, if she gave it her every effort, then surely she could learn to shoot a bow and ride as well as dance and sing? She just needed time to manage that, Joan told herself. And to her mind, the best way to ensure she had that time was to ensure she kept his desire for her burning hot until she'd gained those skills.

It was a plan, at least, Joan thought grimly. An alternative to the proposed annulling of the marriage, and that was better than nothing, she decided and contemplated how best to start that.

The answer seemed obvious. They were already in bed and while Cam had his shirt on, she didn't see any evidence of his plaid. Joan began to push down the linens and furs covering them both, pausing when she got them to her waist and could get a look at the damage she'd taken that morning.

Damn, she thought with amazement. Her side was black and blue and red all over. The bruising hadn't fully formed yet, obviously, but she could already tell it was going to be as bad as her face had been after Toothless had finished with her. It should be less painful though. At least she hoped it would be. After the beating she'd taken, every time she'd spoken or made an expression, or unconsciously reached up to touch her face, it had ached like crazy. She shouldn't have the same problem with her side. Well, so long as she wore loose clothes and didn't bump up against things or touch it.

Sighing, Joan finished pushing the linens and furs down and then eased to her knees with a grimace. Moving wasn't too bad, but it wasn't completely painless either. She could live with it though, Joan thought, and then glanced around, her eyes settling on a pot of ointment on the bedside table.

Leaning over, she picked it up and lifted it to her nose to smell it, smiling when she recognized the scent. It was a numbing salve. Her aunt must have mixed it up when Cam had brought her back. She'd probably applied it then too, Joan supposed, and wondered how long ago that had been. In the end, she decided it didn't matter. It wouldn't hurt to apply more.

Joan dipped her fingers in and quickly began to rub it over her side, wincing at the first touch. Oh aye, touching it would be a good thing to avoid, she thought grimly, relieved when the task was done.

Setting the small pot back on the table, Joan turned back to Cam. While his shirt was still on, his plaid was missing as she'd hoped. Even as she noted that, he murmured sleepily and rolled onto his back.

A small smile immediately claimed her lips. This position was just perfect for what she intended.

CAM WAS HAVING A WONDERFUL DREAM. HE and Joan were by the waterfall they'd camped by on the way north. He was lying on his back on his plaid, and Joan was bending over him, her long hair brushing across his stomach as she pushed his shirt up his chest.

"I love your body," she whispered, her breath hot against his skin as she smoothed her hands over his ribs and then his upper chest, pushing the cloth until it was gathered up under his chin and arms.

"Mmm," she murmured, smiling, then bent to lick teasingly at his nipple. Cam smiled at her teasing and tried to slide his hands into her hair to draw her up for a kiss, but she evaded his touch and slipped further down his body, her hair dragging down his stomach again, and then gliding over his hip bone before she stopped and peered at his stirring erection.

"What have we here?" she breathed, glancing up to him with wide naughty eyes before dipping down to lash him with her tongue again, this time running it quickly over the head of his hardening cock.

Groaning, Cam reached down again, this time managing to glide his fingers into her hair, but then he stopped, merely cupping her head and gasping as she closed her hand around his shaft and squeezed gently.

Her gaze lifted to him again and she smiled solemnly, and then murmured, "I love you, Cam."

"I love you too," he murmured, waking himself up with his own voice and opening his eyes in time to see Joan take him into her mouth. His eyes widened incredulously as dream became reality, and then squeezed closed on a moan as she drew her mouth down his shaft. She'd asked him to teach her how to pleasure him with her mouth after he'd done it to her once on their journey and he'd tried to instruct her, but she'd always been tentative and unsure in those early efforts. This time she was a woman determined, and Cam squeezed his eyes so tightly closed he almost saw stars as she began to move her mouth up and down on him, her hair tickling his hips and thighs, her hand following her mouth's movement, her breasts brushing his legs just above the knees.

Cam took it as long as he could stand it, but was afraid he was going to lose himself right there in her mouth, and without even having kissed her or otherwise seen to her pleasure. His conscience simply couldn't accept that, and he rose up slightly so that he could catch her by the upper arms, and began to drag her up his body.

Joan came willingly, letting him slip from her mouth and moving up his body to straddle his hips, trapping his erection between their bodies. She raised herself, and clasped him in hand to direct him into her, but Cam caught her hand to stop her. Once she was upright, he'd seen the bruise on her side.

"What are ye doing?" he asked with a frown.

Joan paused and peered at him uncertainly. "I wanted to . . ."

Cam arched his eyebrows when she hesitated and blushed. "Lass, ye can no' possibly want to with yer side the way it is. And yer leg," he added, as he glanced down and noted that her actions must have started it bleeding again. Bright red blood was showing through the linen bandage wrapped around her leg.

"I'm fine," she assured him, shifting her hips to rub herself against him.

Cam stiffened as pleasure shot through him, but then he took note of her expression. There was more determination there than pleasure, he decided grimly, and urged her off of him.

Kneeling beside him, she tried to slip her leg back over his hips, protesting, "But, I want to please you."

Cam stilled and met her gaze. "Love, ye already please me. But ye're no' in any shape fer this. Yer side must be sore, and ye've started yer leg bleeding again. Ye need to rest and recover."

"Nay, I'm fine," she assured him, and reached out to wrap her hand around his still erect penis. "Let me please you, husband."

Cam groaned, but forced her hand away. "Nay, woman. Ye need rest."

"I need you," she insisted, leaning up to kiss him as her hand once again found and clasped him, and slid his length.

Cam was not responding to her kiss, but he was weakening. He could feel it. He wanted to force her to stop and rest, but damned if his cock wasn't opting for another outcome. Growling, he opened his mouth to her, then whipped his head toward the door when a knock sounded.

"Ignore it," Joan said quietly, trying to turn his face back to hers with her free hand. "Let me finish what I started. I—eeeeee," she ended on a squeal and released him to dive under the linens and furs as the door suddenly opened.

"What the devil!" Cam barked as his mother and father and Joan's aunt and uncle trooped into the room one after the other, all of them grim faced. *What the devil was happening now?* he wondered with irritation. And could they not have waited until later to tell him about it?

Joan poked her head up from under the furs when Cam dropped down beside her. She peered over the edge of the material at the people who had entered, then sat up a bit with surprise. "Uncle Ross? What are you doing here?"

Ross grinned at Annabel and said, "She called me 'Uncle.'"

"Aye, she calls me 'Aunt' most times now too," Annabel told him with a small smile.

"Would someone care to explain why ye've all decided to barge in here while me wife and me are abed?" Cam snapped.

"We have important news," his mother said apologetically.

Laird Sinclair nodded, but then scowled and said, "'Sides, 'tis the middle of the day, lad. What the devil are ye doing abed anyway?"

"Annabel was injured," Cam reminded him stiffly.

"Aye, she was. That does no' explain why ye're lying about with her." His eyes narrowed. "Ye were no' trying to indulge in some hough-magandie with her when the poor lass is all bruised and beat up, were ye? She's in no shape fer that nonsense."

Cam scowled at his father. "Aye, I ken that! I even told her as much when she tried to have her way with me."

Groaning, Joan pulled the furs back over her head. Well, this was embarrassing.

Cursing as he realized what he'd said, Cam growled, "Just tell us what ye came here for and go so she can rest."

"Laird MacKay arrived this hour past with news," Lady Sinclair murmured quietly.

"Aye?" Cam asked.

"Aye," Ross said. "I sent one o' me men out to

search for the cloth merchant after ye all headed to Sinclair. I thought to buy material to bring with me when I collected me wife and daughters."

"Material?" Cam asked with confusion.

"Fer gowns for Joan," he muttered, sounding uncomfortable.

"Oh, Uncle, that's so sweet," Joan said, coming up from under the furs to beam at him. Much to her amazement, the man actually blushed and looked even more uncomfortable.

Clearing his throat, he shrugged, and said, "I was no' sure what ye'd like, so I picked what I thought would look best with yer coloring. The men loaded it all on a wagon and we brought it with us. They're unloading it now."

"Thank you," she whispered, tears glazing her eyes at the kindness. Joan wished she was dressed so she could get up and hug the man.

"Surely that is no' the news that was so important ye burst in here to tell us?" Cam asked with a frown.

"Nay," Ross said, straightening. "On his return journey with the merchant, me man came across a fellow dead on the side o' the road. He recognized him as a Sinclair, so—"

"No' Douglas?" Cam interrupted sharply.

"Nay," his father assured him at once. "'Twas Allistair. Douglas is fine as far as we ken."

"Oh." Cam sighed.

"Me man brought this Allistair back with him, along with his belongings. There was no violence to the body and he seemed to have died a natural death, so I told them to put him in a wagon and I'd return him to Sinclair when I traveled here on the morrow, and then I dealt with the merchant. But once that was done, I saw the men had left the warrior's bag behind. I bent to pick it up and when I opened it and found it was full o' scrolls. Since I was no' sure who they were to or if they were urgent messages, I decided we'd best set out right away rather than wait until morn."

Cam sighed. "Let me guess, the messages were to the families of the women Mother invited here, and we'll be stuck with the wenches fer even longer than we'd feared."

"But some of the girls have already left," Joan said with a frown.

"I sent out three messengers," Lady Sinclair explained. "Some of the lasses live closer than others, so I divided them amongst the men thinking to speed the process along. The messenger who was to deliver the scrolls to the closest families has already returned. They are the families of the girls who have already left us."

"Oh," Joan murmured.

"So ye came to tell us that we'll have some o' the women here longer than we'd hoped?" Cam asked slowly.

"Nay, we came to tell ye that the messenger was poisoned," his father said dryly.

"Poisoned?" Cam sat up straight.

"Aye, it didn't take but one look for Lady MacKay to determine the lad had been poisoned," Lady Sinclair said quietly.

"His fingers were blue at the tips," Annabel murmured when Cam and Joan glanced to her.

"Aye, poison," Joan said, mouth tightening.

"What kind?" Cam asked.

Joan shrugged. "Ye can get a poison that'll do that from crushed apple seeds, cherry pits, peach pits . . ."

"Laurel leaves or rotting cabbage too," Annabel added.

"But it's very fast acting," Joan said with a frown.

"How fast acting?" Cam asked. "Could he have been given the poison here before he left?"

"Nay," Joan and Annabel said together, and then Joan added, "He would be dead within minutes of eating whatever the poison was in."

"It must have been put in his food," Lady Sinclair murmured, and noting their expressions, explained, "I had Cook pack a bag of food and drink for each o' the lads ere they left so they could eat in the saddle and no' have to stop to hunt up their meals." Grimacing, she admitted, "I was a bit eager to have the girls gone."

"It would have had to have been put in something with a strong flavor to cover the taste of the poison," Annabel said thoughtfully.

"Aye." Joan agreed and when Cam glanced to her in question, explained, "This poison is bitter. 'Twould have been hard to hide the flavor."

Cam nodded in understanding, but added, "And then they would have had to get it in his food bag."

"So someone went to a lot o' trouble to keep the scrolls Allistair carried from being delivered," Laird Sinclair said grimly.

Cam's eyes widened and he turned to his mother. "Whose messages did he carry?"

Ross pulled several scrolls out of his plaid and dropped them on the table. Aunt Annabel immediately picked one up and examined the scroll. "This just has MF written above the seal."

"The MacFarlands," Lady Sinclair announced.

"This one has a B," Laird Sinclair said after picking up another.

"Buchanan," Cam's mother said, and added, "Which means the other three should be Carmichael, Drummond and MacCormick."

"Aye," Lady Annabel said, checking each scroll. "One is marked with a C, one a D and one with MC." Frowning then, she said, "These are all to the families of the girls who fell ill from the cider."

"And Finola," Lady Sinclair pointed out. "But she was no' taken ill."

"Aye," her aunt agreed and then said thoughtfully, " 'Tis possible Finola poisoned Joan's cider in the hopes of getting her hands on the dress while she was under the weather."

"Finola wasn't in the room to put anything in my drink," Joan pointed out.

"Oh, aye." Grimacing, she gave her head a shake. "I forgot about that."

"Then the person who poisoned the messenger can't be the same one who poisoned my cider,"

Joan said reasonably. "She hardly would have drank the cider she'd poisoned."

"Unless she deliberately drank from the goblet to remove suspicion from herself when the others drank it," Lady Sinclair pointed out.

Joan frowned at the suggestion, but supposed that was possible. She considered the four women who had fallen ill with her and then said, "I think we can discount Murine, at least. She was the first to drink from it after me and only did so because I suggested she have some."

"Aye, but she may only have accepted because refusing might have made her look suspicious once ye fell ill," Cam pointed out.

Joan sighed unhappily and sat back. He was right of course, or could be. How the devil were they supposed to sort this out?

Cam suddenly cursed with frustration and stood up. "Frankly I do no' care who it is. I want all of these women out of here and me wife safe. I say we send them all home today with our men for escort."

"I understand why you would feel that way, Campbell," her aunt said solemnly. "But that will not eliminate the problem. If we do not discover the reason behind the attacks, there could be another attempt at a later date when you are not expecting it. If you are unprepared at the time, there is a better chance it will succeed."

"Or they could pay someone else to do the deed," Uncle Ross said quietly. "Which ye wouldn't be expecting either and could no' prepare against."

"Aye," Annabel agreed and shook her head. "The best solution is to sort it all out and find the culprit now."

Cam scowled at the suggestion, obviously not pleased, but nodded in the end. "Fine. How do we sort it out?"

Everyone was silent for a minute and then Aunt Annabel said, "Perhaps we need to spend more time around these women, get them to talk and hopefully they will say something to reveal themselves."

"And how are ye going to get the women all in the same room together with Joan? I'd say she needs her bed rest after today's incident," Laird Sinclair said and then added heavily, "And without the lad here to pester her."

Cam scowled at his father. "I told ye, I was no' the one who—"

"We shall have a sewing party," Lady Sinclair said suddenly. "Ross brought all that material for Joan. We shall suggest to them that she is feeling low after this latest accident and we would like to hold a sewing party in her room to cheer her."

"That might work," Annabel said thoughtfully, and then nodded and smiled and said, "Aye. I think that might work well."

"Ye may be able to get them all together, but 'tis a lot to hope fer that the lasses'll let anything slip," Laird Sinclair said with a frown. "They will be treading carefully now, watching their words and every move."

"Mayhap," Annabel agreed with a nod. "But

mayhap not. They can't know we suspect any-thing. Does anyone outside this room know we suspect Finola's death was not an accident? Or that the hatpin that was put in the saddle was found?"

They all glanced to each other in question until Joan said, "I haven't told anyone."

"Me either," Cam announced.

Everyone else spoke up then, avowing that they hadn't spoken to anyone outside the circle about it and Annabel nodded. "Very well then. I think 'tis best if Joan spends the afternoon with the ladies. Ye can bring up the subject of the cider and Fino-la's death and see if anyone reacts oddly."

Joan was just nodding when Lady Sinclair sud-denly said, "The guards."

"The guards?" she asked uncertainly.

"Father put guards on our door after the inci-dent with the horse," Cam explained quietly. "To keep ye safe against any more attacks."

"Oh dear," she said with a wince. "Well, that probably has tipped them to the fact that we know someone's up to no good."

"Aye," Lady Annabel agreed on a sigh.

They were all silent for a moment, and then Joan said, "Perhaps if you remove my guard and—"

"Nay," Cam said sharply. "They stay."

"Sending them away would not do any good anyway," her aunt said gently. "They have been out there for hours now. I am sure all the girls have either seen, or at least heard of, their presence out-side your room. They already know something is amiss."

"Aye, but if we remove them and—"

"Nay," Cam repeated at once.

"Husband, please just hear me out," she requested quietly.

Cam hesitated, but then nodded reluctantly.

Joan smiled at him, and then turned back to the others. "We could send away the guard and tell them about the hatpin and—"

"What?" Lady Sinclair interrupted this time. "But we are supposed to be making them think that we think that there is no threat, not that we ken there is one."

"Aye," Joan agreed patiently. "But they already know that from the guard, so now we have to explain why we would no longer think that's the case. We shall say that a hatpin was found under my saddle and we suspected someone was trying to hurt me because of that and the cider so Cam arranged a guard. But when Lady Sinclair saw the hatpin, she recognized it as Finola's and we now realize she must have been behind both incidents. In fact, we can say we now suspect it is what she was doing creeping around the castle at night. We believe she was returning from the stables. Therefore she was the threat, the threat is gone and all is well."

"That's brilliant, me love," Cam complimented solemnly.

Joan flushed and ducked her head, but glanced quickly back up when he added, "But I do no' like ye no' having guards."

"She will no' be without guards," his mother

assured him, straightening from whispering with her aunt. "Lady MacKay and I will be with her at all times until this is resolved."

"Aye," her aunt said firmly and smiled at her.

"There!" Joan said with relief. "'Tis all settled then. We women shall get to the bottom of it."

For some reason, none of the men appeared pleased with this announcement.

Chapter 17

"Oh my, Joan, ye're truly the luckiest lass I ken," Lady Murine breathed, running her hands over the rolls of material stacked on the table by the fire in Joan and Cam's bedchamber. "To have an uncle as kind as Laird MacKay . . . I can no' believe he bought ye all this."

"Aye," Saidh said solemnly, walking around the room to take it all in. "Ye've enough cloth here to make a dress fer every day o' the year. Ye'll never have to buy cloth again."

"Aye," Joan agreed, eyeing the material from her position in bed. She had been excited and pleased when the servants had begun to carry the cloth in, but when they'd set down the first load and left, only to return again and again, she'd been flabbergasted. The man must have bought every stitch of material the merchant carried with him. The rolls formed a pyramid shape on the table, but also had been leaned up against the walls and laid across the chairs. There wasn't a surface in the room that didn't hold a bolt of cloth. Even the bed had a couple rolls lying across the end.

"Well," she said now. "While I am lucky, I surely don't need all this cloth. So I thought I'd gift you each with a couple bolts for helping me."

"Really?" Edith asked excitedly, running her hands over a bolt of dark blue material.

"Aye, of course," Joan said solemnly. "You've all been so kind, I'm pleased to share my good fortune with you. Besides, I feel rather like I owe you. After all, you all got sick from drinking my cider."

Aunt Annabel cast her an approving smile for the way she'd brought up the subject of one of the attacks, but Joan managed not to smile in return. She kept her gaze solemn as she peered from woman to woman, judging their reactions.

"Oh, that was no' yer fault," Murine said at once, rushing to the bed to sit on the edge and clasping her hands. "Ye were trying to be kind when ye offered me a drink, and the others only tried it because we complained it was so bitter."

"Aye," Edith agreed grimly. "The fault lies with Finola fer dosing it with whatever she put in."

Joan shifted her gaze sharply to the woman. "You think Finola put something in my cider?"

"Well, who else would do it?" Edith asked with a shrug. "Besides, she stuck her hatpin in yer saddle."

Joan nodded solemnly and avoided looking at her aunt and Lady Sinclair. They'd apparently done well at presenting the explanations she'd suggested.

"Finola could no' have dosed the cider," Saidh said now with the exasperation of someone who had repeated this several times already. "She was no' there in the solar with us."

"Well Finola was no' there when Joan was thrown from her horse because o' the hatpin either, but we ken she did that," Edith pointed out reasonably. "Perhaps she dropped something in Joan's goblet while the servant was gathering the goblets and cider in the kitchens."

"And how would she ken which one Joan was going to use?" Saidh asked dryly and shook her head. "She could no'."

"Saidh's right," Garia said, offering an apologetic smile to Edith. "There were two goblets still when I came back with me pins and I did no' see anything in the goblets." She paused, and then added judiciously, "Though, I confess, I was no' looking. But still, if there had been something in one o' the goblets . . . well, I could ha'e picked either one. 'Twas just happenstance I did no' pick the one Joan got. For that matter, 'twas just happenstance one o' you didn't pick it yerselves."

"Then mayhap she did no' care who drank it," Murine suggested now. Grimacing, she added, "'Tis no' as if Finola liked any o' us. She made it plain she thought herself above us all." She shrugged. "Mayhap she just wanted one o' us sick and did no' care who."

"Now that's just nonsense. What benefit would there be fer Finola to just randomly make one o' us sick?" Saidh asked with exasperation and then answered her own question. "No' a thing."

"I do no' ken," Garia said suddenly, her expression thoughtful.

"Oh, please, Garia," Saidh said with surprise. "Do no' say ye believe this nonsense? Ye're usually the more sensible one o' the three o' ye."

"Aye, but Finola was wearing Joan's gown when she took her tumble down the stairs," Garia pointed out. "What if she just wanted one o' us sick as a distraction to bring an end to our finishing the gown so that she could pinch it fer herself ere we hemmed it and made it too short fer her?"

"Oh, say," Edith said with surprise. "That does seem possible."

"Damn, it does," Saidh agreed on a grumble and shook her head. "I suppose it certainly seems more likely than that we have two people here trying to hurt Joan."

"Aye," Murine agreed and squeezed her hand. "Joan is just too nice to have made enemies."

"Aye," they all agreed as one, smiling at her.

Joan smiled back, but silently cursed. She hadn't learned a damned thing. She glanced to Lady Sinclair and her aunt then, hopeful that they had picked up on something that she hadn't, but both women looked as disappointed as she felt.

She would have to keep trying, Joan thought grimly. The culprit was one of these women. It had to be. Why else would the messenger carrying their scrolls have been poisoned? One of them wanted to stay longer, and who would want that when Cam was married and unavailable? Unless they planned to change that and make him an available widower again.

"QUIT YER BLOODY PACING, LAD. YE'RE MAKING me nervous," Laird Sinclair barked irritably.

"My apologies," Cam said dryly. "But I'm a little worried just now. In case ye've forgotten, me wife is up there with a woman who has already poisoned her once, arranged a riding accident and killed another woman."

"How can we ferget? Our wives are up there with her too," the MacKay said grimly. He turned his tankard on the table, then muttered impatiently, "This is worse than waiting through a birthing."

"Aye," Laird Sinclair muttered, raising his ale to drink it.

Cam didn't comment. He didn't even want to think on that subject. It would just make him more anxious.

"Halt!"

Cam glanced around with surprise at that barked word from Laird MacKay. He then followed the man's gaze to the three lasses who now stood frozen at the foot of the stairs. His sister, Aileen, and Laird and Lady MacKay's daughters Annella and Kenna. The trio had obviously been about to try to sneak upstairs.

"Here," the MacKay snapped, pointing to the bench beside him. "Now."

The girls hesitated, and then all three heaved sighs and moved reluctantly to the table to sit down.

"Where did ye three think ye were going?" Ross asked dryly once they'd sat.

"Jinny said the ladies are all up in cousin Joan's room having a sewing party and we thought to join them," Annella explained.

"Ye'll no' be joining them," the MacKay announced.

"What?" Annella appeared surprised, but when her father shook his head firmly, she protested, "But Papa! She is our cousin and we both—" She paused to smile apologetically at Aileen, and then continued, "All three of us sew well. We should be there too."

"Nay," the MacKay said firmly.

When Aileen pursed her lips, as if she wasn't sure that his nay included her, Cam's father eyed her solemnly and echoed, "Nay."

Aileen slumped in her seat with a sigh.

All three girls then simply sat there, moping and looking miserable, until the MacKay shifted impatiently and said, "Go find something to do. Pick apples or something. Mayhap the Sinclair's cook'll make ye a tart."

"All the ripe ones ha'e been picked already," Annella said miserably. "Cook said one o' the ladies brought in a basket full the other day for him and he made applemoyse with them."

"Well then go find something else to do," Laird MacKay suggested impatiently.

"Can we take our horses fer a ride?" Kenna asked hopefully.

"Nay," Laird MacKay said firmly. "I want the two o' ye to stay close today."

When they simply sat there, fidgeting, he added, "But no' this close. Get yerselves outside to the gardens and take a walk."

Sighing, the three girls stood and headed for the keep doors.

"But no riding," the MacKay barked after them. "I'll be asking the stablemaster later and if I find ye went against me, I'll . . ." He paused, looking blank. Apparently, unable to come up with a suitable threat, he simply muttered, "I'll make ye sorry."

"Daughters, eh?" Cam's father muttered.

"Aye," the MacKay agreed, and then glanced to Cam with surprise when he suddenly stood up. "Where are ye going?"

"Ye can no' go upstairs," his father added firmly, apparently thinking he meant to storm the room to protect his wife.

"To the stables," Cam said, hurrying away from the trestle tables without further explanation. The MacKay's words to his daughters had made him realize that he hadn't thought to ask the stablemaster if any of the ladies had been near the stables of late. He suspected the man hadn't seen anyone near Joan's mount or he would have mentioned it when he and his father were examining the animal for what might have caused her to go crazy as she had. But he might not have thought to mention one of the ladies simply being in the stables. They all had horses there. Actually, it may end up that all of them had been there recently, but he wouldn't know unless he asked . . . and it was better than simply sitting around waiting. Doing nothing was making him crazy.

He found the stablemaster, Robbie, mucking a stall when he got there and immediately asked, "Have ye seen any o' the ladies down here o' late?"

Robbie paused and straightened to face him as he shook his head. "Nay. I would have said as much if I had after finding that hatpin in yer lady's saddle. But I've no' seen even one o' the lasses down here in a couple days. They all have horses and rode them often enough ere ye got here, but once ye arrived, they've no' been back."

"Oh," Cam said, leaning against the stall door with disappointment. He'd told himself it was a long shot, but he'd still hoped . . .

"Is there something else I can do fer ye?" Robbie asked, continuing with his work.

Cam shook his head, but said, "Should no' yer stable lad being doing that, Robbie? Surely ye've more important things to attend to?"

"Aye, but me stable lad's gone missing, so I'm stuck with it 'til I replace him," Robbie said dryly.

"Missing?" Cam asked straightening. "When did he go missing?"

"The morning after the MacFarland woman died," Robbie said grimly. "Ye asked me to prepare yer horse and yer lady's, so I told him to do it and went inside to break me fast. When I came back out o' the keep, the horses were waiting at the base o' the stairs, but he was gone." Scowling, he added grimly, "He has no' returned. And I'll no take him back when he does. I need a dependable lad here, no' a flitter widget who can no' be counted on."

Cam was silent for a moment, thinking, and then he asked, "Did ye ask around after him? Has anyone seen him?"

"I asked," Robbie admitted. "One o' the men on the wall said he saw him walk the horses to the keep stairs. He said one o' those ladies yer mother brought here was walking with him, but once they reached the stairs he paid them no more heed and he does no' ken where he went after that."

"Which lady?" Cam asked sharply.

Robbie shrugged. "He did no' say."

"Which man was it who saw them together?" Cam asked.

"Tormod," Robbie answered, and then paused to eye him curiously. "Why are ye so interested in the lad?"

Cam just shook his head and turned to head out of the stables.

"My betrothed was young and handsome," Murine said on a sigh as she began to cut material at the table.

"Ye met him?" Saidh asked with interest.

"Aye. He was on his way to claim me and had just reached Carmichael land when he died. They brought his body to the castle. He was ever so handsome," Murine said sadly.

"Mine was no'," Saidh said dryly. "Mine was an old bastard."

Joan's mouth twitched at the woman's words.

Saidh was a little different than the other ladies. She had been raised with eight brothers and, probably because of it, talked like a man herself.

"Do ye mean that literally? Or just as a general description?" Garia asked with an amusement that matched Joan's. She too was seated at the table, cutting cloth. They'd moved all the bolts to the floor to make room for the task.

"Both," Saidh said dryly. "He was the bastard son o' the Ferguson. The Ferguson outlived his legitimate son and left all to him. He was a pig," she added with a grimace, and then glanced to Garia and asked, "Can I use the shears? Me thread is in a knot."

"O' course."

When Garia grabbed the shears and stood to take them to her, Saidh glanced to Joan and added, "Other than the fact that it would have been more considerate o' him to wait until after he wedded me to go and die, I do no' mind so much."

"Are ye no' worried that ye might never marry and will be sent to an abbey fer the rest o' yer days?" Murine asked worriedly as Garia set down the scissors and quickly returned to her seat.

Saidh snorted at the thought as she cut off the knotted end of thread. "Me brothers would never send me to an abbey. They ken I'd kill 'em if they did."

Joan released a startled laugh and then glanced to Edith when she made a sound of disgust.

"Me brothers would send me off to the abbey in a trice if it were no' for me father." Her mouth turned down unhappily and she added, "Unfortunately, his health is no' well, so that may happen soon."

"I'm sorry to hear that," Joan said with a frown. She couldn't imagine being forced into the church against her will. Surely it wouldn't make for a good bride of God if she was unwilling?

"What about you, Garia?" Saidh asked, glancing to the little redhead. "Abbey? Or old maid?"

"Neither," Garia said with a shrug. "Me mother already has another husband lined up. The only reason she had no' already arranged it is because she was hoping Cam would take interest and marry me." She shrugged again. "He's wealthier and more powerful."

Joan was about to ask who the man was when her aunt suddenly stood and moved to the side of the bed.

" 'Tis time to put more salve on your side," she said quietly. "Lift your arm."

"Oh, aye," Joan said guiltily and did as she asked. She'd been slipping on the task she was supposed to be performing and had allowed the conversation to shift to subjects that had nothing to do with any of the attacks that had taken place at Sinclair. She supposed this was her aunt's way of bringing them all back to the topic. There was nothing like letting them see the ugly bruising to ensure they started thinking of how she'd gained it. Hopefully it would bring the topic back around to the attacks on her, she thought, as her aunt lifted the side of the tunic she'd pulled on before the cloth had been brought up.

"Oh!"

Joan glanced to Murine at that cry, just in time to watch the woman swoon and slide out of the chair she'd been sitting in. She ended up slumped against the legs of her chair, her skirt up around her thighs where it had caught as she'd fallen out of her seat.

Saidh peered at Murine, shook her head and then stood up to walk over and tug her skirt down to cover her legs. Straightening then, she turned to peer at Joan, her eyes going wide as she took in Joan's side. "God's teeth, woman. Yer side is black as sin."

"Aye, it looks nasty," Garia said with concern, getting up from her seat at the table to move closer to the bed. Shaking her head, she met Joan's gaze and said, " 'Tis lucky it was yer side and no' yer head that took the blow or ye definitely would no' ha'e survived."

"That was probably Finola's intention," Edith said grimly, taking her place to get a better look at it.

"Mayhap," Joan agreed mildly. "But I was the lucky one. I hit my side, not my head and survived. Finola wasn't so lucky." She paused, but when no one said anything, she added, "Actually, I feel rather sorry for Finola. She must have been terribly unhappy."

Garia paused at her seat to peer at her and then shook her head. "I'm sorry, Joan. I do no' feel bad fer her at all. But ye're very kind to, yerself."

"Kind to the point o' stupid if ye truly feel

sorry fer that bitch," Saidh said with disgust. "The woman was cruel, nasty and she was after yer man . . . and she did no' care that he was married to ye either."

Joan hesitated, and then glanced to where her aunt had settled back in her chair by the table. When she arched an eyebrow ever so slightly in question, Lady Annabel raised her mead and gave her head the faintest shake, her expression grim. So did Lady Sinclair when she glanced to her next.

Sighing, Joan lowered her head and pretended to sew a stitch to hide her expression. There was no way she could keep the frustration off her face right now as she acknowledged how stupid this idea had been. Or maybe she just wasn't any good at it. They weren't learning anything from this exercise. Nothing she'd heard so far was very helpful in telling them who was behind everything. These women all just seemed like nice, normal women. Not one was showing signs of being a coldblooded killer who might have thrown Finola down a flight of stairs and had set Joan up for a riding accident that could have killed her. Maybe the girls were right and Finola had been behind everything. Perhaps she had dosed the cider just to put a halt to the sewing session and get her hands on the dress. And perhaps she had stuck the hatpin in the horse that night before she'd fallen down the stairs.

Of course, that didn't explain where the candle she'd been holding had gone, Joan thought, but perhaps the explanation for that was as simple as one of the servants pinching it in all the chaos after Finola had been found dead.

Sighing, Joan glanced up, and frowned when she noted Murine was showing no signs of stirring.

"Shouldn't Murine be waking by now?" she asked with the beginnings of concern. "She doesn't usually stay in her faints this long."

"Aye, she usually wakes quickly," Saidh said, and Joan glanced to her sharply as she heard the slur in her voice.

"Saidh? Are you all right?" she asked, sitting up slightly. Noting the glassy eyed look on the woman's face, Joan glanced quickly to her aunt. "Aunt Annabel, there's something wrong with . . ." Her voice trailed away as she noted that her aunt appeared to be sleeping in her chair. Lady Sinclair was too, she noted, turning her attention to her next.

Chapter 18

CAM LET THE KITCHEN DOOR SWING CLOSED behind him as he spied Tormod chatting up one of the maids at the far end of the room. He'd searched high and low for the bastard until one of the men had mentioned that the warrior was sweet on a kitchen maid, though he hadn't said which one. That had finally led him here.

"Tormod," he barked, striding toward the pair.

"Wha—Oh." Tormod straightened at once on spotting him and turned to face him in question. "Is there something ye want?"

"Robbie said ye saw the stable boy walking me horse and me wife's to the keep yesterday and that he was talking with one of the ladies me mother brought here?" Cam began.

"Aye. I do no' ken where he went to after that, though, and I told Robbie as much."

Cam waved that away. "Which of the ladies was he with?"

"Oh," Tormod grimaced. "I do no' ken her

name. 'Twas the short one with red hair. I think she's a MacCormick."

"Aye. That's Garia MacCormick," Cook announced, drawing his gaze around. "A little peculiar, but a nice lass just the same."

"Peculiar?" Cam asked quietly.

"Aye. She picked me a bunch o' apples the other day. Thought I might like to make a nice tart or something, she said. I made applemoyse instead, it's tastier, to me mind, and—"

"Get to the peculiar part," Cam interrupted impatiently.

"Well, later that day one o' the maids saw her picking through the garden, gathering up all the cores from the apples," he said with a shake of the head, and then explained, "I have the maids throw things like that there, it makes the soil richer and—"

Cam didn't stay to hear more. He didn't need to. Apple seeds had been amongst the things Joan and Lady Annabel had said the poison that had been used on the messenger might be made from. And Garia had been seen not only collecting the apple cores, but also walking with the stable boy as he led their horses to the castle. He couldn't think of any other reason the woman would have wanted the apple cores, and it would have been easy for her to distract the stable boy and slip the hatpin under the saddle as she walked with him. Cam was pretty sure he had his culprit.

Unfortunately, his father and Laird MacKay

were less certain when he shared what he'd learned with them.

"I do no' ken, son," his father said, pursing his lips. "The cook said that a maid said . . . ? Did ye talk to the maid herself? 'Tis one thing to suspect the MacCormick lass did it, and another to accuse her on such flimsy proof. The MacCormicks are powerful. We do no' want to start a war here by accusing the wrong lass."

"Aye, and Tormod did no' even ken the lass's name," the MacKay pointed out. "Ye should at least have him point out to ye which woman he saw. He and Cook could be talking about two different women. Or is she the only short redhead yer mother brought here?"

"Nay, there were two others," Artair said. "Though one left the first day and another this afternoon. Garia MacCormick is the only short redhead left."

"And the only short redhead whose scroll was carried by Allistair," Cam said impatiently.

"Well, that's true enough," his father admitted thoughtfully.

"She's up there right now with Joan," Cam said grimly.

"She'll no' do anything with the other women there," his father said soothingly. "I'm thinking we should call Tormod out here, and get Cook to send out the maid who saw the lass collecting apple cores and have them tell us if the Mac-Cormick lass is who they saw. We can do that at the evening meal," he decided with satisfaction.

"If 'tis the same lass, and is the MacCormick girl, then we'll sit her down and ask her some questions. We'll get to the bottom o' this."

"If the ladies have no' already done so by then," Laird MacKay added.

"Aye," Artair nodded. "If the ladies have no' figured it all out for themselves by then."

Cam narrowed his eyes at the two men and asked, "How much ale have ye had?"

His father stiffened at the question. "No' even a full tankard, thank ye very much. What are ye suggesting?"

"I'm suggesting that earlier neither o' ye were pleased at the thought o' our wives being up in a room with a possible killer, and now ye both seem pretty damned unconcerned."

"O' course we're concerned. But they should be safe enough with all the women together, and this is a sensitive business. We can no' just accuse a lass who belongs to a powerful clan on hearsay," his father snapped.

"Fine," Cam snapped back. "Then I'll search Garia's room and find proof."

"Oh, say, that's a good idea," his father commented. "I'll come with ye."

"Aye, me too," Laird MacKay announced, getting to his feet.

THE HAIR ALL OVER JOAN'S BODY SEEMED suddenly to be standing on end as she stared at her unconscious aunt and mother-in-law, and then she slid her gaze back slowly across the room. To

Murine still lying prone on the floor, then to Saidh struggling to get up from her chair and then dropping back with alarm on her face, then to Edith asleep with her arms on the table, and finally to Garia who had stood and moved to the end of the bed and was eyeing the sleeping women with narrow eyed interest.

"Garia?" she said quietly.

The woman took a deep breath, her shoulders rising, and then she let that breath out and turned to meet her gaze. "Aye, Joan?"

Joan hesitated and then asked, "Did you put some sort of sleeping powder in their drinks?"

Garia nodded.

"When?" she asked. "I didn't see you near the tray. Saidh even brought you your goblet."

"Aye, she did," Garia agreed. "Saidh is surprisingly considerate despite her rough talk and ways. I quite like her. 'Tis a shame she will have to be the villain in all this."

"Saidh will be the villain?" Joan asked with a frown, glancing to the woman in question. She had slumped in her chair, her eyes at half-mast.

"Aye, she was the last to be affected by me tincture and noticed that I was the only one left who was completely unaffected besides you. She still isn't fully asleep, and just look, ye can see the realization in her eyes. She understands it was me," Garia said sadly and then shook her head. "I'll have to kill her and claim it was in self-defense, that I woke up and saw her bent over ye, tried to save ye by stabbing her with the shears, but 'twas too late."

When she then picked up the shears from the table and stepped toward Saidh, Joan quickly asked, "How did you give the sleeping draft to everyone when you didn't go near the tray of drinks after the servants brought it up?"

Garia turned back and stared at her for a long minute. Joan suspected she was debating whether to answer or not. In the end, however, she shrugged and said. "Murine was easy. Seated at the table with me as she was, I merely had to wait for her to start cutting and then quickly drip some in her goblet. I dosed Saidh's drink when I took her the scissors, and then I dosed Lady Sinclair's as I passed her on the way to see yer bruising. She was looking at it too and seemed quite horrified. Had she not seen it before?"

"Not since I was first brought back," Joan said quietly. "I believe she helped Aunt Annabel with me then."

Garia nodded, unsurprised. "I dosed Lady Annabel's goblet on me way back to me seat and Edith's as well since she was over here gawking at yer side still . . ." she shrugged. "And then I just waited to see who dropped next."

"Next?" Joan asked. "So Murine's faint wasn't a faint?"

Garia shrugged. "It may have been, but the tincture will keep her under."

Joan nodded slowly, but when Garia began to move again, asked, "And you did all this to what end?"

Garia blew out a slightly irritated breath and

turned to peer at her again. "Why do ye think, Joan?"

"Because you want Cam for your own," she guessed.

"Aye, o' course I do," Garia agreed. "And much as I like ye, Joan, yer wearing finery does no' make ye a lady any more than putting a dress on a pig would make it one. Ye're a peasant. Yer mother may have been a lady, but yer father was a commoner. She became a commoner when she married him. Ye were born a commoner, raised a commoner, and will always be a commoner. Cam deserves better than that."

"Better being you?" she asked dryly.

"Aye, as it happens," Garia said. "I was born and raised a lady. I have been properly trained in all the things a lady should ken. I sing like a bird, ken every dance there is, can hit the center of a target with an arrow on the windiest day and can ride like a warrior. I was born to rule Sinclair, not some backwater keep with little in the way o' coin and a dirty, smelly old Laird . . . a laird who licks his lips every time he looks at me like I'm a leg o' mutton he can no' wait to bite into," she added with disgust.

"This is the man your mother plans to marry you to?" Joan asked, trying not to be obvious about shifting her eyes around the area nearest her in search of a weapon besides the wee sewing needle she held in her hand.

"Aye. She'd rather marry me off to that odious creature than be saddled with me fer the rest o' me days," Garia said with a combination of bitterness and pain.

"Could you not run away to the abbey or—" Joan snapped her mouth closed at once as fury exploded over Garia's expression and she realized what she'd said. She hadn't been thinking, she'd just been trying to keep the conversation going as she searched for a way out of this situation. But she was thinking now and wasn't surprised when Garia clenched her hand around the shears and began moving toward her instead of Saidh.

"The abbey, Joan?" she ground out furiously. "Yer mother was sent there fer punishment fer killing her husband, yet ye think it must be such a pleasant place I'd want to spend the rest o' me life there? Unwed, me hair shorn from me head, me knees chapped from being on them so much. Never to have children o' me own?"

Joan couldn't help thinking that might be a good thing, but suspected saying so wouldn't be a smart thing to do just then.

"Ye're the one who should be in an abbey. Like yer mother before ye. Ye never should have been in Scotland at all. Why did ye have to come and ruin everything?" she growled.

"There were twelve women here, Garia. What did you plan to do? Kill anyone he showed interest in?" Joan asked quickly, easing sideways on the bed.

"They were no competition," Garia snapped with disgust, pausing at the bedside. "Saidh is so rough ye'd be forgiven for thinking her a man, and Edith likes to think she's smart, but she's dull as dirty water. As for Murine, she could no' keep from fainting long enough to hold a conversation with the man. And they were the best o' the bunch!" She shook her head. "Nay. If no' fer you, he'd probably have proposed to me already and then I could have laughed in me mother's face. She did no' think I could win him," she added bitterly. "Well, I shall show her when ye're dead and we're wed."

"Did you push Finola down the stairs?" Joan asked, trying to change the subject to something less volatile and buy more time.

"Aye. The cow threw herself at Cam. There ye were, lying in yer sickbed and she was throwing herself at him like some tavern wench," she said with outrage. "She had to be punished." Pausing, she frowned and asked, "How did ye ken she was pushed and did no' fall?"

"You took her candleholder," Joan said quietly, easing a little more to the side away from her.

"Oh. Aye. 'Tis in me room. I shall have to put it back in hers after this," Garia decided.

"Is that when you took the hatpin from her?" Joan asked, glancing swiftly to the side and wondering if her goblet was sturdy enough to do any damage if she hit her with it.

"Aye. 'Tis a shame, that. I really liked the hatpin, but it seemed better if the pin used was someone else's, and using hers would reassure anyone who might be getting suspicious that the danger had passed. Which is what I thought happened," she added and then frowned. "I hadn't thought of the candleholder." Shrugging, she turned her full attention to Joan again. "Ye do realize ye're no' going to be able to get out o' the bed ere I stab ye?"

"Mayhap," Joan allowed. "But I can try."

Garia smiled faintly. "I really do like yer spirit, Joan. 'Tis just a shame ye never learned yer place and that ye should stay in it."

The words were barely out of her mouth before she suddenly stabbed out at her with the shears.

Rather than try to flee the bed and be stabbed in the back, Joan grabbed the bolster she'd been leaning against and brought it up to block the shears. Much to her relief, it worked and while the feather bolster suffered a messy death with feathers flying everywhere, she was unscathed.

Joan made an attempt to flee the bed then, only to have Garia grab her by the hair and drag her back. She landed on her back in the bed, saw Garia shake the bolster off the end of the shears and plunge them toward her again, and quickly grabbed her wrist with both hands. She also began to scream her head off. A sound that ended in a grunt when Garia suddenly climbed onto the bed and knelt on her chest, forcing the air out of her lungs in one painful gush.

"Ye're just making this harder on yerself, Joan," Garia ground out, trying to force the shears down toward her chest.

Joan would have told her to go to hell, but didn't have the air in her lungs to say it. Besides, all her strength was presently being sapped by trying to keep the shears out of her chest. She was failing miserably at the effort, the lack of air weakening her, and Joan was sure she was about to die when Garia suddenly collapsed onto her with a startled grunt.

Eyes wide, Joan retrieved the shears from Garia's now lax hands and then pushed her head out of the way to look past her.

"Murine," she said with surprise when she saw the woman standing there with a log from the fireplace in her hands. Jinny had prepared for a fire in case the ladies wanted one, but it was warm enough they hadn't bothered. Still, the logs had come in handy, Joan thought vaguely.

"I'm sorry," Murine said quietly, drawing her gaze again.

Joan glanced to her with surprise. "For what? You saved my life."

"Aye, but it took me so long," she said unhappily and explained, "I woke from me faint a while ago. I didn't drink the mead she dosed. I was too busy trying to cut a straight line. And then when I woke up, it took me a minute to orient meself and try to move, and before I could, I heard what she was saying, what both o' ye were saying and I was so scared. I was trying to look around fer a weapon without drawing her attention to the fact that I was awake, and—"

"Murine," Joan interrupted gently, brushing Garia's hair impatiently out of her face. "You did good. You saved me. You saved Saidh too. Garia was going to kill her as well and claim Saidh had killed me. So you saved us both."

"Oh," Murine said with surprise. "I did, didn't I?"

"Aye," Joan assured her and when the other woman let her arms drop and let the log slip to the floor, said worriedly, "Please don't faint. 'Tis hard to breathe with Garia on me and I think I need help removing her."

"Oh," Murine rushed forward at that, reaching for Garia's arm, but froze and glanced over her shoulder as the door burst open.

"'Twas not Murine," Joan shouted quickly when Cam charged toward them with his father and her uncle on his heels.

"We ken," her father-in-law assured her as Cam hurried past Murine. The man then frowned and rushed to his wife to check on her, even as her uncle moved to Annabel.

"How did you know Garia was the one?" Joan asked with a frown as her husband dragged the woman off of her.

"She was seen picking apple cores out o' the garden and she walked the stable boy to the keep," Cam said grimly, letting Garia drop to the floor so that he could look Joan over. "Are ye hurt? Did she hurt ye?"

"Nay," Joan assured him, and then smiling, added, "Murine saved me."

He glanced around with surprise at Murine and Joan smiled at the woman, then said solemnly, "Thank you Murine."

"Oh . . ." She flushed and waved her thanks away, then promptly fainted.

"There's something wrong with the lass," Cam said with a frown.

"Aye," Joan agreed, slipping off the bed to check on her. "But I think between Aunt Annabel and myself we can sort it out and help her."

She stilled as Garia moaned behind her, and then turned to peer warily at the woman. When she remained unconscious, Joan scowled and told him, "She admitted to killing Finola and putting the hatpin in the saddle."

"Did she say what she gave the women?" her uncle asked grimly, drawing her gaze to where he still stood bent over Aunt Annabel, trying to rouse her.

"A sleeping draft," Joan said quietly. "They will sleep for a while, but should be okay."

"Thank God," Artair Sinclair muttered, straightening from Cam's mother. Scowling at Garia, he asked, "Did she say what she did to the stable boy?"

"The stable boy?" Joan asked with confusion.

"He's missing," Cam explained quietly. "He was last seen walking our horses to the keep steps. Garia was with him."

"Oh dear," Joan said on a sigh and shook her head. "Nay, she said naught about a stable boy."

"We'll find out when she wakes up," Ross said grimly and then glanced around the room at the unconscious women. "We'd best put everyone in their rooms until the effects of whatever she gave them pass."

"What'll we do with the MacCormick lass?" Laird Sinclair asked.

"I'll take her below and put a guard on her," Cam decided, bending to pick up the woman now. "I'll find some men to come help with the other ladies too," he added, heading for the door. He paused there though, and glanced back to Joan to say, "I'll be right back."

Joan nodded solemnly and watched him go. Her uncle and father-in-law were right behind him, their wives in their arms and Joan suspected she wouldn't see them again until the women woke up. They both looked terribly worried and distressed that their wives had been drugged. It did her heart good to see that. She hoped Cam loved her well enough that twenty years from now he would still care that much about her.

"Joan."

She glanced around at that whisper, and stood quickly to move to Saidh. The woman was still slumped in her chair, her eyes only half open, but she hadn't completely lost consciousness.

Joan dropped to her haunches beside her and took her hand as she offered her a smile. " 'Tis all right. 'Tis just a sleeping tincture. You'll sleep for a bit, but that's all."

"Sorry," Saidh whispered and Joan shook her head with confusion.

"For what?"

"Could no' help ye," Saidh muttered wearily.

"Oh," Joan patted her hand. " 'Tis all right. Murine saved the day for both of us."

"Aye." She could not tell if the expression that flickered across Saidh's face then was more surprise or respect for the other woman.

"Rest," Joan suggested. "We'll talk when you wake up."

Saidh's eyes drooped the rest of the way closed and Joan straightened with a sigh, then glanced to the door as Cam returned with several men behind him. He moved directly to her, collecting a fur from the bed on the way to wrap around her, and then held it there as the men silently moved to the sleeping women.

"Garia woke as I carried her below," Cam announced suddenly as they watched the men pick up the women.

Joan glanced to him in question. "Did she say anything about the missing stable boy?"

"Aye. She told us where to find the body," he said grimly.

Joan sighed at this news and shook her head. "Did she say anything else?"

"Nothing worth repeating," he assured her, and then placed the ends of the fur in her hands and moved to follow the men to the door.

"Fetch their maids to them once ye have them in their rooms so they do no' wake up alone and scared," Cam ordered, as they filed out, and then he closed the door behind them.

"That was very thoughtful," Joan murmured as he turned and walked back to her. "I should have thought of it."

Cam just shook his head, scooped her up and carried her to the bed. He then settled in it with her in his lap and simply held her in his arms.

"Joan," he said after a moment.

"Aye?" she asked, tipping her head back to peer at him.

His head was tipped back and his eyes closed. "I love ye."

"I love you," she responded at once.

He nodded, and then lowered his head, opened his eyes and said, "Nay, I mean I really love ye. Everything about ye. Ye've no need to learn anything. I love ye just the way ye are."

"But ladies are supposed to know how to sing and dance and shoot arrows and—"

"Aye, I ken that's what is expected," he admitted, and then asked, "But what good are those things?"

She blinked at the question in confusion. "I'm not sure what you mean."

"What if ye'd kenned those things when I'd met ye?" he asked. "What could ye have done? Sing me sweet songs while I lay dying, and then dance on me grave?" He gave her a slight shake. "Ye do no' ken yer own value. Ye saved me with yer healing skills. Ye kenned enough to get us somewhere safe and out o' the way to heal. Ye've got courage, and while ye may no' be able to shoot an arrow straight yet, yer a damned fine shot with that slingshot o' yers." He paused briefly, and then added, "By the by, we should have made sure ye had that fer this little soiree. Ye could have defended yerself better." He peered at her seriously. "I'd like ye to carry it at all times from now on."

"Aye, husband," she said quietly.

Cam released a deep sigh and then promised,

"I'll teach ye anything ye want to learn—to ride, to shoot an arrow, to fight with a sword e'en—but I'll no' have ye thinking ye *have* to learn anything fer me. I think ye're perfect just the way ye are."

"Oh," Joan said shakily, tears pooling in her eyes. "And I think you're perfect too."

He bent to kiss her gently, then lifted his head again, and asked, "So no more talk o' annulling the marriage?"

"Nay," she agreed solemnly.

"Good," Cam said just as solemnly, and then grinned and added, "No' that me mother would have allowed it anyway. She's decided ye're the perfect woman fer me too."

"She has, has she?" Joan asked with amusement.

"Aye," he assured her. "I think me picking ye to wife has raised me in her esteem. She thinks I'm ever so clever now."

"So do I," Joan said with a laugh, and then her expression turned serious and she caressed his face. "I do so love you, Campbell Sinclair."

"And I, you, Joan Sinclair." He lowered his head then to kiss her and Joan smiled, sure that everything would be all right.

Epilogue

"KENNA AND ANNELLA WERE VERY UPSET that we did not bring them with us."

That comment from her aunt made Joan glance up from the shirt she was mending and smile at the woman. "I don't know why you didn't bring them. They would have been welcome here. We have the room."

"Payton will bring them once we send word that the babe has arrived. I just did not want them to . . . get in the way," Lady Annabel said.

"You mean, you didn't want them seeing the horrors of childbirth and fear having babes themselves," Joan said dryly, and then quickly pushed thoughts of childbirth from her mind. She'd been doing that for months now, ever since discovering that the wild carrot had failed her and she was with child.

To be fair, Joan supposed the wild carrot hadn't really failed her. It tended to become less effective with constant use and she had been using it pretty constantly, mostly because Cam's attentions had been pretty constant. Not that she'd minded . . . until she'd realized she was with child.

Of course, on the bright side, they hadn't had to use it since then. There was no need to protect against getting with child when you were already with child, and she and Cam had been even more constant since finding out she was with child. Both of them were worried about what was coming, they'd been acting like she was dying, living every moment together as if it might be one of their last, which, of course, was what they feared. That she would not survive labor and their time was limited.

Joan shifted uncomfortably as her stomach cramped, and forced herself to breathe through it. Once it eased, she slid her gaze over the women seated with her in the solar. Her aunt, her mother-in-law, Murine, and Saidh. Aileen had wanted to come as well but Lady Sinclair had left her with her father at Inverderry castle where they had settled when the man had passed on the main castle and title of laird to Cam. Joan was quite sure they'd left the girl behind for the same reason her aunt had left her cousins home. None of them wanted the girls to know what they were in for and be so afraid of it that they tried to avoid getting with child. As for Murine and Saidh, they had become good friends in the last months. They didn't see each other often, but wrote back and forth quite a bit.

Fortunately, Cam liked them too, and he was

the one who had written to invite them to come stay and lend their support when they judged her time was near. He'd done it as a surprise and Joan loved the man for it. Or, at least, loved him more. He was forever doing thoughtful little things like that, and every incident just increased her feelings for him, she thought as her stomach cramped again.

"Are you all right, dear?" Lady Annabel asked suddenly. "You look uncomfortable. Do you need something soft to sit on or—?"

"Nay, I am fine." Joan breathed with relief as the cramp ended. Forcing a smile she added, "Besides, no position is comfortable now, I am too big."

Annabel nodded, but her eyes were narrowed slightly as she peered over her and Joan knew the woman would soon realize she was in labor. She was a trained healer too, after all. Still, she'd managed to keep it to herself for some time. Joan had been in labor all morning, the first cramps waking her ere dawn, but they had been mild then and a goodly time apart. They had grown increasingly frequent and uncomfortable ever since. Now they were becoming downright painful. They were also coming so close together, one barely ended when the next began. She wouldn't be able to hide her situation for much longer, Joan thought and ground her teeth together, breathing slowly through her nose as the next pain hit . . . and it was a doozy.

"Would you like to lie down?" Annabel asked, suddenly beside her.

Joan glanced up with a start, her mouth opening on a gasp of surprise that ended in a groan before she could stop it.

"What's wrong?" Lady Sinclair was immediately beside her aunt, concern on her face. "Has it started?"

"Has what started?" Murine asked with confusion and received a swat to the arm from Saidh for the question.

"What the de'il do ye think?" Saidh asked with disgust as she stood to join the others around Joan's chair.

"Please, sit," Joan panted as the cramping ended. "I'm fine."

"They are coming much closer together now, dear," Annabel said gently. "Perhaps we should move to your bedchamber while you can still walk."

Joan glanced to her with surprise. "How long have you known?"

"Since coming down to break my fast this morning," Annabel admitted. "You were rubbing your stomach when I arrived, and then just before we got up to come up here, you went very still and bowed your head for a moment."

"Well why didn't ye say something?" Lady Sinclair asked, wide-eyed.

"Joan obviously did not want anyone to know, so I respected her wishes," Annabel said apologetically.

"Well, why wouldn't ye want us to ken?" Lady Sinclair asked, looking wounded. "We're here to help ye through it. 'Tis why we came."

"Aye, 'tis, ye daft woman," Saidh said with a shake of the head and then moved up to take her arm. "Come on, up with ye. We'll get ye all settled in bed nice and cozy and ye can squeeze our hands 'til we scream with ye when the pains hit."

Lady Sinclair frowned slightly and said, "Perhaps Lady Saidh and Murine should wait here. They're unwed maids. 'Tis no' proper to—"

"Oh, bullocks to that," Saidh said at once. "I did no' travel all this way to sit in the solar while Joan travails in another room."

Joan chuckled at her friend's asperity and allowed her to help her up. "Come on then," she said with a sigh. "I guess Aunt Annabel is right. We should move to the bedchamber while I still can." Getting to her feet had got more and more difficult the larger her stomach had grown, but standing this time would have been impossible if Saidh hadn't taken one arm and her aunt the other to help pull her up. Breathless and panting once she got to her feet, Joan glanced around and paused as she noted Murine lying on the floor.

"That lass needs to eat more," Saidh muttered on a sigh when she followed Joan's gaze to the prone woman.

"I'll send one o' the maids back to help her once we get ye situated in bed," Lady Sinclair said with a shake of the head. "Come along."

"Aye," Joan murmured, eager to get to the other room before another contraction hit. She had barely kept from crying out this last time, and feared once she let loose, she wouldn't be able to stop. Joan did not want to be screaming her head off on the landing. Cam would hear and know it had started. The longer she could keep him from worrying, the better. If she were lucky, he wouldn't have to know until it was over and she was, hopefully, presenting him with his new baby. On the other hand, if she didn't survive . . . well, she didn't want him having to go through watching that. She loved the man too much.

"Just walk slow," Annabel advised as they began to walk her to the door. "We can stop if you need to. There is no rush."

Joan nodded, but was still determined to get to the bedchamber before another contraction hit, and found herself pulling at the hold the two women had on her arms. They were in the hall and halfway to the bedchamber when the next cramp hit. Joan stopped walking at once, her hands instinctively reaching for her stomach. She didn't know if it was because she was standing or not, but it felt like someone was kicking her front, her back and her innards all at once and she staggered, dropping to her knees before Annabel and Saidh could stop her. That was when her water broke.

"What happened?" Saidh asked with alarm as the liquid puddled on the wooden floor around Joan.

"'Tis the water the baby grows in," Annabel said calmly and assured her, "Do not fret. 'Tis normal. It has to come out so the babe can."

"Oh."

That faint cry drew their attention in time to see Murine slumping to the floor just outside the solar door. It seemed she'd regained herself . . . briefly.

"Honestly, one o' these days she's going to hit her head so hard when she falls that she'll no' get up," Saidh muttered with a shake of the head. "She really needs to wear some kind o' cushioned cap that covers her whole head. Mayhap I should make her one," she added thoughtfully.

"I'll help," Joan said on a pained laugh.

"Aye, well, mayhap we could get through this first," her aunt suggested, kneeling beside her. "Can you still walk or shall I call Cam to come carry you?"

"Nay! Don't tell Cam."

Lady Sinclair frowned. "He should ken. 'Tis his child."

"Aye, and he'll know once it's done, but I won't have him worrying in the meantime," Joan said at once.

"But if you need help getting to the bedchamber we shall have to call on him," Annabel said apologetically.

"I can walk," Joan said determinedly and started to push herself to her feet just as another contraction hit. This one came on hard and fast, and—unexpected as it was—tore a startled scream from Joan before she could stop it. Which caused an immediate commotion amongst the men seated at the trestle tables in the great hall below.

"What's happening?" Cam shouted. "Joan?"

"'Tis all right!" Lady Sinclair called quickly, "Joan is—" She paused when Joan caught her arm and squeezed, then sighed and finished, "Lady Murine fainted again."

"But I heard Joan scream," Cam called, sounding closer. He was coming up the stairs.

"Stop him," Joan hissed through gritted teeth.

"She screamed because Murine dropped her drink as she fell, spilling it all over Joan's gown," Lady Sinclair lied. "Go on back to what ye were doing. We're fine here."

There was a pause and then the men began discussing the unfortunate Murine and her constant fainting, their voices growing fainter as they headed back downstairs.

Joan closed her eyes with relief, both that Cam wouldn't worry, and that the contraction had ended. "Thank you," she whispered, managing a smile for her mother-in-law, and then on a burst of gratitude said, "I think I must be the most fortunate of women. I have the most wonderful husband, a beautiful home, amazing friends, and lovely family." She squeezed Lady Sinclair's arm again and smiled. "If I die on the birthing bed, I certainly can not complain that God did not gift me with much first. Including a good and kind woman for mother-in-law." She added solemnly, "Thank you, Lady Sinclair. You've been an angel, teaching me how to run Sinclair this last year, and doing so with the patience of a saint."

"Do no' thank me dear, it's been me pleasure,"

Lady Sinclair said, hugging her. Then, dashing away the tears that had sprouted in her eyes, she added sternly, "But no more talk o' dying. Ye won't die, ye can't. Cam would ne'er forgive me and I would ne'er forgive meself."

"Don't be silly, even if I don't survive the birthing bed, it won't be your fault. You've nothing to feel guilty for," Joan said, and lowered her head as another contraction started.

"Bearnas?" Annabel said uncertainly. "What did you do?"

Struggling with the pain building in her, Joan raised her head to glance at her mother-in-law, frowning when she noted the guilty expression on Lady Sinclair's face.

Cam's mother hesitated, but then blurted, "My maid learned from Jinny about the wild carrot seed and I had her switch it out for—"

"You interfering bitch!" Joan was as shocked as everyone else when she shrieked that. It was a combination of betrayal and the pain suddenly ripping through her that propelled it, and then she was too consumed with the agony overwhelming her to pay much attention when Annabel patted Lady Sinclair's arm and tried to soothe her.

"Joan does not mean that. She is just in pain."

"Aye," Lady Sinclair sighed. "But she's right. I am an interfering old . . . er . . . woman, and if she dies I'll never forgive meself."

"I kenned it!"

Joan blinked her eyes open with alarm and

cursed rather volubly when she saw Cam stepping off the stairs and rushing toward them.

"Ye're havin' the baby!"

"Well you needn't sound so accusatory. 'Tis not as if I snuck around behind your back and got with child without you. You helped make it," Joan snapped, pain and frustration making her cranky.

"She does not mean to snap, Cam," her aunt said at once, turning to pat his arm now. "She is just in pain. You must not pay attention to anything she says."

"Aunt Annabel," Joan began, and then cried out with surprise when Cam scooped her up and started quickly down the hall.

"If ye're going to shout at us and call us names, ye'll do it from our bed," Cam said, sounding a little snappy himself.

"'Tis perfectly normal, Cam," Annabel said reassuringly as she hurried after them.

"Aye. Ye should ha'e heard what Annabel called me when she was birthing Payton," Ross MacKay said, appearing at the top of the stairs. As Cam carried her past, the man pursed his lips and added, "And Annella. And Kenna too, come to think on it." He shook his head. "My sweet little Annabel shrieked like a fishwife and cursed like a warrior."

"Thank you, husband," Annabel snapped, looking embarrassed as she followed on Cam's heels. "Why do you and the other men not go below and wait? And take Cam with you."

"I'm no' going anywhere," Cam announced firmly, continuing up the hall.

"Well, if ye need a break, yer father and I'll be in the solar," Ross announced.

"With *uisge beatha*," Artair Sinclair added, a pitcher in hand as he reached the top of the stairs.

"Good thinking," Saidh said, taking the pitcher from him as she passed. Smiling she added, "'Twill help Joan with the pain, I'm sure."

"Damn," Artair muttered and then turned to peer below and bellowed, "Bring more *uisge beatha*, Aiden. That sassy Buchanan wench stole ours."

Joan heard Saidh chuckle at the words as Cam carried her into their room and set her on the bed.

The moment he released her he began gathering furs and bolsters and pilling them behind her back. Then he sat down on the side of the bed and took her hands in his.

Joan took in his expression and frowned. He was looking at her as if it might be the very last time he would. Sighing, she turned to Saidh, a breathless laugh slipping from her lips when she saw that she'd poured some *uisge beatha* into a goblet and was downing it. "I thought that was for me."

Saidh lowered the goblet and peered to her with surprise. "Did ye want some?"

Joan rolled her eyes and said dryly, "It could no' hurt."

Saidh nodded and looked about, then moved to the table by the fireplace where another goblet sat. Joan watched her start to pour the liquid, but then was hit by another contraction and lowered her head, staring at their entwined hands as she tried to concentrate on breathing until the pain had passed.

"Squeeze me hand if ye want to," Cam said quietly. "It may help."

Joan forced a smile and opened her mouth to assure him she was fine, but instead a long, loud scream came out.

Saidh stopped dead at the sound and stared at her wide-eyed, then raised the goblet to her mouth to gulp some down.

"Give me that. 'Tis fer Joan," Lady Sinclair snapped with exasperation. Taking the drink from Saidh, she moved to the side of the bed, but then simply stood there and stared helplessly as Joan screamed. When the contraction ended and she finally stopped screaming, Lady Sinclair held out the goblet, but Joan just shook her head and sagged against Cam's shoulder, panting.

Lady Sinclair hesitated, but then raised the goblet to her mouth and chugged down the contents.

"Where's my aunt?" Joan asked wearily as she suddenly realized she wasn't there.

"She said she was going to get her medicinals and have her maid fetch some items," Lady Sinclair said, peering into the empty goblet with a frown, then dropped it with surprise when Joan began to scream again as another contraction hit her.

"What can I do?" Cam asked, panic on his face.

Joan shook her head, but then tugged her hands free of his and grabbed at his shirt and plaid to pull herself upright.

"What are ye doing?" he asked with surprise. "What do ye need?"

What she needed was to get to her knees, or to squat. She was pushing, but it was harder to do while lying down and her body wanted to squat.

"Get this off me," she gasped, tugging at her gown.

Cam immediately helped her remove it, leaving her on her knees in nothing but her tunic.

"Help me," she muttered, grabbing his shoulders to shift her position.

Cam stared at her wide-eyed as she shifted to squat on the bed in front of him. "Should ye be doing that?"

"Watch for the baby," Joan gasped.

"Watch?" he echoed briefly and then glanced down with bewilderment. "What do I—?"

Joan interrupted him with long half grunt, half shout as another contraction hit her and she bore down. The pain ratcheted up to an unbelievable level this time and it felt like she was being torn asunder, and then it suddenly ended, or at least dropped back to something that was almost non-existent in comparison.

"Bloody hell. I caught him," Cam muttered, and she peered down to see that he held their child in his hands and that it was indeed a boy.

"Bloody hell! I missed it!"

Joan glanced around to see that Annabel had returned and had come up short in the doorway, several servants behind her carrying water, linens and various other items.

"Not all o' it," Joan pointed out dryly and her aunt gave her head a shake, and then rushed forward, barking orders.

"He's perfect," Cam breathed, reaching out to brush his son's cheek with one callused finger.

Joan smiled tiredly. Her aunt had kicked Cam out for the rest of the activity, and much to her surprise he'd gone willingly. Well, perhaps she hadn't been all that surprised. Birthing was a messy business and he had been rather green around the gills at the time. Now, however, it was all done. Her son was clean and wrapped in swaddling, she had passed the afterbirth, been cleaned and put in a clean tunic and was now sitting in a chair by the fire as the women changed the bed linens. Only then had her aunt decided Cam could return.

"Aye, he's perfect," Joan agreed, peering down at the sweet faced baby in her arms.

"The bed's ready if ye want to lie down again," Lady Sinclair said quietly, moving to stand beside the chair Joan sat in. Peering at her first grandson, she smiled softly and whispered, "He's beautiful. Do ye ken what name ye'll give him?"

When Joan glanced to Cam, he shook his head. " 'Tis yer choice. Ye did all the work."

Joan hesitated, and then met her mother-in-law's eyes.

"Bearnard," she said quietly. "In honor of the lady responsible for his being here. Thank you," she added solemnly, and then rushed on, apologetically, "And I am sorry about calling you an interfering bitch earlier. My aunt was right, I really didn't mean it. Without you, we wouldn't have Bearnard."

"Oh, me dear girl," Lady Sinclair cried, bending to hug her and the baby both. "There's no need to apologize, and pray do no' thank me. I should never have interfered and am just so relieved it all worked out all right. It could easily have gone the other way and then I would have lost someone I have come to love dearly."

Cam frowned from one to the other as Lady Sinclair straightened. "What are you two talking about?"

"Nothing," Joan said quickly, knowing he'd be furious if he found out how his mother had interfered. She'd tell him eventually, of course. But not until he got over the fear they'd both just gone through. She suspected that wouldn't take long, but didn't want to risk it now when everything was so perfect.

"Thank you, dear," Lady Sinclair kissed her cheek, and then peered at the baby again and marveled, "He looks so like Campbell when he was a bairn."

"Would you like to hold him?" Joan asked.

"Please," Lady Sinclair said eagerly and carefully took him from her. She peered down at him and cooed gently, then glanced up to ask. "Can I take him to the solar for the men to see?"

"Aye, of course," Joan said at once.

Nodding, Lady Sinclair quickly left the room, taking Bearnard with her and Joan smiled faintly, and then gasped when Cam suddenly stood and scooped her into his arms.

"It's to bed for you," he said carrying her across the room. Rather than lay her in the bed though, he settled in it with her in his lap, then pulled the linens and furs up to cover them both, muttering, "Ye must be exhausted."

"I fear I am," Joan admitted wryly, then tipped her head back to smile at him. "Exhausted but happy. We survived the birthing bed," she pointed out.

"Thank God," Cam breathed, leaning his forehead against hers and closing his eyes. "Let's no' do this again. One babe is enough."

"Oh, I don't know," Joan murmured. "It wasn't that bad."

Cam pulled back and peered at her as if she were crazy. "Ye were screaming yer head off, woman."

"Well it hurt. But it was worth it," she said with a smile, and then added, "And I was thinking a little sister for Bearnard would be nice."

Cam stared at her silently for a minute, and then said, "A little sister, hmm?"

"A pretty little girl who would adore her da as much as I do," she added.

He smiled crookedly. "I bet ye were a beautiful baby."

"And mayhap we could name her Maggie after my mother," she added softly.

"Aye, mayhap we could," Cam said and kissed her.

Joan kissed him eagerly back. They couldn't do much more than that for now, but she was content. She had survived the birthing bed, had a beautiful son who had all his fingers and toes, and someday he would have little brothers and sisters to join him. She could hardly believe how her life had changed. She really was the most fortunate of women.

Want more Lynsay Sands?
Keep reading for an excerpt
from her classic historical

SWEET REVENGE

Available December 2014
from Avon Books

$\mathcal{K}$YLA WAS THE FIRST TO SEE THEM.

Lying on her stomach in the back of the horse-drawn cart, she was dozing in and out of a fitful sleep when a leaf fluttered onto her forehead. Frowning slightly, she reached out from beneath the furs covering her and brushed the item away. She then tried to settle back into the warm cocoon of healing sleep again, but found discomfort would not allow it.

Forcing her eyes open and blinking as the furs she lay upon came hazily into focus, she shifted slightly, trying to find a position that would ease the awakening pain in her back. It was a mounting, burning pain and was a miserable way to start the day, she decided unhappily, her mind immediately turning to thoughts of Morag's miracle salve. The stuff smelled as putrid as a privy on a hot summer day, but it made the pain in her back disappear immediately after it was applied. Temporarily at least. The effects lasted for only a few hours, then the foul balm had to be reapplied to beat back the white-hot agony. She could do with some of its lovely numbing effect now, she thought with a sigh, shifting carefully onto her side to peer hopefully at the woman who slept beside her.

A drop of what she thought to be rain landed on her face as the fur slid aside and she wiped it away, surprise replacing her irritation as she felt the grittiness on her finger and looked down to see that it wasn't rain but a small bead of mud. Eyes raising instinctively, she gaped at the shapes that hovered in the branches overhead. Silent and still, they hid among the trees, watching tensely as the procession moved along beneath them.

Kyla had just opened her mouth to shout a warning to her escort when a long, loud wail filled the air. Bloodcurdling and ferocious, it set the hair at the nape of her neck on end. The first voice was joined by what seemed like a hundred others, and the mounted party came to an abrupt halt.

Grabbing for the side of the conveyance to steady herself, Kyla watched in amazement as a man dropped lithely from the branches above to land between her and Morag in the cart. Her eyes widened as a ray of sunlight speared through the trees, glinting off of the sword he held and turning his red hair to fire. Her gaze dropped over the plaid he wore. At this angle and with it flapping in the early afternoon breeze, she had an exceptional view of his naked legs all the way up to his thighs. And a fair pair of legs they were, too, she noted with an interest wholly inappropriate to the situation. Shapely ankles, muscled calves, nice knees, and strong thighs distracted her—until he let loose another long, loud wail that drew her eyes upward. He raised his sword high in one hand.

Truly, had she not seen him, she would have thought his wailing the shriek of the dead rising up from the pits of hell. It was loud, long, and ear-piercing, and it seemed to stab right through her skull to her brain, making it throb in contest with her back. It didn't help when his voice was joined by the others still in the branches above. And when the others suddenly began dropping from the trees as well, bedlam broke out in the clearing. Startled warning shouts and bellows of pain rose up around Kyla like the springtime flood waters in the river by her home, and the fellow standing at her feet suddenly leapt off the wagon and out of sight.

Gritting her teeth, she closed her eyes briefly, then pushed herself to her hands and knees. Her arms shook, weak from that small effort, and the bottom of the cart seemed to swim before her eyes, but she took a deep breath and managed to ease back to sit on her haunches. Raising her head determinedly, Kyla peered around as the clang of metal against metal joined the shouts and shrieks already filling the quiet glade they had been passing through.

The miserable burning in her back and her pounding head were immediately forgotten as

Kyla took in the activity around her. They were under attack. What made her mouth drop open and her eyes widen incredulously was the un-believable fact that the mad savages attacking her chain-mailed escort actually appeared to be winning!

Several members of her escort had already fallen from their mounts. The rest were attempt-ing to urge their horses closer to the wagon to form a tight circle around it to defend from, but their attempts were hampered by the panicked rearing of the now-riderless horses that suddenly seemed to be everywhere.

Swallowing the fear tightening her throat, Kyla peered slowly around the glade with a sort of stunned apprehension. Her men were dropping like flies at summer's end. Already a third of them lay injured or dying on the muddy ground.

A roar drew her eyes as a great mountain of a man slammed into the back of the cart, struggling with one of her men-at-arms. With no time to prepare herself for the jolt, Kyla was sent sprawl-ing onto her stomach again in the bottom of the wagon, her chin slamming hard into the floor of the cart despite the cushioning furs.

Cursing, she started to push herself back to her haunches again, but had barely lifted her head when one of her escort rode up to the side of the cart. He forcefully shoved her down again, order-ing her to be still before riding off into the fray once more.

Frowning and muttering under her breath,

Kyla did as she was told . . . for all of a heartbeat. She popped back up into a sitting position again.

"What's about?"

Remembering the woman who had been resting beside her throughout this journey, Kyla tore her gaze reluctantly from the fray and sank slowly back into the wagon. Rolling carefully onto her side, she peered worriedly at the wrinkled, old face of the woman who had been a maid, nurse, and mother figure to her for as long as she could recall, then lied, "'Tis all right. 'Tis nothing. Go back to sleep."

A bloom of pale color tinged wrinkled old cheeks with anger and Morag's black eyes narrowed. "Yer lying, girl. Ye never could fool me."

The maid began to rise, determined to see for herself, but Kyla quickly pressed her back down. "Nay, do not rise."

"Then tell me!" she ordered sharply. "And the truth this time."

"Aye." Kyla sighed, searching briefly for a way to lessen the old woman's imminent terror, then shrugged. There was none. "We are under attack."

"What?!" Gasping in horror, Morag began to struggle upward again.

Kyla was trying to push the woman back down into the safety provided by the sides of the cart when a second jolt gave pause to them both. Stilling, they spun to stare at the warrior now standing on the back of the wagon. He was the same man who had first landed in the cart and as she had before, Kyla found herself memerized by the sight of him. Tall. Strong. Magnificent. He stood poised for a moment surveying the battle, the sweat on his body gleaming in the sunlight, then, just as suddenly as he had arrived, he lunged off the cart again, sword swinging ferociously.

"Gor!" Fanning herself with her good hand, Morag collapsed back against the skins in the bottom of their cart. "Savages!" she muttered crossly. "Highlanders. And 'tis one of them yer Catriona is wedding ye to. Yer dear departed mother must be rolling in her grave."

"Aye," Kyla agreed, then scowled as Morag pushed herself back up so that she could peer over the side of the cart.

"What are you doing?" Kyla hissed, sitting up to pull her back.

"Watching to see if we win."

Kyla opened her mouth to say that it mattered little—even if Catriona's men won, she would not be the winner—but before she could comment on that, two battling Scots crashed into the side of the wagon sending both women tumbling sideways against the far wall. Just as Morag would have raised herself again to continue her watch, a sword swung over their heads, then caught in the wood of the wagon. A man cried out in agony.

The Scot who had landed briefly in the wagon earlier peered over the side at them, a fierce glare on his face. "Keep yer heads down, ye lack-witted harpies!" he bellowed in Gaelic.

When Kyla's eyes widened in confusion, the man then repeated the order in English. Obviously he'd thought she had not understood the order the first time, but in truth, her confusion was due to the fact that he had given it at all. He was not one of her escort, but one of their attackers. What the devil did he care if she lived or got herself killed?

Frowning, she peeked over the edge of the wagon again, dismay overwhelming her as she saw that every single one of her mail-armored escort had fallen. Not one still stood among the battling men. Even the driver of the wagon was now sprawled on his seat, bleeding badly from a shoulder wound. The only warriors between herself and capture were the Scots her betrothed had sent to meet them at the border. There seemed few of them left.

Peering around at the fighting men, she estimated that perhaps fifteen of her escort still stood. Fourteen, she corrected as another man fell. Thirteen.

"What's about?" Morag rasped anxiously. Kyla bit her lip as she glanced down at her companion. Once the last of their defenders were slain, the attackers would no doubt turn their attention to them. Kyla was not willing to contemplate what would happen then. These savages bore no resemblance to the knights of her brother's court.

Muttering under her breath, she ignored Morag's question as well as her own aches and pains and began to move. Climbing over the lip of the cart, she crawled onto the seat beside the slumped driver, grabbed the reins from his slack hands, then gave them a sharp snap. Unnerved by the smell of blood and the battle that raged around them, both animals were more than happy to fulfill her silent order. After a brief spate of snorting and wild rearing, the beasts set out, hooves tearing into the moist earth beneath them as they drew the cart quickly away from the melee.

Movement to her side brought Kyla's eyes around in time to see the previous driver tumble from the bench seat, dislodged by the lurching motion of the wagon. She winced at the thud as he hit the ground, but set her teeth and snapped the reins over the horses again, urging them to greater speed.

"Damnation!" Pushing herself up weakly, Morag peered out the back of the cart. Behind them, their attackers seemed not even to notice their escape.

Kyla scowled and reached back to push her gently down onto the floor of the cart. "Stay down, Morag. You are not well."

The woman snorted at that, but sank down among the furs willingly enough, though not before muttering, "Oh, aye, but ye are, I suppose?"

Disregarding the sarcastic comment, Kyla concentrated on steering their cart through the trees they had entered. They hadn't gone far when she spotted the horses. About twenty of them. No doubt belonging to their attackers. She was just worrying over the idea that they may have left someone to mind the animals when Morag's ear-splitting scream rent the air from the back of the cart. Kyla turned just in time to see a figure drop from a tree branch.

He was huge. A veritable mountain that made the whole wagon shudder as he landed in the back of it. Kyla's gaze found the shiny blade he held in one hand and she panicked. With a broken arm and cracked ribs, her nurse maid was helpless against such a brute.

Dropping the reins, she stood, turned, drew her own dirk from her waist, and lunged—all at once. It was really quite amazing that she hit her target, but not only did she hit him, she sent the attacker backward right off the cart.

It had been an incredibly stupid thing to do, Kyla realized. With nothing to hold on to but the person she was tackling, she went tumbling off the wagon with the man. Driverless, the cart continued on its merry way, Morag screeching frantically from the back.

The savage's body cushioned Kyla from the worst of the fall. Yet despite this bit of luck, her landing was jarring and, for a moment, she could only lie atop the man, trying to regain her breath. It was the shine of sunlight reaching delicately through the summer leaves overhead to touch the tip of the blade she had dropped that moved her to action. She had just managed to grasp the dirk when the brawny man she lay on suddenly released a loud roar and rolled her onto her back, a move that sent all of the air rushing out of her lungs.

Gasping in agony, Kyla blindly jabbed her knife at him. Much to her relief, the great bear cursed and moved off her at once. Taking advantage of that, Kyla rolled quickly away from him and onto her stomach, sighing as the pain that had been ripping at her immediately eased a bit. Still, her vision wavered slightly as she eyed him where he now sat, gaping at her with amazement as he grasped the wound she had made in his side. It really wasn't much of a wound from what she could see; once he got over his surprise at her aggressive action, he would no doubt come at her again.

Turning her head, Kyla peered about, her gaze fastening on a good-sized fallen branch a few inches away from her right hand. It was leafless and pale brown from time spent in the elements. The bit nearest her was obviously the tip, but it widened out as it went, growing until it was thicker around at the end than her upper arm. Stretching, she closed her fingers over it, dragging it toward her even as she began to struggle to her hands and knees. Then, grasping it in both hands, she used it to help lever herself back to her feet.

The man recognized her intent the moment she lifted the stump of wood in her trembling arms and turned toward him. He immediately started to rise, but Kyla was already swinging for his head. The wood connected with a crack, the dead branch snapping in half as it slammed into his head. For a moment, Kyla feared all she had managed to do was anger the man further, then, a gurgle of surprise slipped from his lips and he sank back to lie in the leaves and grass.

Kyla felt nausea rise up inside her, then Morag's screams reached her through her dismay. Turning away from her enemy, she hurried after the fleeing cart, her heart nearly stopping when another figure dropped from the trees directly in front of the wagon. Spooked, the horses reared, the cart tipped, and Morag tumbled out with a cry that turned Kyla's blood cold. The cart righted itself and the horses stopped, stomping fearfully at the ground.

All she could see was Morag's frail body lying on the ground as she rushed forward. Forgetting the other man, she rushed to her maid's side, the knife slipping from her limp fingers as she dropped to her knees and gently touched one leathery cheek. "Morag? Morag!"

The flickering of those old, white eyelashes seemed the most beautiful thing in the world to Kyla. Releasing a gasping sob, she hugged the frail body close and silently offered up a prayer of thanks.

It was only then that she recalled the other barbarian. Glancing up, she saw with some surprise that he was a mere boy. And that he wasn't paying her the least bit of attention. He was looking past her.

Following his gaze, she immediately understood his lack of concern. The battle was over. The warriors were approaching, expressions grim.

Laying Morag quickly back down, Kyla snatched up the dirk she had dropped and got to her feet, moving instinctively between the prone woman and the approaching men. But, like the boy, the warriors paid her little heed. Instead, they hurried to their fallen comrade and encircled him, hiding him from view.

Clenching the dirk tighter in her sweaty hand, Kyla set her gaze darting about the area. It seemed obvious there was no escape, for she could not leave without Morag. Standing and fighting was her only option. In truth she wished it were not. She had never thought to die this way. Nor so young.

The men began to turn their attention to her now. Expressions forbidding, they moved forward, forming a half-circle in front of her as they took in her stance and the dirk in her hand.

Kyla expected an immediate attack, men coming at her all at once. It was a bit unnerving when they merely continued to stare at her, then began to discuss her in Gaelic, unaware that she understood the language.

"Bonnie," one commented, drawing her wary gaze to him. He was tall. Good God, they were all tall. She was of average height herself, and these men seemed giants. They stood, looming like a forest of trees before her. Broad-chested, solid, strong, and terrifying.

"Aye. Bonnie. But wee." The man who said that seemed to be the leader. She had noticed that the others had deferred to him as he led the way to stand before her. He was the red-haired man, the same one who had stood on the back of the wagon, then called her a harpie and ordered her to keep her head down. He was one of the tallest of them. He also seemed to be one of the brawniest, though the man directly beside him, the one who had originally called her "bonnie" was a good deal larger. Good grief, that man could be mistaken for a small building from a distance, she thought, frowning briefly at him before turning her attention back to the leader. She realized that the men were agreeing with him and not very flatteringly.

"Aye. Puny."

"Pulin'."

"All bones."

"Frail-lookin'."

"Pale as death, too and swaying on her feet. I be thinkin' she won't survive the trip home, let alone our harsh winters."

The leader nodded at that observation and they all eyed her gloomily. A dark-haired man behind the leader brightened. "Mayhap 'tis not her. Mayhap we attacked the wrong party."

Those words brought a round of hopeful looks from the other men, but the leader shook his head. "Nay, Duncan. 'Twas the MacGregors we fought with the Sassenach. I recognized at least two of them."

Kyla's sigh of disappointment joined that of the men. For a moment she had glimpsed freedom; surely if they had erred, they would have let her go. Alive? But, aye, it was the MacGregors that had been escorting their party. Twenty of them had met them at the border. It had been an added precaution, though Kyla had thought it unnecessary at the time, since forty of Catriona's men had already been escorting her. Now she saw how wrong she had been; the English men-at-arms had been slow and awkward in their mail. They had fallen quickly against these savages, leaving the MacGregor men alone to protect her. She supposed she was who these men were looking for, though she could not for the life of her figure out why. Unless the entire betrothal had been a ruse to get her away from the castle and assassinate her. That was a possibility. And not beyond her sister-in-law's nefarious mind.

"Well, we'd best be collecting her and moving on," the leader commented finally, drawing her attention back from her thoughts. He did not seem eager to accomplish the deed. In fact the only move he made was to shift his feet as he eyed her. Still, even that was enough to make Kyla stiffen warily. She would not go down without a fight.

"Careful of that blade of hers. 'Tis verra sharp. She gave me a fair nasty scratch with it."

Her gaze turned at once to the speaker, the man she had noted could be mistaken for a building. Shock covered her face now as she took in his features rather than his bulk; he was the one she had stabbed, then knocked out. The man was now standing tall and strong, no discomfort on his face and little to show that she had hurt him except for the blood on his shirt and plaid. And there was not very much of that either, she noted now with disgust.

Mouth tightening, Kyla braced her feet farther apart and bent her knees slightly in the manner she had seen her brother take during hand-to-hand combat.

Tipping his head to the side, the leader eyed her briefly, then suggested in English, "Ye'd best be dropping the blade, lassie, ere ye hurt yerself."

Kyla's only response was to lift her chin grimly. When the leader moved calmly forward, she was ready for him. Or so she thought.

He took two steps in a slow, meandering pace, then suddenly lunged. Grabbing her wrist in one hand, he forced it into the air, snatched the knife from her fingers with embarrassing ease, then tossed it to the man she had stabbed.

Screaming in frustration, Kyla kicked at his legs. She screeched even more furiously as she found herself picked up and slung over his shoulder like a sack of wheat.

"Calm yerself!" The stern order was accompanied by a slap on the behind that shocked her into silence. "We'll not hurt ye or the old witch."

Cursing roundly, Kyla thumped her fists ineffectively against his wide back, then paused to watch anxiously as one of the other men stooped to survey Morag. She nearly sobbed with relief when the fellow seemed to realize the woman's fragile condition and took care to lift her gently before following the man carrying herself.

When the barbarian transporting her suddenly paused, Kyla knew instinctively that they had reached the wagon and that he would most likely drop her into it. She tried to brace herself for what was to come, but no amount of preparation on earth could have readied her for her landing in the back of the cart. 'Twas not that he was unduly rough. Simply that he knew not of her injury and set her flat on her back in the bottom of the wagon with a small bump. It had the same effect as if she had been dropped on a wide board with nails poking out of it. The pain took her breath away, leaving not even a small gasp for her to cry out with. Lights danced briefly before her eyes before everything went black.